THE HIGHLANDER'S SECRET

A Scottish Highland Warriors Novel

ROMA CORDON

Cover art by Dar Albert at Wicked Smart Designs

Published by Oliver-Heber Books

0 9 8 7 6 5 4 3 2 1

For Sabitree, thank you for being the best mom.
To Francis, I'm grateful each and every day for the inspiration.
And for Shiva, thank you for giving me the world.

CHAPTER 1

AUTUMN 1747, CAMBERLEY MANOR, SUTTON COLDFIELD, ENGLAND

"Heat not a furnace for your foe so hot that it do singe yourself."

— WILLIAM SHAKESPEARE, HENRY VIII

A gunshot pierced the air. Phoebe Dunbar, code name *Hawk*, snapped the gossip column shut. Had General Bolingbroke fired the shot? She turned towards the glass doors of the hothouse, where she'd been taking her teatime break. Her view was obstructed by the sharp morning sun glinting off a plethora of greenery and vivid hothouse blooms. Her nostrils flared in anticipation of what she'd come here to do—find dirty secrets.

Phoebe pushed up from her seat, squared her shoulders and exited the hothouse. She turned left, in the direction of the gunshot, ignoring Camberley Manor on her right. She'd told her employer, Lady Bolingbroke, she would take her teatime break in the hothouse, but no one would think it unusual if she took a stroll outside instead.

She took the path towards the tiny swan pond. The slate pebbles were rough under the soles of her delicate leather half boots. Phoebe slowed her pace when discernable voices grazed her ears from across the water's surface. She dipped behind a yellow rhododendron almost as tall as she was.

Always hide in plain sight, Falcon had said. Falcon was Phoebe's spymaster and she'd ended the dictate with, *because they'll never suspect you.*

Phoebe's adrenalin surged as her employer's husband spoke.

"And why would a Scotsman have interest in outfitting the British Army with muskets? Doesn't your ilk have great dislike for the English?" asked Sir Henry, baronet and army general of the redcoats. His voice dripping with cynicism.

"Profit bows to no nation, Sir Henry," came a deep, cultured voice.

The hint of a Scottish brogue sent a fierce shock of homesickness straight to Phoebe's stomach.

The general gave a low chuckle. "Touché."

Phoebe leaned out from behind the bush and peeked, wanting to identify the Scot.

At present she had a view of his statuesque back. His thick hair, black as sin, was tied in a neat queue with a black bow.

The general's typical hard smile turned appreciative as he took the musket from his steward, who'd primed it. Bolingbroke then eyed the Scot. "For what length of time will you be stationed in Burntwood?"

Bolingbroke wasn't a tall man, but during the few occasions Phoebe had conversed with him, he'd held his head high and managed to look down at her. His beady eyes had a way of chilling the blood, even in a banal conversation. Upon meeting him, she'd decided the moniker of *Hangman* was well suited.

"For the foreseeable future. With the camp followers including wives and children of the men, as well as cooks, nurses and sutlery services, it's quite domestic," the Scot said.

"If your camp followers are lightskirts, as we had when I was stationed in Scotland years ago, they also make the nights go by quicker." She could hear the lascivious sneer in the general's voice.

The Scot shifted his stance as if uncomfortable with the comment. His broad-shouldered power stance and uniform were most certainly cavalry. The sheathed rapier hanging off the sword belt on his left hip seemed an integral part of the man himself.

The general aimed and fired at the target, a circular piece of wood about fifty yards away, already bearing a hole from the previous shot. The loud bang resonated in the air echoing through the distant forest. A flock of tiny gray birds dashed into the air from a nearby tree.

"Excellent shot, Sir Henry," the Scot said.

Phoebe ducked back into her hiding space. She twisted the folded copy of the *Daily Courant* in her hands. The gossip column's ink blackened her palms. News of the Crown's latest Jacobite hangings for high treason wasn't forgotten. Her mission: to report weapons technology, and tactical information advantageous in the event of a Jacobite resurgence, while exposing and thwarting corruption in the British Army. But if she were caught spying on General Bolingbroke, she would end up the same, with a rough noose around her tender neck, snapping it in two.

Just then Phoebe saw the slow approach of the kindly old footman Ludlow from the Manor. He was taking the same footpath she'd come by a few minutes ago. She adopted what she hoped was an innocent posture, of one simply perusing the gardens.

But through her peripheral vision she took in the Scotsman's uniform. Dark colored breeches hugged athletic thighs and lean calves, which were clad in tall cavalry boots. He wore a striking gray surtout coat with gilded facings on the cuffs and coat tails used by the Royal Scots Greys, 2nd Dragoons' Cavalry.

The Scot turned around and she caught sight of his face for

the first time. Phoebe gasped in shocked surprise and nearly dropped the gossip column.

Slade MacLean still caused her heart to lurch, to squeeze and twist in her chest. To make want and regret bump each other in her belly. To make her wish she'd been more outspoken and confident as a child. To make her sorry she wasn't as pretty as a dead woman. It had been years, but the subject of her childhood anguish and desires still brought heat to her cheeks.

Phoebe took in Slade's features. The first time she'd met him, his gorgeous dark good looks had made her gawk, for he was perfect, like those tall strong beautiful knights she'd dreamt about as a nine-year-old girl. He'd done the same thing to her little heart a sinful scoop of syllabub or a decadent dollop of plum pudding did. Made it forget to beat.

Her brother Egan had brought him home and introduced him to their family. She had believed in knights then; she had believed in the innate goodness of others when he'd saved her life. But then, seven years ago, she'd outgrown such silly childhood notions as her world had spun out of control and ceased to make sense on the moors.

A loud shot rang out, pushing her recollections aside. The shot was followed by a muffled thump and a weak cry. Phoebe's gaze darted across the pond. The steward held the musket, which was still being primed. But why was there smoke at the tip of his barrel?

"You incompetent fool!" Slade's growl resonated across the surface of the water.

Phoebe swiveled back to Ludlow. He was lying on the footpath, gripping his chest.

"Oh no!" she cried.

Fear sliced through her as she dashed toward the fallen footman, the forgotten gossip column flopping to the ground. A chill ran up her spine as she knelt down beside him. She ignored the sharp slate cutting into her knees through the material of her skirts. His polite, wrinkled face was twisted in pain. Her hands grabbed his as he clutched his chest.

"How … what can I do?" She could barely get the words out.

Too much air left her lungs with the constriction of her chest. Phoebe's eyes fell to the red-stained gloved hands she clutched. Red, the color of her nightmares. Recollections came flooding back. A seven-year-old memory of the malevolent fair-haired, Romanesque-featured Faye Ross dressed in his red uniform, the pain as he struck her in the face. Now, the sticky wetness of the blood registered on her palms. Her body swayed. Ludlow's taut features unfocused in her vision.

Black spots danced in her eyes. The sickening metallic smell of the blood hit her like a punch to the gut. The black spots melted into each other like hot wax. They engulfed her and pulled a black shroud over her world.

CHAPTER 2

"Utter imbecile. Why is he in the gardens while we're conducting a musket demonstration?" The general's sharp voice cut the air as he approached. "And what in damnation is Lady Bolingbroke's companion doing here?"

Colonel Slade MacLean of the Royal Scots Greys, 2nd Dragoons, division of the Scots Guards, knelt before the fallen lass as his lips pressed together in concern. The irate and capricious general stopped his verbal rampage two steps away as his panic-stricken, incompetent steward stood further back. Slade was not surprised at the general's lack of empathy or the man's poor behavioral control. These were traits of an autocratic and dictatorial murderer, after all. The man was more put out at the stalled musket demonstration and less concerned over his footman's injury or the fainted lass.

Slade eyed her, slumped over the bleeding footman. There'd been one wild shot, and he was confident it was lodged in the footman's chest. With care, Slade took hold of the lass's shoulder and waist and turned her limp body over. He hooked one arm under her shoulders and another under her knees and lifted her.

The strangest sense of déjà vu slammed into Slade's chest as the lass's head fell back. Slade pushed the feeling aside and carried her over to a nearby long-chair and laid her down gently, wishing it were made of something softer than cast iron.

As Slade returned to kneel beside the bleeding footman, a second footman came sprinting towards them from the manor.

"Send for a sawbones or healer—better yet both—and I need linens for the blood," Slade said, eying the second footman. The man, with bulging eyes and mouth agape, nodded and darted back towards the manor, almost tripping in his haste.

Slade lifted the blood-soaked lapels of the injured footman to find the bullet hole. The footman's breathing was weak, and he was out cold. Just as well, for the pain would be unbearable if he were awake. Slade pulled his trident dagger from its sheath at his waist and sliced open the footman's shirt to get a better look at the wound.

"I say, is all this necessary? Leave him for the healer. Let's carry on with the demonstration," the general said with a wave of his hand.

Slade looked up at the general and refrained from curling his lips in disgust. Bolingbroke's callousness was astounding. Slade took on a placid expression.

"I've seen enough battlefield medicine to be of help until the healer arrives." Slade kept his voice level.

The general eyed him with some distaste. He didn't appear the least bit interested in getting blood stains on his pristine attire.

"Oh well, if you must," the general scowled, tapping his feet. "I'll be in my study. Come and see me when you are finished. I'd like to discuss a possible contract with Hortons. After I've taken a look at the American longrifle musket of course."

"Of course, Sir Henry." Slade gave the man a crisp nod as Bolingbroke made a swift turn towards his manor. Satisfaction warmed Slade's chest. It appeared the general was taking the bait of securing an arms deal despite the proposition coming from a Scotsman. But then, Peter's exquisitely crafted muskets were most convincing.

Slade glanced at the steward who stood in a hunched posture, wringing his own wrists. He deserved to be throttled for his incompetence. Regardless of the man's ineptitude, however, he appeared not only remorseful, but Slade guessed he'd never shot anyone.

"You. Come here," Slade ordered. "Keep his head and shoulders steady, should he come to. Movement will exacerbate the bleeding."

The small-boned steward, who carried himself like anything but a military man, nodded and approached, his eyes widening in a frog-like face, to do Slade's bidding. Slade inspected the bloodied chest. A sucking chest wound. He'd seen countless such as this on the front lines. He placed his gloved hands over the injury and applied the right amount of pressure. He had to stop the escape of air, and at the same time curtail the bleeding. There was nothing else he could do for the man except keep his hands in place until the healer arrived.

Slade raised his head to face the direction the general had gone. What an astonishing lack of responsibility and concern for his own staff. But then, such lack of concern paled in comparison to the perverse morality he'd demonstrated in the Scottish Highlands during the Jacobite rebellions. Thousands of innocents murdered as a result of his orders. A muscle in Slade's jaw spasmed. Slade was here because of one death in particular. And Slade would have his revenge.

His neck muscles stiffened. It had taken a visit from his former savior and his sometimes tormentor, Bullfinch, for Slade to finally settle on the perfect plan of revenge on Bolingbroke. Slade was always patient, methodical, and calculating in everything he did. Well, the truth was the first five years after he'd lost her, and his reason for breathing, Slade hadn't cared whether he lived or died. In fact, many times he'd prayed for the latter. Then there'd been days where he'd danced with the idea of sticking a blade through the general's heart. His own father and brother would have loved to follow suit, like Brutus and the senators eliminating the egocentric Julius Caesar. The simplicity of such a brutal act had seemed poetic at the time.

He'd failed Sylvia, but Bolingbroke was the one who might as well have handed her the hemlock. Or at least that's what he'd been telling himself over the years, but now he wasn't sure. He'd seen soldiers come back from the war and go on to live prosaic lives as if they hadn't done horrendous things. Maybe he was one of those who had to forget the horrendous things to have a normal life, but he didn't have a normal life, did he? The heavy weight of guilt and self-loathing had a way of slowing a man down.

He'd pictured Bolingbroke's death in a hundred different ways over the years. There'd been countless whisky-filled days and opium-induced stupors when the pain had been so unbearable, he'd almost unhinged into complete madness. Bolingbroke's death was the only thing that kept him alive after it had happened.

But a blade to Bolingbroke's chest was too good an end for the general. Slade had no intention of creating a martyr. *No.* A slow and methodical decimation of a grand political career sounded much more enticing. And Bullfinch had given him the opportunity to do just that.

A few minutes later, the second footman arrived with a tall stack of white linen. Slade took a few of the cloths to press against the wound and instructed the footman to hold them in place while he unfolded the remaining linens and draped them over the injured man. He then took off his coat and draped it over the man's body as well. With a hole in his chest and the substantial loss of blood, the footman's temperature would have dropped. Slade exhaled a breath of relief, for the bleeding had ceased for the most part.

A low feminine groan sounded, and Slade turned to face the lass on the cast iron long-chair under the willow tree.

"Keep pressure on the wound until the healer gets here," he said to the second footman. The man's head bobbed in earnest. Slade strode over to the lass.

Her features intrigued him. They fired a response from every nerve ending in his body. Despite the groan, she still hadn't come to. Her flaming auburn hair was swept up in a bun held by a jeweled comb. Not a maid, but not an aristocrat either. Then he recalled the general's comment about a lady's companion. Curled tendrils outside the chignon hung on either side of the lass's face, framing delicate features and a complexion that was fair except for an enticing sprinkling of freckles. Slade's instincts came alive as he took in her evenly spaced eyes, a tad sunken, giving an appearance of vulnerability. She was in her early twenties, he'd guess.

Why did she look so familiar? Could he have swived her? In his past life, he'd had a taste for innocence, but now his tastes leaned more towards the wicked and experienced. Quite a shame, for there was a dangerous hint of voluptuous curves in the way the lass's prim gown draped her form. Just the type to spark fire in his blood.

He stood next to her and scanned the length of her still body. He couldn't decide if her drab gown was gray or had once been black and had been laundered too many times. Her hands were bloodied, as was the front of her clothing. The blood was the footman's, wasn't it?

Slade gently lifted the woman's blood-stained hands and inspected them one after the other for injuries. Delicate wrists and slender fingers, but no injuries. He was still holding her right hand when her eyes pushed open. A captivating shade of hazel.

With the combination of hazel eyes and auburn hair, she reminded him of—

God's Blood!

His stomach clenched even as light-headedness made him let go of her hand. He took a step back.

"Fifi?" Slade said, shocked.

CHAPTER 3

Slade's body froze while his mind raced back fifteen years. Fifi had slipped while standing on a wet rock too close to the edge of Loch Duich. Without thinking, he'd dived in to save her. The last time he'd seen her, his own world had disintegrated to ashes and blood.

Dear God, had he just minutes ago imagined he could have swived little Phoebe Dunbar, whom he'd taken to calling Fifi, years ago? He should be mortified. Not only was she his friend but Egan's sister, and she could be hurt. And yet, as his eyes swept the length of her shapely figure, he couldn't muster the mortification. She had surely grown up nicely.

She scrambled to sit up on the bench, but stopped short, closed her eyes, and swayed for the briefest of moments, looking a tad green.

"How do you feel?" he said, his muscles tightening in concern. He made a move towards her, but she forestalled him with a raised hand. She then steadied herself at the edge of the long chair and took a few deep breaths as if gathering herself.

After a few seconds she straightened to face him. "I feel like I fainted and made a complete fool of myself," she said. Her head shifted towards the injured footman. "How is Ludlow?"

Slade's eyes followed her gaze. He'd momentarily forgotten the man. "We're unable to move him until the healer gets here, which should be shortly." He paused and turned back to her again. "Your reaction was natural for anyone witnessing a gunshot."

A look of self-derision darkened her features. "You did not faint."

A cool smile tugged at his lips. "I've fought in two wars and have seen far worse."

Speaking of the war always brought back the images. Bloodied and broken bodies felled in booming seas of cannon smoke and musket firings. Slade swallowed the tightening in the back of his throat. The worst part had been living each day as if there'd be no more. And the smell, an acrid stench of sulfur and death.

Fifi sent him a half smile, acknowledging his attempt to make her feel better. Warmth suffused him, for her look held traces of the innocent nine-year-old girl, full of lofty ideals, who he'd saved all those years ago. It sent the images of war right out of his head.

"Is that where you've been all these years? Fighting in the wars?" she asked.

He nodded. "After Sylvia died ..." His words trailed off as that invisible knife ripped through his heart. Slade cleared his throat, swallowed against the tightening, and started over. "After she died, I needed something to do, far away from the Highlands, that would make me forget."

Her expression sobered. "Such a loss I imagine is difficult to forget," she said softly.

Slade let out a weary exhale. "It is. It follows you, even in war."

A need to divert the conversation squeezed his insides. "And you?" Slade's glance swept the encompassing area. He gestured with an open palm to the general's flourishing gardens, impressive hothouse, and elegant manor. "How did you end up here as a lady's companion of all things?"

Disbelief rolled down his spine. Lasses Fifi's age were already married with a couple of bairns. Yet she was here, working. Even more puzzling was the fact that the Dunbars were one of the wealthiest clans in the Highlands. Why would she have to work?

Fifi's expression hardened. There was something different about her now. Her countenance suggested weariness, restraint, and sagacity; such a stark contrast to the open, vibrant, and light-hearted young friend he recalled. He'd never seen this look from her before. Granted, it had been many years. When her fetching features evened out, he wondered if he had imagined the tension in her face.

"I am here in the service of a very dear friend who would never forgive me if her secrets were revealed," she said.

She had evaded his question. Who was this friend? And what bloody secret?

The sound of rapid wheels reached them from a distance. Slade turned from Fifi to see a black gig heading straight for them. *Bloody farthing hell!* He badly wanted to continue the conversation, but the footman had to be attended to.

He faced Fifi. "Are you faring better? Do you require the services of the healer?"

She shook her head. "I'm not hurt, but I would like to sit and catch my breath for a moment. I am fine. Please, attend to Ludlow."

He hesitated for a breath before speaking. "It's a delight to see you after all these years. I do hope we have a chance to continue our conversation. And I wish you a full recovery from this ordeal. Please, do excuse me."

He gave her a courteous nod.

She smiled. "Seeing you has certainly been a pleasant journey into the past."

One he hoped they could continue together. Slade turned and strode towards the approaching vehicle.

The gig pulled up next to them, and a short, stout graying man stepped out from the black transport. Why was it typical for healers to dress in black? Made them look more like undertakers, in Slade's opinion. He appraised the healer of the situation then assisted him, the second footman, and the steward in relocating the injured man into the manor through the servants' side entrance.

The housekeeper directed them where to carry the injured footman. They entered a prepared room at the head of a long symmetrical hallway. The servants' quarters were clean, ornamentally restrained, and modest. After Slade was assured there was nothing else he could do to help, he picked up his coat and asked a maid named Swindlehurst, who smiled rather boldly at him as he exited the room, to direct him to the general's study.

She gave him directions then added, "if you cannot find him in his study, then you will certainly find him in the library," she said. Then went on to give him directions to the library as well.

"You are very helpful. How can I repay you?" Slade said, donning his coat.

"You can buy me a drink at the local tavern." This time her smile was undoubtedly come-hither. He eyed her in a manner not unlike the Greeks must have eyed the Trojan Horse and contemplated it getting them into Troy but he'd have it easier than the Greeks, since his Trojan Horse seemed a talker and the trick would be to get her to give up the secrets. After returning her smile, he dashed off to have a final word with Bolingbroke.

CHAPTER 4

*P*hoebe sat for some time under the willow tree collecting herself after Slade, the second footman, the steward, and the healer carried an injured Ludlow into the manor. When her knees were less like jelly, she rose and made her way to the rear of the manor, not wanting Lady Bolingbroke to see the blood on her hands or the horrendous state of her dress. She scurried through the kitchens, circumventing the cook and maids, and headed straight for the privacy of her small but neat bedchamber.

Her hands shook and her stomach roiled as she scrubbed the dried blood off with the clean, cool water in a porcelain washbasin using a square of orange-blossom soap. She stood by the dressing stand, staring down at the resulting bloodied water stark against the whiteness of the porcelain. Flashbacks of her washing herself after the moors seven years ago hit her. The old, familiar unclean feeling followed, flooding her with self-disgust. This sensation of being soiled had long since burrowed under her skin, branded her soul, and become a part of her flesh. Certain types of filth couldn't be scrubbed away.

Phoebe stripped off her blood-stained dress and put it aside for the laundress. The blood had not soaked through to her shift or petticoat, thankfully. She donned a black dress with a linen lining, a built-in whalebone corset, and flowing skirts. It had a modest white cotton fichu covering her all the way to her neck, just as she preferred.

After putting her hair to rights enough to face Lady Bolingbroke, Phoebe glanced around for the *Daily Courant*. She wanted to secure the gossip column, along with the hidden Jacobite news pamphlets which Falcon's assistant had mailed to her. Falcon occasionally sent communications to spies via specially delivered missives or artificial notices placed in the *Daily Courant's* advertisements in code, which Phoebe hadn't quite finished sifting through.

Recalling she'd dropped the gossip column when Ludlow was shot, she made her way back outside down the pebbled path towards the rhododendron. She'd told Slade she was doing this in the service of a friend. Falcon was formidable, unassuming, and deadly, but friend? She chuckled. As Phoebe approached the rhododendron, she stop short, startled. Standing by the willow tree was Slade MacLean, his arms body width apart, palms resting on the cresting rail of the cast iron long chair, his lean body angled slightly downwards. Taut lines of tension on his forehead didn't diminish the attractiveness of his features.

His beauty snatched away her breath, like the first time she'd met him years ago. But now he was steelier, edgier, and more dangerous. This man made her heartbeat erratic and her lower belly clench.

He must have sensed her approach, for he turned. He straightened, and his features relaxed. His warm gaze swept down her changed clothes.

"I wondered if I'd still find you here. I thought to bid you adieu before I left," he said.

She offered him a pleasant smile. "Has your business with the general concluded?" she asked.

"For today," he said.

Her eyes were drawn to an errant lock of thick, black hair that had escaped his queue. It wavered slightly in the wind, teasing the edge of his earlobe, which didn't look quite right.

"You sustained an injury during the war?" she asked gesturing to her own ear with a tap of her finger, concern tightening her voice.

The need to run a finger over the uneven lobe, to see if it was as jarring to the touch as it appeared, surprised her.

"Nothing more than a minor wound. I was shot by a French infantryman during my first battle. Took half my ear lobe off. It only bothers me when I am in full gallop. The wind sounds like a screaming ghost," he shrugged.

"I am sorry you were hurt," she said, her voice softening, her chest warming at his humor.

Fifteen years ago, they'd shared an easy rapport, one of warmth and young friendship. Could they recapture that ease? As a young girl, she'd told him chivalrous stories of the Order of the Thistle, stories her mother used to read to her at bedtime. And she'd revealed a secret dream of hers to him, of becoming a knight errant who helped the poor Scottish farmers terrorized by the wicked English redcoats. Phoebe was now embarrassed on behalf of her nine-year-old self for such fanciful childhood imaginings. But he'd never once called her silly.

"There wasn't time to inquire earlier, but I wanted to ask. How is your family? How is Egan?" he said, with genuine interest.

He stepped around to the front of the long chair and gestured with his palm for her to join him. She stiffened. For the past seven years she'd been careful to never be alone with a man. Brutal male strength unsettled her. It had caused her to overreact on countless social occasions over the years. She'd become abrupt with one or two of the younger and bolder manor staff, warning bells too loud in her head when they'd attempted flirtations. She'd received strange looks in return. But such overreactions had kept her safe.

But this was Slade, her old friend.

Phoebe still hesitated before sitting, taking in the surrounding gardens. If Lady Bolingbroke happened upon them, she would spout propriety because Phoebe was unchaperoned. But Phoebe spotted the gardener trimming the evergreen hedges nearer to the manor, only fifteen feet away. A groom eyed them from the end of the gardens closer to the stables. He held the reins of a bay courser, possibly waiting on Slade.

A brief conversation with an old friend in daylight while two others were nearby wouldn't buck propriety. Would it?

CHAPTER 5

*B*efore Phoebe moved to sit on the chair, she spotted her discarded gossip column half hidden under the rhododendron. She picked it up, then took a seat. Slade sat to her right. She shifted to face him. His tall, broad-shouldered torso was imposing, causing her to swallow hard as her eyes rose to meet his sharp emerald ones.

"Egan is busy learning the Eileanach business. He will eventually take over the running of things. Father and Mother are not fond of the fact that I am in England. They'd much rather I take a husband and settle down in the Highlands, preferably close to Eileanach Castle where they can lord over my life," she said.

The corners of Slade's lip twitched up, in what seemed like mirth and silent understanding. "Now I start to see why you are here. Perhaps your parents' reach to lording over your life, as you put it, doesn't extend to Sutton Coldfield."

A laugh left Phoebe's mouth, lightening her insides. "Yes. That certainly is an added attraction to my being here," she said.

Her posture relaxed. Perhaps that old rapport was returning after all.

"And how is your family?" she said.

A shadow crossed his fine features. Phoebe sensed Slade's hesitation in answering her question. He didn't get along with his father, Chisolm, or brother, Lachlan and because of that Slade had revealed years ago he'd never gotten use to calling Chisolm "father." His mother had died when Slade was a wee lad, but Phoebe never had the courage to ask what had happened.

Weariness flickered in Slade's eyes. "They are doing well enough, from what Lachlan reports in his missives to me. Both Chisolm and Lachlan are demanding I return to Garraidh Castle. But that's not so easy when one holds a commission in the Royal Scots Greys," he said.

"Is that why you are at the general's residence? Military business?" Phoebe asked, but then regret contracted her midriff. She was fishing for information on Bolingbroke, and she hated it had to be done through Slade.

His green eyes sharpened at her question. She imagined the resulting flutter in her belly was what a butterfly felt like under the inspecting gaze of a natural philosopher. Slade had never provoked this response from her before. But then again, she'd never worked as a spy while in his presence before, either.

She affected an air of insouciance she didn't feel.

"I am attempting to arrange an arms contract betwixt the general and Hortons," he said.

Was this one of the unsanctioned businesses the general was involved in? An arms contract didn't sound illegal unless the general was using military funds to buy personal weapons. Or using such weapons for unavowed attacks against the rebels. But surely Slade wouldn't be a part of that, would he?

Phoebe tilted her head, questioningly. "Hortons?"

"They're a gunsmith company out of Birmingham, in which I hold an ownership stake," he said.

It appeared Slade was involved in business ventures outside of the Royal Scots Greys and Garraidh Castle, his family seat.

"I assume as a general, Bolingbroke is authorized to enter into arms contracts on behalf of the English military?" Phoebe asked, aware that her question was probing. But she'd had to ask the question. *Trust your instincts*, Falcon had said.

Slade sent her one of those piercing gazes of his.

"At present, the general's interest is purely personal," he said.

At least he'd answered her question and not given her any of that male superiority nonsense about her questions being unsuitable for a gently bred young woman. Her eyes took in his expression as it changed. His sleek, well-formed brows climbed. A frown line formed between them, and his nostrils flared slightly at the end of a long, well-shaped nose. "Your interest in my dealings with the general is as puzzling to me as when Britain decided to form an alliance with Russia."

Phoebe lowered her gaze, tapping her chin with her pointing finger. *Blast!* She feigned a rueful look. "Apparently, my attempts at polite conversations were not entirely polite. I beg your pardon."

His slow smile and study of her features were more than she was comfortable with. "The last time you were this evasive was when I caught you and Alex all those years ago stealing the bull instead of the heifer to teach yourselves how to milk the animal," he said, with a chuckle.

A sharp pang constricted her chest at mention of Alex. Yet, recalling the bull incident from when she was nine years old pulled a soft chuckle from her throat. Especially recalling that silly rhyme Alex used to hum when in a particularly devious mood. *Queen, Queen Caroline washed her hair in turpentine, turpentine to make it shine. Queen, Queen Caroline.*

That weekend, fifteen years ago, Egan and Slade were at Eileanach Castle, on a break from fostering. And she and Alex had been wagering sugar cakes on who would be faster at milking the animal when Slade had caught them sneaking around behind the keep.

"Imagine our surprise when we attempted to milk the bull and realized the animal's body parts weren't quite right," she said.

But despite her light tone, her gaze faltered, recalling her brother's ruddy little face. After all these years, she still missed him fiercely.

"I shouldn't have mentioned Alex," he said, his tone faint and regretful.

Phoebe managed a smile as she shook her head in a dismissive manner.

"Of course you should. You were his dear friend," she said, then continued. "No two siblings ever plotted and schemed like Alex and me. I lost count of how many times we landed ourselves in hot water with our father. And you were there for many of them the year of Alex's accident. You even became our conspirator-in-arms on a few occasions if I remember correctly."

His expression was solemn, yet his eyes twinkled. "I had to help you two with the bull. But afterwards, I couldn't very well tell anyone, because if your father found out, he'd no doubt think me a bad influence and forbid me from spending time at Eileanach. And so, your conspirator-in-arms was born."

Her heartbeat quickened, and warmth started in her chest and suffused the entire length of her body. "You came to our aid like a knight in shining armor after we purloined two bags of boiled sweets. And then there was that time when you saved my life."

Warmth and fondness brightened his expression. "I seem to have fallen into a pattern then, didn't I?" He chuckled good naturedly, then continued. "That time involving the boiled sweets, we all shared in the spoils. You loved sweets back then."

Desserts had been, and still remained, one of her weaknesses.

He considered her for a second, then startled her when he reached out and gently touched her shoulder. "I hope you are recovered from earlier—"

She gasped at the contact and sprang from her seat. Her heart lurched and the gossip column fell. He immediately stood up, perhaps out of courteousness, and stepped back, his body momentarily freezing in alarm. Regret sank into her belly. She'd panicked and overreacted again. *But this is Slade. He's a friend,* she reminded herself a second time. It seemed the knowledge didn't dictate her body's instinct, prey backing away from its perceived predator.

Mortification at her action burned her face. Embarrassment and shame made her want to run.

"Are you well? Are you still unsettled by the footman's shooting?" he asked, eyebrows drawing together in concern.

"I suppose I am," she lied. "I just realized I need to return to my duties. Lady Bolingbroke will be quite put out at my long absence."

He bent down, retrieved the gossip column, folded it, and held it out to her. "Of course. I've delayed you long enough." His expression had become inscrutable, no doubt sensing her change in countenance. He must think her abominably rude. But there was no way she could explain her odd behavior.

She took the gossip column from him. "It was quite lovely seeing you again after such a long time," she said, interjecting a lightness into her voice she didn't feel.

"And you. I hope we can see each other again soon," he said, executing an immaculate bow.

She turned and broke into a run. Perhaps if she ran fast enough, it would wipe her awkward behavior from her memory, and his.

Two days later Slade found his friend, former Ensign Peter Horton of the Royal Scots Greys, at the back of Hortons gunsmith building engaged in conversation with a worker. The smell of gun oil and ammonia was strong in the air. Peter was average height with a husky build, warm, whisky-colored, trusting eyes and unruly coffee-brown hair.

As Slade approached, Peter's head lifted and his whole face lit up. Slade smiled at his friend.

"Here you are at last. I expected you a week ago," Peter said.

Slade took the hand Peter extended and shook it. "You know how stingy the general is when granting permissionnaires."

"Like an auld mongrel with a juicy bone. And here I was thinking you got distracted by a lass or two."

Slade grinned. "That as well."

Peter laughed and ushered Slade into a large unoccupied admiralty boardroom. With open palms, Peter beckoned for Slade to take the seat across from the chair he pulled out. Slade took the chair and sat down. The monstrously long wooden table stretched between them below a Gothic, wrought iron, ten-candle chandelier.

Two mounted deer heads high on the unvarnished wooden walls eyed them. The countless haphazard stacks of papers on the sideboards and the book-filled ceiling-to-floor shelves gave the room a utilitarian air.

"I am eager to hear of all the new sales you procured from our friend the general," Peter said.

Slade straightened in his chair and took in a lungful of air, regretting his boastful words to Peter about increased sales when he'd bought into Hortons and proposed approaching the general. "The general took the proposal, but not precisely as we might have hoped."

Peter's eyes sharpened with interest. "How do you mean?"

"The army does not yet have the budget to outfit their garrisons with your elite standard of Brown Besses. At present, they have the budget for the outdated, cheaper versions. Besides, the general is a Charleville musket man."

Peter's brows knotted. "There is a 'but?'"

"He will apply to his superiors for a larger budget. There is still a chance he could order a sizable number of Brown Besses. We will have to wait and see."

Peter clicked his tongue. "It's fortuitous we decided to wait on the expansion, even with the influx of capital when you became a principal. It would have all been for naught."

Slade's shoulders dropped, and he broke eye contact to avoid the disappointment plastered all over his friend's face. A month ago, when he'd used a small portion of the fortune he'd made from his overseas weaponry deals to buy into the Hortons business, it appeared he'd oversold the idea of the army buying guns from Hortons. It had been a means to an end, a legitimate reason to set up the meeting with Bolingbroke. His investment in Hortons was a smart one, with or without a contract from the army. That's not to say it wouldn't be an exponentially wiser investment if the army did have the budget to buy the new muskets.

"He still could get the approval, if not to contract for the number of muskets we envisioned in the beginning, then perhaps a portion of it. In the meantime, he is interested in ten custom tailored Charleville muskets. And he wants a second demonstration with the American longrifle musket," Slade said.

Peter's expression brightened. "Ten of the Charleville muskets? Not a total loss, then. We are finishing up a couple of exquisite American longrifle muskets, maple stock, forty-eight-inch iron barrels with brass etchings on the butt and barrel tip, with more accurate trajectory and increased fire power than the older versions. They will be ready for you in three days."

Slade nodded then reclined in his chair. He intertwined the fingers from both hands behind his neck, his lips stretching into a lazy smile. "Now that business is over with, how does your lovely Lucia fare?" Slade said.

A flush crept up his friend's face. Slade had to remind himself Peter was five years younger than his twenty-nine and didn't care to hide his revoltingly happy state, in love with the object of his desires, his wife. Though he was delighted for his friend, a strange pang snaked its way through Slade's midriff. He didn't care to give a name to it just then.

"Lucia was disappointed you couldn't attend our wedding. She wants to meet you. To thank you for saving my hide during the war on the North Bank in Germany," Peter said.

"I was trying to give the French grief—saving your hide was a happy coincidence."

Peter guffawed, then his expression straightened to seriousness. "The entire unit would have perished if you hadn't risked your neck to divert the French. You deserved more than that medal and promotion to colonel."

A lazy smile tugged at Slade's mouth. "Well, I did get quite a bit of entertainment out of seeing the French camp lit up when their stock of grain exploded."

Despite the lightness he maintained in his voice, Slade

recalled how reckless he'd been. How determined he'd been to get himself killed. Penance for his sin. A deed he'd been incapable of performing with his own hands. Soon after, trifling with death had become tedious.

Slade had joined the Scots Greys right after Sylvia's death, while Peter had joined because of the need to impress Lucia's family. Peter's reason for enlisting was so refreshing they'd hit it off as friends on their first meeting all those years ago. Peter had been an essential light, balancing Slade's darkness during the war.

"Something bothering you?" Peter asked.

Slade shook his head, realizing his friend had been watching him. "I was just thinking back to when we first enlisted," Slade said.

Peter's lips curved in a reflective smile. "I was trying to impress Lucia's father and you were ... looking to escape from the Highlands?"

Peter's answer surprised him. Peter had shared his entire past over the years. He'd even confided in Slade the second Lucia's father had agreed for him to marry her. Peter had, right then and there, resigned his commission in the Royal Scots Greys and came to work at his family's gunsmithing operation. Peter liked sharing details of his life. Slade didn't. However, it hadn't stopped Peter from speculating on Slade's past.

"I wouldn't call going to war an escape," Slade said.

"It can be, if you're running away from something darker than war."

Peter's words punched his gut. A hot mist washed over his body. Guilt, his old friend.

The irony was that the inadequacy of their uniforms against the elements during the war, the inedible rations, and the starving men too weak or ill to fight had still not dulled his memories of Sylvia's death. Many of his fellow officers would share stories of their families around a campfire in Germany when they'd have the luxury of one. Slade had never been one of those. He couldn't bear to be reminded of what he'd lost—it unhinged him. Even after a decade, it made him want to rip his heart from his chest so the nails would stop digging into his soul.

His friend's lips pursed for a breath, before he spoke. "I don't know what burdens you or what made you join the Scot's Greys, but you have to forgive yourself and move beyond your past."

His friend's voice was sincere. It made Slade swallow the tightness in his throat. Slade had only ever told his foster brothers Egan and Daegan the real story about Sylvia. And then later Minister Raghnall and his wife.

Slade arranged his features into what he hoped was bored indifference. "Promotion to colonel and a medal was sufficient for me. Besides, I am considering giving it all up."

Peter's brows lifted. "You are going to sell your commission?"

"Lachlan has been sending missives over the past few months, insisting he and Chisolm need me back at Garraidh." A wave of irritation at his brother's bold request caused Slade to press his lips together. "So yes, I am considering it. But not until I tie up some loose ends and conclude this deal with Bolingbroke."

Slade had ripped up the first five missives from Lachlan, but they'd kept coming.

His father's and Lachlan's anti-English rhetoric had for all intents and purposes branded him a Judas, especially after almost two thousand Jacobites lost their lives at Culloden fighting against the English in April of the prior year. Slade had been overseas, having stayed there after fighting alongside the Hanoverian King George II himself and his son the Duke of Cumberland at Dettingen in 1743, enemies to the Jacobites, and had only returned to Scotland fifteen months ago. But if his father and brother found out where his true allegiance lay, they would no doubt want to hug him.

Slade cleared his throat to suppress his ruminations.

"Speaking of loose ends, can you recommend an inquiry agent in Birmingham? I need to locate someone living in Wombourne."

The previous night Slade had encountered two of Bolingbroke's valets and his maid, Omelia Swindlehurst, at the local pub. After buying them several rounds of ale, and artfully ignoring the maid's boldness towards him, he learned where Bolingbroke kept his most sensitive documents. He also learned that Bolingbroke preyed on the female staff at Camberley Manor, and he'd gotten a young maid with child. Would the young maid be willing to speak to the gossip columns for a small sum of money? And how safe was Fifi, working in the household of such a snake?

Interest flashed across Peter's features. "Yes, I've dealt with one or two inquiry agents. I'd be happy to make the necessary introductions. Are you looking to cause trouble or ease trouble for someone?"

Slade threw his friend a cheeky grin. "A little of both."

CHAPTER 7

Phoebe woke before dawn in the dark in her modest bedchamber at the manor. The morning air was chilly as she stepped from under the counterpane. She shivered in her night rail as she turned up the Betty lamp on the nightstand, next to her favorite volumes of Voltaire and David Hume, between whose pages she'd hidden the Jacobite pamphlets.

She picked up a quill and started penning a missive on the status of her reconnaissance mission in Caesar Cipher. Phoebe used Falcon's special concoction of milk ink to write the body of the missive, then she signed it Hawk—her code name in the Movement. The writing, when dry, was invisible to the naked eye and could only be revealed using heat.

Afterwards, Phoebe donned serviceable attire, collected her letter to her mother, plus Lady Bolingbroke's mail, procured the services of one of the manor's footmen as escort and made her way into Birmingham's city center. As always, her mother expected her home for Phoebe's birthday, and still believed she was staying with an old friend from Ayr Academy.

The stench of waste and horses fused with food from a nearby bakery tickled her nose as she stepped into the Royal Mail hours later. The slate-gray sky and crisp autumnal air magnified Birmingham's congestion. An energetic city filled with smoke and commerce. It wasn't a place like on the moors of the Scottish Highlands where you'd find yourself alone, in broad daylight, yelling for help until hoarse.

After posting her letters and Lady Bolingbroke's, she picked up a package sent from Falcon's assistant, which she was sure contained the finely crafted pair of three-inch metal prongs she'd ordered from the Movement, needed for breaking in undetected to Bolingbroke's desk.

Her thoughts then shifted to Slade. And she cringed for the hundredth time at her overreaction under the willow tree six days earlier. Her cheeks heated. Fear was ingrained in her. It controlled her, changed her behavior. She couldn't have helped it.

First, always learn their habits and routine, Falcon's voice sounded in Phoebe's head as she strode down the street, avoiding a smelly pile of refuse. Lady Bolingbroke was spending the day with Mistress Capnell, her friend and fellow gossip monger. And Bolingbroke was in his study where he always was, except on Thursdays when tupping the laundry maid, capricious Swindlehurst. Phoebe was certain proof of Bolingbroke's unsanctioned activity was in his desk drawer, which she'd gotten a glimpse of by chance while speaking to the housemaid.

As Phoebe crossed the street, she stopped short upon noticing a sprawling two-story wooden building across the street with signage reading *Hortons Gunsmith* painted in bold black and gold letters. Was this Slade's Hortons? Her heart lurched forward, and indecision gurgled in her belly. Should she say hello? Phoebe's mind was made up when she saw Slade's familiar dark figure, head and shoulders above the rest, exiting Hortons accompanied by a man of average height with unruly brown hair.

Phoebe made her way across the busy street toward him, sidestepping an oncoming carriage with squeaky wheels, at the same time Slade turned in her direction. He halted his stride, his friend following suit.

Slade was devastatingly appealing in the crisp gray uniform of an officer for the Royal Scots Greys, much like he'd worn at the manor, his open-front gray surtout coat giving him an air of military command. He moved like a natural leader, tall and arresting, grabbing the attention of all around him, especially the women. Slade seemed oblivious to the two women passing him and his friend, their eyes lingering on Slade a breath longer than propriety allowed. Slade's companion wore a pale waistcoat, matching shirt and dark breeches topped off with a cedar-brown woolen jacket.

A holstered flintlock pistol hung casually off Slade's hip instead of a rapier this time. How secure he must feel with it, a comfort she herself had been unable to experience since the moors.

His cool gaze flicked up from the hem of her dress to her face with such intensity and imperious authority her heart gave a sudden jolt and she felt what it must be like to be a soldier under his colonel's command. When his eyes landed on her face, the side of his mouth tilted up in a devastating smile, making her lower body clench. Perhaps he'd forgotten how awkwardly she'd ended their last meeting.

CHAPTER 8

"What an unexpected pleasure. What brings you to Birmingham?" Slade asked Phoebe.

Phoebe had made it a point to dress in drab colors for the past seven years, never wanting a man to take notice of her ever again. But for some reason, her nondescript gray dress and dark woolen coat topped off with a plain *dormeuses* bonnet made her self-conscious under his explorative eyes.

"Errands for my employer," Phoebe said.

As Slade introduced his friend, Peter Horton, the gray light of day accentuated the chiseled lines of Slade's jaw and cheekbones, which had grown more angular and harder since they were children. He was more self-assured, confident and controlled now, most likely picked up in the military.

Phoebe smiled at Peter, who gave a gallant bow in her direction. He was fully half a head shorter than Slade.

"How do you do, Mistress Dunbar?"

Peter's pleasant expression, marked in his well-disposed features, drew a sense of affability and friendship from Phoebe. As this did not happen often—never in fact—she took it to heart.

"A pleasure to meet you, Master Horton. I take it you are a gunsmith?"

"Indeed, I am. And how do you know our colonel here?" Peter threw a cursory glance in Slade's direction.

"Slade fostered with my older brother Egan at the MacDonells' Invergarry Castle in the Scottish Highlands when they were lads," Phoebe said.

"Then you and I must speak at length. Even though I have known the colonel here for six years, I know next to nothing about him."

"It would greatly please me to—"

"Don't you have an appointment?" Slade cut in, his expression superior and laconic as he eyed Peter. Peter, appearing unperturbed, reached into his waistcoat and retrieved a silver pocket watch.

Peter clicked the device open then gasped. "The meeting with the Gun Trade Association is about to start. I must dash. Enchanted to meet you, Mistress Dunbar. I look forward to our next encounter."

He inclined his head towards her and Slade, his features taking on a warm and unassuming smile.

After Peter left, Slade folded his hands behind his back and shot her an expectant smile. But then after glancing at their immediate surroundings, a shadow of disapproval crossed his features.

"Doesn't your employer provide you with an escort?"

"I always have an escort for Lady Bolingbroke's errands, a footman this time, currently tending to the horses at the stables."

He seemed to consider her answer then his gaze turned direct. "And for personal errands?" A hint of concern in his tone.

Phoebe gave a half shrug. "I hardly ever need one. Many times, I come into town with a few of Bolingbroke's staff on our time off, and after errands we travel back in a group." Phoebe paused, warming at his concern, then added, "For example, on the thirty-first of the month, three of us are going to the Saint Michael's church fair, for my birthday."

"The thirty-first? That's your birthday?" A pained expression darkened his brow.

Phoebe was taken aback, concern squeezing her chest. What would cause such a stark reaction in him? "I know the thirty-first is also the day of *Samhain*, but—"

Slade shook his head. "Forgive me. I didn't intend to cause any concern. It's only that I … I once knew someone whose birthday was the same day."

Her entire body stilled, then she blinked at him even as coldness brushed her spine. At that moment, Phoebe would have staked all the darkest secrets of the Whig Party, the English Government and the Royal Army put together that Slade was referring to Sylvia. She regretted unknowingly broaching the topic of his former betrothed and causing him distress. And she would be damned to hell, for she was jealous of a dead woman.

Phoebe had been but a few feet from Sylvia once, years ago, when Egan and her parents had taken her for new clothes in Portree. Egan had pointed Sylvia out to Phoebe as Slade's betrothed even though they'd never actually spoken to each other. Sylvia had had that perfect clear porcelain skin, with big sparkling cinnamon brown eyes, in a perfect oval doll's face that seemed to have a perpetual genuine trusting smile. Phoebe had already been enamored of Slade and seeing how flawless Sylvia was had made her green-eyed over the other woman ever since.

His expression shuttered, as if he wished to change topics. "Since your escort is currently taken up with tending to the horses, might I accompany you for the remainder of your errands?" he said.

Her spirits lifted. As gallant as ever, despite her faux pas. "All that remains is for me to grab the latest copy of the *Daily Courant* before I head back, and I would welcome the company," Phoebe said.

The gossip columns had recently reported on the Jacobite rebel raids in Claigan village in the Scottish Highlands conducted by the English redcoats. Phoebe was certain Bolingbroke's men were responsible for the raids. What else were Bolingbroke's minions up to? *Always keep your eyes and ears peeled,* Falcon had said.

Phoebe and Slade began a leisurely stroll in the direction of the coffee house to procure the gossip columns when Slade eyed her with concern. "How have you been since the footman's accidental shooting?"

"Quite well, thank you. And Ludlow is recovering, thanks to your quick thinking," Phoebe said, to which Slade gave a gracious inclination of his head.

As they made their way down the sidewalk, the foot traffic around them pushed them close enough together that his gleaming riding boots brushed the edges of her skirts, the action strangely intimate.

Then Phoebe's eyes fell on his holstered pistol, the beautiful design on its butt so masterfully engraved she had an intense urge to do a test fire. But how to get Slade to allow her to fire his pistol without divulging she's a proficient trained by the Movement? "Is it difficult to learn how to shoot with a flintlock pistol?" she said.

His lips pursed as they both sidestepped a group of cackling men dressed like sailors. "It depends on how proficient you want to be. Why do you ask?"

"Will you teach me?" she said. And braced herself for his response which she was certain would be not only oppositional but reprimanding as well.

He stopped walking and stared at her in utter surprise and bewilderment. "Whatever for?"

Phoebe stopped walking and turned back to look at him, determination settling in her stomach. "I assume you are much safer when able to take care of yourself, having defensive skills or a weapon. I realize it's highly unorthodox and extremely unladylike, but I long for a bit of that secure feeling." She was fully prepared to beg if he refused.

Slade shook his head, gesturing with an open palm for her to continue their walk as he himself resumed. "One does not need to learn to shoot to feel secure," he said, his tone adamant.

Phoebe swallowed down her mild annoyance. "No, one does not. But working in the house of a general—which is stocked with all types of arms, I might add—and coming into Birmingham at least once or twice a week on errands for Lady Bolingbroke, it would be prudent on my part to think of security. Why just last week two drunken sailors coming out of a pub nearly knocked us over—"

Slade stopped his stroll, his green eyes glinting with alarm even in the day's pale light. "Were you accosted?"

She stopped as well and rushed to assuage his alarm, while her insides warmed at his concern. "No. No, it was an innocent mistake for which they begged our pardon. But what if their intentions had been nefarious?"

Slade's face tensed. "Although I find it shocking you are implying you wish to carry a firearm, your observation about working in Bolingbroke's household is well noted."

Derision and danger brewed in his expression. Did he not like General Bolingbroke? Weren't they comrades-in-arms? Well, she supposed someone like Bolingbroke inspired anything but camaraderie.

"Very well, I'll teach you how to shoot," Slade said, the words coming out determined.

CHAPTER 9

*P*hoebe's fingers curled around the wooden grip of the pistol, her pointer finger on the trigger. She raised her right arm straight out and pointed at the target about eighty feet away. The ball had already been rammed down the front of the barrel, the charge powder loaded in the pan and the pistol cocked. Falcon's voice rang in her head. *Practice makes progress.* She couldn't tell Slade she was already a proficient markswoman. If she had, she would have had to reveal why.

After they'd picked up the gossip column, Slade had brought her to Hortons second floor, which had a well-equipped and spacious shooting range.

Slade's green eyes observed her keenly. "Now remember all I just said. Aim and squeeze. There will be a split-second delay before the gun kicks back and the shot is released."

The wood was warm against her palm but the trigger cold as ice as she took aim and tightened her finger. Her eyes were riveted forward when the slight kick-back made her dig her feet in firmer where she stood, a split second after the loud pop sounded. The resulting hole appeared in the first ring outside the bullseye.

Slade blinked in astonishment at the target and then back at Phoebe. "Have you done this before?"

Blast! Should she have aimed for the second ring instead of the first?

She shrugged, affecting an air of innocence. "I may have picked up a few pointers from Egan in the not-too-distant past."

She felt rather than saw his searching eyes traveling from her forehead down to her eyes, her cheekbones, and then lingering on her lips. Heat rose to her cheeks. Energy crackled in the air affecting her equilibrium as his eyes remained on her.

"What have you been doing with yourself since I last saw you that day in Eileanach's stables? You certainly didn't graduate from Ayr Academy and immediately start as a lady's companion." Slade's quiet, intimate voice collided with her senses. His green discerning eyes darkened as he continued to study her.

Phoebe's heart stuttered as flashbacks flooded her head. She turned away from him, his gaze too intense. She walked to the table a few feet away where she placed the pistol, her back to him so he couldn't see the rawness in her eyes.

The day he spoke of was seared in her memory. It was the last she'd seen Slade before he'd left for the Royal Military Academy at Woolwich. A bleak and cold day, not only because she'd wondered if she would ever see Slade again but because she was mourning Alex's death, and the encounter on the moors had happened a few days before in broad daylight. No one knew she'd been bruised beneath her clothes. No one knew her world had crashed and combusted to cinders. She'd been too scared to tell anyone. Scared of Faye Ross's retaliation. That day, she'd wanted to tell Slade that, despite her misery and hellish reality, just being near him had brought her comfort and relief from her bleak life. Being with him had given her a chance to forget. But Slade had been in a hell of his own then, having just lost his love, Sylvia.

Now, unaware Slade had closed the distance between them,

the touch of his hand on her arm jarred her senses. The alarm bells were so loud, Phoebe didn't think, just reacted as trained. Phoebe swung around, pulled her hand back and sent the ball of her palm forward, straight into her assailant's gullet.

Not an assailant. Slade!

Oh, dear God.

Slade's eyes bulged as he coughed, sputtered, and stepped away from her, both hands holding his throat.

Phoebe's jaws dropped. Heat and mortification enveloped Phoebe completely as she realized what she'd done and stepped towards Slade. Concern a heavy weight of regret in her chest. "I'm … I am ever so sorry, you startled me. It wasn't my intention to—"

"It's fine. I'm fine, just give me a second." His voice was a painful-sounding strangled whisper. Phoebe's palm went up to cover her mouth. She wanted to weep in dismay.

Slade's palms rested on his knees as he bowed his head and continued to cough. When he finally straightened, his face was red, and his eyes glistened with embarrassment and astonishment.

"Your defensive skills are quite good without the aid of a gun." His voice slowly returned to its usual richness.

"Did I hurt you? Are you well?" Phoebe asked, guilt tightening her chest.

Slade laughed in self-mockery. "I shouldn't have come up behind you like that. Forgive me."

Phoebe hesitantly joined in his laughter, although hers sounded strangled. "I shouldn't have struck you. I beg your pardon."

"Then we are even. Where the devil did you learn to punch like that? It makes me wonder how little Fifi became … you," he said, his brows arching in question.

CHAPTER 10

ROYAL SCOTS GREYS, 2ND DRAGOONS' GARRISON, BURNTWOOD, ENGLAND

Slade concluded his toilette in his colonel's quarters as dawn's noisy chorus of birds outside echoed indoors. He pulled on a white shirt, donned his inky black breeches, then tugged on winter hose and a pair of tall caramel leather boots. As he buttoned his embroidered waistcoat and tied the silk cravat in a barrel knot with military precision, Slade glanced out the window. The fiery trail across the sky begrudgingly dropped golden hues into the early morning's grayness. From the way the branches of the alder tree swayed, it was going to be a windy day.

Today would have been Sylvia's twenty-eighth birthday. It had been a warm spring day under a similar alder tree in the Highlands when he'd proposed to her a decade ago. The sweet scent of wildflowers and resin drilled into his memory. Sylvia's shy but brilliant smile had rivaled the marigold sun. His heart had been beating so fast it had almost broken free of his chest. He'd asked her to be his wife. Her cinnamon brown eyes had sparkled with emotion as she'd flung her arms around his neck with a breathy *yes. Oh yes,* she'd said. He could still hear that enamored voice in his dreams just before the blackness of nightmares took over.

He now pulled on his dark greatcoat as he headed for the

door. His eyes glanced over to the plain wooden table with its folded parchments, quills, ink pots, and a stack of leatherbound books. Atop the stack was Minister Raghnall's folded missive. He'd read the heartbreaking missive so many times its ends were curling outwards. Isaac, Raghnall's only son and Slade's friend had died in a skirmish with the redcoats at Claigan village. His hands fisted. The redcoat's *cleansing* of rebels in the Scottish Highlands had long since changed from viciousness to malicious glee.

Slade reached for the door's handle just as footfalls sounded outside. Seconds later his door swung open, and Reginald Seymour stood in the doorway dressed in his uniform.

"A word, MacLean."

General Reginald Seymour, his direct report, wasn't what Slade would call a kind man, but he wasn't a contemptable arsehole either. From Slade's experience, one had to be a contemptable arsehole to advance to the rank of General, thus it said something about the man. Seymour was approximately ten years Slade's senior, always clean shaven and in fit form, with those discerning brown eyes revealing a casual omniscience.

The general had an exceptional combination of hardness and approachability, giving one the impression of trustworthiness. And mayhap he was trustworthy, but Slade didn't know enough of the man to make the determination yet.

Slade stepped back, folded his hands at his back and squared his shoulders to face his superior.

He hiked a brow at the other man. "Is there a problem, sir?"

General Seymour stepped into the chamber and closed the door behind him.

Seymour's eyes narrowed. "Are you meeting with General Bolingbroke again today?"

"Not today. But I will be soon."

The general grimaced. "I don't make it a habit of interfering with the personal lives of my officers, Colonel, but you ought to know you will make a number of enemies in this garrison if you continue to keep company with Bolingbroke."

Interest sparked inside Slade's gut. Did Seymour not get along with Bolingbroke?

Slade banked the information away.

"Why, may I ask, sir?"

His superior's mouth twisted, as if he'd tasted rancid milk. "Bolingbroke has a less-than-savory reputation after unjustly transporting several of our men to the colonies, among other things. And one becomes tainted by association."

What was the army doing about said less-than-savory reputation? And what did he mean by *among other things*?

"Are you alluding to questionable actions by Bolingbroke?" Slade asked.

The other man nodded with a scowl. "I am."

The curt nod suggested he wasn't prepared to discuss it further. But Slade pushed the issue.

"I take it, sir, disciplinary action against Bolingbroke would be difficult?"

The general fixed his gaze on Slade. "Yes, it would be. Without evidence and testimony, impossible."

A smile tugged on Slade's lips, not unlike the one a cat would have upon locating the hiding place of a rat. "I am obliged to you for letting me know, sir."

Slade then inquired about the procedure for the sale of a colonel's commission. Despite the general's clear surprise, the other man provided the necessary information, after which Slade departed his quarters, and left the garrison on horseback.

Two hours later Slade loosely held Destroyer's reins as he strolled beside the beast. The horse let out a disgruntled neigh.

He patted the animal's shoulder in a soothing manner. "You'd rather be racing across open fields instead of walking through a herd of chattering attendees at the St. Michael's Church fête, wouldn't you?"

Destroyer gave a light toss of his head in the affirmative.

The smell of roasted meat from the food vendors mingled with the scent of fresh hay and the stench from the paddocks of ponies, pigs, and goats. The church's organ played, its notes escaping the open stained-glass windows and filling the grounds with one of Isaac Watts' popular hymns. It reminded him of visiting Raghnall's church during his childhood and finding a measure of peace. And acceptance. Something he'd never had at home after his mother's death.

How was he to find Fifi in this discordant gathering? Several minutes later, he spotted a trio on the other side, stopping to admire the horses for sale. A young couple with a pleasant countenance, dressed in Sunday best clothes. The lanky young man looked very much like a valet he'd seen at Bolingbroke's. But Slade was more interested in the lass standing beside the couple. Fifi.

CHAPTER 11

Fifi wore a nondescript olive gown starting at her graceful neck and flowing down the curves of her elfin figure to trim ankles fitted with dark chocolate leather boots. His eyes rose the length of her, lingering a second too long on her curvaceous chest before he yanked his gaze to further take in her attire, annoyed with himself. It kept slipping his mind this was Fifi, Egan's little sister. And calling Egan's protectiveness over Fifi extreme was akin to describing a gargantuan monolith as a pebble. Why was he not surprised Fifi's ensemble seemed to blend in with the background? She'd picked up a knack for dreary and drab colors. Why was that?

Slade leisurely strolled towards the trio, pulling the reins of a reluctant Destroyer. As he approached, Fifi's gaze shifted towards him. The slopes of her shoulders perked up and she eyed him with surprise and an intensity that made his skin tighten. Was she wondering what he was doing here? The truth was, he wanted to see her for her birthday. Perhaps selfishly, he longed for the familiarity of a bonny face from home. Or perhaps it was simply her friendly company he longed for. Someone he'd loved being with, when he was younger, when life was simpler, and he hadn't yet been poisoned by Old Testament revenge and retribution. One thing was certain—he needed a new memory for the thirty-first, besides it being Sylvia's birthday.

"Slade?" she said, her countenance brightening.

"I've never attended a church fête before. I wanted to join you," he said, in answer to her questioning tone.

Fifi made a cordial introduction to her companions, Reddington, an upstairs maid, and Montgomery, a valet, who worked at the manor.

Montgomery's unpretentious gray eyes flickered over Slade with recognition. "I recall you helping the day Ludlow was shot."

Slade exchanged a few words with Montgomery. He exhaled contentedly upon learning Ludlow was out of bed and recovering.

Reddington, a shy, pale lass, inquired about the horses, which she and Montgomery took their leave of Slade and Fifi to peruse.

After they left, Fifi turned to Slade. "May we take a look at the gentleman's blades on display?"

His eyes widened with surprise at her question. Pistols, defensive skills, and now blades? "You wish to look at the knives?" he asked.

She snorted at his question. "I realize my tastes could be considered boorish, even masculine, trending towards improper, as are some of my other proclivities. But I've had an interest ever since Egan trained me in their proper use."

Why would Egan train her on the use of gentleman's blades? But then he recalled that as a young lass she had been keen to learn swordplay, to the utter dismay of her parents. Hell, the first time he'd met her she'd been nine and was reciting the knight's oath when she'd fallen into the loch.

Slade grinned at her, tugging Destroyer along towards the merchant stalls. "I don't think it boorish or masculine in the least, just surprising. But it does pique my interest on your other proclivities."

Merchants called out, even clanked their displayed silver, tin, and lead goods together to grab their attention as they took a leisurely stroll along the stalls towards the knife and sword sellers.

"Reading, for example. My mother never missed a chance to remind me such an exhibition of independent spirit won't do me any favors in securing a husband," Fifi said.

"Are you in the market for a husband?" He wondered out aloud.

"A husband is the farthest thing from my mind," she said.

"It takes great strength of character to be an independent spirit, going against the norm. Most people are too afraid to step out of the mold of a follower. As for reading, it's rather commendable you want to improve your mind."

She sent him a pointed smile, as if his answer pleased her. A becoming flush of the palest rose colored her cheeks, erasing the lightest of her pretty freckles.

"And you?" she asked.

"Me?"

"Yes. Any vices to share with an old friend?"

Slade considered her question before speaking. "I've been told I snore rather loudly. When we were stationed in Germany during the war, my comrades feared I would lead the enemy straight to our camp," he said.

Her lips twitched. "What an unforgivable vice indeed. And did your snoring lead the enemy to your camp?"

He chuckled at her restrained merriment. "Well, no. We came upon their camp first and disarmed them before they could retaliate."

She looked impressed, yet mirth still danced on her features. "You and your men triumphed despite your loud snores. Well done."

Her face glowed with an adorable warmth, reminding him of when they were younger.

A gust of wind swept the area—it flipped Fifi's bonnet right off her head. His body tightened and heated, filling with an unexpected hunger as her enticing scent suffused with orange blossoms and bergamot teased his nostrils. The wind tossed her hair like wild waves crashing on rocks. And the sun glinted off each fiery red and copper-toned strand, like a cloak of fire hypnotically dancing around her shoulders.

Slade was so spellbound he didn't move fast enough to pick up the bonnet as a gentleman would have.

"Oh no," she gasped.

The prosaic action of her bending to retrieve the fallen bonnet drew Slade's eyes to her enticingly curved backside. He scolded himself, dragging his gaze away and shaking himself out of his momentary stupor. This was Egan's sister, he reminded himself again.

It was then that he took in the reason for her gasp. Destroyer's front hoof had partially crushed the bonnet which she now held in her hand.

He grimaced at the ruined hat.

"Both Destroyer and I beg your pardon," he said.

"Fitting name your horse has," she murmured. Her eyes narrowed at his horse in disapproval.

Destroyer gave a loud snort, tossing his head right then left, as if objecting to the title of Destroyer of women's bonnets.

Slade found himself considering her as they drifted through the crowd. Did her dreary tastes in attire extend to every aspect of her life?

"You spoke of your enjoyment of reading. What are your favorite books?"

She chewed on her bottom lip, seeming to regard his question.

"While I do enjoy poetry quite a bit, philosophy is my first love. Voltaire for example, but my favorite is David Hume."

He scrutinized her, flummoxed. He'd expected her to mention

a French romance novel or perhaps a chapbook, not Voltaire and David Hume. Voltaire and David Hume weren't dreary reads nor typical for lasses. These were men of modern religious, political, and scientific ideas. Possibly even dangerous ideas.

"Why David Hume?" Her choice to read the works of a philosopher and presumed atheist was the bigger mystery, Slade decided.

Her eyes sparked at his question.

"Since he lives in Glasgow, I think he has a firmer grasp of the Scots' plight than Voltaire. I like his idea that without passions, one can avoid pain." She paused thoughtfully then continued. "If I get too excited, or angry, or even happy over something I quell my energies, because I don't want to do anything silly, or regrettable, which is often the case when one is impassioned."

The conviction in her voice speared him down the middle. His heart squeezed and his head buzzed with countless questions. She spoke of pain like it was a familiar friend. Or enemy. He couldn't tell.

"But surely that's no way to live? Only halfway in," he said.

"Being calm and reflective is safe."

"Safe from what?"

"Hurt."

Slade stopped and stared at her. She stopped as well, looking up at him with furrowed brows and a vulnerability that cut his heart with an invisible knife.

"Are you speaking of Alex's death, Fifi?" His tone was soft.

Her throat muscles worked, and pain contorted her lovely face before she looked away.

"I am. But not only Alex's death, life in general." He didn't miss the way her voice cracked with emotion.

"But that's only half a life, Fifi. Alex wouldn't want that for you."

Her jaw muscles worked, but she remained silent.

Slade's mind fell on his own plight. On his need for revenge and retribution. And on his familiarity with the two, like a second skin. Was he capable of approaching the general's culpability with logic, calm and reflection? Without the passion of hatred? Without the pain of loss and the gut-wrenching guilt? Peter had told him to move beyond his past. To forgive. The idea caused spiders to crawl under his skin and cold shivers to run up his spine. If he forgave, what would happen to his redemption?

Slade's fingers curled around Destroyer's reins. "I fear humans are incapable of such advancement in thinking. We are all animal urges and instincts at the core. Passion is far too intertwined in our blood to be separate."

For the next few minutes, they slowly walked side by side, in companionable and reflective silence, Slade seeing Fifi in a way he never had before.

"What other Hume ideas resonate with you?" he asked.

She was meditative before speaking. "The idea that society should approach with suspicion government's need to change long-established customs," she said.

Was she referring to the English monarchy and government? If she was a sympathizer, then why the heck was she working for an English general's wife?

She'd tricked him. She wasn't drab and dreary at all. She'd grown into an enigma, among other things.

The right side of his mouth lifted. "Are you a rebel sympathizer, Fifi?"

His tone was filled with mirth. But as the words left his lips, Slade felt their gravity. Everything faded into the background except his heartbeats as he waited for her reply.

She was about to answer him when Montgomery and Reddington rejoined them at that very moment.

CHAPTER 12

CAMBERLEY MANOR, SUTTON COLDFIELD, ENGLAND

Two days later, as the midday sun bathed Camberley manor's open stable doors in warm amber light, Phoebe waited. She'd just seen Lady Bolingbroke off to her afternoon tea with Mistress Capnell at which time her employer asked her to finish the correspondences and then pick up her sapphire necklace and earrings for the upcoming charity ball she and the general would be attending. But Phoebe didn't start any of it because Slade was finishing up a musket demonstration with general Bolingbroke and would have to come by the stables to pick up his horse. Falcon's voice resonated in her head. *Private connections should not influence the mission.* Phoebe chose to ignore it.

She didn't have to wait long. Slade's tall lean figure strode around the corner from the gardens, heading for the stables. Her vitals spiked at the sight of him. A cool breeze brushed the length of her, mixing with the heat forming along her spine. Slade carried a long canvas bag, looking like it contained muskets, propped on his broad right shoulder, his expression softening with warmth at the sight of her.

Silhouetted against the sun's streaming overhead rays, he

advanced towards her, his stride strong and sure. Her nerves had been jangled since he'd arrived earlier; now they were positively in chaos as he neared. Because of her fear since the moors, men set her nerves on edge. But Slade set her nerves on edge for an entirely different reason.

Phoebe swallowed against the sudden dryness in her mouth and relaxed her features into a smile. "How did the musket demonstration go?" she said, her voice unusually high pitched and breathy.

She wasn't fishing for information, she told herself, simply inquiring whether Slade had a successful meeting.

He frowned. "Not as well as I'd hoped, but not a complete loss either."

Before she could prod for clarification, his gaze landed on the stables then returned to her. "Are you taking a horse out?" he asked.

She considered the correspondence awaiting completion on the desk in the library. "I do have to run an errand today for Lady Bolingbroke," she said.

"I am at your disposal as an escort for errands." He gave a wide smile, and made a spirited bow.

His overtly courteous gesture set off butterflies in her belly, untangled her nerves and warmed her from head to toe.

She decided now was as good a time as any to pick up Lady Bolingbroke's necklace. "I'll just be a moment to grab my coat, hat and gloves."

Half an hour later, after deciding on one of the Bolingbrokes' two-wheeled open-top conveyances, Phoebe and Slade set out for the jewelers. A whiff of the slightly sweet scent of silage from the countryside circulated in the air. She sat next to him as he held the reins in a casual, relaxed manner, guiding the chestnut gelding in a slow clip-clopping trot.

Her skin heated at having to sit so close to him on the small conveyance while his long uniform-clad leg brushed hers, the imprint of toned thigh muscles evident through his fitted breeches. The contact of his leg against the thick outer layer of her skirt sent jolts straight to her skin, blood, and bones. Phoebe debated internally whether to pull away from him and move closer to her end of the seat, but decided the gesture would draw too much attention. At least that is what she told herself. In the secret recesses of her body, she welcomed the warmth of contact despite his imposing shoulders.

The left wheel of the carriage jerked over bumpiness on the road, sending Phoebe sideways into Slade's hard body. She gasped as her pulse spiked and her muscles tightened. Good God, his body was built like steel, his strength and size so much more evident on contact. She picked up the faintest hint of cloves and male spice as she scrambled to sit up straight once more.

Slade's left hand reached out, and she instinctually shrank away, a tiny cry escaping her lips before realizing he was only trying to steady her. Mortification and shame contracted her insides and sent heat to her cheeks. Dear Lord, her body seemed incapable of not being jittery around him. He pulled on the reins, and the carriage jolted to a halt.

He turned to her with knitted brows. "Are you all right?"

She swallowed, the heat of embarrassment flooding her body. She'd overreacted. Again. And worse still, he'd taken note this time.

"I'm quite well, thank you." Her voice was so squeaky it made her lower her head. Where was a hole in the ground when you needed one to disappear into?

When she looked up, he was considering her with a frown. "Do I make you nervous, Fifi? There is no cause to be. We are auld friends, are we not?"

A loud ringing sounded in Phoebe's ears. Did friends make each other's palms dampen, hearts race and bodies react to any least bit of nearness or contact?

"Of course we are friends," she said, letting out a strained laugh.

He sent her a solemn and overtly disbelieving quirk of his brow.

"How did my adventurous and rambunctious little friend from Eileanach Castle grow up to be a nervous lady's companion, working in the household of an English general, when she herself exhibits rebel tendencies?" he asked, his voice deep and probing.

Phoebe blinked and forced herself to meet his gaze. It was difficult to maintain steady eye contact, like gazing at the bright and blinding midday sun. She momentarily lost her words. He not only made her nervous, but she couldn't decide what to do with her hands. And her feet, though unmoving, felt awkward on the footrest. His steady gaze intensified with inquiry. The air between them crackled. Was it tension? Heat? She struggled for an air of composure and for her voice. "I … I told you, I'm here in the service of a friend."

"Yes, you did say." He murmured.

From his tightening lips he clearly didn't swallow what she was feeding him. Slade faced forward once again and snapped the reins. The gelding resumed its trot.

"If you ever require my assistance, besides being your occasional escort, all you have to do is ask," he said.

Her heart warmed at his offer, despite the skepticism in his eyes.

He'd no doubt made the offer because of Bolingbroke's reputation for hating Scots and being a savage executioner in the Highlands. His moniker of *Hangman* was well earned. Regardless of her lies to Slade, her current clandestine occupation, the violent tragedy befalling her seven years ago, and the fact that Slade's presence stirred something unexpected and unsettling inside her, Slade was indeed an old and dear acquaintance.

"I value your friendship a great deal and am thankful for your offer of help. Rest assured if ever I find myself in need, I will come to you," she said, to which he nodded with a satisfied quirk of his lips.

When they arrived at the jewelers, Slade alighted and gave her a hand in stepping down from the conveyance.

"Should I accompany you inside?" he asked, still holding her hand in his much larger one, making her heart hum. His touch was gentle yet strong, and steady, his warmth enveloping her hands even through the layers of their gloves.

"I don't think it will be necessary. Monsieur Gustave is usually very quick and efficient. I will only be a minute."

Inside, the jeweler had Lady Bolingbroke's necklace and earrings already cleaned and wrapped.

On the return carriage ride to the manor, Slade's friendly tone made Phoebe wonder if she'd imagined the previous crackling heat and tension between them.

"I haven't seen Egan in some time. What is he getting up to these days?" Slade said.

"Mother's last letter said he and a Dunbar delegation are on the Isle of Coll negotiating peace with Clan Campbell. There've been some hostilities betwixt our two clans recently."

Slade snorted. "Hostilities no doubt instigated by the Campbells. They're troublemakers. I don't envy Egan his task. I imagine the Dunbar retainers would rather do battle."

Phoebe took in the autumnal, yellowing leaves of prominent trees on either side of the road. "My father is the one who is pushing for peace," she said, knowing that Egan would do whatever their father told him, even if he himself hated the Campbells, like many Highlanders.

"Egan always did the honorable thing, acting for the greater good," Slade said.

Phoebe found herself smiling, as her good-hearted but overbearing brother's past behavior came to mind. "When I was younger, he was so protective of me, barking like a fierce guard dog whenever any lad spoke to me or any of his friends even looked in my direction."

Slade chuckled, sending her a warm, playful glance. "I recalled how Egan use to chase away your admirers when we were younger."

Phoebe laughed at Slade's teasing tone. Warm fondness filled her belly as she recalled the same tone from when they were younger. She'd simply adored Slade's teasing and warm friendship when they were younger, she still did. But then the memory of her brother confronting Ross pulled her mood down. Seven years ago, Egan had challenged Faye Ross, and the ensuing fight had nearly proved fatal to her brother. Phoebe had never told Egan the truth but knew that Egan suspected Ross had done something untoward. She'd been too ashamed and scared of Faye Ross's retaliation. Since then, Egan had been a terror against any man coming near her.

CHAPTER 13

CAMBERLEY MANOR, SUTTON COLDFIELD, ENGLAND

On the night of the Earl of Clarendon's charity ball, an hour after General and Lady Bolingbroke departed in full livery, the activity in the manor died down. But Phoebe's stomach roiled with excitement, dread, and anticipation.

When she was sure all the staff had retired to their quarters, she cracked open her door. The hall was quiet. Sliding the black velvet vizard mask in place so she wouldn't be readily identifiable beneath the dimly lit wall sconces, she exited, closed the door and tiptoed down the hall and up the stairs towards the general's study. She glanced around to make sure no one was about before turning the cold brass knob with clammy palms. Phoebe slipped into the study to the scent of cheroot and whisky and closed the door behind her without making a sound. She placed a hand on her chest to calm her heart as it threatened to escape her ribcage. Falcon's voice sounded in her head: *Remain dispassionate and calm.*

"Simple for you to say," Phoebe whispered to herself.

A loud gong reverberated in the study and Phoebe's heart dropped to her stomach. But then her eyes snapped to where the sound had originated, landing on the gilded face of a long case clock. She narrowed her eyes at the offending hands reading half past eleven. Then ignoring the ceiling-to-floor bookcases stacked with books, the classical bust, maps and globe, she headed straight for the leather-trimmed mahogany desk and its hidden drawer.

By Phoebe's estimation, the Bolingbrokes should be arriving at the ball now, for the earl's residence was an hour's ride from the manor. She would allow herself one hour in the study. She didn't think the Bolingbrokes would ride to the ball to simply return home, but to be conservative she would assume so. Typically, these events lasted until the wee hours of the morning.

The pale light from the gargantuan hearth's dwindling fire and the illumination from the two wall sconces above its mantel glinted off three lustrous silver-trimmed flintlock muskets mounted on the wall. An image of Slade's breathtakingly beautiful green eyes flashed across her mind. *Blast!* She didn't need any distractions now.

But there'd been something in the way he had looked at her during their brief tête-à-tête to the jeweler, that heated her from the inside out.

Phoebe pushed aside her thoughts and sat in the general's enormous, leather-upholstered chair in front of his desk. She reached into her pocket and removed the two three-inch metal prongs which had been mailed to her by Falcon's assistant, code-name Blue Jay. Blue Jay had expertly sewn the prongs into the taffeta lining of a caraco jacket to keep them safe and undetected while being transported by the Royal Mail. They often had to resort to extreme measures to safeguard the tools of their trade.

Aided by the pale light from the wall sconces, she stuck the first metal prong into the keyhole of the pin and tumbler lock. Phoebe gingerly tilted it in a clockwise direction with her left hand while she inserted the second prong with its three ridges into the top of the keyhole with her right hand. Phoebe lightly jiggled and raked the prong back and forth, feeling for an opening.

The resistance gave way. Her mouth relaxed into a slow smile. She turned the prong until it clicked. Phoebe pocketed the two prongs and pulled on the handle of the drawer. It slid open as if on well-oiled slides. There were several sheets of folded paper in the drawer atop a leather-bound ledger. She lifted everything and paused, eying the unlit silver-plated candelabrum. It wasn't safe to light it, so she walked everything over to the dim light of the hearth.

Her hands trembled as she opened the pulpy folded papers one by one and scanned their contents. Phoebe ignored the first few pages concerning routine army matters and focused on the last pages discussing the Abolition of Heritable Jurisdictions. Centuries ago, the law of Scotland granted jurisdiction to privileged persons or heritors and their heirs, allowing clan chiefs to govern their lands and clans. The abolition of this right stripped governing power away from the Scottish clan chiefs in favor of the English crown. The last page Phoebe now held discussed forcibly upholding this law with extreme measures in the Highlands including torture and death for offenders, but redcoats didn't need a reason to torture and kill Highlanders who followed clan tradition like their fathers and their fathers before them. She walked back to the desk, recorded the information on a blank sheet of paper, then pocketed the copy.

The remaining parchments appeared to be of more standard Army matters; as she was about to put them aside, however, one title *New Artillery Cannon* design and another titled *Glenfinnan Mission* stood out. Phoebe's heart hammered against her chest as she pulled it out of the stack and read further. The *New Artillery Cannon* design would be an easy copy but *Glenfinnan Mission* took up most of her attention. It was a rejection note from Field Marshal Pelham to take part in a raid on Jacobites at Glenfinnan, where Charles Edward Stuart had first raised his flag on August 19, 1745. The field marshal ended the rejection by saying while he couldn't sanction such a raid through official Army channels,

it was up to the general if he wished to proceed through unoffi-
cial ones. Phoebe then noted the scrawled names of Bolingbroke's first and second lieutenants, Hughes Cope and Walter
Hawley, with three words below. *Mission a go.* But when?

The rebels should have been shielded by the Indemnity Act of
June 1747 after the Battle of Culloden, yet Phoebe somehow
wasn't surprised Bolingbroke was still conducting raids. *This is it.*
This is what she'd come for.

She'd just copied the *New Artillery Cannon* and *Glenfinnan
Mission* information when approaching footfalls thudded outside
the study, Phoebe froze. Fear coated her spine. She glanced at the
clock. She'd already been in the study for an entire hour! Could
the Bolingbrokes have simply driven to the ball then return? One
of Falcon's codes played in her head. *Know where the exits are at all
times.*

Blast! The fact that there was just one made her heart stop
cold. Phoebe dashed back to the desk, shoved the original documents back into the drawer and pushed it shut. She'd taken two
steps away from the desk with the intention of hiding when the
only door to the study swung open.

CHAPTER 14

*P*hoebe stared at General Bolingbroke currently blocking her exit. He stood in the doorway dressed in pristine evening elegance. All the blood rushed from her head so fast, she feared she might faint. His porcine eyes were frigid and calm as they eyed her up and down. He had the look of a man whose attempts to appear civil couldn't quite belie the distasteful way his mouth turned up or the hostility in his eyes.

"Who are you and what in damnation are you doing in here?" he asked in an eerily quiet tone.

Even though Falcon's voice replayed in her head—*Never look guilty*—Phoebe couldn't command her rigid body to relax. But thankfully the vizard offered her a degree of anonymity, unless he worked out who she was in spite of it.

The general's eyes narrowed at her as he stepped into the study and, without making a sound, closed the door behind him. His body appeared as taut as a noose dangling a dying man. Somehow the chances of her surviving seemed slimmer with the door closed and with him eying her with a rancorous stare. She'd much rather he yelled for a footman to come and throw her out. But this was what she'd trained for.

"Apologies, Sir Henry. I was waiting." Phoebe was surprised at her calm tone. She'd made her voice overtly nasal and squeaky hoping to continue with the disguise.

The general took a few steps towards her, his eyes slowly roving the length of her.

"You are not one of the downstairs maids. And you're not Wetherbee either, she is much rounder. Who are you?" His inquiry was placid and cold.

"Apologies, but I'll remain anonymous for now," she said.

"Who are you waiting for?" he asked.

Several questions rushed into Phoebe's head, but one held her attention. What was the penalty for high treason?

Death by hanging.

She needed something that would shock him so much he wouldn't question.

"Montgomery," she said.

"Montgomery?" His right hand reached up to twirl the side of his mustache.

She hoped the valet, Montgomery, and the maid he was sweet on, Reddington, would forgive her for this blunder.

The general's gaze traversed Phoebe's body and his lips twisted into a lascivious sneer. Her skin prickled with a revolting unclean disquietude.

"Then you must be Reddington. Well, has my early return impeded your late-night rendezvous with Montgomery, my dear? You must blame Lady Bolingbroke. I could stand her insufferable company no longer."

He took two more steps towards her. His face and neck flushed with pleasure, filling Phoebe with disgust. He was so near now the horrid scent of sweat and male perfume made toxic acid rise up from her stomach.

Phoebe gave a slight shrug of her shoulders feigning calm and took two steps back, as the chill of alarm lifted the hairs on her body. Old images of Ross rushed into her head with the force of a guillotine cutting off her breath.

The general chuckled, wetting his lips. "I hadn't figured you for a hussy. You are always such a shy little thing. I am now immensely pleased I left ahead of time. I'd much rather avail myself of your pleasurable company than my wife's. Perhaps I can take Montgomery's place for tonight's rendezvous, my dear?"

He took the final step towards her, grabbed a handful of her hair, and yanked it towards him. Pain riveted through her scalp as every single muscle in her body went rigid with mind-numbing terror. But rage born of self-preservation broke through like a battering ram. Her eyes fell on the silver candelabrum. Phoebe snatched it up with both hands and swung it with all her strength against the general's skull.

From the look on his face, he hadn't expected the first blow. She dealt two more. Their dull thuds made her stomach roil.

"Filthy whore …" The general groaned, crumpling to the floor.

Phoebe put the candelabrum on the desk. She had to quiet the groans before he raised the alarm. She grabbed the jeweled comb from her hair and pulled it apart, snipping out the hidden pin with the spider's poison. *The venom of the brown widow causes temporary paralysis; it's to be used only in emergencies.*

This qualifies as an emergency, Falcon. Steadying her tremulous breath, Phoebe pushed the pin into the pulsating vein at the general's neck.

Seconds later the general's groans quieted. Of all the thoughts bombarding her, one stood out.

Run.

But her body shook with cold fear as she slipped out of his study and closed the door behind her without making a sound. In her bedchamber, she snatched up her reticule and black fur lined cloak, then as silent as a specter sprinted for the stables on shaking legs, encountering no one.

It wouldn't take long for Bolingbroke to work out that it was her instead of Reddington who was in his study after he awoke. Especially once Phoebe vanished. She doubted he would send the constables after her for the humiliation she caused him. His ego wouldn't want anyone to know. Besides, she'd done no permanent damage to his person, nor had she taken anything. Yet she still had trouble breathing through the tightness in her chest as she bridled and saddled Bolingbroke's fastest horse. If the constables did come after her, horse theft would be a certain charge.

CHAPTER 15

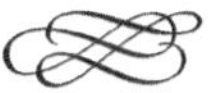

HILL HOOK, SUTTON COLDFIELD, ENGLAND

Slade groaned when the persistent knocking metamorphosed into an annoying banging. Ignoring the blaggard wasn't working. His eyelids pushed open in the dark as he sat up and swung his feet down the left side of the bed. Who could possibly be banging on the door at this unholy hour? When his bare feet sank into something plush and soft, he recalled the bear rug and where he was. He'd been used to the cold floors of the officers' quarters in Burntwood but had availed himself of the Hortons spacious and comfortable hunting lodge ten miles south of Burntwood for the past two nights since selling his colonel's commission.

The banging grew louder. He made his way out of the bedchamber and down the hall towards the receiving area of the lodge, but not before slipping his trident dagger into the back waist of his breeches. Even though only Peter, the stable hand, and the cook were privy to his whereabouts, he wanted to be prepared. But then he rolled his eyes.

"A prowler with ill intentions wouldn't bother to knock, MacLean," he grumbled to himself.

The banging turned into a full-blown assault on the front door. "I'm coming!" Slade bellowed.

Taking the Betty lamp, he marched to the front door, slid the bolt, and hauled the door open. Slade blinked in disbelief, fumbling with the cold metal handle. Fifi? Was he still sleeping? Every single muscle in his body tensed as he stared at her, shocked. Someone cleared their throat and Slade's head snapped to the person standing next to her. Not one of his dreams of Fifi, then. Peter would never be a part of those.

"What has happened? Are you well?" Slade asked, his pulse picking up as his eyes snapped back to her. Alarm stabbed his gut as he scanned the length of her from head to toe for any signs of injury or distress.

"We are quite well," she said. Her tone too calm and her expression far too placid and practiced for the earliness of the hour. Her words abated some of the alarm, yet the muscles on his brows contracted.

It was Peter who spoke next. "Apologies for the inconvenience of the hour, Colonel."

It seemed his rank of colonel would survive the actual position itself. He readily stepped aside, allowing them to pass, then closed the door and pivoted around taking in the windblown strands of Fifi's coppery, unbound hair. She was covered from neck to the tips of her dainty leather boots in a sweeping hooded cloak the color of onyx, the bottom edges lined with fresh brown mud splatters. Pale hands clutched a small reticule.

"What has happened?" Slade said his own voice ladened with concern and disquietude.

"You did say to seek you out if I ever require assistance. You however did not specify it had to be at a respectable hour," Fifi said, with a rueful expression.

Unease prickled against his skin, and his brows shot up. "I don't understand," Slade said.

"I require an escort to a local inn, so I can let a room for a few nights," Fifi said, pulling the lapels of her cloak closer around her as if cold.

Slade ushered everyone further into the receiving area closer to the great hearth. He proceeded to throw two thick logs atop the embers. Then he lit a gray tallow candle from the ledge atop the mantle and stirred up a crackling blaze. He used the candle to light the five-arm candelabrum on the polished wooden table that stretched across half of the receiving area, before blowing the taper out.

The candelabrum's light highlighted Fifi's coat. He'd had the pleasure of undressing a number of women in his adult life and could swear she was missing her hip roll. She was too casually—or perhaps hastily–dressed.

He frowned, pursing his lips when he took in the exhaustion seeping into her expression. Slade dragged a cushioned mahogany chair nearer to the heat of the hearth, making a grating sound against the floor.

"Please, have a seat," he said to her.

She obliged.

Slade pulled Peter aside. "What happened?" Slade whispered.

Wide-eye concern played across his friend's features.

"Mistress Dunbar showed up at the gunsmithy asking for you. It's a good thing I've been sleeping there this week to finish up a late order. I brought her straight here."

Had Fifi ridden from the manor to Hortons Gunsmith and then to the Hortons lodge? *Bloody farthing hell.* Altogether she must have been on a horse, in the dark, for the better part of five hours. His shoulders tightened even as his stomach muscles clenched. What would make her not only risk her safety, but risk running into highwaymen or brigands at this hour?

But then Slade stilled and considered where Fifi had come from and in whose manor she was employed.

He gritted his teeth as icy coldness rose up his spine. One of his knuckles cracked against his curling fist.

CHAPTER 16

"Did he hurt you?" Slade asked Fifi, with a voice that was deceptively low.

Fifi faced him. Her jaw muscles worked as she considered his question, the rest of her countenance calm and cool.

"No, he did not," she said.

His fist slowly uncurled even as he continued to eye her closely.

Peter's feet shifted against the stone floor. "Who are you two referring to?" Peter asked.

Slade would never reveal details proving embarrassing or potentially dangerous to Fifi, despite trusting Peter without reservations.

Slade wasn't going to answer Peter. He turned to Fifi. She said nothing either.

Her gaze fell to her ungloved, upturned palms. When Slade caught sight of their raw blisters and cuts, something tightened in his chest. *Bloody farthing hell.* He didn't have any healing salve.

"Fifi …" he started, worry and concern pulling his tone down. But then he paused when she looked up. For a split second, he

75

saw that uncertain little friend, the one he'd dearly cherished years ago. The little friend he'd had when he'd needed one. When he'd been trying to escape a cold home, lacking the sweet gentleness of a mother. His heart clenched to a painful state forcing him to take deep breaths.

"I will help you in any way that I can. But why not stay here instead of at an inn? There's plenty of room and food and I will take care of you until we can decide what to do," he finished.

He swallowed when the uncharacteristic and unprecedented urge to comfort her took hold of him.

She looked around as if considering. "Thank you for the offer, but we would require a chaperone. Or is there perhaps a cook or a maid who also resides here?" she asked, uncertainty lingering in her expression.

Peter spoke before Slade could answer. "My wife, Lucia, could act as chaperone. The cook and maid at the lodge don't reside on the premises."

"Thank you, Peter. I would love to make the acquaintance of your wife. However, I only plan to remain here for a few days until I can reunite with my friend," Fifi said, a smile easing into her features.

Slade considered her with a keen eye.

"Is this the same friend for whom you acted in service of at the manor?" Slade asked.

Anger heated Slade's insides. He wanted to forcefully explain to this friend of Fifi's that friends don't put each other in danger at the manor of a swine like Bolingbroke. But he had to quell that impulse for now.

Her eyes flashed with something like reticence. "Yes."

When her eyes landed on his chest, her cheeks darkened as she then averted her gaze. Slade tilted his head down. It'd slipped his mind he wore nothing but breeches.

"Pardon me," he said.

As he turned and made a dash towards his bedchamber to don a shirt, Peter's voice sounded as he spoke to Fifi.

"The colonel sold his commission with the Scots Greys and will eventually be venturing back to the Highlands. I'm sure he can serve as your escort to this friend of yours in the meantime. You can trust the colonel with your life and honor. He is the most principled man I know."

Slade returned wearing a white linen shirt. He carried a bottle of whisky in his hand as well as a pail of water he'd retrieved from the barrel in the kitchen and a linen he'd just torn into strips for bandages. He placed the pail down next to the chair Fifi occupied.

"Please, use the water to wash your hands." He placed the bottle down on the table.

Her eyes softened with gratitude.

Peter shifted uncomfortably. "Should I have fetched a healer or a sawbones? Pardon me, I didn't think of it earlier." Peter then threw up his hands in a self-deprecating expression. "I am utterly helpless in emergencies. Perhaps I should bring Lucia earlier rather than later. She always knows what to do in a fix."

Fifi flinched with a hissing intake of breath as she dipped her hands into the water. "A healer is quite unnecessary, Peter. But thank you."

"Please, hand me the bottle," Slade said to Peter, then turned to Fifi.

"This will bite."

She pressed her lips together, nodded up at him, then opened her wet palms above the pail. He took the bottle from Peter and went down on one knee in front of her, took her upturned left palm in his right and proceeded to drizzle the golden liquid on her blisters. The sharp, woodsy aroma flowed up to his nostrils as he resisted the urge to blow air on her palm at her hissing intake of breath. She wasn't a little girl in need of coddling anymore, he told himself.

"Apologies for the discomfort," he whispered as he released her hand and proceeded to the next one.

"Did you get those blisters from riding to Birmingham?" Peter asked, his face crumpled in more pain than was displayed on Fifi's feminine features.

"It's not as bad as it looks. I am very much looking forward to meeting your wife," Fifi said, glancing towards Peter.

Slade didn't miss the way she skirted Peter's question.

Peter's face relaxed. "I think you and my wife shall be great friends. My Lucia is talented, beautiful, and more than capable in every situation."

Fifi smiled. "She sounds delightful, and handy. Do you reside in Birmingham?"

"Yes, we do. Not far from here in fact."

Slade handed the bottle back to Peter then he took Fifi's palms once more. As he inspected the now-cleaned cuts, he pushed down the anger and hatred starting to rise up. Bolingbroke was responsible for this. The raw cuts didn't seem deep or long enough to warrant stitches. This knowledge abated some of the heat within him. He proceeded to bandage her palms with strips of linen.

"Fifi, what happened?" Slade asked, in a gentle tone.

She opened her mouth to speak but closed it without uttering a word. Then reopened it with a sharp inhale. "I was caught in a rather compromising situation. It demanded my immediate departure from the manor. I …" She paused, her eyes dropping to the floor.

Slade turned to his friend but before he could open his mouth Peter spoke. "I should be shoving off. It looks like you have a tight rein on the situation, Colonel. And I am sure Lucia can be of some assistance. I'll bring her by later."

Fifi's gaze rose to meet Peter's. "Thank you for your escort."

Peter stepped around Slade and came towards Fifi. He patted

her shoulder in a friendly fashion. "All will be well, Mistress Dunbar. You are in good hands with the colonel here."

Slade bade Peter goodbye, recalling his friend's words to Fifi earlier. *You can trust the colonel with your life and honor. He is the most principled man I know.*

But it wasn't true that a woman could trust him with her life, was it? Sylvia had trusted him, and she was dead.

CHAPTER 17

After Peter left the lodge, Slade bolted the door and walked towards the sideboard. He filled a slender goblet with sherry, the chestnut brown liquid's warm, fruity scent filling the air as he took it to her.

"Dutch courage," he said.

She accepted it and readily took a sip.

"Was there something else you wanted to say about this compromising situation you found yourself in at the manor?" he prodded.

She worried her thumb against the curve of the glass, seeming to contemplate her next words, then levelled her gaze on his. "Yes, but before I proceed, I wondered, where do your loyalties lie? That is to say, are you for English rule over Scotland? Are you in agreement with the signing of the Union?"

Slade eyed her, understanding her question, yet failing to see the connection.

In 1707, the Articles of Union led to the creation of Great Britain, uniting the Kingdom of Scotland and the Kingdom of England, which included Wales. But many Scots, like his own father and brother, saw it as the subjugation of Scotland under the iron claw of England. He disliked the English the same as his family but couldn't tell anyone that his former position as colonel had been a cover. Jacobites themselves were using the Union to rebel against George II, the German-born King of England. The Whig party-dominated English Parliament and their army of redcoats.

Slade rubbed his chin as he considered her. "People don't fight for governments and crowns; they fight the English because a redcoat killed a loved one, or they fight the Jacobites because they don't want a papist telling them what to do. They align themselves with a side that gets them what they want."

"And which side are you aligned with?" she asked, in a deceptively low tone. Fifi's gaze focused on him with such intensity he had to quell a few warning bells going off in his head. This wasn't the little girl from his younger days questioning him; this was the woman who'd punched him at the shooting range. The one who'd reacted to devastating effect when she'd been caught off guard. When she'd perceived a threat. This was the woman who stirred something devilishly delicious and dark, deep inside him.

"I align myself with my friends, Fifi, like you and like Egan, and with my family. Nothing else matters. Certainly not governments or kings," he said.

He saw the warmness and softening of her eyes before she smiled and added. "And Bolingbroke? Are you his friend?"

Should he tell her that if he could, he would punch a knife straight through the man's venomous heart? He gritted his teeth before inhaling and injecting a breeziness in his voice. "My acquaintance with Henry Bolingbroke is at most transactional. He in no way has my allegiance, certainly not my friendship."

Fifi eyed him. His answer pleased her. But her eyes continued to search his. It occurred to him that she saw more than he wanted her to.

Her gaze shifted down to the remaining liquid in the goblet as if looking for her next words there.

"Before I go any further, I must have your word you will never reveal the source of the information I am about to tell you. Upon your honor as a gentleman and as Egan's foster brother."

Suspicion snaked through Slade at her question. His previous assumptions of what had brought her here tonight had been all wrong.

"You have my solemn word," he said unreservedly.

She tilted her head back and gulped the remaining contents of the glass, gave a slight cough, then eyed him.

"I have it on good authority that the English will now resort to murder, plunder and destruction to enforce the Abolition of Heritable Jurisdictions in the Highlands, in addition to continuing with raids to capture Jacobites. I must warn my friends, my family and my clan."

Slade stared at her in disbelief as something detonated inside his chest. The questions were too many to voice. He turned away from her and started to pace parallel to the long table, the dangerous energy pulsating through his veins too rampant for standing still. This would strip the last vestiges of power from the Scots in favor of the English. What would happen to his father and brother, and what of Garraidh?

He paused his stride and eyed her. "I am almost afraid to ask, but is this friend of yours, for whom you are in service at Bolingbroke's manor, working for the Jacobites?"

Even as he asked the question, realization struck him like the setting-off of a cannon ball in his head.

She was caught up with the Movement. *Sweet Saints!*

CHAPTER 18

"I am not at liberty to answer," she said, her tone low and her words sounding practiced.

Horseshit. But she'd inadvertently given him an answer after all.

"Very well. We will leave it for now." His eyes trailed her from head to toe, then he continued. "I'm afraid all I have to offer you for a change of clothing is my own."

Her expression eased into a smile. "Thank you. Yes. I'd welcome it until I can purchase some of my own."

Slade showed Fifi around the spacious lodge. He pointed out its weapons room, dining area, gaming room, kitchen, stocked larder, and four bedchambers. He then guided her to a guest chamber at the back of the lodge, for it provided her with the greatest degree of privacy. Afterwards, he walked to his chamber to shuffle through his belongings for the cleanest breeches and shirt he could find.

Twenty minutes later he strolled back to her chamber and pushed the door open, holding the fresh clothes in his hands.

"These should be adequate for—"

Slade halted in his tracks as an audible gasp escaped Fifi's lips from further inside the chamber.

The breath left him, and his senses shattered. She had lit a candle on a sideboard and stripped herself of the cloak, leaving her in a long thin night rail. He shouldn't find the outline of her curves beneath the diaphanous fabric so seductive, but he did. Her lips parted in shock, sending a rush of heat and blood straight to his groin. His eyelids slammed shut and he swung around, giving her his back, a foul imprecation escaping his mouth. It was unfortunate the imprint of her delicious looking areolas was now burned on his brain. He would never be able to unsee her luscious figure. And he would never be able to stop what he was starting to feel for his friend.

Hasty scrambling sounded behind him.

"I hadn't expected—" she started, in a breathless voice.

"Forgive me. I'm terribly sorry—" he cut in.

A booming crash and a simultaneous "Ouch!" sounded. Slade swung around despite the threat of a second faux pas. She was on the floor looking as undone as he felt. Her booted feet seemed to have caught on the edge of the rug. He dropped the clothes he was holding and in two long strides he was upon her. Taking her upper arms, he gently but firmly lifted her.

"Are you hurt?" Slade asked.

The lack of finesse he employed to pull her up made him curse himself inwardly. But all words died in his head when his actions landed Fifi's soft curves flush against his hard edges. Her bandaged palm splayed awkwardly on his chest to steady herself. The feel of her body was too bloody sublime. The edgy feminine scent of her scrambled his senses, and the heat from her nearness reshaped his reality. She tipped her head back, eyes widened, and pupils dilated. Her soft breath escaped her lips, brushing his cheeks as if she would speak, but no words sounded.

There was shock and heat in her eyes, but he dared not contemplate the latter. If he contemplated it too much, he would forget that having Fifi in his arms with dark erotic thoughts flying through his head would draw Egan's protectiveness and wrath. He still had to use all his self-control to rein in the screaming urge in his hips to thrust forward or the overpowering desire to lower his lips to hers.

Slade blinked when something sharp nipped into the left side of his chest. All sultry images drained from his head. He blinked and glanced down. The candle's light reflected off an elegant Damascus dagger she held right over his heart. Something cold rippled down Slade's body.

"Let go of me," she said, her voice calm.

The kind of calm right before thunder ripped the heavens apart in a deadly storm. His eyes flew to hers. And it hit him. If he made a single wrong move she wouldn't hesitate to plunge the dagger straight through his heart.

It dawned on him what he was looking at in her face.

Cold terror.

Slade immediately released her and took two steps back.

"I would never cause you harm, Fifi. The very idea offends me," he said, unable to account for anything at the moment.

He'd never given her any reason to be afraid of him, mistrust him—why on earth would she be terrified of him?

Her subsequent grin was void of any mirth whatsoever as she wagged the dagger at him, as if he'd been a disobedient pupil and she his reprimanding tutor.

"You are never to enter this chamber again." Her nostrils flared and her breathing audible.

"Even if you are in need of assistance?" he asked.

"I don't require the type of assistance you are offering," she spat.

And what type was she referring to? Wasn't she the one who'd come to him at five in the morning in need of help? But now seemed an imprudent time to discuss the type of help she needed or the type of help she imagined he was offering. He bent down to retrieve the clothes he'd dropped on the floor and deposited them on the bed.

She gripped the weapon like a shield in front of her as she marched towards the door and held it wide open. She was being exceedingly dramatic, like the day at Hortons shooting range, the first day in Bolingbroke's gardens and even the day of the jewelers. But tonight she'd been through a taxing ordeal at the manor, and her childhood friend had just been about to kiss her and not in a friend-like way.

Slade exhaled audibly. Amiable Peter had told Fifi she could trust Slade with her life, but could she trust him with her virtue?

Fifi eyed him, then pointed to the doorway.

"I'd like you to leave now."

"There's food and drink in the kitchen if you are hungry. Take anything you wish," he said, before exiting her bedchamber.

The door bolted loudly behind him.

CHAPTER 19

*P*hoebe's hands shook so violently she nicked her thigh three times before managing to tuck the dagger back into the leather garter belt. The defeated energy spiraling through her chilled her to the bones. The only explanation for her reaction was, she was damaged. Ross had damaged her. The hard, shocked expression on Slade's exquisite features replayed in her mind over and over sending an invisible razor-sharp knife through her heart. She slammed her eyes shut, palmed her face, and dropped onto the bed's edge. A sob of unmitigated misery and regret escaped her mouth before she clamped her lips shut, changing the sound to a whimper.

Mind-numbing panic and bone-chilling fear had caused her to overreact. Again. She understood the look of a man who wanted her. But she'd never seen it with such intensity on a cherished face like Slade's. She'd only seen it twisted with malevolence on Ross's face and on a few fleeting strangers of no consequence like Bolingbroke.

Had bone-gnawing exhaustion caused her to lose her mind? Had it caused her to reveal to Slade the English plan to use violence in enforcing the abolition of Heritable Jurisdictions Act?

Perhaps. But the honest truth was she trusted Slade never to betray her confidence, despite her body being unsettled around him. Then there was that hatred she sensed in him when he spoke the name Bolingbroke. She trusted that above all else. Besides, the MacLeans were friends of the Dunbars. When she related the English's latest plans to her father, he would warn the MacLeans and many others in the Highlands.

This thought lingered on her mind as exhaustion took over and she surrendered to a restless sleep.

Hours later, Phoebe faced the small, square mirror on the oak dressing stand in her bedchamber. She gasped at how Slade's breeches accentuated the curves of her hips. Utterly inappropriate. And there was no place to conceal the dagger. She couldn't possibly make a trip to the Royal Mail to send a missive to her mother or a coded note to Falcon looking like this!

An awareness pulsated through her at the crispness of the material touching her body, because it had touched his. She imagined she could smell his scent, clean with a hint of cloves and male surrounding her, making her insides liquid. An image of Slade's rumpled hair, lean, muscled torso, and bronze skin from earlier made her skin flush and breath ragged. He was perfect, with a torso like Michelangelo's *David*. The ink mark on his right bicep in the shape of a dark coiling viper had added an air of raw, unbridled danger, so shockingly different from the amiable lad she'd known in her childhood.

Should she have gone to Aunt Penelope or to the Movement instead of coming to him? Those distances were far greater. And her aunt would have thrown a conniption at her state of dress. Falcon had said *Impromptu and direct contact for people in our line of work is unwise.* That had left one remaining alternative.

When a creaking sounded from the front door to the lodge Phoebe stilled.

"Hello! Mistress Dunbar?"

Phoebe's head perked up. The woman's voice was almost

musical. Phoebe exited the chamber and darted out towards the receiving area of the lodge.

She was greeted by a smiling, comely, round-faced young woman, dressed in a fashionable coral and rose colored open-front *contouche* gown, revealing a decorative stomacher and petticoat. It was finished off with scalloped ruffles, trimmed elbow-length sleeves and separate *engageantes.* How impractical for a lodge. The exotic feathers on the woman's extravagant *bergère* hat looked about to take flight.

Phoebe stared at the woman before finding her voice. "Hello, I am Phoebe Dunbar."

"Oh, you poor dear. You poor, poor dear. When Peter told me of your ordeal I had to come. I am Lucia Horton," the other woman said.

Phoebe's lips stretched into a smile at Peter's wife. Lucia Horton's gaze became purposeful with a downturned mouth, as if looking at a little bird with broken wings. Phoebe's appearance must appear pitiful to someone as formally attired as Mistress Horton.

"It's a pleasure to meet you, Mistress Horton. Peter couldn't stop singing your praises," Phoebe said.

Mistress Horton pressed her startlingly white gloved hand to her chest, blushing. Peter's wife placed the fashionable portmanteau she'd been carrying on the long table then came forward, taking both of Phoebe's hands in her own.

"Please call me Lucia. Where is your bedchamber?"

Half an hour later, Phoebe pressed her palms against her ears as everything in the chamber spun around. She stared tongue-tied at the contents of the portmanteau that were now laid out on the bed, various items of colorful clothing, undergarments, and personal effects.

"When Peter said you not only had to make a hasty departure from your employer's home after you found out what bad sorts they were, but that you hadn't had time to pack, I said to myself, I must help," Lucia said.

"But … but this is beyond generous," Phoebe said, sounding breathless to her own ears.

"These are yours to use for as long as you wish. You are but a few inches taller than I am. Otherwise, the size is quite similar. My Peter surmised my gowns may fit you."

Lucia held up an emerald-green muslin *contouche* gown next to Phoebe, then beamed.

"Most becoming. Now, take those hideous garments off so I can assist you into this," Lucia said.

While Phoebe was grateful to Lucia, she bit down on her lip and actively refrained from crossing her hands over her chest after donning the gown. The overpowering urge to rip the shockingly revealing gown off her body warred with her need not to offend Peter's wife. Its low-cut bodice was far too revealing.

At least the gown wasn't red. Phoebe thanked all the saints for that. Since her attack, the color red made her break out in a sweat. Red was the one color she would never don again, ever—the color of Ross's uniform.

After Lucia helped her to snugly wrap and knot the bandages around her palm and the back of each hand, she also assisted Phoebe with brushing out her hair. As Lucia then put up the sleek strands in a chignon, Phoebe spoke of her childhood and first meeting Slade while he fostered with Egan.

"In the Highlands, clan lairds often send their sons for training or fostering with warlords to prepare them for their duties as men. They forge bonds with other clans, train with various weaponry, acquire knowledge on how to do battle, manage their own clans, various livestock and farming plus they are given an enviable education in the process," Phoebe explained.

Then Lucia described how she first met Peter, who was currently with Slade just outside the lodge tending to the horses.

He came into her father's apothecary on Loveday Street years ago. Then the tangible air of wealth surrounding Lucia made sense.

"Is your father either Allen or Hanbury of Allen and Hanbury's apothecary?" Phoebe asked. That establishment was well known and thriving.

"My Father is a Hanbury." Lucia brightened.

After Lucia was finished with her hair, Phoebe rose and walked over to the mirror. Her hand went up to cover her mouth as her eyes widened at her own reflection. Her appearance was head-turning. Weakness slithered down her body, bringing on a slight queasiness in her belly.

CHAPTER 20

For the eventide meal at the lodge, the cook laid out food in various dishes on the sideboard across from the long table. The prominent aroma of the meat and leek soup made Phoebe's mouth water, reminding her she hadn't eaten all day.

As Phoebe stood by the table, her hands resting on the back of a chair, she glanced at Slade across the table. He had just popped opened a bottle of wine with a polished motion of his hands. He hadn't said a word to her, hadn't even looked at her since he'd made an appearance. She couldn't blame him, after the way she'd reacted in her bedchamber earlier.

Phoebe was unable to pull her eyes away from Slade, taking in his square, clean-shaven jaw. He was dressed for dinner in thigh-hugging gray breeches and a crisp white Cambria shirt, his neck missing a cravat.

The play of shadows on the angular lines of his face, cast by the flickering light of the candelabra, emphasized his breathtakingly handsome features.

Lucia shifted from dish to dish, a few feet away at the sideboard. "I am very much looking forward to keeping company with you at the lodge, Phoebe. I think it will be great fun for the two of us. A chance to get to know each other even better, as it were." Lucia's tone was conversational as she topped off her plate of food with an apple tart.

Phoebe hadn't touched the fruit in seven years. Ross's apple scented pomatum had made her cast up her accounts that night on the moors. But then again, it had been the least of the reasons for her losing her stomach content. She shook the recollection away when Lucia eyed her, expectantly.

"I very much look forward to spending time with you as well," Phoebe said.

Lucia's expression brightened as she set her plate of food down on the table across from Peter who, without hesitation, got up to help her with a chair.

Phoebe sensed Slade's approach from behind.

She swung around to see his handsome face lined with worry and regret. Her eyes dipped the length of him, taking in his tall riding boots. They were polished to a gleaming shine, another one of his military habits.

"I sincerely apologize for my behavior earlier," he whispered. "It pains me to think I caused you distress. Forgive me?"

Phoebe shook her head, her heart squeezing at his thoughtful words. "No, no, it is I who must apologize for my overreaction. I was simply exhausted and not myself."

His eyes were warm and searching as they considered her before speaking. "Well, then, perhaps we may endeavor to forget the entire episode?"

"We should," Phoebe said.

"Wine?" he asked. His voice smooth and hard at the same time.

A type of unrestrained energy vibrated from him. She'd never sensed it before. It wasn't threatening, nor was it frightening—on the contrary, it invigorated the length of her. There was something raw and undoubtedly male about him, putting her senses on alert.

"Yes, please," she said.

He proceeded to fill the goblet next to her on the table. As he poured, the full-bodied aroma of the burgundy liquid mingled with Slade's particular scent of cloves and soap. She found herself taking a deep inhale.

"Something about you looks different this evening," he said, his eyes still on the wine.

Had he been looking at her? Instead of hyperventilating, as she would have expected when attention was focused on her appearance, her skin tightened. Phoebe kept the pitch of her voice lower than usual.

"Necessity demanded I borrow one of Lucia's gowns. But my hopes of not drawing attention to my attire is apparently dashed to bits," Phoebe said.

"A man would have to be missing a pulse not to notice you in this gown." His voice was low and gruff.

Her cheeks grew hot at his words. But was it a compliment or sarcasm?

"Are you finding everything to your liking?" he asked, looking up at her after filling the goblet.

"Yes," she said, then thought of her earlier ablutions and how much she wanted to take a full bath. "But I would dearly love a portable tub."

Somehow mentioning something as necessary and mundane as a bath took on an intimate quality as she blinked at him. His green gaze took on the color of emeralds in the candlelight.

CHAPTER 21

"I'll have the stable hand bring in a tub," Slade said with a shuttered expression, before turning and walking away.

After taking a deep steadying inhale she stepped over to the sideboard. Phoebe placed a sample of all the food on her plate, except for the apple tarts.

She did, however, serve herself a healthy portion of plum pudding. Since she was a wee bairn, plum pudding had been her absolute favorite. From the buttery cinnamon scent mixed with the sugary decadence of plums wafting up from this one, it was going to be an absolute treat. She carried her plate back to the table and took her seat.

Peter eyed Slade as he filled his glass. "Since you'll be returning to the Highlands soon, I thought I could accompany you to drum up some more business."

"Oh, I'd love to accompany you and help with the gunsmithy's business. In fact, it sounds like a marvelous adventure for us all to travel to the Highlands," Lucia cut in, in a delighted trill.

Surprise, pleasure and thoughtfulness flashed across Peter's features. "It's a long and grueling journey, my love."

"But you'll take care of me, won't you, dearest?" Lucia pouted at Peter.

"Well … yes … of course my love." Peter managed to look hesitant and utterly besotted all at the same time.

"Then it's settled. Besides, the colonel will be with us. Will you be returning to Scotland, Phoebe?" Lucia said, shifting to face Phoebe.

Phoebe paused mid-chew, considering. She was very interested in Bolingbroke's Glenfinnan mission. She would have to let Falcon know. But it was a good opportunity to warn her father about the English move to break the power of the Scottish Clan Chiefs.

"It's quite possible that I may," Phoebe said.

Lucia looked quite pleased with this answer.

Slade strode to the chair next to Phoebe, a full plate in his hand as he sent a cursory glance in Peter's direction. "Do you have any specific potential customers in mind?"

The awareness of Slade returned, seeping into every inch of Phoebe's skin. She didn't know what to do with it or what it meant, so she concentrated on ignoring it as she took another bite of food.

"Wouldn't your father and brother be interested in a demonstration?" Peter asked.

A grimace stretched across Slade's features. "It's possible. But I'm certain we'll be able to interest some of the neighboring clans."

For most of the meal, Phoebe attempted to ignore not only the pulsating virility of the man sitting next to her but the seamless way his beautifully rugged hands cupped his wine glass or gracefully held the knife and fork.

Phoebe finished her meal and turned all her attention to dessert. With a great degree of reverence, she scooped up a spoonful of the plum pudding, eying its rich, moist texture with an anticipatory sigh. As a connoisseur of plum puddings, she could tell, even before the spoon touched her tongue, it was going to be perfect.

When a burst of delectable flavors exploded in her mouth at the first bite, an unwitting guttural moan escaped her throat. She swallowed then glanced around. Had anyone taken note of her indulgence? Slade alone eyed her, his gaze penetrating, and his body as stiff as a board. She glanced at his plate. Why hadn't he taken dessert?

Phoebe indicated the dessert in her plate. "Would you like to try it?"

Slade shook his head and returned his attention to the remnants of food on his own plate.

After the meal everyone sat companionably with each other and sipped their wine. Phoebe was pleased that Slade and Peter didn't insist the ladies drink tea and leave the men to finish their wine separately, as custom dictated.

Lucia set her empty goblet down and eyed Phoebe. "My father is great friends with the local magistrate in Birmingham, and I think I should have him look into your former employer's questionable behavior. They must have done something dreadful, if it forced you to leave so abruptly ... are you up to speaking about it?"

Phoebe almost choked at the unexpected question. She quickly gulped down the wine she'd been sipping. Everyone straightened and eyed her, waiting for an answer. Falcon's voice slammed into her awareness. *Don't ever get caught off-guard; stay in control.*

She steeled herself and cleared her throat. "Admittedly, it's an intolerable and unpleasant story, one I think would be quite upsetting to discuss now lest we all suffer painful indigestion," Phoebe said.

"Oh, of course you are correct," Lucia said, looking slightly chastised.

Slade considered her, his expression inscrutable. His eyes

stayed on her, making her want to shift in her seat, but he then tipped his head back and finished his own wine.

On the morning of the next day, Lucia's maid Martha, a mostly gray-haired and quiet motherly sort, arrived with Lucia's packed bags for her stay at the Lodge. Then Lucia insisted they visit Birmingham to pick up any additional incidentals Phoebe had left at her employers' home in her haste to depart.

After a two-hour ride in a sleek black Hanbury carriage, they arrived at the jewelry quarter in the vibrant city center of Birmingham. The footman hopped off the back to assist the ladies down.

Phoebe managed to purchase two readymade gowns despite Lucia's criticism for their utter lack of fashion. And while Lucia was occupied with jewelry perusal, Phoebe slipped away next door to the Royal Mail. She posted a missive to her mother and paid an exorbitant sum for an express missive, which she'd written in code, to be sent by messenger to Falcon. For the past eight weeks, she'd had three sources of funds—an allowance as a lady's companion, a stipend from her father and a discretionary allowance from the Movement. Now she was mindful that just two sources remained.

Phoebe guided their walk away from places Lady Bolingbroke or the manor staff would patronize. After the spider poison had worn off, what had Bolingbroke done? If anything. Slade had instructed the lodge's stable hand to return the horse Phoebe had taken from his stable. Therefore, as far as horse theft was concerned, she was innocent.

As the three women exited a store and turned the corner, Lucia stopped short, Martha almost colliding with her.

"Why, it's the colonel!" Lucia pointed across the street.

Phoebe's gaze followed where Lucia pointed, her eyes widening. It was easy to spot the dark, familiar figure among other passersby, for Slade was head and shoulders above many. Slade, who appeared deep in thought, had stepped out of an office building. The sign on the awning above him read *Harbert and Company, Private Inquiry Agents.* Why would Slade require a private inquiry agent?

He'd left the lodge this morning before she'd even awoken.

Lucia waved with vigor at Slade but then stopped and dropped her hands when a boldly dressed beauty in a rather loud orange caraco jacket ran up to Slade and threw her arms around his neck. Phoebe's body went rigid. It was difficult not to notice the capricious Swindlehurst even from this distance. Why was she hugging Slade as if they were more than friends? The notion solidified when Swindlehurst placed a bold kiss on Slade's lips. The heat drained from Phoebe's body. Had Swindlehurst refocused her attentions from tupping the general to targeting Slade?

Slade, who hadn't noticed them, returned Swindlehurst's hug and seemed surprised by her kiss. The scandalous gesture by the maid, however, didn't seem to bother him in the least. And why would it? A kiss from Swindlehurst's perfect lips wouldn't be a hardship for any man to bear.

"Who is she?" Lucia said in a surprised tone.

"Omelia Swindlehurst. She's a laundress from the manor," Phoebe said.

"From your former place of employment? But why would she behave in such a scandalous manner towards the colonel?"

Why indeed. Although Phoebe could venture a few guesses, she shrugged in response. She had trouble understanding why the sight of a woman in Slade's arms sharing a hug and a brief pressing of lips had the effect of making her stomach roil. Yet she couldn't drag her eyes away from Slade and Swindlehurst.

"Well, I don't like her. She's too ... too bold and her outfit far too audacious to be respectable," Lucia scoffed. Lucia gently touched Phoebe's arm. "I am sure she's just a friend of the colonel." Her voice sounding far more consoling than Phoebe was comfortable with.

Phoebe schooled her features. "Oh, I'm sure she is. And even if she isn't, well it's no concern of mine … ours, that is. We should be on our way."

"Of course, my dear. Lead the way," Lucia said.

Phoebe stepped into the closest coffee house, intending to pick up the latest copy of the *Daily Courant*. She wasn't sure why something inside her was sinking.

CHAPTER 22

Two days later, Phoebe gazed out the window of the impressive coach the Movement had sent for her. It was sleek, slim, unmarked, and best of all fast. Reddish-brown underbrush and tall, yellowing-green trees at the foot of picturesque hills flew by. But, after ten hours of jarring motion from the conveyance, as the horses raced northbound over the dirt road with only quick stops to water and change the animals, her teeth and bones were starting to rattle.

Falcon's missive, written in Caesar's cipher with a recognizable script, had arrived yesterday at the lodge by messenger. It contained seven words. *My Dear Hawk, Be ready. Sending transport.*

Today before dawn the six-horse carriage had arrived at Hortons lodge with its driver and two rather brawny-looking uniformed footmen. Phoebe had been dressed and waiting. She had slipped from the lodge while everyone except Lucia was still asleep. She'd had to reassure Lucia several times she'd be back the next day, not to worry, she was visiting her aunt's sick friend who had sent the coach with its driver and footmen as her escorts.

Phoebe had been avoiding lengthy conversations with Slade since seeing him and Swindlehurst together. She shouldn't care about their embrace. She didn't. She was sure she didn't. But her stomach muscles clenched every time she recalled Swindlehurst kissing him.

The coach arrived just outside a quiet country village about ninety miles north of Birmingham, stopping at its local inn, called the Red Lion, just as the golden-orange sun touched the eastern horizon. After disembarking from the phaeton, Phoebe was escorted by one of the footmen to the waiting area on the top floor.

When Falcon's young fresh-faced assistant, code name Blue Jay, appeared, Phoebe eyed her with a smile. "My thanks for the prongs. They were perfect for opening a locked drawer," Phoebe said. Blue Jay was garbed in a smart cobalt dress with a crisp white pinafore, and a white linen coif covering her neatly braided black hair.

In the Movement, everyone had a code name, and Blue Jay's suited her well, for she was not only perky but fiercely opinionated regarding the exiled Jacobite Court, of which her parents were former courtiers.

"*Magnifique*! The prongs did the job they were designed for," Blue Jay said in a polished French accent, looking quite pleased.

Phoebe had learned on first meeting Blue Jay two years ago that the exiled Jacobite Court started its history at Saint-Germain-en-Laye, near glorious Versailles, France, until the Peace of Utrecht ended and it had to relocate to less-prestigious Lorraine, then later Avignon. That history was closely tied to the formation of the Movement, funded by exiled Prince Charles Edward Stuart and the French government.

Blue Jay led Phoebe to a grand and spacious room then left. Phoebe's eyes found Lady Naveau, codename Falcon, right away amidst the elegant décor which sparkled despite the dimming evening light coming in through the white lace curtains from outside.

"Forgive me my dear if I don't get up to greet you, my knees have been protesting," Falcon said, her French accent hardly noticeable amidst her eloquent pronunciation. Her warm countenance made Phoebe forgo the customary greeting of offering deference to the countess. Instead, she leaned down and wrapped her arms around the other woman's solid, slim frame.

Falcon returned the hug adding a warm and affectionate pat on Phoebe's back. Phoebe trusted, loved and respected Falcon. And she was grateful because Falcon had given her the chance to take back control of her life. To fight against the fear and weakness Ross had instilled in her ever since the moors, since Ross's attack. Life wasn't fair. The good weren't always rewarded, there wasn't always justice for the abused, and the bad weren't always punished, but this purpose gave her a chance to make matters less unfair. And if she could make it safer for just one other woman, then she could cope. She would survive.

As Phoebe took the chair next to Falcon's velveted winged back chair, her eyes swept the other woman's length. Falcon's resplendent appearance in the silver and light blue *robe volante* gown, topped off with an immaculate, tall, silver-gray peruke was enough to leave anyone in awe. But for some reason, Phoebe always found reassurance and comfort in Falcon's presence. Or perhaps it was that Falcon's voice never rose an octave above a calm steady timbre, and Phoebe found this rather soothing.

"I trust you and your family are doing well, your ladyship," Phoebe said.

Astute gray-blue eyes twinkled at Phoebe from a refined, square-jawed face.

"Except for my complaining joints, I am as healthy as an ox. My sons are both doing a commendable job of holding the reins of our shipping empire. And my two daughters-in-law are busy with my three rambunctious grandsons. Only more grandchildren and overthrowing George II and the Whig party would make me happier," Falcon said, with an imperious tilt of her chin.

Phoebe chuckled. Falcon never missed a chance to express her derision for the English Crown or their supporters.

"And how is your family, my dear?" Falcon continued.

"Mother and Father are well. Although I can't tell which they are more disappointed in, the fact that I am not in the Highlands, or that I haven't yet taken a husband," Phoebe said.

"Your parents love you and mean well, I am sure, my dear. And how is your brother?"

"Egan is meeting with Laird Campbell on the Isle of Coll because they murdered two of our retainers," Phoebe said.

Falcon frowned with concern. "The Campbells fought with the Royal Army against the Movement at Culloden last year. They are untrustworthy and an unpleasant bunch. I hope Egan fares well."

Egan was a formidable warrior who had trained under the feared and legendary Warlord MacDonnell himself, along with Slade and their other foster brothers. He was more than capable of handling the Campbells.

Phoebe straightened in her chair. "Egan travels with an army of Dunbar retainers and has their unreserved loyalty. The Campbells are the ones who should be wary."

Falcon laughed; the soft warm sound filling the room. "Spoken like a true Dunbar, my dear. Now, what was so important we had to meet in person?"

Phoebe reached into her reticule, pulled out the copies of the General's *New Artillery Cannon* design and the *Glenfinnan Mission* documents and handed them to Falcon. The countess donned a pair of golden spectacles and scanned the documents.

Afterwards, Falcon regarded Phoebe, the spectacles adding an air of superiority to an already impressive presence. "With Henry Pelham being reelected, the Whig party is becoming bolder. I will send a missive to my contact near Glenfinnan to warn the villagers of the raid. Now, tell me all not contained in these documents," Falcon said, displeasure wrinkling her brows.

Phoebe recounted her discovery by the general and her subsequent flight from the manor to Slade at the Hortons lodge.

Falcon's brows arched in concern as she slowly took off her spectacles, placed them on the side table, then regarded Phoebe with a watchful gaze. "I am pleased you made it out unharmed. But I can imagine how difficult it must have been for you, given your particular background."

"Maybe difficult, but I am certainly content with the information this mission yielded," Phoebe smiled.

Falcon eyed Phoebe marked intelligence in her eyes. "This wasn't the only reason you wanted to meet, was it?" Falcon said.

CHAPTER 23

*P*hoebe sat forward, her adrenaline surging as she squared her shoulders and confidently gazed at Falcon, who knew her only too well. An opportunity had just presented itself, and she would grab it.

"No, it isn't. The *Daily Courant* reports Bolingbroke's first and second lieutenant generals, Hughes Cope and Walter Hawley, are moving north to Scotland. It's highly likely one or both will show up at Glenfinnan and other parts of the Highlands to conduct illegal raids on former rebels," Phoebe said.

Phoebe cleared her throat, then sat back against her chair, her relaxed countenance deceptive. "I, myself, was thinking to return home to the Highlands to warn Glenfinnan of the raid and my father of the English move to break the power of the Scottish Landowners. And keep an eye on Hughes Cope and Walter Hawley," Phoebe said.

Falcon's lips stretched into a pleased smile. "You have the Movement's full support, financial and otherwise, to thwart both their plans." Falcon then leaned further forward in her chair, regarding Phoebe with a sharp pointed look. "But be prepared. We don't always get what we want, my dear. If you ever lose control of any situation. What matters is how you move forward. You must—"

"—remain calm, stay focused on my purpose and continue with the available resources," Phoebe finished; her lips lifted in memory of another one of Falcon's mantras.

Falcon gave a low chuckle, and her expression softened. "You are correct, of course. I think my dear Albert would have liked you as much as I do."

Phoebe absently smiled at Falcon's comment about her late husband. But her mind lingered on the words *if you ever lose control*. Was there any guarantee one would never lose control? A cold and gnawing tremor snaked through her body.

Phoebe inhaled a cleansing breath, forcing herself to keep up with the conversation. "I would have liked to have met your husband," Phoebe said.

As a sexagenarian, the elegant and shrewd Lady Naveau had not been quelled by age, nor had she become settled in the security of all she'd accomplished. Winifred Meaux, Dowager Countess of Naveau, matriarch of the Meaux family, spymaster for the Movement's south region, code name Falcon, was as disabused, disgusted, and enraged as Phoebe was with the brutalities committed by the English. Falcon blamed their band of bloodthirsty redcoats for her husband's death during the illegal raid of an Edinburgh shipyard. Not *death* but murder, she'd said.

After Falcon had told Phoebe her story two years ago, during a stroll in a private garden soiree being hosted by Aunt Penelope, Phoebe had revealed her own story. Her soul had been shattered in 1740 when a redcoat named Faye Ross had hurt her. Her dignity and body stained, her peace of mind gone, her virtue tarnished, and control taken away. Control over how she dressed, who she interacted with and where she went. It was then that Falcon explained what she did for the Movement and asked Phoebe if she wanted to fight back.

Phoebe had said yes. And the Movement had trained her to

fight with various weaponry, to lie, to protect herself, and how to escape and evade capture. Learning about spy craft had been the most entertaining.

Falcon's sharp eyes now scrutinized Phoebe. "I assume you feel safe with Slade MacLean, and you trust him, or you would not have turned to him for protection."

"Egan trusts Slade unreservedly. And my gut tells me I can trust him as well," Phoebe said, then explained that Lucia and her maid were staying with them at the lodge.

Falcon considered her for a breath then smiled in a reassuring way. "Well, the important thing is you are safe, my dear."

At the winding down of their discussion, Falcon rang for supper, after which Phoebe was escorted by Blue Jay to a comfortable and private bedchamber at the back of the suites. It took Phoebe hours to fall asleep, because thoughts of her mission were intruded upon by Slade and Swindlehurst.

The next morning, after Phoebe awoke and completed her toilette, she exited her chamber. She found Falcon in resplendent form, reading the *Daily Courant*, the musky-sweet scent of exotic tea filling the dining room of her suite.

Falcon glanced up from her gossip column. "Sit and have some breakfast. The tea is excellent, fresh from the Orient, recently arrived on one of our ships. The Orientals not only can teach us about teas but about the wonderful art of silent warfare."

Phoebe smiled at Falcon's conspiratorial grin and raised right brow, recalling her own introduction to blow darts during her training and their origin. She served herself from the sideboard, then sat down across from Falcon.

Falcon motioned towards a headline in the gossip column then handed it to Phoebe. "You might find this of interest."

Phoebe took the gossip column and eying the article titled *Former maid of Camberley Manor accuses General Sir Henry Boling-broke, Baronet, of unsolicited attentions,* she read on. *A former maid of the Bolingbrokes claims she was forced into intimacies with the general leading to her pregnancy out of wedlock.* Phoebe's breath quickened as she took note of the article's source. *Harbert and Company, Private Inquiry Agents.*

She supposed Harbert and Company had countless clients, but the fact that Slade MacLean was one of them seemed a bit too coincidental.

Phoebe leaned back in her chair, disbelief gurgling in her belly. "I don't doubt for a minute Bolingbroke coerced his maid, but someone must have taken great care to ensure this story reached the gossip columns. It's a bit unusual."

"I agree. This article does good work of tainting Bolingbroke's character and reputation," Falcon said.

After a few minutes of contemplative silence, Falcon raised her chin. "While you are in the Highlands, you must make the acquaintance of Donald Lochiel, spymaster of the north region at the Movement, code name Bullfinch. Lochiel or one of his agents will provide you with any resources you might need."

"Where might I find him?" Phoebe asked. Donald Lochiel was one of the seven men of Moidart, closest advisors to Prince Charles Edward Stuart himself. He was a well-known Jacobite and a hero in the Movement but was currently being hunted by the English.

"He's gone underground. But you can make contact on the isle of Beinn na Faoghla. He'll emerge if it's safe for him to do so. If not, he'll send someone. Lochiel is a wily one. He keeps the names of those who work for him secret, even from me, claiming it's for their safety. So keep your wits about you when dealing with him or his agents."

CHAPTER 24

Slade pushed up through the chilly water and waded out of the lake. The pebbles and stones pricked his feet as he padded towards the cluster of small boulders where he'd left his possessions. The morning was brisk, despite the sharp flaxen sun. Droplets of water sluiced down his naked body, raising gooseflesh on his skin. He grabbed the linen, toweled himself dry, donned his clothes and boots and strapped the trident dagger to the belt at his waist. The weather was becoming too cold to swim outside, but he still preferred it to using a tub in his chamber.

He strolled towards the lodge, a sense of accomplishment warming him. He'd signed a contract with the general for a hundred American longrifle muskets yesterday in spite of the *Daily Courant* publishing the article. What were Bolingbroke's plans for the muskets? The man had been tight-lipped about it. Whatever his reasons for contracting for the muskets, Slade was eager to share the news with Peter.

And he was thankful the *Daily Courant* had kept the identity of his informant, Bolingbroke's former maid, a secret. The woman had few things working in her favor, being unwed and unemployed with a child out of wedlock, but her anonymity was one of them. He hoped the money he'd paid her for the story through Harbert and Company would help her in the interim while the agents hunted for her next employment position, which he'd directed them to do for an additional payment.

As Slade approached the lodge, in the distance, he spotted the reason he'd needed a cool plunge so early in the morning. Fifi stood motionless, her back towards the open stable door, staring at the ground in front of her. She looked like the earth had opened up and Lucifer himself was emerging. His adrenaline spiked. His view of the space in front of Fifi was blocked by shrubbery, so he reached for his dagger and broke into a run, in her direction.

She edged backwards towards the stable door as a feminine hand reached out from inside the stable and pulled her further back, away from where her gaze was fixed.

"Are they adders? I plan to have children and live a long and happy life. Getting killed by snakes will certainly hinder my plans." Lucia's shriek rang out from inside the stable.

"I don't know if they are adders," Fifi said.

"Mistress, please come away! You are standing too close to the vile things," Martha said.

Slade neared the trio, his breathing coming hard. An angry hissing made his gaze drop to the ground in front of Fifi. Two sizable brown snakes coiled angrily in front of her. He exhaled in relief. He was about to tell her they were harmless grass snakes when the sight in front of him heated his blood, rendering him speechless. Fifi tugged up the front of her skirts with one hand, revealing two rather long and elegant dove-colored stocking-clad legs. His eyes widened at the gray lace garter on her left thigh, for it secured a glinting Damascus dagger. She reached for it. *So, that's where she kept it.*

"Wait," he said, her intention with the dagger clear, as he himself re-sheathed his own.

Phoebe's head snapped up. Mortification wiped away some of her fear as she dropped her skirt.

He strode over to the two snakes and lifted them, one in each hand. The reptiles coiled around his hands, their bodies smooth and cold against his skin. One of them struck his hand with its head a few times as Slade carried them over to two large rocks hunkered amid some drying bushes and ferns and released the snakes. No doubt they'd come from some such place. He then made his way back to Fifi and the other two women, who stared at him as if he'd taken leave of his senses.

"Disaster averted, ladies. They are harmless grass snakes in a bad mood because their hibernation was disturbed," Slade said.

"But you could have been bitten. That was a big risk, handling the little beasties," Lucia said, her eyes wide.

"I've handled worse. One does have to contend with encountering the wild in the wilderness." Slade chuckled.

Lucia narrowed her eyes at him. Clearly, she did not find his comment amusing in the least. He'd sensed a certain chill in the air ever since the day he'd returned from his meeting with the Harbert and Company agents in Birmingham. And for the life of him, he couldn't work out why that was.

"We are much obliged, Colonel. Come, ladies, let's get back to the lodge before we encounter any more beasties," Lucia said to Fifi and Martha.

Martha followed Lucia towards the lodge, Fifi trailing them.

It occurred to Slade that he needed to discuss their journey to the Highlands with Fifi.

"Fifi, may I have a word?" he called out.

Fifi turned around and eyed him as if she wished for anything but.

"Yes?" The intonation in her voice was almost imperious.

Slade strode towards her as Lucia and her maid disappeared into the lodge. He didn't know if he was relieved or disappointed Fifi had returned to dressing in drab colors and gowns covering her from her neck to her ankles. Today she wore an unremarkable black ensemble, as if she were in mourning. She'd obviously returned Lucia's dresses. Perhaps it was a good thing. The night of their buffet dinner, he'd had a devil of a time keeping his eyes off her.

"Would you care to join me on a ride? We could explore the moors," he said, keeping his tone casual.

It was an apropos question since they were already standing by the stables. But the look she gave him, like he'd asked her to skin a live rabbit for dinner, made him clear his throat and rethink his proposal.

"How about joining me in the gaming room then?" he asked.

"Lead the way," she said, her tone flat.

When they entered the gaming room a few minutes later, she traipsed around the cards table to the farthest side.

He leaned his knuckles against the edge of the table and regarded her. "How fares your aunt's sick friend?"

When she'd disappeared, he'd had a difficult time extracting details from Lucia. All she had said was Phoebe had left to visit her aunt's sick friend. If Lucia hadn't told him—at his insistence —about the coach, its driver and the two capable-looking footmen escorting Fifi, he would have had to go look for her, worried for her safety. He'd been relieved when she'd returned yesterday.

She now eyed him, seeming to take care with her answer.

"She is much improved. Thank you for your concern," Fifi said.

Slade considered her as he lazily strolled around the cards table, approaching her side. He took note of her delicate throat muscles working. Did his closeness make her nervous?

"I do apologize if I caused any undue worry with my sudden departure," she said.

He stopped next to her. "Not at all. I'm pleased your aunt's friend is improved and you are safe," Slade said.

Her eyes seemed to snag on his hand, then she gasped. "Oh no, your hand!"

CHAPTER 25

Fifi closed the distance between them and took hold of his right hand, concern lining her brows.

Fifi was so near, Slade caught a whiff of her seductive orange blossom and bergamot scent. The sunlight, now more gold than flaxen, streamed through the window, highlighting the fiery strands in her flaming hair arranged in a loose bun.

Her hands were dainty as they held his, so much smaller than his own, and her skin soft, warm and dewy against his callouses. Her blisters were gone.

"Were you bitten by the snakes?" she asked, worry raising her tone.

Slade absently eyed his hand where she indicated, taking note of the reddish bruise where the snake had struck him.

"There's no need for concern. Grass snakes don't bite. They simply strike at you with their heads," Slade said. His eyes returned to hers as the memory of her delectable softness against his hard frame sent a shock of craving like a thunderbolt through his body.

Fifi blinked up at him. Something cleared the concern in her eyes, perhaps the realization she was holding his hand. Or perhaps shocked at sensing the illicitness of his thoughts.

She released his hand as if it had scorched her. "Oh, pardon me. I am relieved you are not hurt," she said, blinking as if uncertain, even as her cheeks flushed.

Fifi stepped away from the cards table and sauntered towards the billiard table.

"Do you play?" he asked, facing her and the billiard table.

She considered the table for a few breaths.

"I was quite proficient while at Ayr Academy. The other girls and I spent much of our free time at a friend's estate, whose family had a billiards table," she said.

"Care to refresh your skills?" He couldn't help the tinge of playfulness and challenge in his voice.

She smiled with interest. "Why not."

He used a rack to arrange nine balls on the table. He placed the white cue ball on the other end of the table then selected two cue sticks and chalked their tips.

Slade strode over to where she stood and handed her the lighter of the two sticks as he considered her. She took hold of the offered stick, but he didn't let go. Her eyes widened in question. His eyes landed on her mouth. The top lip prim and perfectly shaped and the bottom, moist and plump with a tinge of rose blush and the promise of something mischievous, even sinful.

"As a young girl you were always getting into trouble with Alex in some scheme or other. You were an open book, full of mischief. Now you're a closed book and you go out of your way to appear prim and proper. Hiding the fact you're a staunch Jacobite. One could even say a zealot considering the lengths you will go to help this Jacobite friend of yours. What changed you, Fifi?" Slade said.

Fifi's eyes narrowed at him. Something more complex than anger flashed across her delicate features. He stilled. The force of the emotion on her face squeezed something deep inside his chest.

"Everyone changes. I suppose I grew up and embraced the world's harsh realities," she said.

He released the cue, and she stepped away.

"It broke my heart to hear of Alex's accident. Egan was devastated. I can imagine it was much more difficult for you," Slade said.

Fifi stilled, her back to him. She made a move to turn, her chin landing on her shoulder, but then seemed to reconsider. She instead sauntered to the farthest end of the billiard table and turned to eye him.

Her expression was even. "It was. It still affects me in some ways. But I imagine you are familiar with the pain of losing someone dear."

Slade's fingers curled around the cue stick as something sharp and darkly familiar pierced his gut.

He avoided her gaze. "Yes. I suppose you and I understand tragedy well," he murmured.

Slade positioned himself by the white ball and took a deep cleansing breath.

He made the first shot. A loud clack scattered the gathered balls, sending the three into the farthest pocket.

"As you haven't played in some time, I'll forgo my turn and let you go next," Slade said.

She sent him an appreciative smile with a fleeting hint of the mischievous little girl from all those years ago. "Why thank you. Although you may come to regret putting courtesy before winning."

Slade chuckled at the fact he'd failed to mention to her that he was also proficient at billiards.

She strolled over to position herself between the white ball and the one ball, in line with a middle pocket. It was a shot he himself would have contemplated.

"Why don't we make the game more interesting?" he said before she took the shot.

She paused and sent him a curious glance. "What do you have in mind?"

He considered her for a second before speaking. "If you win, I promise not to tell Egan you're spying for the Jacobites, provided you take care not to place yourself in danger again like you did at the manor."

Her eyes widened at him, perhaps at her realization of his knowledge. She should deny it, but something innate held her back. Then defiance etched itself across her features as she raised her chin. "And if you win?"

Slade eyed her lips as something hot stirred deep inside him. He still couldn't get the first night in her bedchamber at the lodge out of his head. The curvaceous outline of her delectable body beneath the diaphanous material and the imprint of her areolas had haunted him every night since. Oh, he was bound for perdition for this, but since he was already heading there for Sylvia's death, what did it matter? His stomach tightened. He shouldn't pursue this. But for the first time in his life, Slade ignored his instincts.

Certainly, if any of the Dunbars found out what he was about to do, he'd be hung, drawn, and quartered, Egan himself doing the deed. But Slade had to know, had to find out once and for all. Was this more than friendship?

He sent her one of his wicked grins. "If I win, a kiss."

Fifi's brows arched in undeniable shock, and her lips parted. He didn't realize she'd dropped the cue until the thing clanked on the stone floor.

CHAPTER 26

The hailstorm of terror at his words never came, as she had imagined it would if she ever found herself in this predicament with a man. Any man. But her body was frozen like ice, even as her pulse raced, shock at his words making her momentarily speechless. If she were honest, perhaps she was more compelled and curious at his words. This was the biggest shock of all. Quite unlike his suggestion of riding with him alone on the moor. She'd been horror struck, recalling where she'd been when Ross had attacked her.

One of Falcon's platitudes popped into her head. *Keep the focus on the mission.* But she was having a hell of a time keeping anything in her head at the moment except the exquisitely gorgeous man standing across the billiards table, his dark eyes focused on her with primal intent. She bent down, snatched up the cue stick, then straightened. Had she thought Slade chivalrous? He'd no doubt kept his roguish qualities hidden until now.

"We all saw Swindlehurst kissing you in front of Harbert and Company in Birmingham a few days ago. What has brought on this need for kissing all of a sudden?" Phoebe said.

His eyes widened, as if something had just dawned on him.

"We?" he asked.

She cleared the discomfort from her throat, aware she was behaving like a jealous woman. "Lucia, Martha and I," she said.

"Ah, I see." His lips stretched into an amused smile, before continuing. "I have no interest in the laundress. However, the becoming flush on your face when you are jealous, is most intriguing."

His dark and sultry tone was quickening her pulse and the pace of her breathing. There was something undoubtedly enthralling about him, even preternatural.

She leaned forward and braced her palms against the table deciding to ignore his last comment. "Am I at a double disadvantage if you win?" she asked.

He gave her an assessing stare. "How so?"

"Well if you win, I not only have to kiss you, but you'll tell Egan about my affairs," she said.

He regarded her with cool superiority. "Let me clarify. Regardless of whether you win or lose, I'll only tell Egan if you do not refrain from putting yourself in danger."

Her knees weakened in relief. Her job as a spy for the Movement, which he clearly had his suspicions about, was a dangerous one, but she had no plans to give it up. However, there was no need to inform him of any of this. The only item on the table seemed to be the kiss.

She scrutinized him. "One kiss?"

He sent her a devilish smirk. "One kiss."

She persisted. "Nothing else?"

"Nothing else," he drawled.

She straightened, defiance piercing her insides. "What if I say no?"

He shrugged. "Well, you'd leave me quite despondent. I must ask, however, if there is anything else you have with which to bargain. Perhaps you can tell me all about this mysterious Jacobite friend of yours if I win?"

She shook her head in vehemence. "Out of the question. One kiss it is."

He sent her a lazy smile. "We have an accord."

If not more interesting, their bet certainly made the game more daring. But since she was practically an expert at billiards, she would best him. And she wouldn't have to worry about kissing him, she told herself. She was mostly not worried about kissing him. Phoebe maneuvered the cue stick in line with the white ball and a corner hole, the one ball in the middle. She took aim and struck with sufficient strength. The white ball clanged into the one ball, sending the latter straight into the hole. The white remained on the table as she'd intended, spinning on its spot while the one rumbled into a side pocket. Triumph made Phoebe straighten and eye Slade, her chin victoriously high.

"You should make yourself comfortable where you are. I, unlike you, will not sacrifice victory for courtesy," she said.

He grinned. His relaxed confidence irked her. "Incidentally, have you accomplished all you needed to before we leave for the Highlands?" he asked.

Phoebe considered her next shot, responding to his question. "I've accomplished all I wanted to and am in fact eager to leave."

Slade leaned against the edge of the table. "Excellent. I'll speak with Peter and Lucia and make the arrangements."

Spotting her next shot, Phoebe leaned over at the waist and aimed with her stick. With a gentle tap against the white ball, causing it to bump ever so slightly against the two, she landed the shot then straightened, taking in Slade from beneath her lashes. He looked amused and not in the least bit worried that she would win.

CHAPTER 27

His look of ease provoked her as she successfully took her next two shots, sending the four then five balls into side pockets of the table.

"I imagine we'll travel from Birmingham, head north through Manchester, and continue to Glasgow and all the places in betwixt, then pass through Fort William, Glenfinnan and finally Skye," he said, contemplatively.

Phoebe was distracted at his mention of Glenfinnan as she walked to the other side of the table eying the six, giving Slade a wide berth as she passed him. She'd have to do whatever she could to protect Glenfinnan but with Falcon's warning missive already on its way, the villagers will be prepared she told herself.

Slade's nearness was proving difficult for her concentration on the game and her consideration of Glenfinnan. Phoebe bent at the waist, pulled back the cue stick and sent it straight into the white, which in turn clinked against the six. Unfortunately, she didn't pull back fast enough and both the white ball and the six rumbled down the side pocket of the table.

"Blast!" she muttered.

Slade made a tutting sound. "Looks like you fouled. And just as I was getting comfortable watching you play."

Despite her cheeks, neck and ears growing impossibly hot at missing the simple shot and for the foul word slipping out of her mouth, she sent him a sweetly sardonic smile. "I yield the table to you."

Slade rose from his reclining position, cue stick in his right hand, and winked at her, seeming to find her tone entertaining as he strode to the side pocket and retrieved the white and six balls.

As Slade leaned forward and positioned the two balls near a side pocket, Phoebe's eyes fell on the way his tight gray breeches stretched across his backside. When she caught her gaze lingering and admiring the raw masculinity of his anatomy, she gasped and looked away. She'd never done that before with any man. Never wanted to.

With one swift thrust of his arms, Slade made the shot straight into the corner hole. His movements were confident, virile, almost brutal in execution. He didn't hesitate. He shifted his body in a calculated motion for his next play.

Phoebe's eyes widened, for the next shot was the seven, but it was partially obstructed by the eight ball. And if Slade hit the eight while aiming for the seven, he would foul. She stared in awe as he sent the white into the table's border at a perfect angle with the seven, avoiding the eight, ultimately driving the white to rebound straight into the seven, sending it into a side pocket. She had made similar shots herself in the past, but he'd done it with such perfect precision. Was there a chance he could best her at this game? She huffed at the thought.

His eyes were cool, clear and calculating as he methodically contemplated the remaining balls on the table for his next shot. She imagined him on the battlefield with a musket in his hand with the same precise surety.

"What was it like during the war?" she asked, curious.

His eyes flickered in her direction. "Dark, cold and bloody," he said.

"Did you kill many French soldiers?" she said.

He frowned. "As a Jacobite you no doubt consider the French as allies. We did not, at the Battle of Dettingen in western Germany. So yes, I killed quite a few. But if I hadn't killed them, they would have killed me." His tone held a hint of sarcasm.

He was not only calculating and methodical but deadly as well. She envisioned a stony look in his eyes on the battlefield before he pulled the trigger, the same one he now turned and regarded the eight ball with.

"I understand as a soldier in war you have to kill the enemy. And of course you must defend yourself. But what of the toll … the cost of taking a life?" she said, gazing at him.

With a gentle tap against the white ball, causing it to bump ever so slightly against the eight ball, Slade landed the shot then straightened and gazed at the surface of the table, seeming to consider her question. The lines between his brows deepened.

"In the beginning, it fractures your soul, one fragment at a time. But then you learn to cope, to become an automaton of sorts."

Gooseflesh prickled her arms at his words because she heard the pain amidst its hardness. The Movement had trained her to kill, and she would have to if the mission required it. The thought left her grinding her teeth, before speaking.

"Did you kill the French infantryman who injured your ear lobe?" she asked, eying his ear. What was he like on the battle-field, merciful or merciless? She was desperately curious to find out.

Slade's expression hardened. He seemed to travel far away in his head.

"He was young, green, came at me with fear and uncertainty in his eyes. I hesitated on the shot. He tripped and fell, losing his musket in the mud. I turned from him to a more immediate threat, a seasoned French officer charging towards me, rage and hate in his eyes. Then the bullet grazed my ear. I looked down. The felled soldier was pointing a flintlock pistol at me, smoke dissipating from its barrel. He must have had it hidden. I can still see the whites of his eyes and the tremor in his hands," Slade said.

The rawness in his voice touched something deep inside her. Her eyes widened. "Did you kill him?" she whispered.

He exhaled in a drawn-out drone. "While I was cursing, blood gushing down my neck, shots were fired. When I looked back, he was dead, taken down by a fellow Scots Grey."

His voice didn't hold the edge of anger or spite, only acceptance, and it spoke volumes to Phoebe.

"You spared him even though he shot you," she said, not surprised he was chivalrous even on the battlefield when faced with death.

His mouth twitched into a sardonic smile. "Don't fill your head with romantic notions of me being heroic. I am anything but."

"I would never dream of doing such a thing," she said, feigning shock.

Slade chuckled and sauntered towards her, on his way to the other side of the table. His movements were slow and deliberate, like a dark wolf on the prowl. He eyed the nine as if it were prey. Then his eyes flickered to her, half-lidded with smoldering intensity making her skin sensitive and her muscles weak. Was the ball the prey, or was she?

She glanced at the green billiard table. *Blast!* Only one ball remained, the nine. She swallowed hard against the monstrous lump forming at the back of her throat. It was highly likely she would lose this game. Then, a kiss.

CHAPTER 28

*P*anic returned, and a cough escaped Phoebe's mouth as her chest tightened enough to pilfer her breath. She fought the urge to bolt from the room and instead swallowed and tried to keep her mind on the game. Not the kiss.

Slade stilled right behind her, she realized when his masculine scent, mingling with the freshwater loch and woodsy outdoors, drifted towards her. Her heart skipped a beat at his sudden nearness. But his whispered "Prepare yourself" in her ear quelled her panic and sent heat rippling down her spine. Warmth from his closeness caused a thrill to shoot through her body.

Her lashes lifted. "Prepare for what?"

Slade strode to the other side of the table, leaned forward and with a loud whack sent the white ball hurtling into the nine, sinking the latter into the corner hole, leaving the white ball on the table like a spinning top.

Phoebe's jaws slackened.

An arrogant and confident smile stretched across his lips. "Prepare yourself for my kiss, of course."

Her eyes narrowed at him. "You are far too bloody good at this," she hissed.

"Why, Fifi, you've sworn twice today. Such colorful language for a lass who goes out of her way to appear colorless." Slade chuckled.

Her muscles tensed with equal parts anticipation and panic. Were they going to kiss now?

He sauntered towards her in long graceful strides, like a great big lazy cat. Her heart pounded against her ribs as if she were cornered prey. When he reached out, Phoebe sucked in a breath. But his hands landed on the stick she held, instead of her. She blinked at him.

The corners of his mouth turned up in wicked amusement. "Should I put this back on the stand? Or would you like to play a second game?"

He was enjoying this. Rogue.

"I've had enough humiliation for one day," she quipped.

He took the stick from her and leaned it against the table then turned back to her. The game was over, but those billiard balls still bumped against each other in her chest.

With reverence, he took her right hand and raised her knuckles up to his lips, gently pressing a soft kiss against the back of her hand. The veneration of the gesture eased knots in her body yet managed to make her insides feel like liquid.

Slade stood there eying her, intensity and inquiry vibrating from him. He made no other move towards her, didn't invade her space further. The knowledge that he could if he wished lingered in her mind.

"Are you still amenable to a kiss, Phoebe?" he whispered, watching her.

Phoebe's mouth went bone dry. If Egan found out she kissed Slade, he would murder Slade and lock her up in a tower for the rest of her life. Her brother was overbearing, overprotective and downright barmy at times. But she loved him and knew he was only trying to keep her safe. And Egan loved Slade like a brother but knowing her brother, Egan would think it wrong for them to kiss, like his brother was kissing his sister.

But Phoebe had chided herself enough for not being confident as a child, or not being more open with her feelings when she was younger. And this was her chance to be confident, open and even bold. Because the truth was, she'd always had amorous feelings for Slade.

Slade's thumb started to draw slow lazy circles in the palm of Phoebe's hand, which he still held. The touch was gentle, but her body's reaction was not. His touch heated and sensitized her palms, sending prickles of energy down the length of her. Her eyes fluttered back up to his. Despite the bright sun streaming through the window, darkness danced with the light in his eyes, making her knees like jam.

"You never call me Phoebe," she finally said.

"I find Fifi to be the name of the little mischievous elfin girl I met fifteen years ago. And Phoebe to be the name of a woman I'd very much like to kiss, if she's amenable," he said, his tone silken.

His words obliterated her senses. In that moment she lacked the ability to think, to draw air into her lungs, or to even move. Both her mind and body under the control of a heady, tantalizing, and terrifying force. She swallowed twice before managing to clear a pathway for air and words to flow.

"I concede," she said, sounding winded.

Her breath stilled as blood raced through her veins. Expectation made her splay her free hand on his chest. She loved the intimate feel of him, hard and unyielding. The wildly pulsating beats of his heart beneath her palm were very much like her own. His hand continued to gently hold her, while the other rested on the table. The innocuous gesture gave her a modicum of security in that she could easily break free and run, if she wanted. Yet she remained as still as a mouse. Exhilarated. Anticipating. And in utter panic.

Slade lowered his head to hers, his eyes intensely focused on her mouth. The first brush of his lips against hers was ever so slight. When the dangerous squeeze in her chest prompted her to breathe, it occurred to her that her lips were tightly shut. Had she been expecting excruciating pain? In fact, the touch of his lips was soft, like the brush of a summer's breeze. It eased the unruly panic inside her, lessened the tension and chased away the cold hard dread.

His lips were velvety soft, in contrast to the hardness of the rest of him.

His lips stilled, as if giving her room to get used to him or to retreat if she so desired. Innately her lips relaxed. Her body, knowing something her mind didn't, pressed into his. After a breath Slade began to softly trail his lips over hers. It was warm, teasing, and tempting. Her hand, having a mind of its own, slipped out of his, then both her palms slid up his chest and lingered on his shoulders.

A strange but sweet lightheadedness overtook her at the taste of cinnamon from his tooth powder. While every nerve ending in her body hummed with desire, he stilled as if awaiting her next move. Her body, heedless of the chaos in her brain, pressed further into him. Her hand unconsciously continued its ascent around Slade's neck. A low masculine rumble of pleasure sounded from his chest as his lips continued their sweet tender assault on her mouth.

Her heart thumped against her chest, shivers of pleasure ran up her spine as heat rippled down to her core. She'd never considered a man's lips could have this drugging effect. Never imagined the mere touching of lips could ignite such a powerful and intense symphony of delight and wonder in her body. Why hadn't anyone told her a kiss could be dangerous, stripping her of inhibitions?

But then Slade's hands slid around the small of her back. And everything stopped. Phoebe froze. Ice cold panic shot through her like red-hot pokers piercing her body from every direction.

She yanked away, breaking their kiss in a panic. Perhaps sensing this, Slade took a step back, her breath coming loud and fast, the same as his.

Phoebe struggled to wipe away the recollection of a vile, red-coated figure pinning the small of her back down into sharp pebbles, just before ripping her most intimate flesh apart with unimaginable pain.

She swallowed hard against the acid rising from her stomach.

His brows lowered in concern, breaking through his dark expression. "Did I hurt you?"

She shook her head, unable to speak just yet. Unable to get a handle on the chaos in her mind and body. She didn't miss the tremor in Slade's hands as he raked his fingers through his thick hair, his teeth worrying his lower lip.

Concern marred his handsome features. "Forgive me if I frightened you. It was never my intention." His eyes searched hers.

As she willed her breath to calm, he spoke again.

"Should I call Lucia to sit with you?"

"Dear God, no," Phoebe said, in a strangled sound, managing to find her voice.

"Very well then, since it appears my presence may prove more of a hinderance than help, I will leave you to compose yourself," he said.

He brushed a brief kiss on her knuckles, the scorching intensity in his eyes sending shockwaves through her body as he exited the gaming room. Her body trembled, her pulse raced, and something stung the back of her eyes. Just one touch of his lips and he had shattered her mind and body and altered her world. Everything she had wanted during the past seven years, being the untouchable pillar of ice, strength, and aloofness where men were concerned all lay broken like a million pieces of a smashed glass jar, impossible to be put back together.

CHAPTER 29

Just under two weeks later, in the dusky afternoon, the sleek, rumbling Hanbury coach dipped and jerked as it ran over a hole in the dirt road. Phoebe worried it might wake Lucia. Her friend, who sat across from her, had dozed off, her head resting on Martha's cushiony-looking shoulder. The sky filled with rolling waves of blacks, fiery oranges, and dulling yellows beckoned the darkness of night and chased away the light of day.

Their journey north through Manchester, Glasgow, Fort William and all the places in between had been excruciatingly slow due to the rough terrain. They'd stopped for breaks during the day to change horses and at night to lodge at traveling inns. Despite the terrible roads in Scotland, they had made good time. Even though the Scottish Turnpike Act of 1713 had called for proper turnpike roads in Aberdeenshire and Banffshire, the roads not yet been built, not only that, but further Acts for the rest of Scotland had ceased because of the lack of funds.

Their group had left Hortons lodge the day after Slade kissed her. And she'd kissed him back. He'd made her body quiver, her skin flare, and her blood burn with desire, despite the panicking side of her. She'd been forced to rethink everything she ever believed possible. She'd been forced to rethink what she wanted. Mortification even now swirled in her belly when she remembered how she had broken the kiss out of pure panic.

Phoebe opened the coach's window and breathed in the cool air. The familiar earthy fragrance with traces of drying heather and thistle overpowered the humidity from nearby Loch Shiel. Poppy red and brown rolling bens, peach yellow and apricot-orange dipping glens, lochs the color of blue sapphire and clumps of tall forest green pine, vivid ruddy alder and oak signaled she was in the Highlands.

Bittersweetness swelled and simultaneously crushed her heart and soul. Here at home, she'd experienced it all, euphoric happiness, the darkest dregs of hell, the saddest, coldest misery and everything in between. The first nine years of her young life with her beloved and mischievous Alex by her side had been happy and carefree. But then, the pain of losing her other half, Alex, in a fatal riding accident had been beyond unbearable. Egan had been away fostering with the MacDonell and Alex had missed him so much, especially since Egan said he would be home for Alex's tenth birthday. He'd sneaked out of Eileanach, heading towards Inbhir Garadh where Egan was fostering. He was thrown from his horse. They found him later halfway between Eileanach and Inbhir Garadh; his neck broken. But Phoebe never blamed Egan. He'd been training, as he would one day have to take over Eileanach.

Then Ross had cracked her world, making her unclean, filthy, and unsafe, letting in sinister nightmares and demons. Unsafe not only because she recognized the possible threat from every single man she'd encountered since then, but unsafe in her own skin, because it didn't fit right since that terrible day. And there had been anger and frustration at her father, for lavishing all his attention on Egan, and then for forbidding her from joining the rebels.

She'd been heartsick when her childhood friend Slade lost his betrothed, causing him to leave the Highlands. Yes, she'd been jealous of Slade's betrothed. She shouldn't have been, but she was. What kind of a friend was she? He'd been lost without his Sylvia, as if his life's compass had been broken. She'd secretly wished she could mean as much to him as Sylvia had. And somewhere in the deepest, darkest part of her mind and in the blackest recesses of her heart, she'd not grieved for Sylvia's death, only for Slade's loss. The honesty and horror with which this now speared her belly was unbearable. She hated herself because of it. But she would do better now, she promised herself.

A flash of wind whipped Phoebe's cheeks just as she spotted the other Hanbury coach in their traveling party, containing Slade and Peter, moving north, a little up ahead on the same deeply grooved earthen road. The other coach, like theirs, was manned by an experienced and uniformed Hanbury footman and driver.

They should be approaching Glenfinnan about now, and nothing looked out of the ordinary. No visible signs of redcoat armies. There should be time to warn the villagers of the pending attack by Bolingbroke's men. But if Bolingbroke's first and second lieutenants were carrying out illegal raids against Jacobite rebel villages, their armies wouldn't be uniformed, would they? The Indemnity Act lifted further legal penalties for Jacobites, but a little thing like the law never stopped Bolingbroke and his men.

Glenfinnan, a hamlet in the Lochaber area of the Scottish Highlands on the shores of Loch Shiel, was both famed and cursed for being the start of the current rebellion. It was where Prince Charles Edward Stuart, leader of the Movement and rebellion, first raised his standard two years prior due to overwhelming support for his opposition to the Hanoverian monarch, George II.

Now, just as their coach made a right on a sharp turn in the road, Phoebe's pulse elevated as her shoulders tightened and chills ran down her spine. A line of smoke rose above the tops of dry trees and disappeared into the sky. No. No. No! She'd hoped to get here in time to warn the villagers before the redcoats arrived. Her heart slammed against her chest, fear and adrenaline alike surging inside her. She pulled her head in and shut the coach's window.

Her first thoughts were of Slade and her friends, and how she didn't want them getting hurt. And then there was the fact that the Movement operated in total secrecy. She could never reveal her mission to anyone. She had to quietly slip away unnoticed, so that they may continue on without her.

Phoebe grabbed the David Hume volume from the seat beside her and used it to hit the roof of the coach, signaling the driver to stop.

Martha, who was half asleep on the seat across from her, blinked slowly, her kind motherly face lined with somnolence and tiredness from travel. "Is aught amiss, Mistress Dunbar? Are we stopping?"

"Nothing amiss, Martha. We will be at the inn in about an hour or two, I imagine. I just require a brief stop to retrieve another book from my trunk. No need to wake Lucia," Phoebe answered in a soft whisper, hating herself for lying. She had to let their group continue on their journey while she took a detour. She didn't want them anywhere near Glenfinnan. She didn't want anyone getting hurt.

Martha nodded in acquiescence as Phoebe grabbed her unusually heavy reticule.

When the big-boned footman pulled opened the coach's door, Phoebe alighted and closed the door. She handed her oversized reticule to the footman, who'd been attentive and solicitous throughout their journey. She made her way to the back of the coach and untied one of two bridled and saddled bay geldings they had in tow.

"Mistress Dunbar?" The footman said, his brows raised in question.

Phoebe hoisted herself onto the horse's back and reached down for her reticule from the footman, who eyed her in stark confusion.

"I am meeting a friend in a nearby Glenfinnan village. I'll come straight to the Black Hog's Tavern right after. That's where we're stopping for the night, isn't it?" Phoebe asked.

For the first time since the commencement of their journey, abject horror carved itself into their footman's features. His brown eyes bulged above a narrow, well-kept gray moustache. "Yes, our destination is the Black Hog's. But I really must protest, Mistress Dunbar. It is quite unorthodox, imprudent, and unsafe for you to leave our traveling party alone and unescorted."

"Keep your voice down, least you wake your mistress," Phoebe whispered sharply.

"But … but …" the footman stammered, seeming at a loss for words.

Phoebe hardened her expression and stared him straight in the eye. "Do you value the life of your mistress?"

Both his brows shot up in a stunned and slightly insulted expression. "Yes, of course I do."

"Then you will get her as far away from here as you can, as fast as you can, and say nothing of this to Slade or Peter. Do you understand?" Phoebe said.

The footman's mouth slammed shut, and his throat muscles worked as he bobbed a nod, eyes as wide as plates.

CHAPTER 30

*P*hoebe guided the bay gelding into a perfect turning transition then dug her heels into its sides, directing the beast off the road and in the direction of the smoke. She urged the horse to move faster and faster. Her black twill travel dress with wide skirts and her sweeping black cloak billowed behind her. Propriety must be sacrificed during missions, since riding sidesaddle, the more respectable option, was nothing but an encumbrance.

She easily circumvented trees and their almost bare branches as she furtively neared the black rising smoke as it grew higher, mingling with crackling orangish-yellow flames. The heat from the burning village, with about twenty wattle and daub cottages, most of them on fire, hit her as if approaching the very bowels of hell.

Horror and fear clenched her stomach at the highly trained men shooting unarmed villagers with army-issued bayoneted flintlock muskets. They were attacking mostly frightened farmers. Cries for mercy in Scottish brogues fell on deaf ears. Seven or eight of them shot in the back for their resistance. The armed attackers bellowing with sharp English accents were fewer in number, but they were fast, aggressive, and ruthless. Most prefer flintlock pistols over rapiers. They slapped away wailing children and caught screaming women. At least five of them being dragged back from fleeing by their hair. Why weren't these poor souls more prepared? Hadn't Falcon's missive reached them? Could the messenger have been waylaid or captured by the English?

The cries of women and children gutted Phoebe, the knots in her body so painful she shook with it. Why would a merciful God allow this carnage? Why were the English so bloodthirsty and savage? Amidst the horror, anger, and hate pulsating through her veins, guilt slithered in. If only she had gotten here a day earlier to warn them.

Her breath came in loud pants, both determination and dread riveting through her. Phoebe jumped down and smacked her horse's rear with a gloved hand so the animal would run to safety. She hid behind a cluster of oak and alder trees at the edge of the village. Phoebe opened her oversized reticule, pulled out the poisoned blow dart from Falcon and slipped it into the pockets she'd had sewn into her cloak. She put on the black velveted vizard mask, then took out the flintlock pocket pistol she'd purchased in Fort William. She primed the pan, closed the frizzen, cocked the hammer, then loaded the powder and ball in one fluid motion.

Pistol in hand, Phoebe silently stared at the chaos. Her breathing now tight and strained. Dust from the heat and smoke debris burning her eyes. Guilt and horror twisting her gut. Not only cottages, livestock, and crops burned, but bodies as well. The smell making acid roil in her belly. Could she save any of them?

Her eyes zeroed in on two tall, broad men speaking in English colloquialism, one with the twisted, angry face of a feral dog and the other with a face like a hissing snake. Feral Dog and Hissing Snake kicked down the closed door of the last cottage at the edge of the village and rushed in. It was nearest to where Phoebe hid and quietly watched, her heart thumping. It was the only cottage not yet on fire. The breaking of furniture and screams sounded from within the cottage.

A third armed man, stockier than the others, with a blazing torch in his hands followed Feral Dog and Hissing Snake. His twisted features protruding from a bearded face struck a chord with Phoebe.

"Drag the dirty rebels out!" Bearded Face bellowed.

Phoebe froze, her skin flaring with the heat of indignation as she placed Bearded Face. She'd seen his likeness in countless Jacobite pamphlets warning of the vilest and deadliest Jacobite enemies and their atrocities. And Lieutenant General Hughes Cope of the British Army, second to General Bolingbroke, was the worst of the lot. Feral Dog emerged from the cottage, dragging a crying, fighting boy who couldn't be more than five, and Hissing Snake followed, kicking an old man out.

"Leave her alone, ye filthy English pig. Leave her alone!" The old man cried. He was struck in the head for his insolence by Hissing Snake with the butt of a musket. The old man fell to his knees on the muddied ground.

A blood freezing scream from inside the cottage made Phoebe's grip tighten around the flintlock pistol. It was a scream from her past, from her nightmares, like the ones she'd made herself on the moors seven years ago. As long as there was breath in her body and blood flowing through her veins, she would never stand by and let a man do to another woman what Ross had done to her. Ever.

A maelstrom of fury and wrath detonated inside her with the awe-inspiring force of a tornado. She bolted from her hiding spot, flying past Ferel Dog and Hissing Snake straight through the door of the cottage, nothing but cold adrenaline and frenzy propelling her.

"What the devil …" Feral Dog bellowed.

"Who the hell was that?" Hissing Snake shouted.

Phoebe found Bearded Face, on the ground on top of a struggling fair-haired woman, sadistic pleasure twisting his oily features. He was punching her, her skirts half hiked up. The flaming torch he previously held lay atop a now mostly scorched and upturned wooden table six or seven feet away. Hughes Cope wasn't wearing a blood red uniform, but Phoebe saw it on him nonetheless, vile, demonic, and hedonistic like Ross's.

Icy detachment overtook the molten fury and wrath inside Phoebe. She aimed for the dead center of his head and pulled the trigger. Her hand jerked at the kickback, a metallic pop sounding. Blood and brain tissue spilled. Her stomach lurched at the red but she steeled herself.

Phoebe pushed the slumping body off the screaming woman and hauled her up. "Come with me. I'll get you to safety," Phoebe said. Urgency pummeling her chest.

"Where's my Nathanial?" the woman screamed.

"Who?" Phoebe asked, tossing the gun aside, knowing she'd be dead before she reloaded. With her now free hand, she reached for the poisoned blow dart from her cloak pocket. Feral Dog, his face twisted with cruelty, came back into the cottage dragging and hitting the five-year-old fighting boy. Phoebe blew the dart straight into the thick pulsing vein on Feral Dog's thin-skinned neck. It would take seconds for the spider's poison to paralyze him. He dropped the boy and clawed at his neck.

"Run. Into the forest. Run!" Phoebe shouted to the boy. The thumping of her heart drowned out the sound of her voice.

But the boy was already running towards the woman Phoebe had just rescued. "Mama! Mama!"

"Nathanial, my precious bairn!" The woman, now sobbing, grabbed the boy in a fierce hug, lifting him off the ground.

Phoebe pointed the woman and boy in the direction of the forest. "Go. Run!"

Outside the cottage, Phoebe saw the older man was now on

the ground, unmoving. Bright red seeped out from a hole in his chest. Hissing Snake stood over him, pistol in hand, unrepentant disdain and savage satisfaction itched in his features.

Her own chest tightened to a degree too painful for her lungs to inflate when the boy, in his mother's arms, saw the dead older man and cried. "Grandpa! Nooo!"

The boy's mother simultaneously shouted, "Papa!"

Without thinking, Phoebe lifted the front of her skirt and pulled the Damascus dagger from its sheath on her thigh. With all her might, she sent it whipping through the air, end over end, straight into the windpipe of Hissing Snake, who was now ploughing towards her. The dagger sank into his throat, stopping him in his tracks. He dropped his pistol, grabbing for his neck.

No one else seemed to take notice of them amongst the rest of the chaos in the village, for which Phoebe was grateful. She was out of weapons. She ran after the darting woman, who clutched the boy and was already disappearing into the forest.

Phoebe and the woman ran as fast as they could through darkness and trees, away from the burning village for an indeterminable amount of time. They'd have the advantage of a head start if any of the English followed. Her chest tightened, her legs throbbed, and she dodged countless branches.

The woman stumbled on a tangled gorse bush and fell forward, dropping the boy. Phoebe reached down for the fallen child to aid the woman, her lungs burning with pain and stitches needling her sides. When they all stood, the woman and boy eying her with flushed faces etched with stark gratitude, she pulled the vizard off to help with her quickening breath.

Just then, the dark silhouette of a tall, broad-shouldered man emerged from the trees ahead of them. Survival instinct and the need to protect made her step in front of the boy and his mother.

"Fifi?" The silhouette said in a hard tone.

Phoebe almost collapsed with relief at the familiar sound of Slade's voice. He'd come after her. Dear God, he had come for her. Despite her wobbling legs and trembling hands, her spirits lifted, stretching the sides of her mouth and unclenching tight muscles.

After a hard swallow, Phoebe managed to speak. "Where are the coaches?" she said to Slade.

"On the road, just up ahead. What happened? Did the redcoats attack a rebel village?" Slade asked, his tone tight with worry as he eyed the woman and child and the direction they just come from.

"Yes. But we must get these two to safety now," Phoebe said.

CHAPTER 31

*L*ater that night, in the Black Hog's Tavern and Inn's large busy dining room, Slade eyed Fifi, who sat next to him at a corner table laid with aromatic powsowdie soup, roasted saddle of mutton, vegetables, breads, cheeses and tarts. The golden light from a ten-candle chandelier high on the ceiling and decorative candle filled cast-iron wall sconces mingled with shadows in the crowded dining room with multiple tables. Those shadows did nothing to hide Fifi's pale complexion and her unusually stiff countenance. When his eyes fell on her soft, supple mouth, he glanced away, redirecting his mind from their kiss at the billiards table and the heat tightening his body. Mingling with that heat was ice growing under his skin, born of fear and worry. What in Hades had she been thinking going to that burning village? She could have been hurt. Many of the dining room's occupants were now discussing the English's horrendous attack on that very village, and the resulting sense-less deaths. It was the English's way of controlling the Scots, through force, abuse, and killings.

Just then a flash of red made Slade lift his head to look across the packed dining room to four English redcoat soldiers who had just entered. The conversations and clinking of cutlery from the approximate ten dining tables at which either families or groups of men dined ceased to a charged silence. A Highlander, dressed in trews in the colors of the Mackintosh clan, well-known Jacobite sympathizers, who sat at the bar across the dining room, spat on the wooden floor, his rancorous stare directed at the redcoats.

"Who the devil invited them in here?" His voice boomed across the dining room.

The tallest and most ruthless looking of the redcoats snapped his gaze towards the Mackintosh clansman. "Watch your tongue, before I separate it from the rest of your body. Your dress is illegal. Tartans were outlawed."

The Mackintosh clansman slammed his goblet down on the bar and shot up from his stool, his ruddy, bearded features twisted into a snarl. "I don't give a shite about English law!"

Before he could reach for his pistol, the bartender and proprietor, a large, round man with a kind face and rosy cheeks, spoke up from behind the bar. "Please, please, gentlemen. All are welcome here. If you have the need to fight, take it outside away from the women and children. Please, I beg you."

His ardent plea seemed to break through the haze of anger and hatred sizzling between the Mackintosh clansman and the redcoat. A young nervous yet smiling waitress immediately approached the redcoats and guided them to one of the last remaining vacant tables, redirecting their attention. The noise in the dining room slowly returned to its previous pitch.

Slade redirected his attention to Fifi. His concern at her leaving their traveling party earlier to go to the rebel village returned. He purposefully clamped his mouth shut lest words he regretted escaped. He'd spoken once before in anger to Sylvia a decade ago causing her death. He'd been young and selfish then. Now, he'd rather cut out his tongue than do it again.

Slade swallowed against the flashbacks from the day he and Sylvia had argued. The guilt hit his midriff; its strike sharper than a blade. Its blackness almost overpowering. He let the acute force spread over his skin, seeping into his bones. And for a few minutes it was a decade ago, the night he'd found Sylvia's limp body and had carried her all the way to her mother's house. The woman had screamed, howled, and condemned him to hell. The realization had hit him then; he was to blame.

The pain, guilt, and hopelessness of it had made him want to take a flintlock pistol to his own cowardly temple, to stop the unbearable bleakness of it from ripping him apart. Instead, he'd spent the next three years drowning himself in whisky and opium.

But by some divine act he had managed to pull himself out of the mire and muck of self-loathing and guilt to join the Scots Guards instead.

Earlier, after arriving at the inn, Slade and Fifi had both given the rebel woman and child coin for food, a room and passage on the public coach. The woman had said she would seek her brother out in the neighboring village at first light.

Slade now reconsidered why Phoebe might have been at the village. From her abilities he'd glimpsed at Hortons shooting range, she was clearly trained. But even with the Movement's training, she could have been hurt or even killed. His heart nearly stopped. It filled his head with such bleak blood-curdling thoughts he had to breathe through the resulting physical pain.

The rebellion wasn't as clear cut as Scottish rebels versus English redcoats. Even though most Highlanders supported the rebellion, there were many loyalists among them. Yes, many Scottish clans fought on the side of Prince Charles Edward Stuart at Culloden, but so did Irish and French mercenaries, the Edinburgh Regiment, and countless Army deserters. And the British Army had English infantrymen, cavalry, and dragoons with artillery, but their battalions were manned by Scots and Irishman. Some call the rebellion Scotland's rejection of the 1707 Union with England which essentially put Scotland under

English rule. Others said Prince Charles Edward Stuart, the Young Pretender, should be on the throne instead of the current Hanoverian king, George II. But Slade called it for what it was—a young rebel Prince's arrogant fight for the throne, using religion, royal blood, romanticism and braggadocio.

Lucia, who sat across from Slade and Fifi, put down her soup spoon and eyed Fifi, concern lining her forehead. "It was courageous of you to save the woman and her child, but what if you'd been injured?"

Slade glanced at Fifi, eager for her answer.

"I saw the woman and her babe running and had to help, that's all there is to it," Fifi said to Lucia with a shrug, affecting an air of nonchalance.

But Slade could tell by the way the long, slender fingers of her left hand fidgeted in her lap that she wasn't telling the whole truth.

While on the road in their moving coach earlier, he'd nearly come undone when he and Peter had turned back and realized the coach carrying the women had vanished. Slade immediately had their driver stop and turn back. Once they'd caught up to the coach with the women, the footman had unintelligibly babbled on about protection and his mistress. It was only when Slade had impatiently threatened to strangle the man, after Phoebe's horse had come back alone, that he'd gotten a straight answer. Slade had gone on foot after Fifi then, thinking a horse would be a hinderance among the trees. Peter remained to protect Lucia and her maid. When Slade had caught up to Phoebe, it had been evident from the distant smoke the English had attacked, but his only thought then had been to get Phoebe, and the scared woman and bairn to safety.

He'd left the Movement after the war, and even though Bullfinch had sanctioned his plan against Bolingbroke, he wasn't officially reenlisted into the Movement. He would do all in his power to protect Phoebe, but if she was a spy, and he was certain she was even though she hadn't confirmed nor denied it, then this was her mission, and knowing the Movement, their secrecy, and rules, he was staying out of it while still keeping an eye on Phoebe. Now that he thought about it, the Movement's secrecy would certainly be a reason for her silence. This only cemented the fact in his mind, that she was indeed a spy for the Movement.

Peter, who sat next to Lucia across the table, put his goblet down and eyed Lucia then Fifi. "The important thing is that you are safe, Mistress Dunbar. But I must agree with Lucia—you could have been hurt. And why didn't you tell anyone where you were going?"

"Please forgive me for causing you all to worry. I only wanted to help the woman and her child, and not place anyone else in danger. I should have been more careful," Fifi said, a remorseful smile touching her lips.

Slade put his tankard carefully on the table and turned to Fifi. Part of him wanted to understand why she'd done it. But more importantly he wanted to make sure she never did it again. The thought that she could have been hurt was slowly unhinging him.

"I'd like you to promise me that the next time something like this happens, you will tell me before doing anything," Slade said, his cool tone belying the turmoil of cold worry and hot anger racing through his veins.

Fifi was silent for a few seconds, staring down at her soup. She turned to him, her expression tense and contrite. She opened her mouth as if to speak but closed it instead and simply nodded. His eyes narrowed with suspicion at her acquiescence.

Everyone ate in silence for a few minutes until Lucia looked askance at Slade. "When do you think we'll arrive? And have we decided whether we'll stop at your home, Garraidh Castle, or Phoebe's home Eileanach castle first?"

"We are closer to Garraidh and should reach there by the end of the day tomorrow," Slade said, picking up his spoon.

His answer brightened Lucia's expression.

Just then, fresh air from the outdoors flowed in and candle-flames flickered as the entrance door swung open. Boots clicked against the wooden floors, and resting weapons rattled against moving limbs. A familiar tall and formidable monolith of a man confidently strolled into the dining room. He was followed by two other men similarly dressed and rugged looking. They all wore emerald-green, royal blue, and burnt umber tartans, the colors of the Dunbars. As the redcoats had alluded to earlier, the Dress Act, part of the Act of Proscription, had recently declared Highland dress to be illegal. But change was slow to come to the Highlands. Then there was the fact that Egan Dunbar was a proud Scotsman and, like the Mackintosh clansman, didn't give a shite about English law. Warmth suffused Slade's chest as he stood up, a wide grin tugging the corners of his mouth.

But it was Fifi who shot up from her seat and spoke first, a warm and surprised gleam in her smiling eyes. "Egan!"

Seconds later Egan had reached their table and grinning, enveloped Fifi in a hug. "It's so good to see you, sister. Welcome back to the Highlands."

Egan twirled Fifi around as if she were still a wee lass. Slade was taken aback by her smile shadowed with a deep indecipherable emotion. He recalled how full of giggles, open, mischievous, and luminescent she'd been fifteen years ago. An intense urge to see that freedom in her smile again struck him. His eyes stayed on her lips for a breath longer than it should.

Slade caught Egan eying him, as he eyed Fifi. Egan released Fifi then grabbed Slade in a back-slapping embrace.

Slade laughed. "It's good to see you, but if you twirl me around like you just did your sister, we will have words."

Egan released him, a chuckle brightening his handsome, ruddy features. "Well now, if memory serves, the last time we had words, it took me but two minutes to knock you on your back. But seeing as you are now an army man, it could take me three."

Slade snorted, recalling their endless training sessions years ago under the watchful eye of the MacDonell warlord. "Yes, it could. But I guarantee they'll be the most painful three minutes of your life."

Egan laughed then sobered as puzzlement crossed his features. He eyed Fifi then Slade again. "I didn't realize you two were traveling together or that you were returning to the Highlands."

Cool caution sparked Slade's insides.

Fifi was the first to speak. "I encountered Slade in Birmingham, and as he was returning to the Highlands, I solicited his escort, to which he graciously agreed. Lucia and Peter have served as chaperones throughout our entire journey."

Slade ignored the question forming in Egan's eyes and proceeded to introduce Peter and Lucia. Slade and Egan had been inseparable during their youth and days of fostering. Egan was fiercely loyal and protective of those he loved, especially his little sister. But he was also brash and pigheaded. Slade loved Egan like a blood brother and would give his life for the man without a moment's hesitation. And Egan would do the same for him even though they fought like barbarians when they were younger. What would Egan do if he found out Slade had kissed his little sister? If he found out Slade itched to do a hell of a lot more to Fifi than just kissing?

CHAPTER 32

Slade eyed Egan as he introduced Keith, his right-hand retainer, and Duncan, Eileanach's new head herder, caring for the cattle and sheep. Slade remembered Keith from previous encounters; Egan trusted him implicitly. Duncan, on the other hand, he'd never met before. From the man's beetle-brows and narrow eyes, he appeared to be in a perpetual foul mood.

Their group called for an extra table and chairs and additional food for Egan and his men. As they started to take their seats, Slade moved to slide in next to Fifi, but Egan abruptly pushed his way in between. It forced Slade to move over one seat. Peter, who sat next to him, and Lucia who took the seat across from Peter, seemed oblivious to Egan's actions. Egan's men sat across from them and appeared too interested in guzzling down ale to notice anything else.

Disquietude hit Slade at Egan's actions, but he set it aside. It had been months since he'd seen his sister; of course he wanted to sit next to her.

After taking a drink of his ale, Slade eyed Egan. "What brings you to this part of the Highlands?"

Egan tilted his head. "After returning from Coll, we had to

meet with the Sutherlands about our grain supply. And I take it you are on a permissionnaire from the army?"

"No. In fact, I've sold my commission," Slade said.

Egan's head tipped back in surprise. "You are a civilian now? What are your plans?"

Slade fingered his mug absently. "Lachlan and my father are expecting me to take up the post of warlord at Garraidh."

Egan scrutinized him closely. "Garraidh? You couldn't wait to leave the place when we were growing up."

Egan, more than anyone, understood how difficult it had been for Slade and Lachlan to grow up without a mother while having a father who had been cold and withdrawn. Chisolm, Slade's father, had been devastated after losing his wife. Some say he'd been obsessed with her before her death, after which, he'd become hard and unyielding. Then there was the fact that Slade had wished Egan was his brother instead of Lachlan. Lachlan, six years older than Slade, had been an arrogant bully when Slade was a lad. And they had gotten into violent fights as boys.

Slade now shrugged in response to Egan's question. "There's no other place like the Scottish Highlands, and I've traveled quite a bit with the army. Besides I've grown immune to the … ah … more disagreeable sides of my father's and Lachlan's personalities."

Egan laughed at the sarcasm. But then Slade realized he did indeed miss the Highlands and his father and brother, even though they weren't the easiest men to get along with. Egan took a drink of ale then put down his tankard; a smirk lifted the left side of his face as he eyed Slade.

"You know, if it doesn't work out for you at Garraidh, we'll find you a place at Eileanach. We can always use a man with your skills. It will also be the perfect opportunity to introduce you to my betrothed."

Slade's eyes widened in surprise, even as his lips curved into a smile. "You are betrothed? This is the best news! Felicitations. *Slàinte*," Slade said laughing and raising his tankard.

Heat radiated through his chest at Egan's good fortune. He was happy for Egan, even though he himself had vowed never to get betrothed again after Sylvia's death.

Images of Sylvia's sweet, bright, unaffected smile flashed across his mind's eyes. How keenly Sylvia had loved him, how enamored he'd been of her. She'd been one of the purest innocents he'd ever known. She would have been a lovely but safe wife. So unlike Phoebe, the most shocking disruption, disagreeable, and desirable surprise of his life. Sylvia took everything to the depths of her heart, the love and the hate. The hate her father had for Scots and the nameless, faceless, Scottish Highlander—as far as her father was concerned—who loved and wanted to marry his daughter wasn't to be borne. That battle of love and hate was what had killed Sylvia, because she'd taken it to heart so deeply. It had killed her. No. No, he and Bolingbroke were responsible, for putting Sylvia through their storms of political hatreds. Slade inhaled in a deep breath, trying to loosen the tightness in his chest, and to calm the heat of anger and coldness of guilt at war inside his belly.

Slade now replaced his tankard on the table, his left brow cocked in question, and a mischievous smile stretching the side of his mouth. "Who is this charitable lass making an honest man out of you?" Slade said to Egan.

Before Egan could answer, Keith cut in with a lopsided grin, his mouth half full.

"A healer from Kilmuir. And the lass is right *bonny*."

Egan's eyes narrowed at Keith. "Mind your gob, *eejit*," he growled.

The full force of Egan's expression would have made a lesser man shake in his ghillie brogues. But Keith simply averted his gaze, a rueful smile broadening his features. Slade had never seen jealousy displayed on his foster brother's features before. This was a new side to the man.

Peter glanced in Slade's direction with a hopeful expression. "If things don't work out in the Highlands for you, I'd be delighted to have you back in Birmingham with me. You can take on an active role in co-managing the gunsmith now you're a principal," Peter said.

Egan perked up with interest, eying Slade. "You've invested in a gunsmithy?"

Slade nodded. "I have. It's Peter's family business. He's here to drum up customers, in fact. Are you in the market for muskets crafted with the latest designs?"

"Absolutely," Egan said, his shoulders rolling with interest.

Peter went into details on Hortons latest muskets to Egan. At the end of Peter's descriptions, Egan invited Slade and Peter to come to Eileanach to give a demonstration.

A few minutes later Egan leaned back in his chair. The earlier question and puzzlement from when he'd first seen Slade and Fifi flickered anew in his eyes. Egan glanced from Slade to Fifi, but he directed the full force of his gaze to Fifi.

"You always send a missive home to the Highlands when you wish to return, and we provide Dunbar retainers for your escort. How is it you are using Slade as an escort, sister?"

Slade's senses shifted, alerted by Egan's question as Fifi blinked in surprise before answering. "As I mentioned, brother, I chanced upon Slade in Birmingham. He was returning to the Highlands, and I decided to return as well. Anyway, I got bored reminiscing over my school days with my auld friend from Ayr Academy and wanted a change of scenery," Fifi said.

Slade's belly clenched; he was sure Egan had no clue Fifi had been at the manor.

Well, in for a penny, Slade thought. "Fifi expressed an interest in returning to the Highlands when we unexpectedly encountered each other in Birmingham. I volunteered my services as her escort. There's nothing else to it, Egan," Slade said.

Slade eyed the muscle twitching in Egan's left eye.

"I say, Master Dunbar, Lucia and I have been with the Colonel and Mistress Dunbar for the entire journey. Everything was done according to propriety," Peter said, perhaps sensing an undercurrent.

That wasn't entirely true, considering the first night he'd spent alone with Fifi at the lodge. But Slade was grateful for Peter's words. If he were the romantic hero Fifi deserved, he would openly express his feelings for Fifi to Egan and properly seek permission to court her. But he wasn't the heroic type. He was the type who had his former betrothed's blood on his hands.

Throughout the entire exchange between Egan, Slade and Fifi, a cloud of confusion had started gathering on Lucia's brows. Now she put down her sherry and eyed Fifi, her brows crinkling.

"But, Phoebe, I thought you left Birmingham because of what happened at the man—"

That very instant, Peter jabbed his tankard of ale right into Lucia's lap, in a movement appearing accidental.

"Oh no, my dress!" Lucia shrieked.

"My love, how clumsy of me—" Peter started to say.

Slade was grateful for Peter's supposed accident. And he couldn't blame Lucia for not detecting the undercurrents. Truth be told, he himself didn't quite understand why Egan had so many questions and suspicions.

Out of courtesy, Slade stood as both Fifi and Peter shot up from their seats to assist Lucia who was frantically trying to shake the amber liquid from her pastel skirts. Egan and his men rose as well. Fifi's cheeks were flushed with equal parts gratitude and distress, and poor Peter looked miserable at what he'd done.

"Let's get you back to the room. I am sure Martha can help us remove the ale before the stain sets in," Fifi said, ushering Lucia away from the table.

After Fifi and Lucia left, Peter sat back down with a plop. Everyone else took their seat. The men fell into a solemn conversation about the nearby village that had been burned to the ground by un-uniformed English. As it turned out, Keith and Duncan had conducted business with farmers living in the very same village.

Slade didn't think it wise to mention Fifi had been at the village. Luckily, it appeared Peter was of a similar mind. Towards the end of the conversation, Egan eyed Slade. "Our camp is a short distance from here. I will return in the morning for Phoebe. I can escort her to Eileanach and save you a trip."

The hard coldness settling in the pit of his stomach, told Slade why Egan had made the offer. Egan's suspicion of Slade's designs towards his sister.

CHAPTER 33

The next morning, as dawn's egg yolk sun broke through threatening clouds on the horizon, Slade slipped out of his shared room with Peter, who had yet to stir. Slade had dressed with military precision and speed in preparation for the day, a little earlier than necessary. He made his way down the narrow hallway with wall sconces holding nearly burnt-down candles.

When he reached the door of the room Fifi shared with Lucia and the maid, he stopped. Was this desire to have a word with Fifi only to relay his suspicions about Egan's impulsive conclusions, or for an altogether different reason? Despite the bed being comfortable and the room spacious, he hadn't slept.

Slade gave a light tap, not wanting to wake anyone in the event they were still asleep. Seconds later the door cracked open, and the stern motherly looking maid Martha pushed her head through the small opening.

"Yes, sir?" Martha said.

"Is Mistress Dunbar awake?" Slade asked.

The maid's brows furrowed. "This is highly unorthodox,

Colonel MacLean, knocking at a lady's door before the sun is fully up."

Slade offered her a rueful smile. "I apologize; however, I need to inform her of changes in our travel plans."

Her disapproving expression did not budge. "A note would have sufficed, sir."

"You are correct, of course. However, since I am already here?" This time he threw her a debonair smile, the one guaranteed to make any tavern wench swoon.

She was unmoved.

"One moment," she said in a flat tone, narrowing her eyes just before closing the door in his face.

He took a step back and glanced down the narrow corridor as he waited. Thankfully, no one else was up and about.

When the door reopened, Fifi stood at the room's entrance in one of her typical bluenose gowns, buttoned up to her neck. Slade's eyes inadvertently dipped the length of her then wished he hadn't, for the fabric sat with tremendous allure on the slightly voluptuous arc of her chest and hips. Her warm, soft, enchanting scent mingled with a sweet bergamot and orange blossom fragrance drawing him in, doing strange erratic things to his pulse. She was too close, or perhaps not close enough. He cleared his throat, in an attempt to recall why he was here.

Her brows rose as if startled by his speechlessness. "Slade, is aught amiss?"

The shadows under her vibrant hazel eyes suggested she hadn't slept either.

"Please be at ease. I only wanted to inform you Egan will be arriving soon to escort you to Eileanach," Slade said.

The tip of her straight dainty nose wrinkled in puzzlement. "But I thought you would be our escort."

At the very last moment, Slade decided not to relay his suspicions of Egan's rash conclusions. Why cause her unnecessary worry?

He offered a warm smile. "A simple alteration of travel plans, nothing else."

Pushing Egan to the back of his mind, he recalled something else discussed at the eventide meal last night and decided to warn her. "Keith and Duncan spoke of Bolingbroke's men's attack on the rebel village in Glenfinnan, after you and Lucia left the dining room," he said.

Fifi stepped into the hallway and quietly closed the door behind her, the shadows on her face darkening. "How much do they know?" she whispered sharply.

"Egan and his men know of the attack on the village, but they are unaware you were in the vicinity."

Something spiraled painfully into his chest at the agony displayed on her features.

Fifi slumped back against the wall, her shoulders sagging.

"I saw it all. I was there. And I couldn't sleep, wishing to God I could have done more than just saving one woman and her child. The English continue to try and control the Scots with brute force and murder. If only I can do more," she whispered.

"You were in the fray?" he said in a disbelieving tone, his worry from last night returning, stronger, almost choking him.

Bloody farthing hell. This was confirmation she was a spy. It also made him realize how exceptional she'd have to be to be recruited by the Movement. Despite his worry, he was impressed as hell. She'd have to be amongst the best. Although, not as good as he was.

He recalled when he'd first met nine-year-old Fifi. She'd been reciting the knight's oath, dedicating herself to fighting tyranny and oppression, to fight against evil, in good faith and without prejudice. He'd never told her all those years ago he'd caught the last part of her oath before she'd stretched her arms out and ended up slipping from the rock outcropping into the loch. He'd been jolted, rendered speechless, and not a little surprised that she'd been more interested in knights than dolls.

"Promise me you won't ever put yourself in danger like that again," he said, his voice sounding harsher than he'd intended.

She blinked up at him. "You are angry with me."

Regret for his harsh tone speared his chest. He shook his head, letting out a frustrated exhale.

"I haven't any right to be angry," he said.

He caught her staring at his lips as he spoke. She shouldn't have. She most certainly should not have. Something achingly sensual and sweet tugged at his chest. It tightened every single muscle on his body.

Her eyes rose to meet his, just as he caught sight of her delicate throat muscles working as if sensing his arousal. Her lips parted, and the sudden raggedness of her breathing sounded. Desire flooded his blood.

Fifi's eyelids dropped, half-lidded, but he still spotted their hazel flecks of golden browns and greens deepening. There was fire there, dancing like sun-drenched copper strands in her lovely hair. Her eyes returned to his lips and an unwitting groan escaped his mouth.

"Tell me I won't scare you again if I kiss—" he started.

"Kiss me," she finished.

Before his brain could process the fact that this was ill-advised and cease the actions of his body, he gently palmed her cheeks as his lips took hers. His hard mouth against her soft, tartly sweet lips was enthralling and exhilarating. It charged his body like nothing had ever done before; his lungs struggled to keep up with the wild pounding of his heart, and the blood rushing through his veins felt like the shock from a lightning bolt. When she sighed longingly and sank into him, he all but lost his mind. But somewhere in his dazed brain heavy footsteps registered.

CHAPTER 34

Cold steel touching his temple made Slade go deadly still. It was the unmistakable feel of the barrel of a flintlock pistol. Ice replaced the fire in his veins.

"Remove your bloody hands from my sister." The quietness of Egan Dunbar's voice hit Slade like a blacksmith's hammer.

Slade stepped back from Fifi, and before he could turn, bone and flesh slammed into his jaw. The full impact of Egan's fist had hit him years ago, many times in fact, during their training sessions. But it had never mirrored a steeled battering ram before.

"No! Egan. Please stop!" Fifi cried.

Slade staggered away from Fifi, worried for her safety, as he turned to face Egan. Another punch landed on his nose. He gasped at the ungodly pain. The unmistakable crunch of a breaking bone sounded as his vision blurred.

Slade raised his hand in a gesture of surrender. "Egan, wait …"

An unimaginable growl preceded another punch landing on his left eye. Slade's head snapped back. The force of the blow knocked him with a painful thud onto his backside. His head rang. His whirling thoughts came into focus. He looked up.

Egan's angry red face loomed over him. His foster brother raised his hand and pointed a cocked pistol straight at Slade's chest. The adrenaline to defend himself never surged inside Slade, nor did anger at being judged a libertine. He understood Egan's reaction. Guilt and remorse stayed his own fists.

An outraged Fifi rushed forward and snatched the pistol from Egan's hands. Duncan and Keith peeked out from behind Egan's menacing stature. Wide-eyed shock showed on their rugged features. He could have even grinned at their astonished and comical looks if his damn face didn't hurt so much.

"Egan Dunbar, have you taken leave of your senses?" Fifi's voice was sharp.

She held the gun by its barrel and shoved it at Keith who immediately took it and pointed it down, away from anyone. Slade had learned the previous night that Keith was a new father of twins. And even though he had only one or two strands of gray hair at his temple, he appeared a cool, level-headed mature sort.

Fifi rushed to Slade's side and assisted him up. She reached into her skirt pocket, took out a pearly white lace handkercher and pressed it to his nose before he could tell her it would just get ruined with his blood. But he ended up wincing audibly at the stinging contact.

"My apologies …" she whispered, pulling her hands away. The intensity of her pursed lips and worry in her expression touched something deep in his heart. It made the pain of his smarting jaw, left eye and nose, which now dripped blood, worth it.

Egan menacingly closed the distance between them. "This is betwixt Slade and I, Phoebe. Return to your room and prepare to leave, posthaste!"

Fifi remained where she was, her head snapping toward her brother, defiance and determination etched in her bonny features. "You're behaving like a ruffian and a barbarian!" Her voice was loud and angry.

Slade couldn't help the adoration and pride ballooning in his chest at her defense of him. But still, guilt and a little bit of shame at being the cause of the siblings now glaring at each other niggled him.

"Fifi …" Slade started, nudging her hand holding the half-bloodied handkercher. She turned to him, the worry on her face returning. "… do as Egan bids," Slade said.

She frowned. He saw the uncertainty flashing across her features, but there was understanding there as well. Neither of them wanted to make an even bigger scandal than this already was. She silently nodded and flinched at the bloody handkercher in her hand. He ventured a guess it was the sight of the blood, recalling what happened to her when Ludlow was shot. She turned towards the women's bedchamber door where Lucia was now peeking out. Lucia's hair was up in a ridiculous mobcap, and pure wide-eyed shock was etched on her face. She grabbed Fifi's hand, shot Slade an accusatory glance, then pulled Fifi into the chamber before shutting the door.

Slade turned to Egan. Egan's mouth had gone slack, and his eyes wide. He was eying Slade and the closed door Fifi had disappeared through.

"Did you … take her to bed?" Egan asked. The twisting red anger and ugly snarl returning to his face.

"No." Slade said, not that he hadn't fantasized about it at least a thousand times.

But Egan didn't seem to hear as he fisted his right hand and bared his teeth like an angry dog.

Slade took a step back but raised his own fists in a defensive position this time.

"Egan. No," Slade said, a steely warning in his own voice.

Just then a door slammed open further down the corridor. This coupled with Slade's voice seem to break through Egan's rage, because his right fist lost all its tension.

Peter came barreling down the hall barefoot, his shirt tails half tucked into his breeches. "Can we discuss whatever this is like civilized men?"

The red on Egan's features lessened in intensity, but his scowl remained hard, cold and unyielding. He eyed Slade steadily for a few seconds before folding his huge arms, showcasing his bulging biceps even through the sleeves of his jacket. "Propriety dictates two options to you, MacLean. Marry my sister to save her from ruin or face me in a duel."

Slade stared wide eyed, frozen and speechless, heaviness expanding in his belly.

"What!?" Peter bellowed in shock, as he came to stand next to Keith and Duncan. The latter two had thin-lipped disapproving expressions focused on Slade.

Slade's head spun. Or perhaps it was the hall that was whirling around. The sensation of walking on quicksand hit him, and ice started to grow under his skin, spreading the length of his spine. He didn't deserve happiness with Fifi, not after what he'd done to Sylvia. Would he repeat his past sins if he married Fifi? Fifi needed a husband with impressive ideals like herself, not one set on revenge like him. But then the image of Fifi with another man sent a hard punch straight to his gut, stiffening the hairs on his neck and causing his ribs to squeeze so tight he had to straighten to breathe.

What if he chose to duel? Ignoring the fact that it was illegal, and he or Egan might end up dead, it would shame Fifi in the eyes of her clan, because it would send the message she was reckless, fast and loose.

What if he tried to reason with Egan? He glanced at his foster brother, the man's hard unbending jaw and nasty snarl getting more pronounced each second Slade remained silent.

Slade took a deep cleansing breath, causing his nose to smart like the very devil.

"I'll marry Phoebe," Slade said.

CHAPTER 35

EILEANACH CASTLE, ISLE OF SKYE, SEAT OF THE DUNBARS

Phoebe stood in the second-floor solar, the pale-yellow morning sun streaming through the towering oculus window behind her father, who sat at his impressive desk. The familiar scent of old leather-bound books from the ceiling to floor bookcases, beeswax candles from the sideboard and wood polish from the gleaming mahogany furniture filled her nostrils. They'd arrived the previous night, and while Peter was staying with Slade at Garraidh, Lucia, currently still asleep, had decided to spend time with her at Eileanach.

The sounds of barking from Odin and Loki, Egan's frolicsome deerhounds, echoed from down below in the courtyard. They were no doubt expressing playful displeasure at the clip-clopping of horses' hooves or the rolling wheels of a wagon.

When her eyes landed on the distant yellowing grass-covered ground and sparse skeletal trees through the window, flashbacks of Faye Ross's malevolence hit her. Ripples of self-scorn ran down her body. It made her want to scrub her skin with soap and water until it was red, raw, and close to bleeding. But that had never helped.

Phoebe pushed the thoughts aside, swallowed the bile burning up her gullet and turned from the window. Her eyes landed on the towering, gilt-framed painting of the freckle-faced redheaded boy with hazel eyes like hers and Egan's, his nine-year-old features fixed in time forever. The expression in his almost sympathetic eyes tightened her chest. Her father had brought the painting from the Great Hall and hung it here after Alex's death, selfishly keeping it for himself. It had been painted almost sixteen years ago, she recalled, because it was the week Alex had temporarily nicked Egan's dagger to secretly show her. She'd been eight and they'd both stared at the dagger in silent awe. It had been a long gleaming blade, sharp enough to cut a single strand of hair on contact.

"I want one just like it as soon as I'm auld enough." Alex had said.

But Alex would never be old enough, would he. Tears pricked the back of Phoebe's eyes. Both she and Alex had been vying for their father's attention, during that same year, hoping to woo it away from his favorite son Egan. She turned away from the painting and blinked across the huge desk at her father.

Well, she had his attention now.

Padraid Dunbar, her father, was like an aged lion, one with graying hairs at the temples, but his bite was more ferocious now than when she was a wee bairn. For he'd been scarred and hardened by wars and the death of his second son.

Her father eyed her as she walked to stand in front of his desk, the papers he'd been reading in his hands forgotten when she'd entered the solar minutes ago. "The English have plans to enforce the Abolition of the Heritable Jurisdictions Act, Father," she said.

He scrutinized her. "You learned this from a reliable source?"

"I did," she said.

He frowned. "So, they are finally acting to take power away from us clan chiefs." He then gave a heavy sigh and continued.

"Clans will disperse. Chiefs will no longer have the legal authority to protect their people."

Her brows pulled together in concern. "What are we going to do?"

Her father touched his temple, closed his eyes for a second before speaking. "The Dunbars are well positioned with the English for future trades with the East India Trading Company. They, themselves, granted us a trading license. We will have to rely more on trade and expanding our cattle and sheep pastorialisation, and less on cottars."

Her father leaned forward and steepled his hands on the desk, his gaze returning to her. "But Egan and I will deal with this. No need to worry your bonny head, *m'eudail*—my dear."

She ground her teeth and refrained from pointing out it was she who'd brought the news, not Egan.

Just then the dogs' barks turned louder and fiercer than before. Curious, she walked back to the window and glanced down into the courtyard. Three men were speaking to a Dunbar retainer. She recognized the short, round one as Hamish Ross, who was about two decades older than Phoebe herself, and next to him was his rawboned younger brother Broden. They were a neighboring clan to the Dunbars. But then Phoebe's eyes fell on the third man, with the pale Romanesque features in the redcoat's uniform, which had caught the dogs' attention. Unlike Hamish and Broden, their cousin Faye had been raised in England and wore his red uniform with pride and arrogance. Phoebe froze. Dizziness overtook her, and her muscles went cold and numb. She palmed the window's sill to steady herself. *Spies don't fear. They fight,* Falcon had said.

CHAPTER 36

"What is it?" Her father asked, still seated at his desk.

She hadn't even been back a full day. How was it he was already here? Hadn't he relocated to the south years ago? The coldness on the length of her spine turned to sweat, Falcon's words forgotten.

She turned to her father. "What are Hamish and Broden Ross doing here?"

"Oh. From the expression on your face, I thought you'd seen a *glaistig* … a ghost. They've come to discuss fencing off their lands from ours, to avoid mingling of livestock." Her father exhaled audibly as if exhausted, then continued. "Duncan has been fighting with the Rosses again because their sheep and cattle keep crossing over to our side of the moors."

"But why is their redcoat cousin with them, if they've come to talk about livestock?" Phoebe asked, her voice sounding higher and harder than usual to her own ears. Was she cursed to be plagued by vile redcoats even inside her own childhood home?

Her father looked towards the window, his mouth twisting with distaste. "For the sake of keeping the peace with our neighbors, let's leave our political biases at the portcullis, shall we, Phoebe? Besides, the English are garrisoning more and more of their soldiers in the Scottish Highlands; we simply have to get used to the *Sassenachs*."

Her father never understood the depth of her dislike for the English, or *Sassenachs*, if she wanted to be disparaging like him. And perhaps that was her fault for being unable to tell him. Part of her bias came from her hate for the English brutalizing Scottish rebels and their families, including innocent women and children. But the other part was currently standing in their courtyard, dressed in a red uniform. He'd threatened to hang her mother, father and brother and murder the rest of her clan if she ever told the truth.

Rigidity coalesced on her entire posture as her heartbeats boomed in her ears and her muscles tightened painfully. "Where is the meeting to be held?" Phoebe asked.

"Right here in the solar."

Oh, no. No. She couldn't face him. Phoebe glanced at the door. The need to flee was so powerful her breathing stuttered. "I'll leave … leave you to it."

Phoebe turned and half walked, half sprinted for the door to escape.

But the door clicked from the other side. Phoebe's heart landed in her stomach. How had they reached this floor so quickly? But when the door swung open, instead of the Rosses and their vile cousin, her mother appeared in the door. Despite the relief that enveloped her entire body, she sank down into the nearest velvet-cushioned mahogany chair for fear her knees would give away.

Her mother glided in on the faint scent of rose water, a warm smile on her face, her graying red hair up in a flawless chignon. The graceful swish of her sky-blue mantua gown sounded as she neared Phoebe and planted a sweet kiss on her forehead.

"I trust your sleep was restful after your long journey, my dear?" her mother said.

"It was, mother. Thank you," Phoebe lied, she'd been too worried about Slade's bleeding nose and the ensuing scandal after her supposed kiss with Slade. She was already the center of the clan's gossip. If only she'd known Slade's injuries, and the supposed kiss, weren't the only things she'd have to worry about today.

"I am glad. Now that you are well rested, my dear, we need to settle the issue of Slade MacLean," her mother said with kind eyes, walking over to stand next to her father, placing a gentle hand on his shoulder. Her parents exchanged a soft, intimate smile before facing her with unwavering parental concern in their steady gaze.

She understood. Her parents were a unified front against her.

She braced herself for what was coming from her parents, even though every cell in her body screamed at her to leave the solar before Faye Ross entered.

"Egan gave me quite a startling report right here in this solar yesterday when he arrived. Considering the compromising position you and Slade MacLean found yourselves in at the Black Hog's, there is but one solution to avoid a scandal. You will marry Slade," her father said, his tone resolved.

The thump of her heart jarred painfully against her ribs. Slade for a husband was any girl's dream come to life. But she couldn't marry him. She wouldn't. Society and the law dictated a wife was her husband's property and she would be no man's property. Giving up control of her life would kill her.

When Faye Ross had hurt her, he had taken away her peace of mind and control over her sense of self, of how she dressed, who she interacted with and where she went. But these past two years she had regained control by being part of the Movement, fighting against what Faye Ross represented; ruthless subjugation, and cruel control. She couldn't give this up. It would destroy her.

Her fingers curled against damp palms, and she leveled her gaze with her father's. "I cannot."

His jaws set in a grim line. "You disregarded propriety. You were seen kissing him in plain view of everyone. And in front of the biggest gossip and troublemaker in our clan, Duncan. Have you no care for your reputation? For the illustrious reputation of our family? Our clan?"

The tendons on the back of her neck tightened. "I can't marry him, Father. Please," Phoebe pleaded.

A crease appeared between his brows. "Why not? Slade MacLean is quite a prize, from what I hear of the women gossiping. And you clearly have feelings for him, ever since you were a wee girl."

She stared at her father, struggling to get a grip on the nightmarish quicksand of her life. Her blood roared in cold panic.

"*Athair*—Father, please. I don't wish to marry. Try to understand," she said, fisting her palms against her sides.

Her father's features were soft but unbending. It was her mother who spoke next."Custom dictates you must marry for us to avoid a scandal, my dear. And the other options for a husband for you are not worth mentioning. A special license is needed. Is it not, darling?" her mother said, looking askance at her father.

The panic was too loud in Phoebe's ears to hear her mother's words.

A raw cough escaped Phoebe's throat. Her chest constricted as if it had the weight of a mountain on top; her lungs unable to draw breath. Panic. She was panicking. She coughed again, and then again, trying to pull in air. But none came.

Immediate concern lined her mother's beautiful features, as she stepped around her father's desk and came towards Phoebe. "My darling, are you unwell?"

Phoebe stood up, shaking her head. She backed away from her mother. She had to get out of this chamber. Black spots threatened her vision, but she willed them away, ran to the door, pushed it open and ran right into Hamish Ross.

CHAPTER 37

$\mathcal{H}$amish Ross reached out, gently steadying her with a hand on her shoulder. "Are ye ok, lass? Where are ye going in such a hurry?" His voice was lightly amused.

Phoebe looked up, swallowing down the bile erupting inside her belly. Coldness sank into her skin as she glanced past Hamish's round shoulders to the flash of concern in Broden Ross's bearded face, and then to the expressionless features of Faye Ross, next to Broden. She extricated herself from Hamish's grip but stood there, her feet rooted to the ground, reliving the darkest day of her life.

Her skin had gone clammy, hot and cold swirling inside her body. Hamish and Broden seemed to dismiss her silence, turned, and walked into the solar greeting her father and mother in polite tones. But Faye Ross lingered behind his cousins, his twisted smile not reaching his dead eyes. She'd imagined this meeting happening countless times during the past seven years. She'd practiced a million things to say. But no words came, just heat and hatred simmering inside her belly amidst cold fear.

He might have guessed her fear, because his features leveled into what she could only describe as malevolent satisfaction. A flash of anger flickered across his features before he turned and followed Hamish and Broden into the solar closing the door behind him. He'd been seething the day he'd attacked her, she recalled.

Phoebe ran until she found herself in her bedchamber on the fourth floor. Her fingers shook so much it took her four tries to slide the bolt fully into the hole and lock herself in. She wasn't safe, was she? She would never be safe while Faye Ross was in the Highlands. She wanted to take a bath after just laying eyes on him for less than a minute. The familiar unclean feeling sank into every inch of her body like hundreds of slimy leeches sucking the light, blood and joy from her soul. But Phoebe took deep breaths and willed herself to calm.

After the moors, she'd rarely taken her boots off in her bedchamber because she'd known he would come when she least expected him to. And she had to be ready to run, when she least expected to. To run from predators. But now, now she'd armed herself to fight.

She reached for the newly replaced dagger tucked away in her garter. Just to feel the coldness of safety in her palms. Her fingers traced the dagger's edge over and over, as she waited.

A few hours later, a knock sounded at the door. Phoebe's heart lurched in her chest and her head snapped towards the door.

"Who is it?" Phoebe asked, sounding calmer than she felt.

"A missive just came for ye, Mistress."

Phoebe recognized her maid Aila's cheery voice. She walked to the door and unbolted it.

Aila, young and fresh-faced, sent Phoebe a wide smile as she stepped into the bedchamber, one of Phoebe's freshly laundered gowns draped over her outstretched arms. A few years younger than Phoebe, she had been none too happy a little over two years ago when Phoebe had left her behind to help with service to the

Dunbar clan while she'd traveled to her Aunt Penelope's, then to Birmingham.

Her maid walked to the bed, laid the gown out carefully, smoothing it, then reached into her skirt pocket and pulled out a sealed missive. Phoebe immediately recognized the wax seal of "F." Her pulse quickened.

As Aila busied herself with putting the gown into the mahogany wardrobe, Phoebe broke the seal to find a blank note. *Blast!*

"Aila, can you run down to my father's solar and see if the Rosses have left?" Phoebe asked.

The second Aila left, Phoebe pushed the door in, went to her nightstand and lit the candle she used for late night reading. Then, holding the blank note close to the flame, she gazed at the paper. Slowly, a single sentence showed itself. It took her a few minutes to work out the cipher. *Dear Hawk, W.H. plans to invest in a number of Highland distilleries.* Phoebe's inside vibrated with intrigue. So, her next quarry, Bolingbroke's second lieutenant general Walter Hawley, was in the market for Highland whisky. She worked on a plan, welcoming the opportunity not to dwell on her present woes.

Phoebe burned the note and threw the ashes in the huge unlit hearth of her bedchamber.

Minutes later Phoebe recognized Aila's light knock on the door. Phoebe bid her to enter.

"They left the keep an hour ago," Aila said, making her way to the wardrobe.

Phoebe let out an audible breath and smiled. "Does your father still work at Strathail Distillery, in Broadford? I hear their whisky is unmatched on Skye. I'd like to order a few casks."

Her maid turned to face her, her expression brightening. "My papa does indeed, Mistress. He was recently made foreman. Should I ask him to pay you a visit?"

Falcon's words played in her head. *Pick the time and place for meetings whenever possible.*

"I'd rather visit Strathail in person, perhaps tomorrow. Can you accompany me and facilitate an introduction?"

Aila gave a spirited nod. "I'd be delighted to, Mistress."

Later, after a quick search, Phoebe found Lucia sitting on a cross-backed wooden chair in Eileanach's apothecary, sipping from a fine white teacup. She'd sought her friend out hoping for commiseration on her likely marriage to Slade. Phoebe's eyes widened at the midday light permeating the colorful stained-glass window, lighting gleaming shelves with more majolica jars and glass bottles than she recalled from the last time she'd been here. There were a number of improvements, like new wooden apothecary chests and countertops filled with freshly dried herbs. There wasn't a speck of dust now, like there had been when she was growing up.

Last night when she had been introduced to Breena MacRae, Egan's betrothed, there'd been mentioned she was a healer and an expert on medicinal plants and herbs.

Phoebe's eyes were drawn to Breena, who stood behind a countertop tying sprigs of fresh herbs together to be hung for drying.

Phoebe gestured to her surroundings. "Are you responsible for all this? It's a vast improvement from when I was in here last."

Breena sent her a bemused glance. "For such a grand and illustrious castle as Eileanach, there was a shocking lack of attention given to the apothecary when I first arrived. I made it my mission to stock up."

Breena was a stunning woman, with her long, raven-black hair, her creamy complexion, and her slender figure, at the moment showcased by a simple but elegant open-draped gown with an exposed petticoat in dark burgundy. There was a quiet sort of grace with the way she carried herself.

What was such a woman doing with her overbearing, mutton-headed oaf of a brother? An unbidden unladylike sound escaped Phoebe's lips. Irritation at her brother for his handling of Slade needled her.

CHAPTER 38

*L*ucia straightened in her chair eying Phoebe with interest. "Is everything all right?"

Phoebe walked over to the wooden chair next to Lucia's and sank down. "My parents are adamant I marry Slade, since Egan reported to them what took place at the Black Hog's. They are not willing to discuss it," Phoebe said.

"Oh. What are you going to do?" Lucia asked, her eyes widening.

Phoebe gave a hopeless shrug. "Maybe I'll run away to hide in a convent. Or find a position as a governess and leave the Highlands."

She was being outlandish of course. But then again, maybe not.

Concern etched its way into Lucia's features. "You can always return to Birmingham with me."

Phoebe sent Lucia an appreciative smile. "Thank you. You are kind. But I have to think. And quick—my parents mentioned a special marriage license. They are not going to wait for the reading of the banns," Phoebe said.

Lucia looked askance at Phoebe. "Have you heard from the colonel?"

Phoebe's gaze dropped, worrying her left thumb and pointing finger. "I have not."

Her plan to avoid hurt these past seven years burnt to ashes around Slade. She was not hearing the warning bells anymore. Her blood, bones and entire body wanted him. Her soul wanted his soul. He would never harm her body, but as her husband it would be his right to control her, and that would destroy her. She wanted Slade but was terrified of what would come of it.

Lucia silently set aside her teacup and saucer, and put a light hand on Phoebe's shoulder, a patient smile stretching her lips. "The colonel has been a kind and true friend to you and is quite handsome. He is a fine catch. Would it be so terrible to be his wife?"

Lucia's opinion of Slade seemed to have improved during their journey to the Highlands, for right after seeing the beautiful Swindlehurst and Slade together in Birmingham's Jewelry Quarter, she'd been quite disapproving.

Breena, who had been eying them both, offered Phoebe a fresh cup of tea from the tea service on the countertop.

Phoebe took the cup obligingly and shook her head to refuse the offered honey. The fresh, sweet scent of the chamomile teased her nose, as she took a few sips and then surrendered to the calm settling in her stomach. She turned to Lucia, then to Breena. "Every part of me rebels against giving up control of my life to a husband."

A well-formed brow arched on Breena's features. "It is maddening, isn't it? We as women are under the control of our fathers or husbands. We cannot enjoy much of the freedom men have. We cannot go to universities, are dissuaded from speaking our minds or becoming too learned. We cannot operate lands if we are lucky enough to own them and in the few professions women are allowed, we are not afforded equal wages."

Phoebe couldn't help but appreciate the irony of Breena's situation, for she would soon be married to Egan.

Lucia sat up straight in her chair. "My Peter is honorable and kindhearted, and I love him. I love being his wife. I don't see it as control in the least."

Phoebe narrowed her eyes at her friend. Despite the fact Lucia was generous and sweet-natured, she had to remind herself they were from different worlds.

"If women were allowed to be in charge of all aspects of their own lives, they wouldn't be hurting anyone, would they? I look forward to being in charge of my own home and managing how and where the income comes from as a married woman," Breena said in a mild manner.

Puzzlement snaked Phoebe's insides. "But you are getting married … giving up control of your life to my brother."

Breena threw her an unperturbed glance as she returned to tending to her herbs. "Well, yes. I love Egan. I want to marry him and share my life with him. I, like Lucia, don't see it as being controlled. But even if it was, giving up control is freeing, with the one you love and trust."

CHAPTER 39

GARRAIDH CASTLE, ISLE OF SKYE, SEAT OF
THE MACLEAN CLAN

*E*arly the morning after Slade arrived home, he sat at a small wooden table next to his beloved five-year-old niece, Sadie. They occupied two of the four miniature chairs surrounding the table in her nursery, which was mostly decorated in white and warm pink flowered wallpaper. The chair was so small Slade had to steady himself by pushing with his booted feet against the floor so he didn't slip off. Her nursemaid, an older woman with a cheerful countenance, florid complexion and graying black hair mostly covered by a lacy mobcap, sat next to them, quietly knitting, and occasionally smiling at Sadie.

Sadie's rosy cheeks, framed by blonde locks, were stark against the white and black frilled tunic she wore as she held the toy and beamed up at Slade.

"Thank you for the present, Uncle. It's a beautiful pony!" Sadie said, her voice high with excitement.

Her delight stretched the sides of his mouth into a huge grin. Sadie had changed so much since the last time he'd visited the Highlands on a short permissionnaire two years ago, right after Fontenoy. She'd sprouted at least a foot in height and was more self-reflective now rather than ready with spontaneous giggles and smiles.

"The shopkeeper in Birmingham said it's carved from the trunk of a single oak tree, known for housing the most mischievous elves and pixies," Slade said to Sadie.

Sadie gazed at her new toy, her eyes widening and her dimples deepening. "Do you think the elves and pixies are still here?"

Slade shrugged, enjoying her wonderment. "Well dearest, you never know."

Sadie skeptically considered the wooden toy, then looked at Slade. "I think I want to learn to ride a real pony. But I don't want to fall off. Did you fall off your pony, Uncle?"

Slade's head tilted down at her. "I didn't fall, little one."

Worry marred her little face as her bottom lip swallowed her top lip and a pronounced frown appeared before she spoke. "You look like you fell off your pony."

A chuckle bubbled up from Slade's belly. "I suppose I do look like I fell off a pony, don't I? he said.

The stiffness in his facial muscles reminded him of the black and blue ring around his left eye and his swollen nose from Egan doing his worst. It was more painful to see the thing in the mirror than the actual sting of the injury itself. At least his sight hadn't been affected.

He'd been worried his black eye and swollen nose would scare Sadie, but her nursemaid had said he was being too cautious. And the physician Peter had made him consult last night said his nose was broken but the bone hadn't shifted and should heel back in place except for a bump.

Slade cleared his throat and continued. "I didn't fall, in fact I had an accident."

She straightened in her chair, her expression turning grave, and her bright eyes bulging. "An accident?"

Even the nursemaid had stopped knitting and was eying him expectantly.

"I bumped into something hard," Slade said. Egan's fist had indeed been solid.

He then sent her a reassuring smile, which caused a tiny stab of pain in his left eye. "But you are not to worry. When you learn to ride a pony the proper way, you won't fall, little one," he said, with confidence.

Sadie placed the toy pony on the tabletop, then turned to him, taking his hand with two of her little ones. Concern etched tiny lines between her brows as her eyes flickered intently from his nose to his left eye. "Does it hurt, Uncle?"

Her concern warmed and constricted his chest all at the same time. For such a young bairn, she had an immensely compassionate and kind nature, which would serve her well as MacLean clan chief someday, if Lachlan didn't have a male heir.

Slade shook his head. "No, no, it doesn't hurt in the least, dearest," he said, sending her a reassuring smile.

Just then the door to the nursery opened and Tara MacLean, his sister-in-law and Sadie's mother, walked in followed by two maids carrying trays of food.

Tara's blonde hair was pulled back in an unadorned knot. Her thin face seemed uncharacteristically sad and pale. In fact, it had been so since his arrival. She'd always been energetic, bright, and ready with a warm smile, but something had changed since his last visit. Lachlan's and Tara's marriage had been arranged by his father, but they had seemed happy in the beginning, both parties very pleased with the arrangement. Her clan had willingly paid a more than generous *tocher*—dowry for the marriage.

"Will you be joining our breakfast, Slade?" Tara said, her tone cordial.

Why wasn't she eating with the rest of the clan in the great hall? He politely declined, gave Sadie an affectionate hug, then excused himself.

A short while later Slade sat at the long trestle table atop the dais in the great hall, taking in the bustle of the breakfast meal. The mouthwatering scent of tattie scones and sausages filled the air. His brother, future laird to the MacLean clan sat to his left. Next to his brother sat Peter. On Slade's right sat his father, Chisolm MacLean, twenty-second laird and chief of Clan MacLean.

Sitting in the great hall with his father and brother, surrounded by their clan, a tinge of bittersweetness contracted Slade's insides. Despite his father and brother's ornery attitudes towards him when he'd signed with the Royal Scots Greys, it shocked him to realize he had missed them. How was it possible that tied up with that love were irritation, anger, bitterness, grief and displeasure? He'd experienced it all with his father and brother. Love was never just love, was it? It had sweetness, but claws and daggers as well.

He'd missed the towering frescos, swords and colorful shields of the clan's past war heroes adorning the hall's lofty stone walls, its size easily capable of entertaining at least two hundred. This was a source of MacLean pride, its purpose to make a grand statement about the MacLeans' wealth and prominence which it accomplished to perfection.

Slade started to tell Peter they should venture into Broadford later to pitch Hortons business to other clans when Lachlan eyed Slade.

"You let Egan Dunbar rearrange your face? I'd have relieved the man of a limb or two," Lachlan said.

CHAPTER 40

Growing up, Slade had often found his brother's brash and blunt attitude annoying. But now he simply threw his brother an unperturbed glance.

"Well, I would have tried relieving Egan of a limb or two after he punched me had he not been pointing a musket pistol at my head," Slade droned.

Peter's knife and fork clinked on the side of his plate and his head snapped towards Slade's brother. "Slade's actions disarmed a potentially volatile situation," Peter said forcefully, looking annoyed at Lachlan.

Lachlan, ignoring Peter, eyed Slade. "Why in Hades was Egan pointing a musket pistol at you?" Lachlan asked.

"Because I was kissing his sister," Slade replied, a slow grin pulling the corners of his mouth.

He had never burned for a kiss like he had for Phoebe's in the hallway at the Black Hog's. It had hit him, mindless and irrepressible. He'd been ablaze with its rawness and fire. And if someone had told him the price for a taste of Phoebe's sweet lips would be a shot in the head from her brother's gun, he wouldn't have hesitated. In that second, it had been as essential as air to breathe.

Slade was still reconciling his little friend Fifi with the woman she'd become, Phoebe. One thing was for certain, he wanted Phoebe like he'd never wanted any other woman. But he couldn't fail Phoebe like he'd failed Sylvia, because the cost had been Sylvia's life.

Lachlan snorted. "You used to be discreet with your amorous intent, brother. What has happened to your discretion?"

Slade had never told his family about Sylvia all those years ago until after he had proposed. Maybe because he had wanted to be sure of his feelings and hers.

Slade's father smiled, picking up his coffee mug. "I imagine when the heart is engaged, subtleties like discretion are forgotten."

His father's words caused him to pause for the briefest moment, because his heart was indeed engaged.

When his father finished his coffee, he eyed Slade. "I, for one, am happy you are back home and safe. Your fighting in the wars caused me grief and worry to no end. And if the English will be enforcing the abolition of the Heritable Jurisdictions Act, like you say, we will need to decide as a family how to refocus the clan's business, outside of cottars."

"With the ongoing war over the Hapsburg dynasty, Jacobite riots here and the riots in the Americas, we'll need a secure income apart from the estate. Getting into the arms business is one option for the MacLeans," Slade said to his father.

Peter straightened in his seat. "Hortons has the best craftsmen in England. We would welcome more investors. Your profit from investing with Hortons would be greater than the profit on your lands."

In the next hour, they discussed alternative lines of businesses as well, whisky distillery and overseas trading, any way to keep up with the British's taxes. At last, Chisolm turned to Slade.

Chisolm had more lines in his refined features than Slade remembered. But his father also seemed less discontent with life. Since Slade's mother had died, his father had been inordinately cold, hardened, and unyielding. Slade had been too young to see the change, but Minister Raghnall had told him how happy his father used to be before his mother's death. Chisolm had worshipped his mother when she was alive. Growing up, Slade had argued a great deal with Chisolm on varying topics from politics to clan matters. Once Slade had tried to convince his father that being in a British army didn't necessarily mean he was aligned with Britain. His father hadn't believed him and had all but disowned him for an entire year. Slade's love for his father had almost festered to hate that year during which their arguments had been harsh and even malicious. But over the last few visits his father had mellowed out. Slade was happy to see his father becoming more relaxed and easy-going. He suspected his father, after all these years, was coming to terms with losing his wife.

"I need to speak with you on a matter of importance. Come join me in the library when you're done with breaking your fast," Chisolm now said to Slade.

CHAPTER 41

Two days after returning home, Phoebe and Aila set out in a horse-drawn cart for the village of Broadford and Strathail Distillery.

Phoebe's thick, fur-lined black cloak helped buffer against the cool, early-November morning. The missing sun and gray clouds left the browning grass in a dull light. And as they crossed over an old, creaky bridge, the water of the Inner Sound on their right seemed more silver than blue. She had left early enough that she didn't have to explain to Lucia, her parents or Egan where she was going, since she had no desire to do so. Falcon had impressed upon her that *Missions are to be discussed only with fellow operatives.*

They passed the noisy bustle of the cattle market with its haggling buyers and sellers, the smell of hay and manure, and the frustrated mooing from Highland coos. A short while later, Phoebe gazed up at the majestic *Ben na Calliach.* Villagers refer to the hill as the *old woman*, because of its shape. But Phoebe couldn't recall the dull light ever falling on it in such a shadowy, foreboding manner.

An hour later, just after passing the quiet parish church, they arrived at a large, reddish stone building overlooking the Broadford River, carrying signage for Strathail Distillery. The man who rushed out to greet them had a full head of graying hair, neatly pulled back, and a pleasant countenance. He also had Aila's smile and clear complexion. He hugged Aila and then her maid introduced her father, Master Fitzroy. After Fitzroy ordered a distillery worker to feed and take care of their horse, he turned to Phoebe.

"It's a pleasure to meet you Mistress Dunbar. Aila sent one of the Dunbar kitchen lads yesterday with the message that you are interested in Strathail whisky."

Phoebe smiled with appreciation at Aila.

"Depending on the price, I'd first like to purchase a single cask to start with and see how it is received by our clan," Phoebe said, turning to Aila's father. Why spend the coin upfront before determining if the Dunbars liked it or not?

"Our whisky is the finest in the Highlands, and I have no doubt you will be pleased," Fitzroy said.

He then led them on a brief tour of the well-managed modern distillery, explaining the cooking of the grains, the fermentation and distillation process, then the aging in their charred oak barrels.

Phoebe asked apropos questions during the tour, then towards the end of their conversation, keeping her tone casual, Phoebe chose her words wisely. "I gather Walter Hawley, a lieutenant general of the British Army, is interested in investing in your distillery. You may very well get a visit from him soon."

Fitzroy's eyes widened, his expression brightening, seemingly impressed and taken aback. "Why, he was just here yesterday, Mistress. However did you know? He's planning a sizable investment, and he ordered a few casks of our single malt forty-year-auld whisky, which I am delivering later this week. Do you know the gentleman?"

Phoebe's head spun at Fitzroy's answer, excitement and dread alike mingled in her chest. But she didn't want word getting back to Hawley that she was inquiring about him.

"I've never met the gentleman. A redcoat I encountered in Birmingham spoke of Hawley's investment. But do be careful—there have been highwaymen robberies in these parts of late. I hope your delivery wagon doesn't have to travel too far," Phoebe said, in a slightly bored matter-of-fact tone.

"Thankfully, no. The lieutenant general is letting the gray manor on Bayview Crest. It's the biggest property not too far off the main road. I imagine the British Army is paying well for him to afford it, even though it needs work and he has no wife or children to support. It belongs to the auld Lord Melville, who moved to Edinburgh years ago. But then I don't like to gossip, Mistress," Fitzroy said, a rueful grin reddening his cheeks.

A short while after Phoebe and Aila left the distillery for home, the main dirt road forked. Phoebe took note of the wooden sign, labeled Bayview Crest, pointing in the direction of the less-traveled road.

"Aila, can you turn toward Bayview Crest for a short detour? I'm curious about the gray manor your father mentioned."

Surprise flashed across Aila's features, but nonetheless she guided the horse onto the side road.

The speed of their wagon markedly slowed because of the unevenness of the road. Their surroundings notably quieted, to where one could hear the wind against gnarly branches of pine trees and the echoes of their creaking wagon.

Up ahead, a gray English-style stone manor came into view to their left. Darkened clouds had started to drift overhead causing sinister shadows. A chill caused Phoebe to pull her cloak closer. The two-story building, with close to fourteen windows, two broken, was utterly unkept. Overgrown bushes, brambles, and tall yellow grass crawled up its sides like snakes. It raised the hairs on the back of Phoebe's neck.

Aila must have sensed it too. "There's something evil about that manor, mistress."

"I feel it too. Let's turn around," Phoebe said.

As Aila turned the wagon around, Phoebe spotted two men with flintlock muskets, perhaps guards, emerging from the spindly trees at the rear of the manor and running straight into the barn. Her eyes were drawn to the unusual number of familiar tall crates stacked near the barn's door. Loud voices drifted from the barn, but the exact words were muddled by the distance.

A rotund middle-aged English officer emerged from the building. He marched straight into the front door of the manor, carrying a dangling horsewhip in his hand, a half-smoked cigar imprisoned between his teeth and lips. Malicious lines on his features looked engraved. He wore a blood-red uniform. Phoebe ground her teeth as the fire of hatred sprang up her body, burning her like a bitter sickness from the inside out. She loathed the color red. She'd never met Hawley before, but her gut and the countless Jacobite pamphlets she'd read of his extreme cruelty told her she was looking right at him.

Aila guided the horse back onto the main road. The clopping of a horse's hooves towards them made Phoebe lift her gaze. Her heart stopped. Recognition hit her stomach like a punch. The red coated rider stopped in the middle of their path, forcing Aila to pull on their reins.

CHAPTER 42

Fair-haired Faye Ross, dressed in his garish English uniform, sat atop a massive snow-white stallion, stark against the backdrop of green pine trees, wind quaking their branches. The crimson of his uniform fill her with burning hatred, laced with ice cold terror. Her skin tingled with a familiar uncleanliness, making her stomach roil.

Phoebe's fingers curled into fists. Ross's empty blue eyes locked onto hers. A sneer stretched across his pale features. "Well, well, if it isn't the little Dunbar brat. Fortuitous meeting you two days in a row after all this time."

His polished English accent was sharp and cold, the same as her nightmares.

The first time he'd called her a brat for her insolence, she'd been attempting to flee him on the moors seven years ago. She'd disliked it then and downright hated it now.

He dismounted from his horse and approached her side of the wagon, standing a few feet from her. All her energies were concentrated on not showing any weakness, despite the cold sweat forming on her back. She hadn't gotten a good look yesterday, but it hit her that his fair hair was thinner than seven years ago and his middle rounder, but his eyes were still soulless in their dead gaze.

The restless stomp of their horse's hooves startled Phoebe. It also reminded her she wasn't alone and Aila was with her. She wouldn't allow anything to happen to Aila.

"Mistress, please, we don't want trouble. Should I go around him?" Aila whispered, next to her.

"We'll leave shortly," Phoebe said. A part of Phoebe wanted to grab the reins and take off with Aila, but she wasn't about to let this vermin get a whiff of her fear.

Phoebe leveled him with an unwavering stare. "Sir, I won't greet you or ask after your health, because the truth is, I have no interest," Phoebe said to Ross, her voice confident with an intonation of mockery.

His slow smile lacked any mirth whatsoever. "Disrespectful as ever. What are you doing here?" he said.

Phoebe's stomach hardened. Did he guess she'd just come from Bayview Crest?

She swallowed against the rising bile in her throat. "How is my presence here any of your concern?"

A glint of malice and anger flashed across his face. "You are like your parents, thinking you are superior to the British," he hissed.

Why would he believe her parents thought themselves superior? Her parents weren't like that at all. Hadn't the Rosses just discussed the shared moor and sheep with her parents when they'd come to visit? He must have seen how cordial and polite they were. Except when they were forcing her to marry, that is.

Her terror increased tenfold when Ross's hand went to rest on the holstered pistol at his hip. Her adrenaline spiked, readying her body for action, but the dagger tucked in her garter would be no match for his pistol

She had no doubt he would relish shooting her and Aila in

broad daylight if he suspected she was a Jacobite spying on an English lieutenant general.

She would never forgive herself if any harm came to an innocent like Aila.

Phoebe's head snapped towards approaching riders when distant clopping hooves sounded. When Phoebe made out the familiar figures coming towards them from the direction of the cattle market, her sigh of relief was audible.

Phoebe jumped down from their wagon and ran into the direct path of the two oncoming riders. She promised to chastise herself later for her reckless action as she called out for Slade and Peter.

They both reined in their horses mere feet away from trampling her and dismounted, eying her with surprise and confusion.

Phoebe ran towards Slade. In her peripheral vision she saw Peter, an amiable expression on his face, strolling towards Ross who had dismounted.

When Phoebe reached Slade, she took note of his blackened eye and swollen nose. Despite the emotions assailing her, guilt broke through to squeeze her chest.

"I am so sorry for what Egan did," Phoebe said to Slade.

Slade's features took on a bemused expression. "I cannot find fault with Egan championing his sister."

Peter and Ross approached. Without conscious thought, Phoebe drew nearer to Slade away from Ross. Slade shot her a perplexed look before facing Peter and Faye Ross.

"Colonel, this is Lieutenant Faye Ross of the second division of Horse Grenadier Guards," Peter said in an amiable tone, oblivious to any undercurrents of tension.

Slade's nostrils flared and he scowled as he took in Faye Ross, then switched his gaze to Phoebe, then back to Faye Ross.

Peter cleared his throat rather loudly as if waiting for something. Slade appeared reluctant as he extended a stiff hand in greeting, but Ross's face twisted into hardness as he snapped to attention and saluted instead of shaking hands. Ross's proper display of a formal greeting for a lower-ranking lieutenant addressing a higher-ranking colonel seemed rather overdone.

From Slade's expression, he seemed to think so as well. Nonetheless he rigidly returned the salute, his eyes sharpening on Ross. "At ease, Lieutenant. In actuality, I've sold my commission. I am a civilian now."

Ross's brows leveled and his lips curled in insolence. "You are a Scot?"

Slade's scowl hardened. With the tightening of his jaws and the narrowing of his gaze he looked downright intimidating. Was his reaction due more to Ross's derisive tone or the question itself? Phoebe swallowed hard when it occurred to her that Slade might have sensed something off between her and Ross.

Ross may have assumed a colonel of the British Army had to be English, until Slade spoke, betraying his Scottish brogue. And the truth was, nothing in Slade's attire suggested he was Scottish. His form-fitting breeches, crisp white shirt, unbuttoned black great coat, and riding boots, would have looked typical for any well-to-do English gentleman in Birmingham.

Slade ignored the question as his unflinching gaze speared Ross. "How do you know Mistress Dunbar?"

Slade's hard tone was edged with an unmistakable challenge. He was an arm's length away from Ross and stood an ominous half a head taller. Phoebe couldn't help but note how much leaner, darker and more dangerous Slade looked standing next to Ross, Slade's facial injuries giving him a harsh visage.

Ross pulled himself up to full height. His answer came with reluctance and a hint of resentment. "The Dunbars are neighbors to the Rosses, my cousins."

Slade scrutinized Ross for a brief moment before speaking again. "You're from the Second Division? You're in Owens' group?"

Ross blinked. "Yes. I report to Colonel Wilfred Owens."

The smile stretching across Slade's lips was unequivocally predatorial. "Owens is a good friend of mine. I'll be sure and mention our meeting, Lieutenant."

Heat flashed across Ross's cold eyes, but he gave a curt nod. "Pleasure to make your acquaintance, Colonel. But if you will excuse me, I must be getting along."

Ross mounted his horse and rode off in the direction of Bayview Crest without a backward glance.

Phoebe let out a second audible breath of relief at seeing Ross's back. Her body ached to fall apart, but she kept herself under fierce control.

Peter, who was standing next to them now and staring at Ross ride away, clicked his tongue. "What a strange man."

Slade gave her a pointed look. "How do you know this man Ross?"

She swallowed back the sand that seemed to have gathered in her throat and made a dismissive flick of her wrist. "Like he said, we met years ago when he visited his cousins, who are neighbors of the Dunbars."

Her dismissive gesture didn't work on Slade, for he continued to consider her closely. "Did he upset you?"

Phoebe licked her dry lips. Dear Lord, she was sweating and weak with queasiness. And she longed for the sanctity of her bedchamber where she could curl up alone and give in to the tremors threatening her entire body. Her stomach roiled, and she suspected if she didn't calm herself soon, she would cast up her accounts right there in the middle of the road. She took a few deep, cleansing breaths then looked up. Slade's cool green eyes held considerable concern. She blinked, for the sight of it squeezed the air from her lungs.

He'd taken on Ross as if the man was beneath him. He'd looked at the subject of her nightmares for the past seven years and treated him like he was an insignificant insect. Slade had instilled fear in Ross without raising a single finger.

The realization hit Phoebe like a blow to the midriff. If she were to survive any length of time in the Highlands doing Jacobite work for Falcon, she could run into Ross at any time, she would need Slade. She would need his protection. Phoebe made up her mind what she needed to do. However, it did not make the queasiness subside.

Slade eyed her expectantly. "Fifi?"

She shook her head in an attempt to dislodge her ruminations. "No, he did not upset me. I was just considering the fact that I have to visit the mantua-maker in Portree to get a wedding gown."

A squeal of delight sounded from behind Phoebe, and it hit her that Aila was still seated in the wagon a few feet behind her and was listening. Aila was well aware of Egan's and her parents' dictate she marry Slade.

Peter smiled. He was atop his horse now, pulling on the reins, for the beast was snorting with restlessness. "Are you two giving in to Egan Dunbar's ultimatum then … you will be wed?"

Phoebe's heart pounded like the setting off of cannon fire. She faced Slade, his eyes intense and so sharp, they could cut glass.

"Yes, Slade and I are getting married," she said.

CHAPTER 43

GARRAIDH CASTLE, ISLE OF SKYE, SEAT OF THE MACLEAN CLAN

Slade's heart squeezed as if gripped by an iron fist. *Slade and I are getting married,* she'd said just days earlier. He wanted her, more than he'd ever wanted anything in his life. But he could fail her like he'd done Sylvia, and she could die and leave him, broken, destroyed, and praying for death. That tended to happen to the women he loved. He had loved his mother. Even though he was very young when she died, she had been his world. He'd barely survived Sylvia's death. Fifi's death would kill him. It would drain the light from this world, burn the heavens to ashes and leave his soul in eternal hell. He blinked at the gray light outside a northwest-facing window of the fourth-floor solar breathing through the tightness in his chest. The silvery-blue waters of Garraidh Loch outside the window crashed onto barley colored sand.

But he couldn't afford this fear of failure.

"I want you to take a wife and settle down," his father had said to him in the library that same day before he and Peter had gone into Broadford and ran into Fifi and Faye Ross.

His father had explained. "Tara had a riding accident. She can no longer bear children. When Sadie comes of age and takes a husband, she will lose her movable goods through her husband's rights of *jus mariti*. She'll retain ownership of MacLean's vast estate, but her management will be limited by law," Chisolm had said.

So, Slade's father was putting the MacLean's estate in a trust for Sadie, to be managed first by Lachlan, second by Slade, and third by Slade's male heirs.

Slade would do anything for Fifi. And he would do anything for his father and Sadie, and so, fear of failure wasn't an option.

The deed had been done, this very day, three days after Fifi had said *Slade and I are getting married*, and two days after he and Fifi had handfasted. He'd wanted his friend and clergyman Raghnall here, but because of old losses and animosities, his father had chosen the local minister most used by the MacLeans.

A knock sounded at the solar door breaking into Slade's thoughts. He pushed away from the windowsill and strolled to the door, pulling it open. Light fluttered in from the lamps in the corridor. The faint noise of revelry and bagpipes filtered up from the lower floors of the south wing of the castle where lingering wedding banquet guests remained.

The MacLeans' cook Iona stood outside the door. She was a heavyset woman in her fifties. Her round cheeks looked flushed, no doubt from being one of the busiest people of the day.

"What are ye doing here alone in the dark?" she asked.

Slade grinned at her when a warm cinnamon scent rose up from the covered tray she held. "I was waiting for this," Slade said.

Her smile was crooked. "Ye'll be telling me ye need plum pudding to seduce your new bride? What about using that handsome face the good Lord gave ye?"

He took the tray from her. "Well, I prefer to be fully armed with all available artillery tonight."

She threw back her head, a hearty melodious laugh escaped

her mouth. "Ye better get a move on. Your guests will come knocking soon to inquire about you bedding the bride."

As Iona turned around and headed down the corridor, Slade made out three familiar silhouettes ascending the stairs, heading in his direction. The burly outline of Egan at the back of the three was easy to spot. Slade placed the tray on a nearby sideboard, turning to the trio. Egan's attitude towards him had been chilly at best since the Black Hog's. Next to him was the lean outline of Daegan MacDonell, his second favorite foster brother. The three of them had been inseparable during their training days with Angus MacDonell, until Slade had joined the army and left the Highlands.

Leading the three in his direction was Peter, who tilted his head towards Slade. "I was told Scots regard the groom's bedding of the bride with importance. Can I be of assistance, Colonel?" Peter said.

Slade cocked his head towards his friend. "The day I need help from you to bed my new wife, I expect there'll be snowflakes flurrying in hell," Slade said.

Daegan, who stood behind Peter, guffawed. "I believe Peter here was referring to guard duty. Nonetheless, it appears you are standing at the wrong door. Why don't we provide you with a safe escort to the door of the marriage bedchamber?" Deagan said, with a wink.

Slade regarded Daegan with mild amusement. "I am capable of finding it all on my own."

Egan, standing next to Daegan, narrowed his eyes at Slade. "We'll still be escorting you to make sure you don't get lost on the way," Egan said, in a hard tone.

Egan still hadn't fully forgiven him for the scandal that injured Fifi's reputation. The Dunbars had all but branded Fifi fast and loose when gossip of her kiss with Slade had been cast about. The rumors had turned to ashes thankfully when word of their wedding had started spreading three days ago.

"How long are you going to hold that one indiscretion against me?" Slade asked Egan.

Egan harrumphed, folding his massive arms glaring at Slade.

Daegan threw up his hands in mock surrender. "I don't know what happened at the Black Hog's, but you two need to bury the poleaxe, preferably not in each other's backs, and move on. This strife betwixt you is starting to give me gray hairs, and I am far too young and attractive to have them."

Peter chuckled while a smirk broke out on Egan's face.

Slade sensed an opening and extended his arm in a friendly gesture towards Egan, the proverbial burying of the poleax. Egan's jaw muscles worked for a split second before he accepted Slade's hand. "You did the honorable thing in the end. I can't remain angry at you. We are brothers now by marriage, after all," Egan said, yanking Slade towards him for a slap back hearty hug. The gesture was warm, and brimmed with brotherly affection.

After Egan released Slade, Peter cleared what suspiciously sounded like emotion from his throat. "It may not seem like it, but we are clogging up your door on your wedding night for a sound reason."

"And the reason is?" Slade asked, picking up the tray he'd set aside.

Peter's expression turned earnest. "Your brother is deep in his cups and is telling everyone he intends to put the newlywed couple together in the marital bed in front of numerous witnesses as the bedding ceremony tradition dictates. We came to warn you."

Slade's shoulders stiffened, and he pressed his lips together. That was just the gauche type of behavior he'd expect from his brother. As it stood, Phoebe was already skittish. He didn't want anything else to frighten her.

His entire wedding flashed by in a murky medley of images. The tremor in Fifi's hands as they'd signed the marriage contract this morning. Her nervous coughs during the reading of their vows, as if she'd been short of breath. The flash of panic in her eyes as they'd parted an hour ago, for her to go and prepare for the bedding ceremony. Was she afraid of the marriage bed? Or of him?

Daegan made a rather overdone chivalrous bow. "I humbly offer my services as guard for the night to keep your brother and other guests away from the marriage bedchamber," Daegan said.

"And I'll be guarding too," Egan said to Slade. "While I know you'll be a good husband and protector for Phoebe, I don't want anyone upsetting my little sister."

Slade refrained from telling Egan that Fifi was anything but defenseless. Egan clearly had no clue his sister was more capable than most women, certainly more capable than any women he himself had ever met.

"I'll join the watch too, Colonel," Peter said, in an amiable tone.

The rigidness in Slade's shoulders eased. He took in each of the men standing in front of him as warmth permeated his chest. "Well gentlemen, I accept your offer, and moreover I thank you for the magnanimous gesture. Now let me not keep my bride waiting any longer."

Slade left his three sentinels heading down the stairs to guard the entrance to the floor from below. He then made his way down the hall to the wedding chamber and knocked. The door cracked open, and Lucia popped her head out, bouncing curls framed her beaming face.

"Oh, Colonel, it's you. Breena and I were preparing your bride, but as you are now here, we'll leave."

She looked back, motioned to someone, then slipped out of the chamber past him, followed by her maid Martha. Breena, Egan's betrothed, followed them, her countenance pleasant but her gaze on Slade watchful as if trying to determine what sort of man he was.

Slade entered the lofty wedding chamber. Still holding the

tray with one hand, he closed the door with the other. He turned around and his eyes landed on Fifi. His pulse hammered, and his desire flared. Good God, he was a fortunate man.

Instead of the modest, creamy silk taffeta wedding gown she been adorned in earlier, she now wore a plush, forest-green velvet dressing gown tied at the waist, accentuating its tiny circumference compared to the shapely swells of her breasts and the luscious curve of her hips. His mouth watered and his nethers stiffened.

He leveled his eyes with hers. "I brought you a present," he said, indicating the tray in his hand.

Her auburn hair was brushed to a shimmering satin gleam, falling down her upper body in glorious fiery ringlets. He couldn't wait to sink his fingers into its rich thick silkiness, to touch her, and draw her mouth to his.

CHAPTER 44

Fifi approached him and eyed the covered tray with a stiff, questioning glance as he deposited it on the sideboard next to a vase of fragrant green lady's mantle and pink cyclamen.

"You brought me food right after our wedding banquet?" she asked, her voice tinged with uncertainty.

The corner of his mouth lifted lazily. "A five-course banquet, where you shifted food around on your plate without eating anything."

Slade proceeded to pour her a glass of sherry.

She uncovered the tray and gasped with delight. "Plum pudding!"

Fifi threw her arms around him and planted a sweet unguarded kiss on his mouth, all stiffness and uncertainty gone. His tactic had worked. But before Slade had time to blink, she'd already released him and was delving further into the tray. But her bergamot scent mixed with the warmth of her flesh lingered on him. It sent a surge of blood straight to his groin.

"How did you know I liked plum pudding?" she asked as she picked up the small bowl and spoon.

He set the sherry down next to the tray. "I recalled your exuberance during dessert at the hunting lodge the day Lucia arrived."

There had never before been a more erotic sound to escape a woman's lips than her moan after she'd taken her first bite that day. The sound had heated his blood and haunted his nights since.

He proceeded to pour himself two fingers of whisky. "It was also a peace offering of sorts," he added.

Fifi planted herself on the edge of a gray velvet ottoman at the foot of the canopied mahogany four-poster bed, with blue velvet hangings and a plush cream counterpane. The subdued firelight from the candelabra glinted off the polished wood, but also danced temptingly in Fifi's hazel eyes.

She stilled before taking her first bite, a delicate brow arching. "A peace offering?"

Slade meandered over to the mahogany chair next to the ottoman and sat down with his whisky.

He leaned back into the chair, took a sip of the golden liquid, savoring its fire as it rolled down his throat. "I take full responsibility for throwing us into this hasty marriage. I didn't have a chance to properly court you."

Fifi's entire countenance softened, and her gaze lowered, her expression intimate at his declaration. "I was the one who ask you to kiss me at the Black Hog's right before Egan showed up, if you recall."

She had shocked the hades out of him. "Yes, I do," he said.

Slade had never been as aroused as he was that morning in the hallway when she'd asked him to kiss her. Her sensuous request had lit a fire in him.

Fifi took her first bite of the plum pudding. Her eyelids completely dropped, and the familiar little erotic moan of pleasure escaped her lips hardening his already stiff groin. His hand tightened around his glass as he took another sip of his whisky and shifted in his chair.

After chewing and swallowing, she considered him from beneath lowered lashes. "I wanted to marry you regardless of Egan's ultimatum," she said.

Her words shocked him, yet again. He never imagined that his little friend from all those years ago would grow up to be a beautiful, desirable, and seductive woman, who would set her sights on him. And even more shocking was the fact that he realized in that moment she had always belonged to him. She danced in his blood, his flesh craved hers, and his soul had always been seeking hers. The parts of his entire being all coalesced to a pure sweet harmony that was Fifi, a tune played by his beating heart.

"Did you?" he whispered.

She cleared her throat as if considering her answer. Her action of licking plum pudding crumbs off her lips, gave him the ridiculous urge to suck the sweet dessert off her tongue.

"I find it's better to have the protection of a husband while in the Highlands," she said.

He chuckled, fingering the cool smoothness of the glass. "Well then, I'm pleased I could offer my services."

Her cheeks turned a darker shade, and it occurred to him she was staring at his legs. Slade glanced down, recalling he'd worn a MacLean tartan kilt, with its distinctive black stripes upon a field of yellow, for their wedding. His knees were now wide apart in a relaxed albeit exposed manner.

She blushed in the most adorable way. "I've never seen you in formal Scottish regalia before. It becomes you," she said.

Male pride stretched the corners of his mouth upward. "You no doubt find me devastatingly handsome," he teased.

She rolled her eyes yet grinned, in a pure, unguarded way, an indelible remnant of the carefree lass she'd been.

Slade swirled the remaining whisky in his glass and eyed her as she finished up her dessert and drank from the sherry he'd poured. He tilted his head back and finished his own drink.

He rose and meandered over to the nightstand. His glass clinked as he set it down. Slade stepped over to the bed and sank into its luxuriousness, one elbow propping up his lounging body. "Come, join me," he said.

He saw the second her countenance stiffened. But she slowly and with caution in her fluttering eyes, moved towards him. She stopped an arm's length away, avoiding his gaze. His eyes were drawn to the tremor in her hands as she untied the knot at her waist. She removed the dressing gown and tossed it on the nearby divan. The uncertainty and hesitation in her movements made Slade's body go very still. Wasn't it the groom who undressed the bride?

The removal of her dressing gown revealed the same diaphanous night rail he had seen the night at the hunting lodge, the same one that had been in each and every erotic dream he'd had of her. And just like that night, her areolas were now tantalizingly visible through the thin material. Slade was now as hard as iron, and wildfire rushed through his veins.

She stood straight and faced him. His heart thumped a maddening rhythm as his eyes moved, slowly devouring the entire delicious outline of her exquisite figure through the thin material, ending in shapely, stocking-clad legs and tightly fastened creamy soft leather boots. If he were capable of stringing coherent words together, he might have asked why she still wore her boots.

He was utterly and completely entranced as she took a deep inhalation as if for courage and lifted her night rail off in a single swoop revealing her naked body.

The room tilted as if unhinged. His fingers curled inward, actively refraining from pouncing and devouring her. The thump of his heart was dangerously rapid. Slade momentarily closed his eyes, praying for mastery of a hungry ferocious beast within.

She cleared her throat as if settling her nerves, and his eyes snapped open. "We must consummate the marriage, but first, I have a few requests," she said.

Slade didn't catch Fifi's words, for his attention was riveted on her tantalizing body. She was made for his undoing, beautiful and perfect. He took in each little divot and curve of her voluptuous figure, soft, lush and appealing. Lust and possessiveness slammed into his chest. A desire to bury himself deep inside her hammered in his blood, his breathing loud and ragged.

Her eyes were watchful as she crossed her arms over her breasts, her movements jerky. He sensed her doubt and fear. With strength he thought himself incapable of, he tempered the blaze within. They were man and wife now, so why would she fear him? And if she did fear him, why had she disrobed without giving him that pleasure?

CHAPTER 45

Phoebe's heart slammed against her ribcage. The terror thumping through her was so potent, it threatened to drop her in a quivering puddle. The only truth keeping her fully erect was the certainty that Slade wouldn't hurt her. After seeing him at the manor six weeks ago, this truth had cemented itself inside her. She *could* trust him. Yet the way he was staring at her now, dangerous, raw, with unbridled lust brewing in his dark hunter-green gaze, she had to wonder. The pre-wedding-night talk she'd had with Breena and Lucia earlier had been wholly inadequate to prepare her for the burning fire in Slade's eyes.

She had to seize control of the consummation, but how? She couldn't allow another man to control her body. Ever. Even for a brief moment. Even the first and last one she'd ever had amorous thoughts of. Granted, Slade was her husband, and this was her duty as his wife, as Breena and Lucia had reiterated several times in this very chamber. Yet Phoebe still wanted control. She had to have it. And keep it. But the unbridled molten hunger in Slade's dark eyes weakened her.

The seven-year-old memory of hard metal buttons from Faye Ross's open breeches digging into the soft flesh of her thigh invaded her head. The sharpness of the insignia on his cuffs had abraded the thin flesh of her restrained wrists. The old shadow pain made Phoebe grab her right wrist. Ice cold panic surged through her, at the prospect of being bedded by a fully clothed Slade.

Phoebe inhaled a deep breath. She had to push through her nerves before she lost all her courage. Without her night rail, she'd lost half of her body's warmth, and a great deal of her bravado.

She ignored the dampening of her palms and the sheen of sweat forming on her brows. "I'd prefer us to be unclothed," she said.

His eyes blinked up from traversing the length of her naked body with frightening rapacity. "I beg your pardon?" he said, his voice the lowest octave she'd ever heard.

His gaze, like obsidian, caused a heated liquid sensation to flutter low in her belly and warmth to return to the length of her a hundred times over.

"My first request for consummation is for us to be unclothed," she repeated, a slight tremor slipping into her voice.

The darkness in his gaze shifted to watchful and restrained, with a sensuous curve to his lips. "Quite reasonable, my love, even preferable. What are your other requests?" he said.

Phoebe's stomach gave a nervous lurch as she swallowed before speaking. "Above all, I'd rather be in control. That is to say, I'd rather … ah … lead in our dance."

The corners of her husband's mouth tipped up further in a sinfully handsome smile. "Any other requests?"

"No," she said, grateful he wasn't looking at her as if she was addled.

Slade threw her a devilish look. "Well then, come over here and undress me, love," his voice soft, silken and sultry.

Phoebe's legs were like a jellyfish as she edged towards him. She felt raw, vulnerable, and bare. Could he discern the act that had tainted her? No, he couldn't, could he. The stain was under her skin, in her flesh, seeped into her marrow. It had long since reached the depths of her soul. She'd done him a disservice, hadn't she? Was he expecting a virgin wife? Well, he'd soon find out she was anything but.

He remained seated but straightened, giving her better access to his neckcloth. He eyed her closely as she willed the tremor in her hands to still, certain he could hear the frantic pounding of her heart. The crisp white material was cool to the touch, in complete contrast to the heat emanating from the rest of him. She untied the intricate knot of his cravat and laid it on the nearby ottoman.

Next, she clicked open the twinkling cairngorm jeweled pin holding the woolen tartan in place over the left breast of his black velvet jacket. Phoebe fumbled clumsily in removing the pin and ended up pricking the flesh of her thumb.

"Blast!" she whispered, snatching her hand away at the stab of pain, dropping the pin on the bed.

His brows furrowed as he took the wrist of her injured thumb and turned the finger towards him to get a better look. A single bead of red had formed on the pad of her thumb, and before she could protest, he'd placed her thumb in his mouth and started to suck.

Phoebe gasped, her eyes widening at him. Despite her nerves, the slick, wet feel of his mouth, in particular his tongue encasing her sensitized finger, sent a rush of weakness down the length of her.

His eyes fixed on her as the rough surface of his tongue dragged long, slow licks over the skin of her imprisoned thumb. The sensation did funny things inside her belly and created chaos in her head. His rapacious gaze was more seductive than she was prepared for. Making her want to retract her two requests. Her breath caught at the unexpected and maddening urge to redirect his lips from her finger to her own mouth. But Phoebe willed herself to be strong and stay her course.

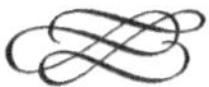

CHAPTER 46

Slade removed the thumb from his mouth and inspected it. "There, the bleeding has stopped," he said.

He plucked a white handkercher from the front pocket of his jacket and tied it gently around her thumb.

He cocked a grin at her, his gaze half-lidded. She didn't know when, but she'd inched closer to him, to where her bare thighs brushed against the smooth but grainy material of his kilt. His tempting, warm, clean male scent, mixed with a hint of cloves, made her too conscious of the exposed skin of his toned lower thighs, knees and upper shins, all with an alluring dusting of sable hair. She shook her head and straightened, as if breaking free of an enchantment, and shifted to put a few inches between them.

He removed the pin from the bed, placed it on the nightstand, then eyed her, his long lean body at rest. "Pointy things can be quite dangerous," he said, with amusement.

She smiled despite herself. "Apparently."

Phoebe resumed fingering her husband's trappings. She removed his jacket, waistcoat, shirtsleeves and sporran. And even though his hands never moved except to help her, it occurred to her that he could be refraining from touching her because of her request to be in control. This pleased her immensely. It also confused her that she'd liked it when he'd sucked her thumb and wished he'd done more, but she'd requested to be in control, hadn't she?

His body was a masterpiece, well-defined striations of sculpted muscle and sinew on his arms, chest and lean stomach like Gian Lorenzo Bernini's incomparable *David* which she'd seen in an art book at Ayr's library.

Her eyes snagged on the dark ink on his bicep in the form of a coiling viper. She stared, utterly mesmerized, and curious, her heart pounding frantically, assailed by an overwhelming urge to touch the inked skin. Phoebe stepped closer, between his spread knees to get a better look. A sudden flush of heat erupted from within her, yet she was incapable of stopping.

Slade's hard muscles tightened on contact, as her fingertips glided over the smooth, darkened skin. She traced her finger up the viper's long tail, over the coil of its body, into the oval of its opened mouth and protruding fangs, ending at the single line of its sharp tongue,

Slade's breath had become more ragged than earlier. It mingled with her own. The air between them sizzled and vibrated with sultry energy.

"Phoebe …?" Slade's low hard voice brushed softly against her neck, sensitizing her skin. A bolt of heat shot through her body as the dark viper swam in her vision.

"Did a sailor do this?" Her own voice sounded uncommonly breathless.

"No. An artist did it, in a little ink house near Aschaffenburg, in Germany, during the war." His voice was low and gravelly.

She cleared her thickening throat, struggling for coherent thoughts amidst a sea of hot conflicting emotions and icy fears.

"Wh … what should I do next?" she whispered, staring at his

mouth and recalling she was supposed to be in control yet feeling anything but.

When she eyed him, his gaze had dropped to her lips. "Kiss me," he whispered.

Phoebe touched her lips to his. Sensations exploded inside her body like a hundred barrels of gunpowder detonating. Lust pushed her to give in to wanton desires, but fear pulled her back. Eagerness for skin-to-skin contact warred with the dread of impending pain. The sweetness of their lips and teeth grazing each other collided with the burning dread in her stomach. Yet she fell further into him, picking up the pace when the hard strength and warmth of his embrace engulfed her.

He tasted of whisky and sin, and she drank him in, as if she'd been starved and thirsting all her life. While anxiety and lust battled for superiority in her mind, body and soul, she battled for control of the coming together. But Phoebe feared that in giving in to the lust and carnal desires, she was giving up control. Pleasure for control. She allowed it to consume her and pull her under.

When his tongue licked her lips, Phoebe gasped at the wicked contact but wine had already flooded her veins instead of blood, dizzying her head and pushing her to reciprocate.

In the back of her mind she was aware of Slade standing and shrugging out of his kilt. But she was too caught up in the kiss to care. She became aware of his thick erection pressing into her lower belly, as hard as steel. Fear struck her like iron spikes spearing her entire body from every direction. A shiver shot through her as if it was the dead of a bitter winter and she was outside and unclothed. But she swallowed down, pushing with all her might, through the paralyzing recollection of the ungodly pain from seven years ago. This was her husband, not her attacker.

Husband, not attacker. Husband, not attacker. She repeated over and over in her head, ignoring her sweating palms. The tremor returned to her hands as she traversed Slade's toned back and chest, but she ignored that too, throwing herself harder into his lips and caresses.

Slade's mouth became hungry, impatient, and hard against hers.

She had to have something. She needed to maintain something, something important. But she couldn't remember what it was, because her mind had abandoned itself. The thumping in her heart became so loud she gasped for air just as he lifted her and sat with her on his lap without breaking the kiss. Slade's steely erection pressed hard and thick into the back of her thigh, and she found herself rolling her hips against his legs wanting more and more friction. Somewhere in the back of her mind the movement of his thigh against her exposed core seemed deliberate and calculated but she didn't care. Her own hunger was like the sparks from a sledgehammer's strike hitting black powder.

The tips of her breasts pebbled against his calloused palms, and she pressed further into him wanting more heat, more skin to skin, more of him.

Phoebe pushed against Slade's chest. Her world turned weightless as his body gave way, going horizontal on the bed, she on top of him.

His fingers were annoyingly slow as they kneaded her hips and derriere. And she wanted to laugh, because in her drunkenness his fingers seemed methodical in their slowness, as if he was restraining himself.

What was happening to her?

His hands traveled up to cup her breasts. He molded the delicate skin and flicked her nipples. The motion was soft and tortuously inadequate.

"More … more …" Her voice was desperate. Needy. Starved.

It was then she realized her mistake. She'd been goading a beast, and he'd been holding back. In the blink of an eye, her husband flipped her entire body onto her back. His weight pinned her into the bed, his eyes wild with carnal lust. His breathing hard.

She froze. All the heat drained from her body. Cold terror gripped her. She scrambled like a frantic prey snared by a predator.

"No. No. No." She shook her head.

Slade stilled and blinked. The black haze in his eyes turned confused.

"What's—" he started.

Bitter hysteria gripped Phoebe. She slammed her bunched fists into his chest. "Get off me!"

Her scream cracked the heavy air like a bolt of energy.

He sprang off her and stood next to the bed, his expression drawn tight with shock. Phoebe's entire body quaked at an alarming rate. She leapt out of the bed and darted on unsteady legs for her dressing gown.

What the devil just happened? Slade's body clamored for release as he struggled for calm, staring shocked at his wife. Lust gushed through his veins. He wanted her like he'd never wanted any other woman before. But he held back with strength he didn't know he had, fighting to understand. With blood pounding in his head, it was difficult. Her scream hadn't been loud enough, or Egan would have already broken down the door.

As the boiling in his blood cooled, he saw it. The fear, perhaps even terror, in her eyes. He'd seen that look before, in the eyes of British prisoners of war at the Battle of Dettingen. Men who'd been through severe mental and physical injury. Men who were damaged. Broken. He'd also seen the scared desolate faces of women after he'd stopped soldiers from violating them in remote villages outside Aschaffenburg. But Phoebe had never been to war, he told himself. His mind refused to comprehend or accept that possibility.

His eyes desperately searched her pained features for answers.

"Fifi, I would never hurt you. Never do anything you didn't want me to. Did I misunderstand?" he said.

She wrapped the belt of the dressing gown around her waist in a single violent motion. But then she seemed to lose steam and stumbled over to a corner chair. She sank down, looking small. She pulled her booted feet up into the chair, hugging her knees. He ignored the fact that she still wore her boots. Fifi started to rock back and forth, staring at the dark woolen rug on the floor.

The sight of her in anguish wrecked him.

His need to comfort her, to hold and gently soothe her in his arms was a painful, gut-wrenching ache. He yearned to touch her. But it warred with the echoes of her last words to him. *Get off me.* Slade actively restrained himself from going to her.

"Are you well? How can I help?" he asked.

She didn't seem to hear him, her expression vacant.

He needed to understand before he could decide what to do next. He walked over to the sideboard and poured himself two shots of whisky in a tumbler. He tilted his head back and drank it all in a single swoop. The familiar burn of the liquid steadied him. Yet his hands shook.

He then filled the tumbler and walked it over to her. "Drink, it'll settle you."

She looked at him blankly. As if she'd been far away. As if five minutes ago she hadn't been hot-blooded and desperate for him. As if he were an utter stranger. Worry, regret and pain speared his heart. He had to close his eyes for a second, to steady himself.

She eyed the glass he offered with suspicion. "I've never had whisky," she said, a tremor in her voice.

With a jut of his wrist he gestured for her to take the glass. "It's medicinal. Good for shock."

Or whatever in hades was going on.

She took the glass and stared at its contents, as if deciding what to do. When she did take a sip, she coughed and held her chest with one hand.

Her eyes watered. "Oh my," she breathed.

But her blank expression was gone.

He turned and strode to the ottoman where she'd laid his shirt. After donning it, Slade crossed over to where his kilt lay on the floor. He picked it up and pulled it on.

When he was more himself, he turned to her, spearing his hand through his thick, tangled hair.

"What just happened?" His tone was gentle.

She stared at him. A plethora of emotions danced across her face. Pain. Fear. Sadness. Misery. Then the blankness returned.

"I … I don't know," she whispered.

He didn't believe her. She knew. Whatever it was that had made her act so unexpectedly. He wasn't angry with her, nor did he blame her. He just wanted to understand. He'd never told anyone the crippling fear Sylvia's death had ignited in him. The fear of failing another woman. What was Fifi's fear?

His mind went back to where it had refused to go earlier. Had someone hurt her? Blood red rage ignited in his gut. His fists clenched and his heart rate shot up so fast, its pumping boomed in his ears. If someone had, he would find the demon and take pleasure in patiently and methodically dismantling him limb from wretched limb.

Slade took several deep breaths before the red dissipated from his vision. He didn't want to be anything but gentle with his new wife, but he also wanted answers.

"We can take it as slow as you need to in the marriage bed. There's no rush. A week, a month. A few months," he said.

His father could wait a little longer for male heirs.

Anxiousness etched its way into his bride's expression, and she took another sip. "Your brother seemed eager for proof of our marriage's consummation."

He gave a derisive snort. "I'll deal with Lachlan. Please don't worry about him." He rose and sauntered over to the nightstand, picked up his dagger and unsheathed the blade. He then nicked his palm, hissing at the sting. He returned the dagger to its sheath and waited for the blood.

She shot up from her chair, setting the glass down on the sideboard, and came to him, her brows pulled together in stark concern. "What are you doing?"

When a few drops of blood started to gather in his palm, he stepped over to the bed and smeared the blood on the counterpane. "There. We've consummated the marriage."

He eyed her, a tug pulling at the corners of his mouth. Her cheeks reddened with embarrassment. "Oh," she murmured.

She picked up his dagger, went to her night rail on the back of a chair, picked that up, cut a long thin strip from its hem, then walked the strip back over to him. Setting his dagger down, she eyed him.

"Your hand, please?" she said.

He gave her his nicked palm. She proceeded to wrap his hand with the strip of cloth. Her touch was gentle. Caring. Tender. After she was done, she looked up at him. Warmth softened her features, even though regret overshadowed her eyes. "You have my eternal gratitude, husband."

Was he her husband if they hadn't consummated the marriage?

Her blank expression returned. And his rage at the possibility that another man hurt her returned, stabbing his gut and twisting in his chest. He swallowed back the bile threatening to come up his gullet.

She picked up her glass, sank back down into the chair and hugged her knees with one hand, then took another sip of whisky. Slade returned to the divan, the question of how to find out what happened to Fifi bombarding his mind.

The blankness dissipated. It was erased after they'd sat in silence for a while, as she took little sips. Whisky tended to put a few layers of false strength between a person and the world. He recalled it only too well from right after Sylvia's death.

CHAPTER 48

The flash of stark pain and gut-wrenching agony in her furrowed brows, tight lips and glassy eyes was fleeting but it sent a jagged knife straight to his heart, obliterating his insides. He would do anything to never see that expression on her lovely face again. Lie. Torture. Kill.

Slade shifted in his seat, wanting to change the topic. "We'll have a few wedding guests to attend tomorrow."

Fifi stared into the hearth. The fire was now mere glowing fragments of coal. "Aunt Penelope from Edinburgh is always looking for any little thing to disapprove of. To criticize. She disapproved of me leaving her home to go stay with my friend Charlotte from Ayr and her family, even though they are well liked and respected in the community. Of course, I went to work for the Bolingbrokes instead," Fifi said, her tone laced with irony.

Slade recalled the blue-eyed woman with the blonde hair done in a ridiculous fashion in the chapel during their wedding. He made a motion above his head. "Was she the one with the ostrich plumes who sat next to your mother at the banquet?" he asked.

Fifi nodded unsteadily. "The very one. Lucky for me she was

visiting the Sutherlands in the Highlands and was able to attend our wedding on short notice." Fifi scoffed, not sounding lucky in the least. She then continued. "She's the legitimate daughter of Sir Donald Lindsay, Baronet. My mother is his illegitimate daughter. Aunt Penelope has never let me or my mother forget that fact."

"She sounds unpleasant," he murmured.

Fifi made a motion toward him with her now empty glass. "Did you know my aunt is the mistress of the Earl of Stair?"

"Is she now. Well, well, Aunt Penelope does get around," he said, feigning shock.

Her lips stretched into a genuine little smile. A smile was good, even though it was a little one. Slade's stomach loosened.

The Earl of Stair, James Dalrymple, moved in the same circles as General Bolingbroke and the Duke of Cumberland, William Augustus, son of King George II. It was a social circle a Jacobite spy could extract quite a bit of useful information from. No doubt Phoebe's mysterious spymaster, the one she was so willing to place her life in danger for, also traversed the same circle.

He frowned. "Was your aunt the one to introduce you to this mysterious Jacobite friend of yours?"

He purposefully didn't use the term spymaster, for it would put Fifi on her guard.

Fifi flushed. Either from the whisky or his question, he wasn't certain.

"Yes. We met at a soiree put together by my aunt in Edinburgh," she said.

Slade decided he didn't like Aunt Penelope.

He narrowed his gaze. "Why do you help this Jacobite friend?"

"Because I hate the redcoats," she said, the hardness of her voice surprising him.

"Why?" he persisted.

She hesitated, as if considering before speaking. "They shoot defenseless farmers, rape their women, burn their homes, kill their children and livestock. Why *don't* you hate them?"

She was holding something back.

"Hate is a strong word. I reserve it for people who have crossed me," Slade said.

Like the demon who hurt you.

She didn't seem to hear him. Fifi reached over to place the empty tumbler on the side table but missed. It fell and landed with a dull thud on the rug.

Slade went over to her. She looked up at him, pain returning to her beautiful eyes. His chest tightened as he picked up the glass and placed it on the side table then knelt in front of her chair, wanting desperately to touch her. She looked so small and a little lost; he didn't know what to do.

"You shouldn't let what happened here tonight upset you," he whispered, as he gently tucked a wayward lock of fiery hair behind her left ear.

Her lips narrowed into an achingly forlorn look. It gutted Slade. All his good intentions of not touching her fell to the wayside. He gently scooped her up. She fit perfectly in his arms as if heaven had made her just for him. She was his, and he would take care of her. Her weight was warm and comforting against his body. She made a weak protest but then seemed to let it go and settled against him instead. He breathed in the inviting scent of her, letting it fill him completely. He inhaled through the tightness in his chest and with care and reverence carried her towards the bed.

"I only intend on putting you to bed, nothing more," he said softly.

"Are you rescuing me again? I was nine the first time you rescued me. Do you remember? I'd fallen into the loch after repeating the knight's oath. You saved my life," she said.

He'd never forgotten what impressive ideals she'd had as a

wee lass. Ideals she still had. Ideals that made him want to be better, just for her.

"In the ancient Orient, they believed that if you save a life, you are responsible for that life for the rest of yours," he said. And as he said it, the words amalgamated like unbreakable steel in his soul.

Her head rested against his shoulder and her arms slid around his neck. Her bosom pressed against his chest. Her voluptuous hips rested against his belly. His body responded to her softness, like a famished beast given a delectable morsel. But Slade steadied himself.

"You are heroic, husband. Despite your claim to the contrary," she said.

"Only for you," he whispered.

The tension in her seemed to ease by the time he reached the bed. The ease seeped into him and relaxed his own body. He helped her under the counterpane. Slade couldn't say why, but he ended up lying on top of the counterpane next to her. Perhaps it was to make it difficult for him to reach for her body, to keep her safe from him.

He wanted to distract her from the shadows he could sense swirling about in her. "Tell me your fondest memory," he said.

She blinked at his question. Then her lips stretched into a somber smile. "Alex running away from our cook, who brandished a rolling pin at him. He'd stolen a meat pie from the kitchen. He'd stolen at least ten of them that same year before my father had a stern word with him. But our cook never caught him, I don't think she really wanted to. He used to make her laugh too hard with his antics. It sums up Alex, mischievous but loveable. He made it impossible for you to stay angry at him for too long," she said.

Her eyes twinkled with love, but her features darkened with the weight of loss. "What is your fondest memory?" she asked.

Slade swallowed back the emotion in his throat and shuffled

through his memories before speaking. "I don't remember my mother very well. I was too young when she died of winter fever. But I do have vague images in my head of a pale, fragile, flowery scented woman, her ethereal voice singing me to sleep with the Apple Pie rhyme. The love, caring and warmth in her voice made me feel like nothing in this world could ever hurt me, like I was her entire world, and she would never let harm come to me," he said.

Fifi's eyes were half-lidded, but brilliant with unshed tears. "She must have been a wonderful mother."

Slade pushed the emotions aside. He had to concentrate on cheering up Fifi, not rehashing the unfortunate sadness in his life. He made another attempt. "Who is your favorite person?" he asked.

CHAPTER 49

Her eyes widened and she gave him a lopsided smile. For a breath it looked like she was about to say something, but then her brows pulled together and she was deep in thought for a few more seconds, before finally speaking.

"Lady Naveau, ah … a dear friend of mine from Edinburgh. We have a great deal in common, she and I. And she knows my darkest secrets but still thinks I am trustworthy, capable and can do whatever I put my mind to. She gave me strength to fight, when I wanted to do nothing but give up."

Dark clouds formed in Fifi's eyes, and she averted her gaze for a second. When she looked at him again the bright smile stretching her lips looked brittle as she continued. "But recently my favorite person has been Lucia. She is uncomplicated and unburdens me in an intangible way. But also, Breena. Even though I've only just met her, she strikes me as terribly intuitive and caring. Eileanach's servants whisper that her impressive botanical knowledge makes her a witch, but its laughable to call a woman a witch just for her knowledge," Fifi said.

Slade's mind had snagged on her use of the term *dark secrets*.

He desperately wanted to know more. But the cold painful twisting in his gut told him he already knew. He was trying to banish some of the old pain from her eyes and poking at dark secrets didn't seem apropos.

Fifi palmed his cheek, her touch sweet and gentle. "Who is your favorite person?" she asked.

Slade struggled to focus on her question and not on the consuming warmth her touch elicited. After a protracted silence, he spoke. "At the moment it's Peter. He is cathartic to my soul somehow, it's difficult to explain. Ever since the war, he's been a light to my dark. At Dettingen in 1743, I would have given in to my dark thoughts after Sylvia, if it hadn't been for him. But I have to say Daegan and your brother Egan are close seconds. We've known each other for over fifteen years and formed strong bonds of trust, brotherhood and friendship while fostering with the MacDonell warlord. Those bonds will never break, regardless of arguments or disagreements," he said.

She covered a yawn. He too was feeling the weight in his own body and eyelids, it had been an emotional hurricane of a day. Something snaked through his gut and tightened his nethers when her eyes landed on his lips but then she trained them back on his eyes.

"I always meant to ask you, who are your favorite authors? That day at the Saint Michael's church I badly wanted to find out but I never got the chance," she said, her eyes searching his.

Slade smiled at the question. "As a boy, I thought the stories about the insane Roman tyrant Caligula and his cruelties, extravagances and sexual perversions were shocking but an eye opener to the depravity of humans. But then I used to spend hours captivated by Homer's tale of wanderings and omens in the *Odyssey*. I'd say the latter was much more enjoyable and probably my favorite. I love the idea of a grand life-altering adventure. Life in itself is one after all," he said.

The slow stretch of her lips was gentle, commiserative, and breathtaking. Her radiance was as deep and wide as an ocean. It stopped his heart. And he wanted to swim in that ocean forever.

Her eyes fell on his lips again. "I enjoyed kissing you," she said, her voice a low murmur.

He gazed at her, sleepiness lowering her eyelids almost closed. His heart ached at her unguarded loveliness, relieved the pained expression had vanished. "I enjoyed kissing you too, my love," Slade said.

She then puckered her lips, edged closer and planted an innocent kiss flush against his mouth. The sweetness of the gesture melted his insides to warm honey. It altered the landscape of his heart, mind and soul forever. But then her body stilled, settling into sleep.

He lay on his side next to her and, with the backs of his fingers, gently stroked the curve of her soft cheeks, the tip of her chin and the sides of her forehead, watching her sleep. But somewhere in his belly, a dangerous fire blazed as he left Fifi sleeping and silently went to the adjoining bedchamber.

Early the next morning, before the adjoining marriage bedchamber door opened and soft sure footsteps of leather boots heading down the stairs sounded, Slade was already up and dressed.

Minutes later, when another pair of footsteps entered the adjoining marriage bedchamber, Slade pushed up from the desk where he'd been finishing up his correspondence, strolled to the adjoining door, pulled it open and stepped in.

Fifi's maid, a diminutive girl with a clean and tidy pinafore, busied herself. She dropped the edges of a counterpane she'd been stretching over the bed, and with a startled expression turned to face him in a jerky motion, her brows almost lifting to her hairline.

Slade relaxed his features into a pleasant expression, not

wanting to scare the girl into bolting for the door. "Tell me, Aila, how long have you served my wife?" Slade asked.

"Ab … about nine years, Master MacLean, except when Mistress Dunb … pardon me, except when Mistress MacLean was down south," she said, her voice slightly tremulous.

"Then you would know who hurt my wife, wouldn't you?" Slade asked, expending an inordinate amount of energy to keep murder from his expression.

The maid's features went deathly pale before they crumpled in absolute and unmitigated distress. She started shaking her head, her chin and lips wobbled, and she took a step towards the door, looking like she was about to run.

"No, wait, please. I promise you are not in trouble. And I know how loyal you are to your mistress. I only want to help Phoebe. I only want to protect my wife and make sure it never happens again. Ever. You have my solemn vow," Slade said, putting his right palm on his chest above his heart and letting his distress show for a breath before shuttering his expression.

Her throat muscles worked again and again just before she stammered out sentence after sentence through tears, explaining her suspicions regarding Faye Ross.

After the maid was finished, Slade thanked the girl, assuring her she wasn't in any kind of trouble. He returned to the adjoining chamber and closed the door behind him without a sound while the rush of blood through his veins hammered like thunder in his ears. A dark, dangerous and desperate guttural howl sounded, and it took a second for it to hit Slade that it had escaped from his own throat. But then the need to contain the lethal predator inside him cracked and he punched walls, shattered tables, and broke chairs before collapsing to his knees in a heap of deadly fury and raging hatred. As his rapid pulse subsided and his racing breath slowed, an insistent knocking sounded at the door. He called out some platitude to assuage the servant's concern, knowing he'd have to hide the aftermath of his rage from Phoebe, and deal with the wreckage himself.

Slade had always been a methodical and patient man. But his exalted patience was in tattered shreds a short while later. He hurriedly penned a missive to his former comrade, Colonel Wilfred Owens of the Second Division, Lieutenant Faye Ross's commanding officer, requesting an immediate meeting.

CHAPTER 50

As Phoebe traversed the entire luxurious south wing of Garraidh expressing gratitude to her wedding guests staying at the castle, nausea gurgled in her belly and a tight pain stabbed her chest. Could they tell her smile wasn't real? Her disastrous wedding night replayed in the back of her mind, making her muscles stiffer than when she'd left the bed this morning after a night of troubled sleeplessness.

If someone could die of mortification, agony and regret she would have long since been buried. The agonizing pain, shock, and sympathy on his beautiful face from when she'd yelled *get off* burrowed into her soul with the force of a hundred iron spikes skewering her, over and over again. Had he left the marriage bedchamber to avoid her?

After speaking to the MacLean's guests, Phoebe spoke to her family before they left. She had to assuage a worried mother and a hovering father that the wedding night was successful. "I am perfectly hale, there is nothing to worry about," she said to her parents.

She had been hurt at their inflexibility when the scandal regarding the supposed kiss first happened. But she realized they were constrained, the same as everyone else. They too had to follow propriety.

"Even though custom dictated you and Slade had to marry, and you are now a wife, I will forever remain your father. You can come to me for anything, always," her father said.

And her mother had tears in her eyes as she fiercely hugged Phoebe goodbye. "Oh, my dearest, I will miss you terribly, please promise me you will come home for a visit as often as possible."

Phoebe had to swallow back the thick emotion in her throat as she hugged her father. Deep in her bones she understood her parents loved her, the best they knew how.

No longer would she live with her mother, father and Egan at Eileanach, Garraidh was her new home now. The thought filled her with sadness. What type of home would she build together with Slade when her mortifying behavior hadn't even allowed for consummation of the marriage?

After her parents, Egan enveloped her in a soft bear hug. She was still irritated at his barbaric behavior at the Black Hog's, although it had lost all of its fire. But being overbearing and high-handed was the way Egan showed he cared.

"I trust Slade with my life. He will make a fiercely protective husband for you, dearest sister. It's there in his eyes. He loves you. But if he ever makes you cry, or hurts you in any way, you only have to say the word, and I will take immense pleasure in flattening him into shape on your behalf," Egan said.

Phoebe chuckled, instantly forgiving him for Black Hog's. "I am sure that will not be necessary, but I love you for saying it."

As Phoebe watched her family leave in a Dunbar coach escorted by twenty retainers on horseback, her chest squeezed partly from love, but partly from regret. Was not telling them what Ross had done to her seven years ago protecting them from the redcoats should her family retaliate? Or was it born of her own selfish need or perhaps fear, that it might tarnish their love for her.

After Egan and her parents left, she had to pacify an overly concerned Aunt Penelope who was fearful there could be only one reason Phoebe and Slade got married so hastily.

"Only the most scandalous marriages take place with such haste, without even reading the banns. Such a shocking disregard for custom could only mean one thing, my dear," Aunt Penelope said, her face unbending and her brows arching in obvious scorn.

"Rest assured aunt, I am not with child. Slade and I are just terribly eager to begin our new life together, with the full support of our families," Phoebe said. She smiled so sweetly at her aunt, her face hurt.

Her aunt looked convinced by the end of their conversation. And Phoebe had to marvel at how good a liar she'd become after training with the Movement.

Then it was time to bid dear Lucia and Breena adieu because they were heading to Eileanach, Breena to be with Egan and Lucia to be with Peter, who was pitching custom made muskets to her father and Egan.

"Your solicitous advice on what to expect in the marriage bed was very useful," Phoebe said to Breena and Lucia, hoping they couldn't tell she was lying. Their unfiltered talk on lovemaking in preparation for the bedding had gone to the wayside. But she wasn't sure she believed their tales of pleasure.

"I knew it! You and the colonel were fated to be together. The way his smoldering gaze follows you, and the way he chivalrously rescued your reputation after Black Hog's is proof, he loves you," Lucia said.

Lucia had become more than just a chaperone and well-to-do wife who was overly concerned with fashion. She had become a cherished friend.

"I'm happy the wedding night was a success," Breena said, towards the end of the conversation.

Although Breena sent her a second glance before they left for the Hanbury conveyance, as if she wasn't entirely convinced with

Phoebe's story. What was it Falcon had said? *A lie is nothing but the truth in disguise.*

The rest of the day in the south wing passed in a blurry haze with thoughts of Slade squeezing her chest every few minutes, leaving her entire body in a bundle of nerves.

The south wing of Garraidh Castle was elaborate and busy. It contained the chapel and a complete set of residences for the laird, his extended family, guests, and their servants. As she made her way back to the quieter north wing, she wondered why Slade had chosen it for their residence. It had its own library, solar, kitchen, great hall, garderobe and a skeleton staff of servants, including Aila, who'd come with Phoebe from Eileanach. Though it wasn't as elaborately furnished as the south wing, Phoebe herself would take quiet and peaceful over elaborate and busy, any day.

CHAPTER 51

As the sun slipped below the western horizon, Aila lit a candelabrum on the sideboard, as well as a robust fire in the hearth of Phoebe's bridal chamber. She laid out Phoebe's change of clothes and arranged for a large wooden tub filled with steamy water to be sent up from the kitchen for Phoebe to wash. Aila added a few drops of bergamot oil to the water and placed a bar of orange blossom pressed soap and fresh folded linens by the side of the tub.

Aila helped Phoebe remove her high-necked day dress with corset stays, underskirts, shift and hose, then left the chamber pulling the door closed behind her. Phoebe pinned up her hair to avoid it getting wet and stepped into the deliciously warm bath, settling into its bone-melting luxuriousness, some of her earlier stiffness easing.

But then the door to the chamber pushed open.

Phoebe didn't turn. Her reclined position was far too soothing and comfortable. "Did you forget something, Aila?" Phoebe asked.

When the door bolted shut from the inside without an answer, Phoebe's heart dropped into her belly, and she jerked around. Slade stood there, his majestic height almost equaling that of the door. A dark pained look flashed across his arrestingly handsome features before becoming shuttered. He was dressed in a long greatcoat and leather riding boots, his warm green gaze darkening to the color of juniper leaves in winter.

Phoebe swallowed back the intense shudder of awareness at her nudity. She forced herself not to shift or make any move to cover herself. She was a wife now.

But as his eyes traversed the length of her in the bath, something inexplicable clouded them. She silently thanked all the saints she hadn't driven him away with her unforgivable but unavoidable behavior. She vowed to do better.

For some strange reason she didn't trust the relaxed smile stretching his lips or his banal next words, something was too contained and restrained about his movements. "How was your day?" he asked as he divested himself of his waistcoat, then unbuttoned the first few buttons of his shirt, apparently getting comfortable. His exposed neck created an air of intimacy. But then again, she was completely naked, under the bath water.

"I tended to the remaining wedding guests most of the day. And bid farewell to Egan, my parents, Lucia and Breena. How was your day?" she said, utterly mesmerized by the graceful way he moved to stand by her tub.

"I spent most of the day conducting training sessions with the guards, part of my duties as new warlord. I also had an unexpected visitor today."

She straightened with interest. "Oh, who was it?"

"Mistress Willoughby, the mother of my late betrothed, visited this morning to congratulate me on our nuptials," he said.

Surprise and sympathy contracted her chest. "She is well, I hope?"

Phoebe considered the question ridiculously inadequate. The woman had lost a daughter and her former 'almost' son-in-law had moved on with his life.

"She is doing better than previous years. Perhaps coming to peace with what happened," he said.

The flicker of sadness across his features made her wonder if he still loved Sylvia. But then the sadness was replaced with something else. Heat. "May I assist you in your bath?" he said.

Her mouth went completely dry.

She swallowed back the thickness of trepidation and intrigue. "Oh, ah … of course."

Slade proceeded to roll up the cuffs of his sleeves, and her eyes fell on the veins of hard toned forearm muscles, fascinated with its sprinkling of dark hair.

He knelt down by the tub. Excitement and fear shot up her spine. She inhaled his masculine scent of leather and cloves as he picked up the soap and small square of linen, dipping them in the water before forming a lather all the while his eyes seared into hers.

Molten heat pooled at her core mingling with anxiousness and anticipation.

He clinically considered the entirety of her body's position before speaking. "Please sit forward a bit."

Her body shivered slightly at the smoothness of his tone; it couldn't be from a chill because she was quite warm.

"May I?" he asked, indicating to the soapy square of linen in his hand.

She edged forward, her fingers digging into her palms beneath the water.

"Ah, yes," she breathed.

Slade gently stroked the area of her back she offered in slow circles and lazy zigzags. His touch both calmed her and created chaos in her body. One second her heart forgot to beat and the next it was speeding while the bedchamber's temperature rose a notch or two. All the while her nails dug into her palms forming half-moons. The contracting of her core caused her to squeeze her knees together sending a shiver down her spine.

"Are you cold?" His voice rasped.

"Ah … no … no," she breathed.

His hand lifted. "Lean back."

His command was soft yet laced with steel.

Slade dipped the linen in a measured, almost calculated motion down the valley between her breasts, leaving trails of fire on her wet skin. Her areolas peaked as he rubbed the linen over each of her breasts in smooth gentle strokes. His outward appearance continued to be clinical, yet his breathing became audible.

Phoebe's breath hitched when her gaze landed on the large bulge in his trousers. She breathed through the fear and her own arousal, determined not to panic.

His hand lingered at her stomach.

"Should I continue further down?" His voice was deceptively low, as his eyes speared hers.

Phoebe gulped. "Ahem … yes," she whispered.

Good. God. This bath was deliciously destroying them both.

Slade didn't deserve Fifi. His little friend had grown up to be a warrior goddess among mere mortal women. She pushed against her fear. She met it head on and did battle. She didn't cower. She didn't hide. From the steely determination in her eyes now, he understood. When she'd yelled *get off,* she'd been bellowing at her fear. He was enthralled by her. Her soft, flaming hair, her smooth creamy skin and her seductive curves were wreaking havoc with his resolve to gently ease her into lovemaking. She was brave, bold and stunning. She had an astonishingly unbendable strength of will which he had never seen in any other woman before. He didn't think she realized just how strong she was. He didn't deserve her, but he was going to take her anyway. He was going to make use of this opportunity and do whatever he had to, to not fail this time. He had killed Sylvia. He deserved to burn in Hades. But he was going to live instead. Fifi was his redemption.

The maid didn't know exactly what Ross had done to Fifi, but Slade had imagined the worst since last night. He'd been living a dark tortured nightmare since his suspicions. It was torment and agony of the acutest kind, when he imagined Ross hurting Fifi.

And he imagined it all. Every single time it sent a gunshot through his heart, and iron nails down his back, shredding his soul. He wanted to gouge the images from the back of his eyes with his own rapier. And his fists had clenched so many times, he might have fractured a knuckle or two. Oh. But there would be the sweet pleasure from killing Ross. It was a certainty. The only question was, how long could he draw out the sweet pleasure of it.

And how would he make his wife feel secure in the bedchamber again? How would he help her to heal? His plan was to give her so much pleasure Ross would be a distant unintrusive thing. He may not be able to wipe the attack from her memory all together, but perhaps he could fill her head and body with enough pleasure that it overshadowed all else. The fact that she was letting him touch her after Ross was testament to her strength and willpower. Her fortitude, resolve, and determination took his breath away. She robbed him of breath, as only a goddess could. And she didn't even know it.

His own disloyal body longed to kiss, lick and suck her wet, soft, satiny skin. He wanted to fill every part of her delectable body, her mind and soul, with only him. He wanted it so bad he was in pain, his body straining to be free of its confines. But not now. And mayhap not for a long time. Not until that fear and uncertainty in her eyes vanished. He would only take her when he was certain she was ready to let him have her fully.

The warm water had gone cloudy with soap bubbles. But the sweet red curls at the apex of her thighs, the fullness of her breasts and the curve of her hips were seared on his brain. They would add to his torment. This pleasurable torment he could bear, but the hell of his hatred for Ross he couldn't. There was only one way to end Ross and make sure the demon didn't hurt Phoebe or other women and Slade intended on seeing that to the lethal end.

Now, Fifi's eyes burned with a warm shade of earthy umber,

the candelabrum's light illuminating streaks of fire dancing in their depths. But her gaze held other things as well. Inexperience. Uncertainty. Apprehension. The inexperience and uncertainty he could work with. But the apprehension killed him a thousand times each second.

"Are you certain?" he gently prodded, to her answer of yes to him washing her intimate flesh. His voice was smooth despite the tumult raging inside. Despite the fear she would stop him.

Her cheeks were a delectable rosy crimson and the delicate muscles at her throat seemed to work for an eternity before she spoke with a breathy, "Ye … yes."

The force of relief and desire hitting him was a precarious combination. But he sent her his rakish smile, eager to bring her pleasure. And eager to ride the waves of lust vibrating through his own body.

"Open your legs," he whispered, with the softest hint of a command.

Slade had to swallow the moisture watering his mouth.

Her clenched legs parted slowly.

He proceeded to tease the smooth luscious skin of her inner thighs, his motions lingering until the apprehension in her eyes was almost replaced with heat.

Then with the pressure of a butterfly's wings against a rose petal, he brushed the linen over the center of her pleasure. She gasped and arched her back. Her eyes widened with a plethora of emotions. Surprise. Pleasure. And perhaps awareness of her own body. The smooth, wet, slick feel of her made his already hard body push painfully against his breeches.

"Shall I continue?" His voice was low and rough.

"Ah … yes," she whispered.

Her lips were slightly parted, moistened, and reddened with the hue of her fear and arousal. Her fear steadied his hands. Despite his simmering rage for Ross, his reverence for Fifi held him together. Also holding him together was the naive fourteen-year-old boy he'd been when he'd first met a nine-year-old lass he'd dubbed Fifi, because of her elfin mischievousness, untainted ideals, and open friendship, when he himself had grown tired of his father's coldness, resulting from his mother's death.

Slade brushed his fingers against her again, this time parting the soft curls at the juncture of her thighs. His movement slower with marginally more pressure. Her eyes darkened, smoldering, and fixated on him. He flicked and pinched but his fingers were infuriatingly constrained by the linen. The rise and fall of her breasts quickened, almost making him lose his focus. She groaned.

Slade was relentless and methodical, but slow, as if he had all the time in the world. She rolled her hips to meet his fingers as her hands gripped the sides of the wooden tub. Her breathing and soft guttural sounds of pleasure became louder. He kept his pace exacting and careful, the same as the pace of her quickening breath.

There was no greater aphrodisiac than the way her half-lidded gaze focused on his. It was the most erotic experience of his life, perhaps because he was focused on her pleasure.

As the pace of her breathing became ragged, he growled with frustration at the linen and ended up tossing the damn thing aside and using his thumb and forefinger. The silken soft feel of her against his bare fingers, coupled with her tight wet heat made Slade's mind and body almost come apart. He imagined his mouth replacing his hands. Slade was skilled at making a woman find her release but one that had been hurt was a challenge. He had to wait for the exact moment the fear left her eyes.

When her lids dropped, and she gave into the pleasure completely, he increased the intensity of his ministrations.

Phoebe came apart in soft broken moans, her body shuddering with tremulous vibrations, her core squeezing in pulsating spasms around his fingers. A hot gratifying feeling washed over Slade, despite being still as hard as steel, and painfully erect against the fabric of his breeches.

After her body went limp, Slade gently lifted his wife and placed her to stand at the side of the tub, supporting her with his arms.

"I … I've never had a bath like that before," she said, sounding adorably surprised, and innocent, her cheeks turning crimson.

Slade sent her a devilish smile as he picked up a large dry linen from the stack at the side of the tub and wrapped it around her. "The first of many, if you'll have it," he said.

He eyed the seductive and delicious afterglow on her skin as she donned her dressing robe. She then glided over to the polished mahogany dressing stand, with its gleaming mirror, gold-wreath designed hairbrush, and tiny delicate scented bottles. He casually leaned against the bedpost taking in her relaxed countenance with great satisfaction.

But then Fifi faced his reflection in her mirror as she brushed her hair. "I must visit a friend on the isle of Beinn na Faoghla," she said, her tone casual.

Something cold doused the heat strumming through his body. No one had friends on Beinn na Faoghla. It was an isle with a few fishing villages, a sparse regiment of redcoats hoping to catch the rebel leader Prince Charles Edward Stuart and a wily old Bullfinch called Donald Lochiel. He'd met the man in Fontenoy, and in many ways, the Bullfinch had saved him, saved him from his demons, and from himself.

"When?" he asked.

"I have to make the journey in a few days."

"I'll accompany you," he said in a clipped tone.

Fifi's brows shot up, the rosiness from her cheeks draining, as she swiveled around on her seat. "It's quite unnecessary for you to take time away from your work, I'd be safe enough with Aila and a MacLean escort," she said.

The thought that she could run into Ross had his insides

turning to ice. "Forgive me, but I really must insist. I would feel better protecting you myself. Who knows what kinds of high-waymen, or brigands are lurking about on such a deserted isle," he said.

The disappointment in her eyes cut him to the quick. She'd no doubt wanted to keep her work for the Movement a secret. But on this point of her traveling alone, he wouldn't budge.

"Of course," she said quietly.

After bidding her good night, Slade headed for the door connecting their marriage bedchamber to the adjoining chamber. He couldn't spend the night in the same room as her, not when his body ached for hers. Not when her work for the Movement could pit her against Ross or get her killed. He had to fight tooth and claw not to get dragged back into a black void. After Sylvia's death, it had been one of self-hate, hopelessness and a bitter chill in his bones and soul. He had swum in the nothingness with whisky and opium. Only Peter and two wars had helped him to crawl out.

CHAPTER 53

Two weeks later, early in the morning, after the kitchen packed their saddlebags with food and other supplies, a fully armed Phoebe and Slade trotted atop horseback. They rode alongside each other north bound from Garraidh, parallel to the coastline of Skye. The briny scent of sea water filled the air, and seagulls' wings fluttered above them before swooping down towards the rocky, tempestuous shoreline to their left.

For the past two weeks, Slade had brought her to a body melting release during every single one of her baths, his deft fingers unleashing multiple climaxes from her. Gently at first, but fierce and intense during the past few nights. She was conflicted she'd had to abandon control to experience pleasure. But willingly giving up control for pleasure wasn't the same as suffering violent abuse when control is taken from you.

Slade's kisses, while sweet, had been restrained. Why was he keeping such a tight hold on his emotions? She'd found her release every single time, he hadn't. She'd been on edge, sensing Slade's body was wound so tight it could snap at any second. She had to do something but was out of her depth.

A distant sound of thunder made Phoebe look up, taking in

the sunless sky and rolling dove-gray clouds far beyond the Isle of Skye. With any luck, the cold northern winds would blow the clouds past them.

She'd been shocked at first that he'd insisted on coming with her. What if he learned that her Jacobite friend was really her spymaster. He already suspected she was a spy, based on their discussion at the lodge. A sliver of something sharp pierced her gut.

Phoebe's eyes strayed to Slade. He sat strong and solid a few feet from her, his greatcoat billowing in the breeze from Destroyer's momentum, her own mount keeping pace. Her husband's magnificent visage was thrillingly disheveled, tense energy vibrating from each and every inch of his stiff and quiet frame.

Her heart squeezed with aching warmth for her childhood friend, now her husband. He'd been tender with her, considerate, patient, and gentle, albeit merciless in his pursuit of her pleasure. Like she was precious to him, not like he'd been forced to marry her. He'd made her want things she'd never wanted for the past seven years, like to touch and be touched.

After two hours of riding, her face was cold and her legs had started to cramp. And it occurred to her that Slade was leading them away from the wharf where they could charter a boat for Beinn na Faoghla and instead towards the Claigan fishing village.

A short while later they arrived at a manse. Its stone walls looked pristine from having been recently whitewashed. Puffs of gray smoke rose up from one of its chimneys.

The sheathed rapier and holstered pistol on Slade's hip clicked against each other as he dismounted.

The cottage was charming, but she sent him a questioning look. "Do you know the local minister?"

"Yes, the minister and his wife are auld and dear acquaintances. More importantly they know every one of the villagers, those with boats and those who can be trusted," he said, tying Destroyer's reins to a post next to the gate.

Phoebe dismounted and followed suit with her own reins. They went through the gate and strode up to the front door. Slade knocked.

The door was opened by a homely older woman. Her wrinkled lips stretched into a warm wide smile. "*M'eudail*—my dear, boy, it's good to see you."

Her charcoal gray hair was held beneath a white linen coif, a few strands out of place. The front of her comfortable-looking black dress was covered in a white pinafore. Her open, even features and warm maternal countenance drew a sense of respect and friendship from Phoebe.

Slade took the small-statured woman in his arms and gave her a gentle hug. "Margaret, it's been too long."

He released her, and she palmed his cheeks in a maternal gesture. "Congratulations are in order, for you are now a married man," the woman said to Slade, fondness making her voice melodious.

Slade smiled and leaned into the woman's touch. His entire countenance softened. He welcomed this woman's warmth and tenderness. Whoever she was, she was important. This was a side to her husband Phoebe hadn't seen before.

CHAPTER 54

Slade's lips thinned. "I was devastated to hear of Isaac's death."

Pain registered on the woman's lined face. "The good Lord giveth, and He can taketh as well." Her voice thickened with emotion.

Slade gave her another hug but held her for a few breaths longer this time. The lines of pain on her face eased.

He released the woman and beckoned with a gesture of his palm to Phoebe. "I've brought my bride to make your acquaintance. This is Phoebe."

Margaret stepped forward with a welcoming smile. Phoebe was getting ready to extend her hand in greeting when the woman pulled her in for a warm hug instead, as if they were old friends.

"I'm happy to meet the woman Slade has chosen to be his wife."

A whiff of lavender and clean linen tickled Phoebe's nose as her arms encircled then released the woman. "It's a pleasure to make your acquaintance, mistress."

The other woman took her by the arm and gently nudged her

inside. "Please call me Margaret, *m'eudail.*" Her tone was warm and soft.

The cozy interior of the cottage, heated by a crackling fire in the hearth, removed the chill from Phoebe's cheeks. Eggshell-white lace curtains were pulled open, letting in the early afternoon light, which reflected off modest oak furniture.

Margaret indicated the chairs near the fireplace. "Please, make yourselves comfortable."

Phoebe removed her cloak, hung it on one of the wooden pegs by the door then took a seat in one of the well-worn but comfortable chairs. Margaret took the one across from her.

After Slade removed his coat and closed the door, he took the chair next to Phoebe. "Where's Raghnall?" Slade asked Margaret.

Margaret gestured towards a window facing the back of the cottage. "He's in the back feeding the chickens. We were so busy this morning with taking supplies to the orphanage then the service right after. We just returned. Isaac used to feed the chickens ..." Margaret broke off, tight pain flashing across her features again.

Her expression tugged at Phoebe's heart. Who was Isaac, and what was he to Slade and to Margaret? Phoebe quirked a brow, feeling helpless and looking sidelong at Slade.

He squeezed his eyes shut for a second, as if berating himself internally. "Forgive me for being so remiss, my dear. Isaac is ... was Margaret and Raghnall's only son. He was a friend and a great reader. Through him I learned of *Robinson Crusoe, Gulliver's Travels* and the *Odyssey*. He was killed months ago in a skirmish led by Bolingbroke's men."

The flash of sadness in Slade's eyes brought a heaviness to her chest. But then his nostrils flared at the mention of Bolingbroke.

She'd sensed a dark, deep-rooted hate for Bolingbroke from Slade at the lodge. It was now there in his scowl.

She took his hand giving it a gentle squeeze. "I hadn't realized you lost a friend, dearest, I'm so very sorry ...." Her words drifted off as she dragged her gaze away from the pull in Slade's eyes to face Margaret. "I am so very sorry for your loss, Margaret."

Margaret offered a tight-lipped smile yet looked resigned to her grief.

A few minutes later, a tall graying man entered from the back. He was dressed in dark clothing but had a pleasant, albeit tired countenance. His expression lit up, and a smile stretched his lips on seeing Slade. *"M'eudail*—my dear, boy."

Slade stood up and went towards the man. They greeted each other like the closest of friends. The man's presence was exceedingly paternal and comforting, the kind that could put you at ease enough to confess your sins. Did this man know of Slade's past? Of Sylvia? Her husband introduced the man to Phoebe as Minister Raghnall Edwards, Margaret's husband.

After introductions were made and condolences expressed, Slade returned to his seat, eying Raghnall. "Phoebe and I were sorry you couldn't make the wedding, but it's understandable under the circumstances," Slade said, looking from Raghnall to Margaret then back to Raghnall.

Raghnall sat next to his wife to whom he smiled warmly before raising his eyes to Slade. "The truth is we would have attended, but we didn't want to upset Chisolm and cause any unpleasantness on your wedding day," Raghnall said.

Puzzlement at the minister's comment caused a tightness in Phoebe's throat. She glanced from Raghnall to Slade then back to Raghnall. "But why would your presence upset Slade's father?" Phoebe asked the minister.

Raghnall studied his hands for a brief second before eying Phoebe. "It's a long story, starting years ago. Elizabeth, Slade's mother, used to attend Sunday service at my church before she died. She confided in me as her minister. Chisolm loved his wife deeply but also wanted her to confide in the minister used by the MacLeans instead. Both Margaret and I had known Elizabeth since she was young, she was accustomed to us. But it was a point of contention between Chisolm and Elizabeth."

Phoebe shook her head in confusion. "But surely to confide in one's minister and friend is natural," Phoebe said.

Slade's voice broke through Phoebe's confusion. "My father loved my mother very much, in his own way. But he was possessive and controlling to the point of obsession. It was important to him that my mother fully embraced becoming a MacLean when they got married, which meant using the MacLeans' minister. This was important to him because he wanted his clan to accept her as one of their own. He was unyielding with this and many other things. I was too young to realize what was happening of course, but I heard the stories growing up. My father's regret for the way he behaved while my mother lived put him in a very dark place in the years after her death. It made Garraidh, during my childhood, a very cold place. Something that has only recently started to change," Slade said, staring at the fire in the hearth as if revisiting the past in his thoughts.

Phoebe's chest tightened as she eyed her husband. "Oh, how very sad for your father, and your dearest mother. Regret is a terrible thing, especially when the opportunity for remedy is lost forever."

When they were younger, she'd often heard Egan say how difficult it was for Slade at Garraidh, which is why he was at Eileanach so often. Not only did he have to contend with losing his mother at a young age, but with a father who was heartbroken and bitter.

Margaret shifted in her chair, her expression soft and maternal. "Chisolm was young when he got married. His idea of a marriage was to control everything his wife did. He loved her dearly, but I don't think he understood until after her death, that to love someone is to give them the freedom to be happy," Margaret said.

After a few more minutes of conversation, Slade inquired about a boat to Beinn na Faoghla.

Raghnall's gaze turned questioning to Slade. "Beinn na Faoghla? Are you sure?"

The Minister gestured outdoors. The earlier dove-gray clouds had turned ominous and a few threatening shades darker. Instead of blowing the clouds further out to sea, it appeared the northern wind was in fact bringing the storm right to them.

CHAPTER 55

Slade and Fifi bid farewell to Margaret and Raghnall, left their horses in the chapel house's stables, then grabbed their saddle bags and set out on the earthen path towards the wharf.

A decade ago, having an understanding and sympathetic ear to unburden his woes after Sylvia's death had helped him to keep his sanity, to drop his habitual use of opium and overindulgence in whisky. Yet Slade hadn't revealed the whole truth of his intentions to the Edwards or to Fifi. Raghnall would have told him to dig two graves before he sought revenge against Bolingbroke; one grave for Bolingbroke and one for himself. And that soft glow of friendship in Fifi's eyes all those years ago would have died, because in telling her he would have revealed to her the monstrous things of which he was capable. But the only way for him to revenge Sylvia's death and redeem himself was to knock Bolingbroke off his pedestal. Then he would take immense pleasure in revealing to Bolingbroke exactly for whom he'd done it.

Slade now glanced in Fifi's direction as they walked. The alluring pink lines of her lips and the gentle curve of her delicate jaw were the only things visible under the black hood of her cloak. Flashbacks of him bathing her lush body hit him. Recalling the sounds of pleasure she'd made even now stiffened his nethers. His perpetual stiffness over the past two weeks was slowly making him lose his mind. When he wasn't with his wife, his thoughts were of her. When she was near, he couldn't take his eyes off her, wanting so badly to make love to her. When he dreamt, it was only of her. Her smell, taste and feel were consuming him and slowly driving him mad. But they would go at her pace, even if it killed him.

When they reached the wharf and asked after Master Ames, a wee lad scraping barnacles off an upturned skiff pointed them in the direction of a stout, bearded man at the end of the pier.

Ames was an older man, barrel-chested and paunchy. His craggy features were every bit the weather-beaten fisherman. Slade inquired about passage to Beinn na Faoghla.

Master Ames raised his eyes, disbelief in his unshaven oval face as he pointed skywards. "Haven't you noticed the black clouds?" Ames asked.

Clouds had indeed blanketed them in an unusually eerie darkness, yet it was still day. Sunset wouldn't come for another three hours.

Before Slade could respond, Fifi spoke. "Please, sir, it's a matter of great importance. You did come with high recommendations from Minister Edwards."

Ames pulled himself up to his full height, his chest puffing out in what looked like self-importance. "The minister sent you to me? Well then, I suppose I can take you. But we must be quick about it. Where on the island are you heading?"

Fifi leaned in closer to Ames as if revealing a secret. "We're going to Saint Mary's. Do you know of it?"

Ames nodded. "Aye. It's on the east side of the island. Lucky for you, because I hate going to the west side. The redcoats are garrisoned there, and they ask too many questions."

Fifi's shoulders visibly tensed at the mention of redcoats. "Yes, lucky indeed."

They boarded Ames' jolly boat, just as the rain started to drizzle.

The journey to Beinn na Faoghla took just shy of an hour. As they neared the wooden jetty stretching over part of the sandy shore and the water, the rain turned from a drizzle to a heavy downpour. Slade's hair was soaked. Cold rivulets ran down the back of his neck, dampening his cravat.

Despite the gusty winds and thick fog, Slade managed to make out a pair of short birches not far from the shore on a mostly treeless isle, the wind violently tossing their branches. The only sign of human habitation was an empty wooden canoe bumping up and down in shallow water tenuously tied to the jetty.

Slade reached into his pocket, took out a few coins, more than the price Ames had quoted, and handed them to Ames. Slade then grabbed their saddle bags and helped Fifi from the small boat onto the wet sand of the shore. He thanked the Lord she had a hood, for it seemed to be protecting her from a complete drenching. Slade was starting to think it was not only ill-advised to come to the isle, but doubly so in a storm. But Slade had done it for Fifi. He suspected if she had to go to the moon, he'd find a way to do that as well.

Slade stood next to Fifi a few feet in from the rolling waves and turned back to Ames.

"How far is the church?" He had to shout above the gusts of wind and pelting rain.

Ames remained standing next to his boat on the wet sand and pointed west. "Straight inland, about an hour's walk."

Slade eyed Ames, raising his brows in question. "Will you wait for us?"

Ames shook his head. "I can't. I have to get back to my wife and bairns."

Slade swore under his breath but cocked his head at the man. "When can you come back?"

Ames patted his pocket where he'd deposited the coins and smiled. "I'll return a couple of hours after dawn. You can wait for me in Glenn's cave."

Slade looked around with uncertainty. "Where is Glenn's cave?"

Ames pointed to their left, past the sandy shore, where weathered slabs of limestone stood atop a hill behind the twin birch trees.

The fisherman then pushed off his jolly boat, rowing back in the direction they'd come from.

The whipping wind was now causing water to crash violently against the jetty. Slade tasted the salt of the sea on his lips.

He turned to Fifi. "Can you run?"

Fifi's rain drenched face was half covered by her hood, but she readily nodded. "Of course."

They made a mad dash for the trees. Then Slade guided them around the thick trunks, where for the first time he noted a narrow, almost hidden vertical opening in the limestone. They slipped through and found themselves standing inside a cave.

It was wider than it was tall, the floor sandy and about twenty paces across and half that in height. But because of the angled entrance the interior was mostly dry. It smelled of musty earth, briny sea, and fresh rain. He leaned back against the cold rock wall not far from the entrance to catch his breath after their exhilarating sprint.

A smile tugged at the sides of his mouth as a soft laugh escaped Fifi's lips. She'd enjoyed their little charge through the rain as much as he had.

Her hood was swept back revealing lustrous hair which had come undone from its pins, its wet fiery tendrils clinging to the sides of her freckle-kissed face. Fifi's hazel eyes sparkled, and her skin glowed with moisture, even in the dimming light. Her long, thick lashes seemed darker, a few clumped together with rain drops, one such drop hanging precariously off the tip of her nose. Slade couldn't resist the pull to close the distance between them and kiss her nose's tip. His mind fixated yet again on the previous night when she'd been wet and naked. The stiffening beneath his breeches caused him to pull back.

She smiled intimately at him but also hugged herself.

His shoulder muscles tightened in concern. "Are you cold?"

The second she opened her mouth to speak, her teeth chattered. "A little."

"A problem I shall soon solve." He sent her a gallant and confident grin.

Slade deposited the saddle bags on the ground, unbuckled his weapons, and laid those down as well. He noted with no little interest the blackened area from an old fire several feet from the mouth of the cave. It was quite fortuitous that the previous occupants of the cave had left behind a pile of dry, broken branches.

Slade opened his saddle bag and pulled out the steel and flint. After a couple of tries, he was able to generate enough sparks on the small pyramid of shavings he'd made with his knife to get a flame. He carefully added branches one by one, so as not to smother the flame but feed it. Soon he had a healthy fire going.

He took off his coat and laid it on the ground to dry. He then eyed Fifi. She had unbuttoned her wet cloak and laid it out next to his, not far from the fire. Her expression softened.

The inner glow in her eyes as she gazed at him squeezed his heart. "Come warm yourself," he said.

Slade's mouth went dry. His gaze followed her movements as she came to sit next to him by the fire. His fingers still carried the memory of her soft, lustrous intimate skin at their tips. And his lips still recalled the sweet plumpness of her mouth. His hands now craved exploring the dip of her waist, and the glorious swells of her hips and breasts hidden under the riding habit. His breath audibly rushed in and out of his nostrils as his body temperature spiked.

CHAPTER 56

Awry sort of expression settled on her features as she considered the flames. "You are very skilled at building fires. Have you been stranded in many caves?" Fifi asked.

Slade chuckled. "I have, in fact. When we were in southwest Belgium during the War of Austrian Succession, at Fontenoy in 1745, we often stayed overnight in caves. It was safer from enemy soldiers during the night. I became quite adept at building campfires."

Her delicate brows furrowed. "Was Dettingen different from Fontenoy?"

"Both were cold and unpleasant. But after Dettingen in 1743, I knew what to expect and was better prepared when we arrived in Belgium. In addition to battling the French, some soldiers battled dysentery, smallpox and malnutrition. The prisoners had it worse. Many had to be shot rather than confined. Prisoners required rations and soldiers to guard them, both of which had been in short supply," he said.

The flashbacks made his shoulders tighten.

He didn't mention his cavalier attitude near enemy lines. Nor did he mention it nearly got him killed a time or two—his goal after losing Sylvia and before learning about the Movement. Their aim, which is that of the French government, being to undermine and weaken the British monarchy and government.

Slade got an introduction to the Movement and Donald Lochiel, codename Bullfinch, while he was in Fontenoy. Bullfinch, one of the seven men of Moidart, are special advisors to the rebel prince, Charles Edward Stuart. His savior, Bullfinch, had given him a new goal, to make trouble for the British. The man had been his savior but couldn't be trusted, because he'd feed you information to get you to do what he wants, which wasn't necessarily the truth. The people who got along well with Bullfinch, were the ones who knew this about the man. Slade had made a fortune during the wars supplying the Movement with weapons because he believed in their cause and being a British colonel was the best way to help them with information on the latest British weaponry and to make money in the process. No one but Bullfinch knew he was a double agent and now, he'd bet his life Fifi was here to see the crafty old Bullfinch.

Fifi was eying him, but she'd gone still. The gentle lines on her forehead were somber. "I am sorry you were thrown into fighting. It sounds dreadful. Have you ever regretted joining the army?"

Slade shook his head. "No. I needed a shock to dislodge me from myself. It wasn't pleasant, but it accomplished that much," he said.

Before he could stop himself, he continued. "And you, what is the most dreadful experience you've ever had?"

Her eyes widened, and her lips slackened at his question.

Slade held his breath for her answer.

A sliver of intense anguish flashed across her pretty eyes. He imagined he saw fear, turmoil, and anger there as well, but it was so fleeting, he couldn't be sure.

Her anguish ripped him to shreds. And her fear made him

vow inwardly to slay all her demons. But he liked the anger. It was the fighter, the warrior goddess in her.

He shifted on the sandy ground to face her, gently taking her left hand in his. Her skin was smooth, but her fingers chilled. He rubbed her palm in between both of his, then placed it close to his lips to blow his warm breath on her skin. He didn't miss the hitching of her breath, as she stared at his lips. His body tightened in response because it was the same hitching of breath every time he'd touched her intimate flesh during the past two weeks. He loved all the sounds she made, but this one especially. He enjoyed knowing he affected her as much as she affected him. After finishing her left hand, he moved to her right.

Her next words surprised him. But they shouldn't have.

"Alex's death was beyond bleak. A ray of sunshine snuffed out from the earth. A great loss, it ripped a bleeding hole in everyone's heart, that will never heal, including in mine."

There was pain in the crack of her voice.

"You are stronger than you think, Fifi. You have the heart of a goddess and the strength of a warrior. You bend. But you will never break. It's your ability to survive and adapt after bleak things that steals my breath and leaves me in awe of you," he said, his tone soft with an undertone of steel.

His words left an intense softness in her expression.

She shook her head. "You don't know—" she started to say.

"I do know." He cut in.

He saw the uncertainty in her expression. She wasn't sure of what he spoke.

She considered him, then her mouth slackened into a wry smile.

"You've always made me believe in impossible things like knights, chivalry, heroes, and love. Even now, after all this time. After all the bleakness," she whispered, her head tilted down to watch their hands connecting as she interlaced her fingers with his.

"You inspire those things in me, my love" he said.

She blinked up at his use of the endearment, her cheeks turning pink. He couldn't recall when he had started using it. But it was the most natural thing to have ever slipped from his lips.

A gentle radiance came through in her softened expression. She loosened, then rethreaded her fingers with his again. The feel of her warm skin against his was sublimely tortuous. Her gaze locked on to their connecting hands again, as if fascinated by how they fit together.

The feel of her touching him was like sparks to a tinder-box. Keeping the increasing sparks from exploding to a full-blown blaze was tenuous.

The fervor in her voice when next she spoke, made him go still.

"Fifteen years ago, when I saw you riding tall and dark through the portcullis at Eileanach with Egan, it was the first time I ever thought a boy was beautiful. And when you were seventeen and you told me you were about to be betrothed was the first time I'd ever been jealous of another girl. I've never wanted to get married. My greatest fear was a husband wanting to control me, my household, what I wore, where I went, who my friends were and how many children I would have. But you are the least controlling person I know," Fifi said.

Something in him took flight at her words as she paused, her throat muscles working before she continued. "You told me on our wedding night that in the ancient Orient, they believed if you save a life, you are responsible for that life for the rest of yours. You said it meaning you were responsible for me. In truth, you've had my heart since I first saw you riding through our portcullis. My love for you has changed since I was nine, but you've had it all along, in all its different facets."

Slade's heart raced, while his mind and soul melted. "Oh, my darling love," he rasped.

He took her in an ardent hug, crushing her body to his, squeezing her with the rapid fire of blood strumming through his veins. Slade planted a kiss on the top of her head, inhaling the familiar warmth of her. Even though his body burned for hers, he found peace in her arms, and bliss in her scent of orange blossom and bergamot. She sighed contentedly, slackening completely in his embrace.

"My greatest fear is that I will fail you. Failing to protect you, even from myself would break me," he said, his voice sounding raw, as if his throat was abraded.

"You won't, you can't, you are too good, I see your halo," she said, burrowing further into his embrace.

If she only knew, he'd killed Sylvia. And the thought that he could unintentionally hurt her was choking the life from his heart and soul.

The fire crackled in the cave while the rain thumped the ground outside and the wind's howls echoed through the air surrounding the cave.

"Have you warmed up?" he asked, still holding her tightly to him.

"Deliciously so," she uttered.

Fifi released him and sent him a sly mischievous smile, one infinitely more potent and devastating than when she was a wee lass. A smile that was carnal, in a way it had never been before. His heart slammed so hard he feared it would break free of his chest.

She took his left hand, turning it palm down and raised it to her lips, planting a kiss. Her moist lips pillowy soft against the hardness of his first knuckle. His body stilled but his eyes locked onto her mouth, starved.

"What are you doing?" he asked, his voice gruff.

"I should think that's quite evident. I'm kissing you," she whispered. She kissed the second knuckle.

"Phoebeee ..." he growled, drawing out her name.

The use of her proper given name was a warning which she ignored.

CHAPTER 57

Phoebe kissed Slade's third knuckle, her mouth lingering much longer than was necessary. She liked the taste of him. The dark feral gaze he threw her was intoxicating, and a little frightening at the same time. He looked like he wanted to devour her.

Was it a betrayal of sorts to compare Faye Ross and Slade MacLean? It happened, regardless. One humiliated, hurt and violently took her free will. Killed her innocence and had nearly killed her spirit. In fact, it had been dead, until the Movement. The other, whose body was a lethally trained weapon, had the strength to do all those things but never had. And deep in her frantically beating heart, the knowledge solidified, that he never would.

One gave her terrors and made her unclean. The other made her ache with carnal desire and sacrificed his own pleasure for hers. Slade forever altered her perception of what men were capable of.

Slade's body was granite hard, yet his touch was petal soft. His scent, which she now inhaled in great big lungfuls, was tantalizing and seductive. A mixture of spice and rugged male. So, unlike her attacker's repugnant stench of sweat and apple-scented pomade from seven years ago, forever seared into her nightmares.

One had taken. The other had given pleasure. Slade had soothed her sparks of fear and turned them into different sparks. And now, she wanted more.

Lightning pierced the sky and flashed across the mouth of the cave, highlighting the molten desire in Slade's gaze.

Sweetness melted her heart mingling with her desire, creating a swirling masterpiece of heat and sensations racing through her body, making her drunk. Drunk on love, desire and a sense of safety, which she hadn't experienced in seven long blistering years. And then it hit her like the shot of a bow straight through her chest. She was unequivocally and undeniably in love with Slade MacLean.

Phoebe never got the opportunity to kiss his fourth knuckle.

Because his hand slipped from hers, taking her chin in a gentle but firm hold, bringing her lips closer to his. But his didn't touch hers, they lingered a hair's breadth away, his warm breath in soft rushes of air sensitizing her mouth. His beautiful face lined with desire, torture and restraint squeezed the air from her lungs. The rough pad of his thumb brushed along her lower lip. It was gentle, tantalizing, and hypnotic. Her lips parted and the tip of her tongue touched his finger. He made a guttural sound as if in pain.

Her insides turned to liquid fire propelling her mouth onto his. The blood rushing to her head was so loud it drowned out everything except the softness of his lips, the rushing puffs of her breath mingling with his, and his divine taste which made her body boil with hunger. She pushed so hard into him, his teeth grazed her mouth. He nipped her lips in response, first the top then the bottom, drawing it towards him, releasing with a sucking sound. Her arms went around him roughly seeking contact with his hard, toned body.

He tasted of male, sea, and rain. And she desperately wanted more. But then he pulled back, and she gazed confused at the dark intense storms of desire brewing in his eyes. It would take little to unleash those storms.

"Are you sure? Tell me what you want" he said, sounding hoarse and winded.

Phoebe had to inhale a few breaths before she could manage rational thoughts. But she had to speak now, before all courage and sensibility evaporated.

"I want us to be husband and wife in all sense of the words, but first ask me again. Ask me about the most dreadful experience of my life," Phoebe said.

Slade blinked at her, her question taking him by surprise. She imagined his pallor turned gray, but she wasn't sure if it was just the way he was angled away from the fire's light.

"What is the most dreadful experience you have ever had?" he asked, quietly.

She took his hand again, the pads of her fingers smoothing over his skin as she stared at their rugged perfection. Or perhaps she just couldn't meet his eyes for her next words.

"I've been a reluctant wife, but it's naught to do with you. In fact, you've eased my fears ..." Phoebe paused to allow air to inflate her shriveled lungs and to calm the rampant beats of her heart. "I was forced against my will seven years ago, and it filled me with hate, made me distrustful, fearful and wary," she said.

He said nothing. Her eyes flickered up to meet his. He'd gone dangerously still, his face as hard as marble, equally white and cold. But his eyes were pools of burning green, and in them she saw encouragement, support, and love. She was safe.

Her heart warmed at the fact that he hadn't pulled away. But why wasn't he shocked?

His jaw muscles worked before he spoke. "At first, I dismissed your nervousness when we were alone. At the manor I thought you were simply unsettled by Ludlow's accidental shooting. Then it happened again on the way to the jewelers, and it puzzled me to no end that you were nervous with me. We were friends after all. But at Hortons I could no longer dismiss it. I wanted to believe you were simply being melodramatic, but that wasn't it. Then I saw you with Ross. And I hated how you were with him. On our wedding night, out of sheer desperation and self-induced torture, I worked it out. After speaking with Aila, I knew. It was Ross, wasn't it? Slade hissed.

His low voice raised gooseflesh on her skin and sent cold shudders down her body. His jaw muscles sharpened and she saw the barely leashed fury and murder in his eyes.

Her heart staggered. Fire joined the cold shudders. Dear God. He'd already known. "You spoke with Aila? Does she know?" Her voice rose with shock and disbelief.

Slade's eyebrows drew together, and he used the hand she was holding to gently squeeze hers reassuringly. "She hates Ross, and she already had her suspicions. But I would imagine after my questions, there's no doubt in her mind he hurt you. The same as there is no doubt in my mind either. I now understand why you hate the British, why you so adamantly side with the rebels. I understand why it's a fight close to your heart and emotions. That woman you saved near Glenfinnan, were Bolingbroke's men attacking her?" Slade asked.

His eyes searched her face as shadows from the fire danced across the lines of his jaws.

"Yes. I would give everything I have to ensure no other man does to a woman what Ross did to me," she answered.

Everything around Phoebe shifted, as if she was watching herself in a dream, starting seven years ago. Her descent into emotional and physical turmoil after Ross's attack. Her bleak blackness of a life until she signed up with the Movement and started fighting.

"Ross is a big part of why I hate the British. But the other part is, I can't abide that they subjugate, murder and torture farmers and their children, and rape womenfolk," Phoebe said.

Phoebe watched the dancing flames of the crackling fire. She felt raw, exposed, and emotionally naked and blistered. But her body and mind were lighter for having spoken out loud her darkest secret.

The seconds ticked by as both Phoebe and Slade gazed at the fire. She'd ended up leaning into his embrace, his body forming a safe warm haven, lending her support and strength.

"My body isn't as a new wife's should be, but it's yours ..." Phoebe started to say.

He took her shoulders gently but firmly. "A million twinkling stars in the dark sky pale in comparison to your beauty. I will never stop wanting you. Your value comes from your spirit, your fight, and your strength of will. No one can ever take that from you. I am deeply sorry for what he did," Slade said.

There was murderous fury in his eyes, but when his gaze fell on her again, she saw the empathy, regret and love. It eased all the knots in her.

"After it happened, I locked myself in my bedchamber. I couldn't go out for days, weeks, months. But during all the time of my self-imposed prison I kept my boots on, ready. I was always ready. Ready to run from predators. When I did emerge from my bedchamber, every time a man came near, I'd break out in cold shivers. It took me years to realize I needed to fight for control of my life. I learned to dress drab, to be invisible. I learned to arm myself, I learned to fight," she said.

"Why didn't you tell your parents, Egan or me?" His voice was heavy with anguish.

Phoebe shook her head. "I couldn't. He threatened to kill my family, to wipe out my entire clan."

"Why didn't you come to me?" He repeated, a cavernous groove forming between his brows, his expression haunted.

Phoebe looked away. The first day she'd seen Slade after it

had happened, it had been ten in the morning and Slade had been bleary eyed and drunk. He'd been in a hell of his own, having just lost Sylvia. She might have decided not to add to his burdens then, but there was another reason she hadn't told him.

"I was ashamed, felt dirty, and broken," she whispered. The truth cut her like a dagger.

He shook his head at her words, yet she found solace in his eyes before he gently pulled her in for a hug. Phoebe's cheek rested against his chest, and in his warmth, with his beating heart soothing her, a measure of peace settled on her.

"You have nothing to be ashamed of and everything to be proud of. You are a fighter Phoebe, a beautiful warrior Goddess, and a survivor. No one controls your emotions but you. No one has the power to make you ashamed, angry, sad, or feel less than you are worth, unless you allow them. And you, my love, are nothing short of extraordinary," he said, his words quiet, but each landing with the strike of a gavel.

Her mind soaked up his words. And as her heart soared, a measure of serenity settled on her soul, as if she'd arrived home.

CHAPTER 58

As blissful as Phoebe was in Slade's embrace, she pushed forward with the past.

"When I was younger, I disobeyed my father quite a bit. He reprimanded me on more than one occasion for going off on my own to the moors. At one point he even threatened to lock me up in a tower at Eileanach if I didn't heed him. Of course, I didn't. One day, I found myself on the moors alone riding, that was when I encountered Faye Ross. He'd been at Eileanach a few times before that, with Hamish and Broden, to see my father and mother, I know not what for. I can't say why but whenever Faye Ross's eyes landed on me, it was like spiders crawling under my skin. But I simply ignored him," Phoebe said.

She had loved riding. One of the few freedoms and enjoyments she'd had after losing Alex. And in her innocence, she'd wanted to hold on to that enjoyment for as long as she could, despite her father's warnings. It was all she had after Alex, after Slade had fallen in love with Sylvia and after Egan had taken on more clan responsibilities from their father. She never found enjoyment from planning dinners, sewing, crocheting, or any of the feminine things her mother pursued. She remembered thinking life had unfairly taken away her wonderful Alex, the least it could do in return was allow her these solitary rides on the moors.

Slade's hands caressed her back soothingly as she spoke. She burrowed further into his arms and continued.

"When I encountered Faye Ross on the moors, I wanted to ride away, but then decided, out of courtesy, to stop and pay my respects. He told me I was rude for not stopping immediately. He said I was like all Scots, thinking themselves better than the English. I didn't like him, his words or the way he was looking at me."

Phoebe paused, when Slade's embrace stiffened. Tension rolled from his tall, broad frame in waves. But she kept going, resolved to get it all out.

"By the time I realized his intentions, it was too late, I was all alone on the moors with this malevolent creature. I tried to get back on my horse, but he knocked me down and ... and forced himself on me," she said, her voice quivering

The last sentence was the most difficult. She'd never told another living soul except Falcon. She couldn't continue. Her skin had gone cold, her stomach was nauseous, and her body was shaking. A final exorcism of her past, she thought.

Slade's arms tightened around her, he was stroking her back and she realized he was also mummering. "Shhhhh ... You are safe my love. I promise, you are always safe with me. And you will never have to worry about him ever again."

If she'd had more presence of mind, she might have asked what he meant, but she found herself wanting to tell Slade why she hadn't told anyone what had happened.

"After he was done with me, I dragged myself home. I hid from everyone. I blamed myself. It happened because I disobeyed my father and went riding alone on the moors, and I was so ashamed. It was my fault," she said.

"The only person responsible for Ross's actions, is Ross," Slade said.

Phoebe's gaze flickered to meet his. His eyes glinted fiercely. His body was as tense as a bow string. She questioned the wisdom of putting him through this. But he'd already known, hadn't he.

"I wanted you to know what happened, before we went any further. I owed you that," she said.

"This doesn't make me want you any less, but it does make me love you more, for your bravery. You are a survivor and an extraordinary woman," he whispered, just before he kissed her forehead.

When she looked up at him again, the intensity of emotion in his steady gaze struck her like a lance through the heart. It connected with her soul. He loved her. Energy thumped inside her stomach even as her own ardor and emotion pricked the backs of her eyes. Slade loved her. She savored the overpowering warmth of its reality. His acceptance and love rebuilt all her broken parts.

"I love you too," she said.

She palmed his cheeks and her lips found his. It was a soothing, gentle and mouthwateringly sweet kiss. She had laid herself open and bare for him, and he had accepted her and her tainted past. And Phoebe would never stop counting her blessings.

Phoebe surrendered to the pull of the kiss, taking a long, deep, delicious drink of Slade's mouth. His lips moved enticingly, slowly, and seductively over hers. She gave in to her desire, then the desire became hunger. And hunger became deprivation.

Phoebe kissed Slade as if her life depended on it, as if he was the air and she had been running for seven long years.

His lips became more demanding, and then as frantic as hers. He was firmly encircling her breast, then squeezing her buttocks. Phoebe's body came alive in a blaze of heat, desire and need as his hands roved, and fondled her. Somewhere in the back of her mind she marveled at the enormous pleasure of their coming together. But there was also tremendous triumph there as well. Triumph that she had conquered her fears. That she had gone through hell seven years ago, and she had not only survived, she was thriving.

His tongue invaded her mouth in deep urgent strokes. His intensity contracted her lower belly and curled her toes, sending her heart and head into a dangerous spin. Her quim craved friction and release, like the delicious release he'd given her each night during the last two weeks. He kissed her earlobe, her nape, and her clavicle. Then his teeth gently nipped her pulse point before soothing the same spot with a lick of his tongue. Pleasure riveted down her spine, eliciting a low groan from her mouth.

Slade hesitated at her jacket's collar, making a frustrated sound as if the material offended him. "I heartily agree with your request on our wedding night to be without clothes, but we are in a cave," he said, his voice light with mirth.

"I could leave my shift on?" she said breathlessly.

And then they were both eagerly tugging at the jacket of her riding habit. She was happy to get rid of it, for it was constricting her quickening breaths. Buttons popped, snapping against the ground. And as she removed her stays and petticoats, remaining in her shift, stockings and half boots, Slade yanked off his coat, waistcoat and shirt, remaining in his hose, boots, and breeches. The latter had a very prominent bulge, making her heart pound even faster than it already was.

Intensity glistened in his eyes, almost frighteningly, as he watched her watching him arranging the discarded clothes into layers on the sandy ground.

The firelight burnished the toned muscles of his arms and taut stomach in a way that compelled her to reach for his biceps, chest, then stomach. His skin burned her like the heat of a furnace as she stroked, the inked viper on his arm mesmerizing.

Then he was pressing her down on the layers of clothes, his

gaze raw, almost anguished in its reverence, causing her to shiver with desire.

His mouth dipped to her breasts, covered by the thin shift. He licked, sucked and gently rolled her nipples between his teeth, one after the other. The erotic sensations he drew from her created a frenzied need in her belly.

"Do you know these have tormented me since the lodge?" he murmured, his breath hot against her areola.

Her head whirled, forgetting for a second how to speak. "I … ah … no … didn't," she whispered, breathing heavily, feeling like she wanted to do everything with him all at once.

He planted kisses on her stomach through the thin fabric, then kissed lower and lower. Her eyes widened in surprise when Slade lifted her hem and dipped low between her legs. His devilishly dark eyes focused on hers as the backs of his knuckles grazed her inner thighs then brushed the most sensitive spot of her body. Oh. Dear. God. Her eyelids momentarily dropped. She whimpered, recalling the pleasure his fingers gave during her baths.

Slade shoved his hands under her derriere, effortlessly lifting one of her legs over his shoulder, then lowered his head between her thighs. The bunched soft material of the shift at her waist blocked most of her view of him. When his soft lips and tongue opened her intimate flesh up like the petals of a rose, Phoebe gasped at the blistering pleasure. It slowly dismantled her piece by agonizing piece. She moaned and writhed as her entire world incinerated into a million tiny free-floating constellations.

CHAPTER 59

Slade grinned, when his wife's body came apart from the ministrations of his mouth and fingers, despite the fact that his own body was stretched as taut as fiddle strings. If he wasn't inside her soon, his control would snap. His body was on fire. He'd never been so desperate or wanted anything so much. Nor had he ever wielded such a powerful control over his own urges before. But he did it for Fifi. Yet, as lust threatened to undo him, so did a killing rage towards Ross. He would take particular pleasure in meticulously gutting Ross, very soon.

But for the moment, Fifi's pleasure was the only one he was concerned with.

He divested himself of his boots and breeches, all the while watching Fifi, a thin sheen of sweat on the glorious skin of her face and inner thighs. Her skin glowed like a goddess emerging from firelight, her luscious limbs shapely, long and beautiful. Even covered by her thigh high stockings and boots, they beckoned his ravenous eyes and greedy touch. Now he understood why she kept her boots on.

He came to her, kneeling beside her. She reached for him, palming his cheeks, and he leaned into her touch like a relaxed but primed lion seeking warmth from his lioness. Her touch like a life force he needed to survive. With his hands spanning her waist, he slowly maneuvered her to sit on him, straddling him as he lay flat on his back.

"I know how you crave control," he said, sure there was an anticipatory wolfish grin on his face.

Her cheeks flushed as she positioned herself more comfortably, while he had to resist the urge to flip her on her back so he could lick each and every inch of her dewy body.

His painfully erect shaft made a tent with the delicate material of her shift as her luscious round derriere shifted on his pelvis, straddling him. The apex of her shapely thighs opened up provocatively, and her delicious breasts teased him mercilessly, mere inches from his mouth.

He suppressed a hungry groan, wanting to take each of their peaks in his mouth and suck. Too weak to resist, he did just that, eliciting a moan from her.

"I believe I'll like being on top," she said, with a half-lidded smile of wonderment.

He took wicked delight in her smile. And deep inside he thrilled at the fact she trusted him enough to be audacious with him.

"I suspected you might," he said, his voice gruff with desire.

He reached for her under the delicate, diaphanous shift. His hands roved her smooth upper, then lower body, cupping, massaging, and squeezing. Fifi's skin was soft and inviting. Her eyelids dropped, giving in to her pleasure as he fondled, feeding his craving.

Despite an untamed urge to thrust deep inside her, he stilled. There was incredulity in her sweet vulnerable face as he thumbed her sensitive spot. It beguiled, transfixed, and held him in its thrall as his fingers worked with rhythmic intent, until she came apart again.

He lifted his upper body so he could kiss her mouth. Their tongues tangled and tasted each other with dizzying effect.

His voice was ragged as he broke the kiss. "Put your hands on me," he said needing to feel more of her.

Her passion-infused gaze partially ebbed.

"Tell me where …?" she asked, her tone breathy but uncertain.

"Anywhere. Everywhere. Just touch me, my love," he rasped.

She palmed his shoulders and chest, from her slightly parted lips and the subtle shift in her smile, he could tell she liked the contact as much as he did. She raked his tight pectorals and abdomen with her fingernails. The pleasure so agonizingly sweet, he would die a thousand deaths to feel her. She sparked his already aroused and barely restrained body. A savage part of him took pleasure in the pain as her fingernails dug a little deeper.

Slade held her hips above his and positioned himself at her opening holding his breath while his heart pummeled his rib cage like a wild animal. His breath rushed in and out of his nostrils even as control threatened to slip.

She eyed him, sensing his hesitation. "It's all right," she whispered, her breathing coming as fast as his.

With painstaking slowness, he inserted himself halfway into her wet, inviting heat, the pleasure indescribable. His hips roared for him to thrust. But he stilled, feeling the sweat forming on his brows, letting her get used to his size. His need to protect her from pain was stronger than his own urgent lust. He dared not move, he dared not breathe, his eyes searching hers for signs of discomfort.

"My sweet?" he asked, his voice tight with restraint.

Before he could act, she took control and moved, tentatively at first, then fully impaling her body with his.

"Dear, God," he growled, shocked and breathless, at the pleasure of being fully inside her, unlike anything he'd ever experienced before.

Their fit was glorious. Perfect.

Her lips parted as if registering their connection. Then a slow smile lifted the corners of her sweet mouth. She was the most beautiful thing he'd ever seen as she discovered her own pleasure. He couldn't speak, his body burned yet momentarily frozen, struck by the sheer awe of her.

The pleasure aglow in her half-lidded gaze confirmed he wasn't ruining this. Slade grinned. His fear of hurting her dissipated.

He carefully and meticulously rocked his pelvis back and forth.

"Oh. My." Her whisper was hoarse, her eyelids lifted with disbelief, and astonishment, and her little smile signaling a bit of excited devilry. Encouraged, he increased his thrusts. Tentatively at first, then more surely. His pleasure increased exponentially when Fifi started to move as well.

He'd never been this aroused or held himself back this much. But it was glorious, and he wouldn't have had it any other way. The pressure at the base of his spine had reached excruciating proportions, yet he maintained his pace, sacrificing his own need for release for her pleasure. He learned what angles and thrusts pleased her by the erotic moans and little hitches in her breath.

He held her sultry, half-lidded gaze as his hand slipped between their bodies to thumb her sensitive spot. The male pride inside him wanted her addicted to the pleasures he could give her. He slowly and methodically paid homage to her quim, raising his upper body to take her mouth in a slow seductive and possessive kiss.

Then it happened. His brain and body suspended its pleasure as her moans turned louder. Her core squeezed his shaft with a staggering grip. As she found her release, his own thrusts turned hard and erratic. Slade saw stars when his own climax came. He danced weightless among unchartered constellations for endless seconds as heat rushed out of him and his seed spilled into her.

CHAPTER 60

Sometime later, Slade and Fifi lay on his discarded clothes near the fire, he on his back and Fifi on her side. The way she was snuggled next to him was adorable, her head on his chest and one of her legs sprawled across his thighs. One arm lazily encircled her waist, while his other hand gently flexed a particularly bouncy curl of her gloriously disheveled mane, which spilled over his upper body.

Fifi's unguarded posture warmed his heart. "I like seeing you so at ease. It's quite a contrast to our wedding night," he said in a soft and slightly amused tone.

She lifted her head, sending him a smile he could only describe as intimate. "My body realized what my heart already knew," she said.

"What did your body realize?" he asked, curious.

"It can trust you."

The immensity of her revelation struck him, given what she'd suffered. It made his chest squeeze tight with an achingly sweet warmth.

He lifted his head and kissed her forehead, inhaling her familiar scent. "When I first encountered you at the manor, I wondered why you weren't married yet with bairns of your own," he said.

Slade was about to add he now understood why, when she spoke.

"After Ross's attack, I vowed never to marry. But now I think perhaps ... I just hadn't found the right man, until you came back into my life," she said.

"Oh, my sweet love," he whispered. A jolt of warmth squeezed Slade's insides.

He moved on top of her, bracing his weight on one arm, so as not to crush her. He captured her lips in a slow, melting kiss. Her body's response was immediate. She threw her arms around him, pulling him further down.

And as his body hardened again and he proceeded to seduce his wife a second time, Slade reveled in one indisputable fact. They had conquered Fifi's fears.

At dawn the next day, after they ate the dried food from their saddle bags, they set out under a pale sun for Saint Mary's Church.

An hour into their walk west, an old gray brick building on top of a small hill, its steeple topped off with a looming cross, came into view. A smaller chapel house connected to its left, an empty wagon hitch near its side door, no one in sight.

They closed the distance to the church's tall weather-beaten door, Slade all the while glancing at his wife. His body hardened even as a devilish smile tugged the corners of his mouth as he recollected their earlier lovemaking and wished they were still in each other's arms in the cave instead of out here.

When they reached the church, Slade pulled on the door handle, a cold metal ring. The door creaked on its hinges as it opened. It was quiet and musty inside. A single lit candle up ahead gave no aid to the gray interior, little light coming in from the ten lofty stained-glass windows, five on either side of the building.

Halfway down the nave, a pair of distant footfalls joined their own.

A tall, gray efficient-looking man in dark clothing stepped in from the side door connecting Saint Mary's to the chapel house.

His thin face with its angular features held a polite expression. "Good morning, welcome to Saint Mary's. I am Minister Emmanuel. How may I be of service?"

Slade stepped forward, extending his arm in a cordial greeting. "Good morning, minister," Slade said. He was still working out what to say next when Fifi came to stand beside him.

A practiced smile lifted the corners of her mouth. "Good morning, minister, we are ardent bird watchers. We were told there are particularly spectacular bullfinches to be seen on this part of the isle."

The minister blinked at Fifi, looking startled. But then his eyes narrowed at her, and he shot Slade a suspicious glance. "Who told you there were bullfinches in this part of the isle?"

Fifi exhaled, sounding a tad impatient. "Our research in the library, of course. We were ardent falcon watchers, but you know how blood thirsty they are. One nearly pecked my head off two years ago. We decided bullfinches were safer."

The minister's entire countenance relaxed as he laughed. "I'll be sure and tell her you said that. Wait here."

Slade ventured a guess that Falcon, whom he'd never met, but knew of by reputation, was Fifi's spymaster.

Minutes later, Donald Lochiel, the Movement's north region spymaster, code name Bullfinch, joined them.

Bullfinch looked the same as he did in 1745 at Fontenoy where Slade had first met the man, and again, a few months ago. Bullfinch had a tall frame, and his thin, distinguished face was lined with wrinkles. But his eyes always struck Slade as all-seeing. His most endearing qualities, however, were his rumpled gray hair and his cocksure smile. The Movement trained their spies to be unassuming, but lethal. However, Bullfinch was in a different category all together, his manner of deception was legendary. Only one or two agents knew Bullfinch like Slade knew him, which was to say, barely scratching the surface of the man's true character. But even with that, Slade understood he must stay on his guard and expect the unexpected. Despite all the cloak and dagger, Slade had always liked the man, given Bullfinch had made Slade a fortune in arms deals.

What Slade wanted to know now, as he clenched his jaws together, was what dangerous missions Bullfinch would orchestrate for Fifi.

Lochiel threw both Slade and Fifi a quizzical look. "Yes? Did someone inquire about bullfinches?"

Slade's eyes narrowed at Bullfinch's smiling ones, daring the other man to call him out. But it appeared Bullfinch wasn't in a daring mood because he showed no signs of recognition when his eyes landed on Slade. And why would there be, the Movement's rules on secrecy were strict, even among its own spies.

"I'll await you by the door," Slade said to Fifi.

"Thank you," she murmured.

He slowly and soundlessly headed for the door, while straining to hear the conversation.

It was unusually quiet in the church—Slade could hear his own breathing—but Fifi's whispers were frustratingly low. He couldn't make out a single word.

Bullfinch's response, on the other hand, carried, and Slade knew it was on purpose.

"He's your husband, you say? How utterly delightful." Bullfinch threw back his head and gave a hearty laugh. His laugh made Slade want to throttle the man.

Slade stole a backward glance. Bullfinch's eyes were on Slade before returning to Fifi as she continued whispering.

Slade groaned. But then Fifi threw Slade a curious glance, before snapping her head back to face Bullfinch.

A minute later, Bullfinch's voice again carried. "For the

Hawley mission, I'll partner you up with one of my agents, code-name Eagle." Bullfinch's voice was nauseatingly merry. "The Eagle will contact you when the time is right. I am confident you two will get along quite well."

Slade's own breath caught in his throat, but the painful grip his jaws were in relaxed. He was grateful as he walked with Fifi back to Master Ames and his boat on the beach. Bullfinch's dictate not only meant that Slade was now officially reenlisted back in the Movement but it allowed him to keep an eye on Fifi while Ross roamed the Highlands. Although he suspected Bullfinch's reasons were more crafty than pairing a husband to watch over his wife. Bullfinch no doubt got twisted pleasure out of creating ripples in Slade and Fifi's marriage.

CHAPTER 61

The next day Slade eyed the swordplay of a group of young guards in the yard at Garraidh, when he noticed Lachlan and Chisolm approaching the yard. The rain had subsided, but the air was brisk, and the sky thick with rolling stone-gray clouds. As the new MacLean warlord, one of his duties was to lead training sessions. But today he was distracted.

Making love to Fifi consumed his body, mind, and soul when he was with her and overwhelmed his thoughts when she wasn't near. She was his redemption. A chance to add light to the darkness in his soul. To balance the scale. And keeping her safe was his priority. When he was with her, he was more than capable of protecting her, but what about when he wasn't with her? She could encounter Ross. Or what if she was injured on a mission? His muscles quivered and ice stabbed his heart at the thought.

Minutes after overhearing Fifi's and Bullfinch's conversation yesterday, he'd worked out her target was General Bolingbroke's second lieutenant general, Walter Hawley. What would his wife do when she found out he had more in common with her than just being childhood friends? He couldn't tell her he used to work for the Movement and had just been reenlisted by Bullfinch, until the time was right. The less she knew, the safer and less distracted she'd be. Distraction can get a spy killed. Besides, knowing the Movement's rules on secrecy, even among their own spies, they would want it this way, because it was safer for all involved.

Slade's glance registered a recurring error in a young guard's swordplay. "You are parrying too much with the flat of the sword. Your opponent can blow through your parry easily. This leaves you vulnerable. Parry with the edge of the sword instead," Slade said.

Lachlan, who stood across from them and not far from where Chisolm was in quiet conversation with a guard, gave a dismissive wave of his wrist and yelled across the yard, loud for everyone to hear. "I don't agree. Edge parrying is no better or worse than flat parrying."

Slade's body tightened with annoyance, not only at the interruption to the group's practice, but at the manner of Lachlan's contradiction.

While the issue of parrying with the edge versus the flat was a contentious topic, Lachlan contradicting Slade's training in front of the guards was a direct challenge to his authority as warlord. If his brother had any tact, he would pull Slade aside and state the contradiction where they could discuss it one-on-one. But ever since they were boys, Lachlan always had about as much tact as a herd of charging cattle.

In fact, knowing Lachlan as he did, his brother's intention was to exert his authority over Slade. And to do that, he would undermine him in front of the guards. Slade was used to Lachlan's pride, in fact, he'd grown a tougher skin since the army. It had an abundance of arrogance.

Slade sent Lachlan a cursory glance. "Why not explain to the group here why flat parrying is no better or worse than parrying with the edge?"

Lachlan's lips curled with impatience. "Because it just is!"

Slade decided the most efficient way to deal with Lachlan's drivel was to meet it head on. Especially since he just decided, he could use Lachlan's arrogance to his benefit.

"Care to demonstrate with me?" Slade asked.

Slade's casual tone made Lachlan's face redden.

"Why not," Lachlan snorted.

The pitch of the hushed voices of the guards rose around them. It appeared his exchange with Lachlan was garnering an audience. Lachlan reached for his longsword, strapped at his back. Slade himself turned and strode toward the yard's gate where he'd rested his own spare rapier in its scabbard. As he unsheathed his weapon and turned to face Lachlan, he noticed in his peripheral vision that Chisolm had ceased his conversation with a guard and was now among their audience. It was a pleasant surprise that his father's presence didn't distract him now, as it had done countless times during his youth, when he'd been trying to impress his father with his fighting skills.

As he took a step towards Lachlan, his brother's lips stretched into a mocking smile. "You sure you want to be using a rapier? As far as I'm concerned, those foreign weapons are far inferior to the Scottish longswords," Lachlan said.

Sniggers sounded in the background. Now why didn't Lachlan's comment surprise him? Lachlan had no love for foreigners, least of all their weapons. But Slade had mastered the longsword years ago under the tutelage of the MacDonell warlord. And he'd become quite adept at using the rapier during his years in the army. The truth was, he could prove his technique with either. As a matter of fact, from the way Lachlan was holding his longsword, Slade ventured a guess Lachlan's fighting technique hadn't changed much from when they were lads. It was always driven more by brute force and intimidation than skill.

"Well then, my rapier should make it easier for you to prove your point, shouldn't it?" Slade said.

His sarcastic tone drew a sneer from Lachlan.

Slade responded with an unperturbed smile. "En garde," Slade said coolly.

Lachlan started out spinning his sword. This was reserved for clearance or to drive several forward-charging opponents back. Or in this case, done for show.

Slade paused, warily eying his brother. When Lachlan turned his spin into a powerful undercut strike towards Slade, he was ready. Slade blocked it with an echoing clash, using the edge of his rapier, but he was also pushed back from the sheer power and force of Lachlan's strike. His brother was built like an ox and had the charging force of one as well. With some effort Slade expertly trapped Lachlan's strike with his cross guard, forcing his brother to slide his blade away.

Lachlan's smile was derisive. "The next time I come at you, you won't be so lucky," Lachlan said.

Slade decided to adopt non-typical maneuvers. Surprise would be his ally.

Slade followed with a downward strike of his rapier, and Lachlan responded with a piercing clash, blocking with the flat of his sword. Lachlan's parry, although powerful, allowed Slade to slide along Lachlan's sword, reversing his own sword's direction into a slash straight for Lachlan's skull. With a loud grunt and immense restraint, Slade halted his sword's trajectory an inch away from his brother's head, who was now frozen except for his hard and fast breathing. Slade ignored the petulant voice in his head saying he should have knocked Lachlan out to prove his point. But it would have meant Lachlan had succeeded in goading him. As a lad he would have dealt the blow, but now he had Fifi to consider, and an aim to achieve.

Slade withdrew his blade and inclined his head towards Lachlan, a smile easing the side of his mouth. "Care to try again?" Slade asked, starting to enjoy himself.

Lachlan's face twisted with anger. Slade had learned years ago never to attack in anger, a lesson his brother seemed to have missed. Lachlan came at him with a hard downward cut. Slade blocked it, his edge trapping Lachlan's sword in his cross guard. His brother withdrew. Slade pushed forward with a strong offensive strike towards Lachlan's crown. Lachlan parried with the flat of his sword. Slade used all his strength to slide past, then followed up with a reverse strike of his pommel towards Lachlan's face. But again, Slade halted an inch away from his brother's body.

Their breathing was audible, but their audience had gone deadly silent.

Lachlan let out a series of curses and withdrew. Begrudging surrender etched its way across his brother's face. Despite himself, triumph, and satisfaction pierced Slade's gut. Slade eased his hold on his sword. He'd proven his point with just four thrusts of his weapon. He decided tact was better than gloating, especially since he needed his brother's help.

Slade turned to the group of guards who were staring at him with rapt attention and admiration. "In a fight, you need to use whatever maneuver is available to you in order to escape injury. Sometimes you have no other choice than to block with the flat, depending on the position where your opponent's strike catches you. But when feasible, blocking with the edge will work in your favor," Slade said.

The young guards cheered in awe at their swordplay demonstration, and Chisolm joined in, with a hearty series of claps. When Slade glanced at his father, his chest warmed, for approval shone in Chisolm's eyes. "I am happy to see you are settling into your new position as warlord quite well," Chisolm said. He might not have been seeking Chisolm's approval, but his heart squeezed to know he had it.

Lachlan narrowed his eyes at Slade and sheathed his longsword. "You have to give me a chance to redeem myself, brother. How's your aim with the musket?" Lachlan said.

Slade heard the note of humility in Lachlan's voice. Perhaps there was hope for Lachlan's oversized pride after all.

It was quite possible that under all the crusty arrogance his brother wasn't a total horse's ass. Nonetheless, Slade decided against telling Lachlan he considered his musket aim to be far superior to his swordplay.

"I'll grant you a re-match, in exchange for a favor," Slade said.

"Of course. What do you need?" Lachlan asked.

"I need your approval to pull a few guards from Garraidh guard duty to escort Fifi, whenever she leaves the castle."

Lachlan's eyebrows arched. "You're expecting trouble?"

Slade contemplated how best to answer without giving too much away. "Fifi has no love for the redcoats, and has garnered some unwanted attention," Slade said, finally.

Surprise flashed across Lachlan's face. Like their father, Lachlan was an ardent Scottish nationalist and was ready to assist in any resistance whatsoever against the redcoats. "You and your wife can count on me, brother. You will have your guards."

"My thanks." Slade shook his brother's hand, grateful to have achieved his aim. He would prefer to protect Fifi himself, but when he couldn't be with her, she would be guarded at all times, especially while Ross was in the Highlands.

After training, Slade took Destroyer from the stables and rode towards the local church and burial ground. He pulled the collar of his greatcoat closer, feeling a chill in the air. Or was the chill coming from the coldness of his decade old memories? He needed to move beyond his past, in order to move forward.

CHAPTER 62

Four days later, as a long strip of bluish-orange dawn painted the edge of the eastern horizon, a fully armed Phoebe and Slade cantered side by side on horseback. The air was chilled crisp against her face as they headed in the direction of Hawley's gray manor.

Concentrating on the mission was proving difficult for Phoebe because an aggregation of heated sensations swirled in her body and erotic images flashed in her head. She had nothing to compare it to. Perhaps the euphoria when she had first hit the dead center of the bullseye, multiplied a thousandfold.

Slade had eased her into lovemaking during their night on Beinn na Faoghla and each night since they had learned more and more about enjoying each other's bodies. Like the fact that she took pleasure in his heated naked weight on top of her, or that he was insatiable when it came to putting his tongue and mouth all over her secret and intimate parts, waking her up several times during the nights to make love. He thrillingly redefined her entire sentient awareness.

If her mission had been foremost in her mind as it had in the past, she would have been disappointed that the Eagle still hadn't contacted her, as Bullfinch said he would. Anticipation and apprehension should be bombarding her gut, considering the danger she and Slade were heading towards, not to mention the fact that her husband was about to find out exactly what it was that she did for what he called "her mysterious Jacobite friend." But instead of disappointment, anticipation or apprehension, all she felt was a weightless giddiness when her eyes fell on Slade. Like diving into the loch for a swim, at that free falling moment midair just before hitting the water.

A few days ago, Phoebe had gotten a coded missive from Bullfinch that an illegal sale of flintlock muskets would be changing hands from Hawley to mercenaries today. He'd gotten this information from a reliable source, a servant that worked at Hawley's manor who'd confirmed there were usually two to three guards at the manor. Luckily the man had ten bairns to feed and welcomed the extra coin in exchange for information. Bullfinch had written for her to keep an eye out for the servant, he'd be the one with the white handkercher.

An hour ago, just as she was getting ready to leave Garraidh's stables on a black gelding, one of her newly appointed MacLean guards had alerted Slade. Slade had dismissed her guards and come with her instead.

"Tell me more about why we're here," Slade now said. Dawn's dim light filtering through dark clouds emphasized the way his beautiful lips thinned. He must realize what they were about to do.

"We're here to witness Hawley's sale of stolen army weapons to mercenaries and take proof of his illegal dealings to my Jacobite friend, who has the means to expose his treachery where it will cause the most damage to his reputation," she said.

Slade was facing forward as both their horses slowed to a walk alongside each other. His jawline hardened.

A flash of intense worry crinkled his brows, shifting to

anguish as he glanced at her. "I don't want to see you get hurt. I don't think I could bear it," he said.

A breath stealing emotion crowded her chest as her heart compressed painfully. The intensity of love that washed over her was so overpowering it stung the back of her eyes as she met his gaze. "I promise to take care. Please don't worry. But we have to do this. Hawley must be stopped." Her voice cracked with raw emotion, but it was also laced with steely determination.

When they were close enough, they tethered their horses to trees well off the road and crept the final hundred or so yards to Hawley's manor. Then they settled quietly out of sight behind the thick trunk of an alder tree, an excellent vantage point from which to view the gray manor and barn where Phoebe had spotted the crates previously with Aila. Ten crates were visible, each the perfect size for holding Brown Bess muskets. They observed at length the two able-bodied plainly dressed guards patrolling the property's perimeter.

It surprised her how well she and Slade had worked together so far, as they waited on the arrival of the musket buyers. There'd been no discussion about how far away they should leave their horses from the site, or the best location to hide and wait, or the fact that they had to mark the comings and goings of the manor while they watched from their hiding spot. Nor had they agreed to count the number of weapons the guards carried, or how best to surreptitiously approach the barn from their location. They just did it.

Two hours later, a military-looking wagon built to transport troops and weapons came down the lane with three occupants. The driver and one of the men at the back were what Phoebe would expect cutthroat Irish mercenaries to look like. But the third man was wide-eyed, much younger, and seemed out of place.

Phoebe pulled her vizard from the special pocket she'd sewn in her coat. As she donned it to conceal her facial features, her muscles went weak, and her mouth dropped open. Words failed her as Slade donned a similar mask.

She hadn't much time to process Slade's mask, because her gaze was yanked back to the occupants of the wagon entering the manor's front yard and making their way to the barn and the two Hawley guards.

A moment later, Phoebe saw Hawley himself strutting out the front of the manor towards the barn with a surly smile.

"That's Walter Hawley, lieutenant general of the British Army, second to Bolingbroke himself," Phoebe whispered.

Slade took the man in, then faced her. She couldn't tell his expression behind the mask. "You've clearly done reconnaissance here before." He paused then continued, "It appears we are two against the six of them. I would think, for proof of Hawley's illegal dealings, all that's needed is the muskets and perhaps one or two of their men to give witness?"

Phoebe nodded. "Yes. Let's wait for them to get far from the wagon before we do anything. Those wagons make for a quick getaway."

Slade's directness was in his eyes and in the curtness of his nod. "Agreed."

As adrenaline pumped through her veins, she positioned her previously loaded pistol and the musket within easy reach. Slade had clearly done this sort of work before. Was the army's training similar to the Movement's? But that wouldn't explain his mask, would it? Phoebe's brain screamed something at her, but she ignored it. She couldn't afford to be distracted.

Phoebe, musket in hand, quickly worked the angles, deciding on the best position for shooting as Slade drew his own pistol and musket, and laid them next to where she'd put her own.

Phoebe eyed him quizzically, a heavy cold sinking into her belly. "What are you doing?"

Slade considered, but it was difficult to read him through the vizard. "Once the alarm is raised, I want you to incapacitate as many men from this position as you can. I'll leave you the firearms. I will go and see how many I can quietly eliminate before they know we are here."

Something hummed inside Phoebe's chest as she voiced one of Falcon's mantras. "I agree. Secure success by subduing the enemy before the fighting begins."

There was amusement in his voice when he spoke. "Yes, but if fighting is required, you fight."

Phoebe eyed him for a breath before speaking. "I'm good at close combat. I can help if I go with you."

His jawline hardened. "Yes. But here you will have a bird's eye view of everyone and can incapacitate more effectively. I know how good you are disarming your opponent face-to-face and with a pistol. I recall Hortons shooting range. But I don't want you getting hurt or distracted."

"I don't want you getting hurt either," she said, pushing past the blockage in the back of her throat. She couldn't imagine her life without him.

CHAPTER 63

$\mathcal{P}$hoebe's gaze darted from the manor back to her husband. Slade was trying to protect her, and she loved him for it, but he was taking the most risk. This was her mission, she should be in the line of fire.

Yet, there was no time to discuss. They either moved forward as a cohesive force, or not at all. The delay could cost them the success of this mission.

Her chest tightened, torn between fear and logic, blood racing through her veins.

"All right, I'll remain here with the guns, but at least take one of them," she said.

"I'm better with a blade," he said.

They'd wasted enough time discussing it, and she didn't want any delays with further discussions, so she acquiesced.

As she positioned all the firearms within easy reach, he grabbed the collar of her cloak. Yanking her to him, his mouth crushed hers. His tongue plundered her mouth. It was quick, rough, and exacting. Her head spun, and her breath was coming fast and hard when he released her.

"Stay safe, my brave love," he whispered, his eyes boring into hers. Before she could speak or catch her breath, Slade had already slipped away behind the next tree trunk, and then to the next, staying low, like a graceful predator on the prowl, all the way to the back of Hawley's barn.

With heartbeats hammering in her ears and her body starting to sweat under her cloak despite the cold, she took up her position behind the trunk of the tree and waited. She'd risked her own safety before on missions but had never risked the safety of someone she loved. The danger of it hovered around her, thinning the air. She realized her knuckles had gone numb with her death grip on the musket before she relaxed her fingers. She wouldn't give in to the fear because then it would make her useless, slowing her reaction and mental clarity which would be a sure way to increase the risk to them both.

Hawley and one of his armed guards were now standing closer to the manor, next to two mercenaries, one armed, all deep in discussion.

Phoebe made out the remaining two men, one unarmed mercenary and an armed Hawley guard, by the back of the barn. Just then, a tall, dark, broad-shouldered figure slipped out from behind a tree, approaching the men from their rear. It was Slade. He silently drew his rapier and thrust it swiftly into the back of the mean-looking armed guard, the bloody blade protruding from the man's stomach. The unarmed mercenary standing next to the now-slumping guard bellowed a loud invective, raising the alarm.

Stunned, her heart pounding her chest, Phoebe didn't have time to react to Slade's second move as he knocked the bellowing man in the head with a blow only a trained spy would use. She was already taking aim closer to the manor and firing at the chest of the guard standing next to Hawley. Her musket ball dropped him. Phoebe grabbed the second musket and shot the armed mercenary in the head as he bolted, acrid tangy smoke wafting from her musket's barrel.

She dropped the second expended musket and grabbed the two loaded pistols. With pure adrenaline pouring through Phoebe's veins and fear a forgotten emotion, she bolted for the fray.

Between her and Slade, they'd eliminated four opponents. Only Hawley and the out-of-place mercenary remained. Recalling the informant's confirmation that there were usually two to three men with Hawley, she was confident they'd accounted for everyone who'd be a threat to them from the manor, except Hawley himself. The former had disappeared into the manor and the latter was scrambling towards the wagon.

She positioned herself in front of the mercenary just as he rushed for the seat of the wagon. Terror and wildness were plastered on his young face.

"Move that wagon and I'll shoot you," she said, training her pistol straight at his head.

The young mercenary's eyes bulged, and his hands went up in the air in total surrender just as Slade sprinted past her from the barn on his way to the manor and Hawley. "Situation in hand?" Slade asked.

"Situation in hand," she said, her breath coming fast. In that second, Hawley stepped out the manor's front door with a loaded musket trained right on Slade's chest.

Several things happened all at once. Blistering heat and cold fear collided in Phoebe's stomach as Hawley fired on Slade. An excruciating pain in her chest almost stopped her heart. But Slade had already ducked out the way. She drew breath again, as the bullet hit the edge of the wagon. A deafening roar in her ears made her head snap towards the young mercenary, making sure he was not running, and then her eyes found Slade again. Praise all the saints, Slade wasn't shot.

Hawley tossed his expended musket. With pure hatred on his twisted features, he went for the rapier sheathed at his waist. But from Slade's half-risen position, her husband whipped out a trident dagger from a sheath at his waist and jabbed forward just as Hawley unsheathed his rapier.

The dagger went through Hawley's shoulder, and the man bellowed curses, dropping his rapier. Slade immediately followed up with a steely punch straight into Hawley's face, felling the man.

After finding rope in the wagon, Phoebe and Slade restrained Hawley, the guard Slade had knocked out cold, and the young, scared mercenary, leaving them out of sight inside the barn. The other three men were already dead.

"One of us has to alert the constables while the other keeps an eye on the three men," Slade said to Phoebe.

At that very moment a wide-eyed, ashen faced man nervously stepped out from the front door of the manor waving a white handkercher, and Phoebe remembered Bullfinch's missive and its description of the informant.

"We can send him to bring the constables," she said to Slade, pointing to the small-boned man with the handkercher.

Slade nodded his approval and said as much to the man. After pocketing the white handkercher, and the coins Slade handed him, the man scampered off towards the village to get the constables.

"I'll wait here until he returns. But I think it's safer for you to return home. If it was any other woman I wouldn't let her travel alone, but now that I've seen you fight, I pity the brigand who tries to interfere with you," Slade said.

Phoebe sent her husband a long assessing look. She was grateful they'd both done this with nary a scratch. All due to the same training, she realized.

Adrenaline still warred with blood in her veins from what they'd just accomplished. So did shock and amazement.

"You're Eagle, aren't you?" she said, swallowing back the moisture in her mouth.

He sent her a cocksure grin as he took her in his arms. "I

wondered when you'd figure it out." His voice was soft, almost teasing.

"You worked as a double agent during the wars?" she asked.

He nodded, his eyes darkened. "I did."

Phoebe blinked up at her husband, astonished and breathless, just as his lips landed on hers, not giving her much time to react to his admission. The kiss sent a blaze of fire straight through her body, singeing her to the core while her spinning head grappled with her new reality and struggled to bring her back to earth.

CHAPTER 64

With reluctance, Phoebe left Slade at Hawley's manor waiting for the constables with three dead men and three men physically restrained. She slipped her vizard back into its pocket and was just about to guide her horse onto the main road from Bayview Crest when the hoofbeats of another rider caught her attention. Her grip on the reins tightened when she took note of his red uniform. Instinct told her the redcoat was heading for Hawley's manor. But when she made out the empty blue eyes and fair hair of Faye Ross with a musket pistol hanging off the holster at his waist, she froze in ice cold terror. No. No. No. This couldn't be.

Her knee-jerk reaction was to flee. This snake had broken her spirit, made her feel unclean, and dragged something nefarious into her soul. But Phoebe inhaled against the tight terror blocking her windpipe. Slade was at Hawley's manor. She had to delay Ross.

If she hadn't just thwarted an illegal firearms deal orchestrated by a corrupt lieutenant general and come out unscathed, and if Slade wasn't still waiting at the manor, she might have run.

But then, she was a lot more capable now than she had been seven years ago.

Pure hatred and malevolence emanated from the twisted scowl on Ross's face as he reined in his white stallion, right next to her black gelding.

"I don't imagine bumping into you twice in this exact spot is any coincidence, is it?" he asked, his tone tight with suspicion.

Phoebe's teeth clenched. Her chin lifted. "Your imaginings are none of my concern," she said.

Something unhinged shone in his expression. A wildness in his eyes that made chills run up her spine. With teeth bared, he reached across and backhanded Phoebe across the face.

"Insolent little bitch." He hissed.

Phoebe gasped as her entire face screamed in pain. Her eyes stung, and even her nostrils smarted. But no more. Enough of this snake's intimidation.

Fury roared in her ears and pounded against her ribs. Phoebe pulled out the primed pistol, previously hidden in the pocket of her thick black cloak and pointed it at his head. She pulled the trigger the second he whacked it out of her hand.

The shot went wild, and her horse reared up, emitting a piercing neigh. Phoebe's grip on the reins tightened, and her booted feet held fast in the stirrups as her hip and abdominal muscles engaged so she could stay seated. And she would have remained on her horse, but Ross grabbed the collar of her cloak and viciously yanked her off.

The breath was knocked right out of her as she landed, pain shooting out from her side through the rest of her. Her horse's hooves kicked out in fear, connecting with Phoebe's leg. Phoebe screamed at the unholy pain as her horse bolted for the trees.

She lay on her side gasping, her body howling in agony and shock. Phoebe's leather-gloved palms pushed against the ground to lift herself up, but she didn't get very far. The debilitating pain in her leg wrenched a growl from her, and she dropped back to the ground. Frustration, anger and hatred burned her belly as Ross sauntered towards her, having dismounted. His animal, no doubt used to gunfire, stayed calm.

A twisted smirk stretched his pale mouth. "I recall having you on your back seven years ago. Apparently, you liked it so much, you readily got on your back again."

"The only reason a woman would get on her back for a vile piece of excrement like you is if you paid her," Phoebe said, her teeth clenched.

His expression turned malicious and he pulled back his booted leg and slammed it into her side.

Phoebe gasped at the sharp pain. Tears stung the backs of her eyes. A trace of his apple scented pomade from his close proximity caused a stomach spasm. She swallowed against the need to retch. Phoebe would fight this serpent with her last breath before she let him hurt her again.

"You are like your parents, thinking you are better than me. They didn't agree to my proposal seven years ago for your hand, but I had you anyway, didn't I?" Ross said, contempt lifting the left side of his mouth.

Phoebe blinked at him, shock, and confusion churning in her belly, amidst the pain riveting through her injured leg.

"Wha … what proposal?" she asked, her voice weak.

A mirthless laugh escaped his mouth. "Didn't they tell you? I asked for your hand seven years ago. And again, three weeks ago. But your parents denied me. We wouldn't suit, they said." He scoffed.

Anger flashed in his eyes, similar to seven years ago, and again three weeks ago.

Pieces of a sickening puzzle started to drop into place. His seething anger that day seven years ago when he'd attacked her. He wasn't just angry she'd refused to stop riding when he'd called after her on the moors seven years ago. He'd been seething because her parents had refused him. She'd thought it was anger from her slight. And then again three weeks ago her mother had said she had to marry Slade because they'd been seen kissing. And because the other options for a husband were not worth mentioning. At the time the words had struck her as peculiar, but she'd dismissed it in her panicked state.

Phoebe's eyes bulged. "Why in all that is holy would you want to marry me?"

Hostility and rancor curled his lips into a sneer. "Because I had been watching you for weeks after Hamish and Broden first told me who you were. Riding the moors seven years ago, without a care in the world. Wild and uncultured like an animal. Animals like you must be controlled, broken in," he said, coming to stand directly above her, his chin raised sending her an unnatural smile. Its eeriness unsettled her.

"I liked the look of you, I imagined I could take you for my wife, but you needed to be trained, like a man must train a horse or a dog how to take commands and behave when in the presence of their masters," he continued, his eyes traveling the length of her, making that unclean feeling crash over her like a tidal wave.

His expression had been the subject of her nightmares. It had made her cry, scream, break out into cold sweats, and shake with terror and fury. It had left her in dark hopeless moods and made her lock herself up in her room for days on end. Not only had she distrusted every single man she'd encountered, but she'd hated every single redcoat for the past seven years because of Ross. He had gotten his wish of control, although not as he might have imagined.

She desperately wanted to grab the pistol he'd wacked out of her hand which lay a few feet away, but the seconds it would take to reload with the extra powder and ball she had in her pocket would cause her dearly, either her life, or much worse like seven years ago. Then there was the dagger strapped to her thigh, but she would have to lift the hems of her cloak and riding habit to reach it. He would knock it from her grip before she could strike.

Blast it all to hell!

But then she noticed a blur of movement and a familiar tall figure about twenty paces away jumping down from his moving horses' saddle without slowing. His animal's hooves muffled against the earthen ground.

Phoebe turned back to Ross. *Never interrupt your enemy when he is making a mistake*, Falcon had said. Ross was too busy licking his lips and unbuttoning his breeches to take note of anything else.

"You are making it very easy for me this time, brat." Ross sneered.

But she must interrupt Ross, for the sake of distracting him from Slade.

"I'll do whatever you want, I'll lay with you, just please don't hurt me again," she said, lifting the hem of her cloak and then the hem of her riding habit.

Ross's hands stilled, and his eyes widened staring at her stocking clad thighs. So distracted was he that he didn't notice her husband lunging for him.

CHAPTER 65

Red blurred Slade's vision at the sight of Phoebe's injured leg and Ross looming over her, her discharged pistol on the ground a few feet away. Bloodthirsty rage howled through his veins. An unimaginable roar cracked the air. It took Slade a split second to realize he'd made the ungodly sound. He dragged Ross away from Phoebe and slammed him down on the ground. When he'd heard the shot minutes ago, his only thought had been for Phoebe.

Propelled by an instinctual inferno in his belly to protect the woman he loved, Slade slammed his booted foot into Ross's head.

Ross dodged the second kick, rolled and jumped up, blinking from Phoebe to Slade, realization and a lewd smile twisted his lips apart, revealing bloodied teeth.

"You know I've had her before you?"

Slade growled at Ross, just as Ross's right leg came at Slade. The first kick sent a shock of pain through Slade's side. He gritted his teeth, too focused on ending Ross to care. He was ready for the second kick. He entrapped Ross's right thigh to keep him unbalanced and in place as he punched Ross's face.

Again, and again. Ross angled his elbows in a defensive position, causing Slade to drop his leg and to step to Ross's rear. He grabbed Ross's waist from behind, heisted him up and slammed him down with an ear-piercing crash.

Slade hovered over Ross, his breath coming hard and fast like a growling beast, his usual patience and methodical nature shredded. He held back from punching and kicking Ross until the man's body was a bleeding mass of skin and bones, even though that's all he wanted to do.

"I learned something about you from Colonel Wilfred Owens." Slade snarled at Ross.

"You spoke … spoke to my Colonel?" Ross asked, his voice shaking, contempt twisting his face.

"You like to hurt women. A bruised serving girl in your army's camp three months ago. A seamstress whose arm was broken a year back, leaving her incapable of caring for her ailing mother. And your own father is rumored to have disowned you and forced you into the army eight years ago," Slade said.

Ross's nostrils flared with hostility. "How dare you question my superiors, you dirty Scot?"

Satisfaction speared Slade's belly when Ross sprung up and came at him with a right hook. Because he no longer had to hold back. Slade effortlessly blocked Ross's fist, letting his rage propel his own fists again and again into Ross's face. His movements were too quick for Ross's retaliation. It gave Slade the opening to grab the back of Ross's head, slamming it down against his pushed-up knee. Ross's head bounced back, making him lose his balance, and taking him down on his rear.

Slade descended on Ross holding Ross down with his knees, but a thought jabbed through the haze of his blinding fury. He needed to get Phoebe away before the constables arrived. Explaining Phoebe's presence would be difficult. As a former colonel he might be able to lie his own way through his involvement, but not Phoebe's. He needed to end this now.

Slade drew his trident dagger from its sheath, but his gaze shifted when he noticed movement in his right periphery. Ross was withdrawing his own primed pistol from its holster. Before Slade could knock it from Ross's hand, a loud shot sounded. Slade half expected to feel a piercing pain in his right side from the shot but felt nothing except for a few wet splatters on his face. He blinked down at Ross, and it was then that he saw the hole in the side of Ross's neck, gushing red. The life was slowly draining from Ross's eyes. As Ross gasped for air, his slackening half open mouth and sideways glance registered shock. When a soft crash sounded a few feet away, Slade looked to see Phoebe still holding her pistol, smoke dissipating from its barrel. But she was now on the ground, her delicate features lined with pain, and her breathing labored. Her injured leg must have failed after she had retrieved, reloaded, and fired her pistol.

"I will get you home, my love, and have a physician tend to you, please, just hold on." Slade quickly removed any sign of Ross's uniform and tied it in a bundle on the saddle of Ross's horse, then slapped the animal's hide with his palm, sending it running for the trees, he then briskly dragged Ross's body behind a large yellowing larch bush.

Slade carefully lifted Phoebe and carried her to sit across Destroyer's back. Her shallow breathing sounded more like a wheeze. Sweat now dripped from her brow and her face was ashen, despite her weak smile of, dare he say, victory and peace marred with physical pain. His stomach was in knots with worry for her injured leg.

"Thank you for helping me slay my nightmare," she wheezed.

"For you, I would gladly slay a thousand Rosses, but in the end, you did the deed," he said, his throat feeling like it had been sandpapered. He straddled Destroyer behind her, gently cradling her in his arms, setting out for Garraidh. Guilt had thickened the back of his throat. And condemnation flayed his skin from his bones for letting Phoebe ride off alone. He should have protected her.

Each clop of Destroyer's hooves jostled her leg, causing her to wince. And each wince was like a stab to his heart

When he arrived at Garraidh, Slade carried her up to their bedchamber. He sent Aila to fetch the physician while he gently and carefully removed Phoebe's outer layers then put her in bed, propping her leg up on pillows.

Slade's gut twisted in helpless knots as his eyes fell on Phoebe's left shin where she'd explained on their ride home that the gelding had kicked her. It was swollen around a deep gash, in a multitude of ghastly reds and purples. The sight of it shredded his insides.

What if he hadn't gotten there in time? Would Ross have raped her again? Killed her? The unmitigated rage and horror surging through him at the thought almost felled him. What would happen the next time he wasn't with her, and she encountered someone like Ross or Bolingbroke? Dear God, he'd never been this helpless.

"Don't …" Phoebe whispered.

Slade blinked at his wife, who had been eying him through her contorted sweat drenched expression of pain.

"Pardon me, my love?" he asked.

"This injury is not your doing. Don't take it on your shoulders."

Just then the physician arrived.

The bespectacled, graying man inspected her injury from every angle possible, asking Phoebe a series of questions about the type and location of the pain. He hovered, impatience gurgling in his belly. Why didn't the doctor simply give her something for the pain?

Slade said as much to the physician, but the man ignored him, mumbling something about overbearing and overprotective husbands.

After an inordinate amount of time, the man opened one of the bags he'd arrived with and put together a splint of wood and leather. The pained noises Phoebe made during the process utterly and completely devastated Slade. It must have shown on his face.

"Please do not worry so, Master MacLean, I've seen worse. Your wife's ribs are bruised, not broken and the fracture in her leg is clean. The chances of infection are low. But it can take up to three months for the bone to fully heal. I'll leave her laudanum tincture for the pain and will return regularly to check on her," the surgeon said before leaving the bedchamber.

Three months. Dear God.

Despite the chances of infection being low, fever did come. And Slade spent the next two days gently wiping Phoebe's heated skin with a cool water-soaked linen to keep her fever down. He spoon-fed her broth in bed whenever she awoke. And he repeated soothing words to her as she slept and thrashed about, and until the crinkle in her brows eased.

"You are my life, my reason to breathe," Slade whispered to Phoebe, as she slept. "If anything happens to you, I will burn this entire Godforsaken world down, because it will be nothing but ashes without you."

Breena and Lucia came from Eileanach on the third day, after hearing about Phoebe's condition.

"Please let us tend to her, Colonel," Lucia said, her brows arched in concern.

"You need to sleep yourself—you've been up for two days," Breena said. "She'll be in good hands, I know exactly what to do." Breena's smile was reassuring, but Slade still couldn't leave Phoebe's bedside.

He recalled Breena was a healer and an expert on medicinal plants when she put a curious concoction to Phoebe's lips to drink. Still, he stayed by Phoebe's side until the fever finally broke. He thanked all the saints he could name—and Breena. Phoebe was out of danger.

Slade sent a missive to Bullfinch updating him on the mission and requested that he do everything he could to ensure Ross's body either wasn't found or couldn't be traced back to the Movement. Over the next two weeks Phoebe's color returned, and during the following three months her leg slowly healed. They celebrated Hogmanay together, quietly in their marriage chamber. It was the best Hogmanay Slade could recall.

At the end of the three months, after the surgeon pronounced her healed and left, Slade sat next to her on the edge of the bed and took Phoebe's hand in his. He was too close to her, he couldn't think straight, he couldn't reason rationally with her by his side, he loved her too much, and she consumed him with passion, light, happiness, and all that was good in this world. His love for her was like being perpetually drunk on alcohol. He needed distance, he needed time to think objectively without her love and loveliness distracting him. He needed to come up with a plan to safeguard her on missions. He needed time apart to think. A perfect time to finish his own mission.

"I must leave you for Sutton Coldfield. I've been putting it off for three months, but I can put it off no longer," he said, an uncomfortable feeling settling in his belly. He'd received word from Bullfinch that Bolingbroke was still sanctioning illegal raids in remote Scottish farming villages to not only eliminate rebel threats and instill intimidation and fear among Scots, but to exert English dominance and control.

Her gaze dropped, but not before he saw the tender worry in them. "Of course, you must have business to take care of. I've proven to be a distraction these past few months, haven't I."

He placed a finger beneath her chin gently lifting her face until her eyes landed on his. "You are my wife. And while your loveliness is indeed a most welcomed and tantalizing distraction, I do have to go."

He finished the sentence by crushing his mouth to hers. He devoured her lips and tongue with his own, inhaling his wife like a dying man gasped for air, knowing this kiss would have to last him a long time.

After he pulled away, breathing hard yet ignoring the urgent throbbing need in his body, his eyes registered the solemn smile lifting her delectably ravished mouth.

"You will be careful."

"And we must discuss our future, and the Movement. I will not stand by and watch you put yourself in danger again, as you did this last time with Ross. If your injuries had been irreversible, or if he had taken your life, I … I …" Slade broke off when the jab of pain to his chest became too much to breathe or even speak.

"But Ross is dead."

"There are plenty of men like Ross still out there."

He saw her throat working, before she spoke, a glint of something in her eyes. "It is the burden we must bear for the work. Even now, you will be riding into danger on a mission. And I will have no rest or peace of mind until you return safely."

"Yes, but you are my wife. It's my responsibility and my honor to keep you safe."

"No more than I want to keep you safe."

"But as a husband, I am the one who must bear this burden."

The glint in her eyes was now clearly visible as indignation, and from her flared nostrils and heightening color, it was going into full blown anger. "Are you now to tell me, husband, that it's your duty to control my work, my comings and goings under the guise of keeping me safe?"

Slade let out an anguished breath, but it did nothing to calm the heat rising in the pit of his stomach or the tension growing in his body. "No, that is not what I am saying."

He was trying to tell Phoebe he wanted to keep her safe because he loved her. He was her husband, and it was his privilege and duty to protect her. His life would be dark, desolate and less than nothing without her. But he was bungling it. And from the look on her face, he was fast realizing this was a conversation they had to have when he wasn't about to leave on a mission.

"I must leave now, but we have to continue this conversation. We must discuss our marriage." He kissed her forehead, trying to ignore the stiffness in her body, before he turned and left.

CHAPTER 66

The day after Slade's departure, Phoebe visited the Edwardes. She'd told herself she was being sociable, and they were so warm and comforting to be around, she desperately needed some of that since Slade had left. But there'd been another reason. Ever since accidentally catching Sylvia's perfect oval doll-face, flawless skin, and stunning brown eyes years ago, Phoebe had wished she was prettier. And now, after disappointing Slade, as was evident by his manner when he'd left for Sutten, Coldfield, Phoebe wondered if Slade also wished he'd had a different sort of wife. Someone who was not only prettier but more traditional, more controllable and appropriate.

Phoebe turned at the sound of footsteps. Margaret walked towards the chair she occupied near the fireplace inside Margaret and Raghnall's cozy manse with an amiable expression, carrying tea service.

"I'm so happy you can join me for afternoon tea, my dear. I am only sorry Raghnall is not here. It's his day for making house calls."

Phoebe smiled. "I am sorry to show up unannounced, but

with Slade being in Sutton Coldfield I was feeling a bit out of sorts."

Margaret placed the tray on a piecrust-shaped tea table next to the oak desk where Phoebe sat.

"I can't tell you how grateful I am not only for your company but also for your donation to the orphanage. It will be used for much needed supplies for the children," Margaret said.

Phoebe hadn't told anyone she'd donated her entire first month's stipend from the MacLeans. She'd wanted to do something good, inspired by the Edwardes and all the good they were doing at the church.

She took a slice of fruitcake off the white porcelain plate offered by Margaret. An idea started to take shape. "I am happy to help. You mentioned earlier you were in the process of collecting donated quilts from the villagers for the orphanage. Have you many remaining to collect?"

Margaret shook her head as she poured tea. The pleasant malty scent of the steaming dark brew filled the air.

"No, I have all the quilts, in fact, just the last one is left to be collected," Margaret said.

Phoebe dipped her head in assent to sugar and cream as she took a bite of the cake. Margaret then offered her the filled white porcelain teacup.

"Let me help, I can pick it up for you, I have the use of a horse drawn cart and three of the MacLeans escorts with me," Phoebe said.

Margaret served herself tea and then took a seat in the gently worn chair nearest to the tea table. "Mistress Ames who lives down by the port is our last remaining donor."

"Mistress Ames? Is she related to Master Ames, who owns the jolly boat?"

Margaret sipped her tea, then nodded. "Yes, indeed. She is his wife."

"It will be nice to meet Master Ames's wife. He's quite a sailor," Phoebe said.

"It runs in his family, they've been sailors going back five generations," Margaret said, conversationally.

Phoebe's heart rate picked up as she swallowed, getting ready to put words to a question that had brought her to Margaret's doorstep. "Did you meet Slade's betrothed, Sylvia, before she passed?"

Margaret stilled, her teacup pausing halfway to her lips. "Yes, dear. I knew Sylvia. Her mother and I are well acquainted. Sylvia was such a sweet innocent girl, but she took the burdens of the world to heart."

"How so?" Phoebe said, trying to understand.

Margaret placed her teacup down on the table, seeming to consider the question. "Well, when she was a little girl, she took care of a pair of chaffinches after their mother abandoned its nest. But they were too young, and despite her attempts at feeding them, the poor things perished. She was inconsolable for months and months. She stopped eating. Mistress Willoughby came to see Raghnall asking for help. He went to speak with Sylvia a few times, before he was able to pull her out of her melancholy," Margaret said.

A twinge of pity sat in Phoebe's stomach even as something pinched inside her chest. "Was she prone to melancholy?"

"Very much so. She felt too deeply. Mistress Willoughby often tells me her daughter was just too good for the harshness in this world."

"I imagine Slade loved her very much." It took a second for Phoebe to realize she'd spoken those words out loud.

"He did. But it was an innocent sort of love, not like the way he loves you, my dear, if the look in his eyes when they fall on you is any indication," Margaret said.

After the conclusion of tea, as Phoebe finished donning her cloak by the door, Margaret came to stand by her side.

"Have you met Mistress Willoughby before, my dear?"

Phoebe pulled on her gloves, shaking her head. "I don't believe I've had the pleasure."

"She is neighbor to the Ameses. You may very well run into her when you are there."

The back of her throat tightened. "Oh. Do you think a visit from me will be unwelcomed?"

Margaret shook her head. "I don't think so, but I thought I'd warn you. After Sylvia died, Victoria … Mistress Willoughby, was bitter and unhappy. She even abandoned her post as governess for one of the Sutherland girls and came to the village to be alone. For a long time she blamed Slade for Sylvia's death. But recently she seemed to have found some measure of peace."

Something prickled at the back of Phoebe's neck. "Why would she blame Slade for Sylvia's death?"

A look of uncertainty crossed Margaret's face. "Perhaps Slade should be the one to tell you this … I don't know the particulars, but Sylvia took her own life."

"Dear, God." Phoebe raised her hand to her mouth. Something heavy and cold expanded at her core.

Her heart ached for Slade. Ached for what he must have had to endure. What he must still be enduring. Phoebe leaned back against the doorframe, the air seeming to leave her lungs. She'd never guessed this. She began to understand the reason for her husband's dark moods.

"But why would Sylvia's mother blame Slade? Weren't Slade and Sylvia happy, in love, about to get married?"

Weariness flickered in Margaret's eyes. "They were in love. I don't know how or why Sylvia took her life. I suspect only Slade or Victoria know the answer."

Countless queries swirled inside Phoebe's head. Why would Sylvia take her own life? Why would Victoria Willoughby blame Slade? The more she learned about Sylvia the more questions she had.

She grabbed her saddle bag from the peg by the door where she'd hung it earlier, then eyed Margaret with a tight-lipped smile. "Thank you for telling me. I'll return with the donated quilt."

Half an hour later Phoebe arrived at the port where she and Slade had spotted Master Ames over three months ago. She dismounted from the horse cart with care letting the MacLean's escorts know she was paying a visit to a friend. The briny, cold wind was stronger this close to the water. It whipped the hem of her skirts and coat about her ankles. A bushy-bearded lanky seaman directed her to a grayish-brown stone cottage with a dark thatched roof a short distance away on a row of dwellings visible from the port.

When Phoebe arrived at the Ames's cottage, she raised her gloved hand to knock on the weather-beaten wooden door. But the clip-clopping of a rider made her still her hand. She turned. A female rider, atop a dark bay gelding, stopped in front of the cottage to the left of the Ames's. The woman was garbed in a black mourning bonnet covering half of her face, and a black coat, which billowed as she dismounted.

The woman's profile was statuesque, her ash blonde hair in a thick knot half hidden beneath the bonnet. She must have sensed someone studying her for she turned and looked right at Phoebe, and somehow the truth hit Phoebe head on. The arresting woman with the striking patrician features staring back at her was Sylvia's mother. She was just as stunning as her daughter, despite being older. How was Phoebe to measure up against such a martyred beauty as Sylvia?

Phoebe cleared the tightness in her throat, turned from the Ames's door and walked over to the woman who was intermittently eying her curiously while tethering her own mount to a towering old oak tree.

"Mistress Willoughby?" Phoebe asked, nearing the woman.

"Yes?"

"I am—"

"You're Slade's wife?" Mistress Willoughby interrupted her, her voice clear, crisp, and cultured.

Phoebe nodded. How had the other woman guessed who she was?

Perhaps interpreting her questioning look, Mistress Willoughby answered. "You are as my neighbor Master Ames described. He mentioned he'd taken Slade and his wife to Beinn na Faoghla."

Up close Phoebe noticed the fine lines on Mistress Willoughby's soft features and the gray hairs at her temples, however none of these things detracted from the woman's elegant beauty. She had the most piercing brown eyes Phoebe had ever seen.

Remembering Sylvia, Phoebe drew closer to Mistress Willoughby. "Please know you have my deepest sympathies for the loss of your daughter. Losing her still haunts Slade. He must have loved her a great deal."

Perhaps he still does.

The other woman's eyes turned empty as her gaze shifted away from Phoebe, but not before Phoebe took note of her trembling chin.

When her gaze landed on Phoebe's again, her features had evened out. "A woman in your position must have a certain strength of character to say those words to me. Thank you. Why don't you come inside for tea?"

Phoebe wanted to, but she didn't think she had the strength of character Mistress Willoughby seemed to think she had. "Nothing would please me more, but I am on an errand for Margaret Edwards. Perhaps another time?"

Disappointment and perhaps something like a sliver of relief etched its way into the woman's features. "Of course." She paused then continued. "Slade and Sylvia were in love. My Sylvia was an innocent but ardent girl. I raised her as a good Christian. But she took things to heart too keenly, she loved too deeply and agonized too much over everything. She worried about their future, my future, and her cruel and absentee father."

"Her absentee father …?" Phoebe started to say.

"My Sylvia was the illegitimate daughter of General Bolingbroke."

Shock momentarily froze Phoebe's entire frame; she opened her mouth to speak but no words came out.

Mistress Willoughby continued. "I met the general when I work for the Sutherlands, years ago. He was rather forceful in his attentions towards me. He made promises of marriage, which I was too inexperienced to see were all empty."

"Does Slade know?" Phoebe asked, finally finding her voice even amidst the lightheadedness and discomfort churning in her belly.

"Of course he does. I've tried to assuage Slade's guilt over Sylvia's death. Guilt I myself put into his head because of my grief. But I know Sylvia wouldn't blame him, and neither should I. She would be happy he has a wife that loves him. Please, make him understand."

"I shall try," Phoebe said.

She felt only half present as she said her goodbyes to Mistress Willoughby.

CHAPTER 67

CAMBERLEY MANOR, SUTTON COLDFIELD,
ENGLAND

id-morning, eleven days after leaving Phoebe, Slade was shown to General Bolingbroke's study. From the reconnaissance reports he'd received from Harbert and Company, this was the time for Bolingbroke's morning ride. But it would end soon, and Bolingbroke would return. He had to move quickly. With excited gratitude, Ludlow, the footman, recounted the other servants' tales of how Slade had administered aid to him when he'd been shot and unconscious almost five months ago.

"They said you were a bona fide war hero, colonel. And that you and the healer saved my life. I am forever in your debt, sir."

Slade had been on a mission of revenge five months ago, using Peter's expertly crafted muskets to ingratiate himself to Bolingbroke. Plotting Bolingbroke's downfall in revenge for the part he'd played in Sylvia's death had been the only thing that mattered. And no one except Phoebe could have made him deviate from his plan. He'd had nothing to lose then. Now, five months later, he had a beautiful wife and a grand future with her to look forward to, and things were changing for the better with his father and brother. He had so much to lose now if this didn't go well.

Ludlow was only too happy to show Slade into the general's study to await the general's return.

After Ludlow exited the study and closed the door, Slade spotted the desk Bolingbroke's valets and his maid, Omelia Swindlehurst, had mentioned at the local pub months ago when he'd bought them enough ale to drown a herd of wild horses.

Slade stepped between the desk and its upholstered chair. His hands went for the handle of the desk drawer. He pulled and wasn't surprised when it didn't budge. He withdrew the ring of master keys, courtesy of Harbert and Company, from his saddle bag and started to try key after key. He'd been in contact with them during the past three months regarding bribes Bolingbroke had taken, encouraging them to leak the information to the gossip columns. On the fifth attempt, the lock clicked open.

His lips curled upwards as he slid open the drawer and sifted through its contents. Slade was pleased when in no time he found a document titled "Glenfinnan Mission." He slipped it into his saddle bag and buckled its flap. Slade closed the drawer, pocketed the keys, then sat down on a nearby leather Chesterfield chair. And patiently waited.

Fifteen minutes later the door swung open. The man who walked in didn't look like the pristinely attired aristocrat and army general he'd negotiated an arms contract with months prior. Slade noted with satisfaction this man looked haggard and tired.

General Bolingbroke eyed Slade with a hint of surprise. "MacLean, to what do I owe the pleasure?"

Slade stood up and they exchanged a cursory handshake. "Are the American longrifle muskets still performing to your liking, Sir Henry?" Slade asked.

Bolingbroke appeared distracted, as he answered. "Yes, yes, I still receive compliments on their excellent craftmanship."

Slade took a seat once more. The general walked over to his desk and perched on its edge, exhaling in a long-drawn-out sigh as if exhausted. "No doubt you've seen last week's *Daily Courant?*"

The level of rancor and contempt strumming through Slade's veins in Bolingbroke's presence was surprisingly lower in intensity than he'd expected. His priorities had shifted since he'd taken Phoebe to wife. Perhaps, she had loved the hate right out of him. In truth, all he yearned for at that very moment was to go back home to his wife and start their new life together.

Slade suppressed a triumphant smile. "I have."

Agitation swarmed the general's harsh features. "Lies! All lies. The soldiers I sentenced to transport were all criminals. The *Daily Courant* falsely represented those men as innocents. Someone is trying to destroy me, MacLean. And when I find the bastard, I will rip out the man's gullet."

Every bone in Slade's body should have clamored to reveal who the person was. He should have reveled in the satisfaction and basked in the glory of bringing this mountain of corruption, in front of him, to his knees. He should have hissed venomously in Bolingbroke's ear "This is for Sylvia, your daughter, born out of wedlock when you slept with the Scottish governess in the Highlands twenty-four years ago. The one who killed herself because of what you and I did."

Slade also suspected that Bolingbroke had either scared or attempted to hurt Phoebe the night she'd fled from Camberley. But he had no way of knowing for certain, and confronting Bolingbroke about it would reveal too much. He would much rather Bolingbroke stew in his ignorance.

Slade reclined in his chair and eyed the general, a casual smile lifting the side of his lips. "It's my sincere hope you find the one responsible," he said as he brushed a fleck of lint off his sleeve. "In the meantime, are you in the market for additional muskets?"

The general clicked his tongue. Muskets appeared to be the farthest thing from his mind.

The rest of the meeting with Bolingbroke was innocuous.

Slade returned to his room at the local inn, a copy of the latest *Daily Courant* folded and tucked away in his pocket. Its front-page headline detailed Hawley's transportation to the penal colonies after a three-month imprisonment and trial for stealing army weapons. Slade set to work making a copy of the documents he'd taken from Bolingbroke's study. He took the originals to Magistrate Higgins two days later. The introduction to Higgins had been made by Lucia's father, prompted by a note from Lucia, who'd thought Slade was taking revenge against Phoebe's former employer. Which was only half the truth. Then, several days later, Slade rode into the Royal Scots Greys' garrison at Burntwood. He strode into General Seymour's office and slammed the copy of the documents onto his former direct report's desk saying, "Here is your non-existent evidence against Bolingbroke."

CHAPTER 68

Spring had arrived. But while white snowdrop buds pushed open outside Garraidh, Phoebe's heart was still frozen in winter's ice. *Waiting is a skill all spies must master,* Falcon had said. But worry was a heavy palpable thing, weighing her down. Threatening to drown her. It was difficult to breathe without Slade. She silently begged the heavens to keep him safe and send him back to her, like she'd done a million times before. She hadn't slept a peaceful night since he left. Wasn't he finished with Bolingbroke? Blue Jay had sent her a copy of the *Daily Courant* publicly condemning Bolingbroke for falsely transporting innocent soldiers as political favors. So why hadn't he returned?

She replayed their last conversation in her head, like she'd done countless times before. *We must continue this conversation. We must discuss our marriage.* They needed to work out a solution where their lives weren't in danger all the time. Where they could cause less worry to each other while working for the Movement. This is what she'd thought at the time. But what if Slade regretted marrying her? What if he wanted a traditional wife, one who did what her husband wanted. One who didn't fight like a man or create unrest in a marriage. What if he wanted a wife like Sylvia would have been?

She would selfishly do anything to keep him as her husband. If he asked her to give up the Movement, she would. Her fight had started because of her hatred of herself and of Faye Ross because of what he did to her, but it had since become a calling. It wasn't just to report weapons design and tactical advantageous information while exposing corruption in the British Army. It was thwarting illegal raids and helping the victims wherever she could. Could she simply abandon it now that Faye Ross was dead?

Yet, the very idea of losing Slade punched a hole in her heart so cavernous, so painful, she staggered towards the window, her breathing strained. She could live without the Movement, but she couldn't live without Slade. She slumped, her forehead resting against the cold, smooth glass. She had to tell him. If only she could tell him. Regardless of how painful it was, she would give up the Movement for Slade. Five months ago, the very idea would have bowled her over. The very idea of having a husband would have made her laugh, or cry.

Phoebe swiped at something wet on her cheeks. She'd been crying all unaware.

A knock came at her door. "Come," she said, absently.

Bright and bouncy Lucia and quietly confident Breena walked in, one after the other. Lucia carried a food tray, and Breena carried a small jar of salve. It was the same salve Breena had used on her leg to fade the scarring.

Lucia's eyes fell on Phoebe with concern. "Aila just informed us you missed breaking your fast, again. And you are refusing food in your chamber. You have to eat. You're wasting away."

Phoebe lacked the energy to properly greet her dear friends. It seemed too great a task. She turned away from Lucia and Breena and returned to blindly staring out the window. "I'm not hungry."

Her stomach was heavy, like rocks had taken up permanent residence in her belly since Slade left.

She heard rather than saw Lucia placing the tray on the nightstand. Phoebe startled when a gentle hand touched her shoulder. She turned.

"Let me have a look at your leg?" Breena said, her voice low, her expression soft with friendship and commiseration. Phoebe swallowed against the thickening at the back of her throat. She didn't want kindness. Kindness would make her fall apart, more than she already was.

Steeling herself from further tears, she favored her left leg more from habit of the past few months rather than pain and walked over to the bed. Phoebe sat on the edge and exposed her left leg for Breena's inspection.

Breena crouched down in front of Phoebe, her wide spring-green skirts forming an inflated circle around her. Breena rolled down Phoebe's hose. Her touch was warm and comforting, her expression pleased. "The scar is practically gone. How's the pain?"

Phoebe had to think about it for a second before answering because it had been the farthest thing from her mind. "The pain stopped weeks ago."

Lucia sat on Phoebe's right, putting an arm around her shoulders. "I know you miss Slade, but you will make yourself sick if you continue like this. Has he written?" Lucia asked.

Phoebe let the crown of her head dip, too heavy to hold up. "No. I am sure he is taken up with work. But, not knowing if he's well, all these weeks, is torture," she whispered.

"I'm sure once he's taken care of your former employer he'll be back. These things take time." Lucia said.

Phoebe blinked confusedly at Lucia. Had Slade told Lucia about Bolingbroke? "My former employer?" Phoebe asked.

"Why, yes. Slade asked for an introduction to my father's

friend, Magistrate Higgins, so he could make a formal complaint against your former employer. Didn't he tell you?"

"Oh … yes. Of course," Phoebe said, recovering, then adding. "But I don't know if he will return. He's not happy with … with our marriage."

Lucia frowned. "Not happy? Why would you think that?"

Phoebe let out a weary breath, not being able to elaborate further without telling Lucia that Slade was worried about her dangerous lifestyle with the Movement. "He said we must discuss our marriage. He was displeased with it," Phoebe said.

Lucia stood, going towards the food tray. "Slade loves you. He can never keep that dark smoldering gaze of his off you. Whatever the problem is, you two will find a solution. You simply have to work together, and compromise. For two people so in love, problems are not impossible to solve. Difficult maybe, but never impossible. Now please eat so I can stop worrying about you," Lucia said, her bottom lip pushing out in an endearing pout as she held out a small dish with a scone.

Phoebe attempted a smile. Not wanting to disappoint her friend she reluctantly took the scone. She bit into it, ignoring the fact that it tasted like sand, she chewed and swallowed.

After Breena finished applying the salve to fade the scar, she tugged up Phoebe's hose and dropped down the hem of her skirt. "Lucia is right. It's clear to everyone you and Slade MacLean are terribly in love," Breena said.

Phoebe let Breena's clear confident tone sink in. Her chest expanded, even as gooseflesh rose on her skin.

"My Peter was just saying yesterday, he knows Slade well enough to know he would do anything for you, Phoebe, which is why he went to Birmingham," Lucia said, sitting back down on Phoebe's right.

Breena took Phoebe's hand in hers, her touch gentle but firm. Her bright tawny eyes closely considered Phoebe. "I don't mind admitting that I was worried for you on your wedding night. You seemed so nervous, even terrified. Or maybe it was my imagination. I immediately voiced my concern to Egan, but he assured me Slade MacLean was an honorable and courageous man, that he would never cause harm to the woman he loved. He also said your husband had a nauseatingly over-inflated sense of what was right and wrong. And he would always protect you, even at great risk to himself. I am happy to see Egan was correct. Whatever the reason for Slade's extended absence, it isn't because he doesn't want to be with you, or that he doesn't love you," Breena said to Phoebe.

Phoebe swallowed back the intense emotion that engulfed her. She'd always known Slade's honorable qualities, of course. Perhaps this was where her jealousy of Sylvia started over a decade ago. She had yearned to be the woman he loved, to be the object of his passion, intensity, love and protectiveness. Phoebe had wanted Slade for herself.

And Breena didn't know how accurate her imagination about the wedding night had been. Or perhaps she did know. Breena's intuition not only surprised her, it left her quite speechless.

"Thank you. I am so grateful my brother is marrying you," Phoebe said. "How is Egan? How are my parents?"

Breena sat on the bed to the left of Phoebe. "Egan and I are trying to agree on a date for our wedding. He wants a spring wedding, but I want it to be in the summer."

Genuine emotion stretched Phoebe's lips up for the first time in weeks. "My brother is nothing if not pigheaded. But I am at your disposal for anything you need, be it help with invitations, planning, going through wedding patterns, or hitting my brother over the head until he agrees to your terms."

Breena laughed. "I may need you to do just that. And I'd love for you and Lucia to be my bridesmaids. My dear friend Eva has already given herself the maid of honor distinction."

Lucia squealed in delight just as Phoebe embraced Breena, and Lucia ended up embracing them both in turn.

"This is so exciting! I love weddings, and I am really good with sewing patterns, and flower arrangements," Lucia said, her tone high with excitement.

After Lucia and Breena exchanged a few words on the latest wedding patterns, Phoebe looked from Lucia to Breena.

"How goes it at Eileanach?" Phoebe said, her spirits lifting for the first time in weeks.

Lucia, who'd been staying at Eileanach Castle with Peter while they concluded various arms deals for Hortons, was the first to speak. "Your parents are well; they do seem eager for you and Slade to have children. I think they yearn to be grandparents."

Phoebe recalled her mother's visit during her recovery, when she'd said the very same thing Lucia was now saying. None of her family or friends knew about Faye Ross and the Movement, except Slade. They all thought her horse had just gone wild, kicking her and fracturing her leg.

Her own accidental meeting with Mistress Willoughby popped into Phoebe's head. The stark declaration from the woman's lips still shook Phoebe to her core. *My Sylvia was the illegitimate daughter of General Bolingbroke.* Afterword, parts of a puzzle seem to fall out of place. She'd thought Slade hated Bolingbroke for killing his friend, Isaac, Raghnall and Margaret's only son, and that he was possibly conducting a mission for the Movement which spies weren't supposed to discuss, even with fellow spies. But now learning that Bolingbroke was Sylvia's father, she realized she had been mistaken.

Phoebe realized Lucia was still talking while she'd been woolgathering. "… Peter and I will be leaving Scotland later this week. He completed discussions on his last arms contract with the Sutherlands yesterday, and my family is eager to have us back in Birmingham. But I will return soon to help with Breena's wedding."

"Oh. I'm going to miss you terribly while you're gone. Do hurry back," Phoebe said, her chest squeezing. Phoebe hugged Lucia. Lucia had been such a comforting constant in her life these past few months, and she was just now realizing how much she had relied on her presence.

After Lucia and Breena left, Breena promising to return in a few days to check up on Phoebe, Phoebe slumped down at the writing desk and attempted to read a David Hume volume. But when she realized she'd been reading the same page over and over, images of Slade popping into her head, instead of the words on the page, she put the book down and decided to complete her correspondence instead.

The sun had slipped behind the western horizon by supper time. Aila came to inform Phoebe they were serving the eventide meal in the great hall. Phoebe was in no mood to take part in polite conversation with her in-laws, but she supposed it would be rude if she continued to be a hermit in her bedchamber.

Phoebe dressed for dinner then left her bedchamber. She had just stepped down from the stairs and turned the corner towards the great hall, when the familiar silhouette of a man came into view. Phoebe's heart surged and she ran, launching herself into Slade's arms, her legs wrapping around his body like a monkey's.

He caught her and held her close to his chest in an iron grip. He took her weight like it was nothing. Her heart beat so fast it threatened to escape her body. She swore it hadn't beaten so since he left. Its erratic rhythm closely mirroring the thumps of his own heart against her chest. The familiar scent of cloves and male spice enveloped her senses as she burrowed deeper into him, wanting to consume him as he consumed her. His arms were warm and steady. He'd brought the sun, and the spring with him. She felt it in her bones.

Seconds, perhaps minutes, ticked by as she tightly held him, rubbing her cheeks against his shoulders and neck, feeling him, inhaling him, over and over, reassuring herself he was here, not wanting to let go in case she was still in her bedchamber, asleep and dreaming.

"You came back, *mo ghaol*—my love," she said, her voice a breathless and disbelieving whisper.

His hands held her derriere while his lips kissed her brow, forehead, and temple. The sound of his deep inhales of her hair warmed her.

"Sweetest love, how are you faring, how is your leg?" Slade

asked. His deep, silky voice sending waves of delicious energy rippling down her body.

"It's perfectly well. All healed," she said, her voice low. Everything was perfect now that he was here.

And her heart broke and mended itself back a million times over the instant he whispered. "I couldn't exist another miserable day without you."

CHAPTER 70

Phoebe was stunned at the genuine outpouring of warmth from Lachlan, Tara, and Chisolm at Slade's return. Little Sadie, Tara and Lachlan's daughter, erupted in innocent giggles over Slade's kisses to her ruddy cheeks after he picked her up and twirled her around to greet her. Phoebe hadn't missed the fact that when Chisolm hugged Slade, Slade leaned into his father's embrace just a little more than necessary, affection tightening Slade's handsome features. It was the most beautiful and poignant moment she'd seen among the MacLeans. And when Lachlan gave Slade a hearty slap back hug, it brought a happy tear to Phoebe's eyes as her throat practically closed up with emotion. The MacLean men were slowly bridging the coldness between them stemming from the death of Slade's mother all those years ago.

Later, Phoebe was acutely aware of the heat from Slade's gaze as they walked side by side up the stairs together to the fourth floor of the north wing, and their marriage bedchamber. Every time his eyes fell on her lips, she found herself moistening them with her tongue.

After he closed the door behind her, she turned around to

face him, her heart squeezing with panic and her lungs bursting with words that had to be said.

"I will give up the Movement. I don't want to lose you because of my work. I couldn't bear it if you left."

Her eyes frantically searched his handsome features for an answer before he spoke.

Slade's brows crinkled in puzzlement.

"Why would I leave?" he whispered.

"You were gone so long, I thought perhaps you were displeased with me for working for the Movement, and then I thought perhaps …" Phoebe started to say.

"If I could have returned earlier, I would have."

"You weren't disappointed…angry?" she asked.

"Yes, at the dilemma we find ourselves in, but not at you. Never you."

Relief washed over her, taking away an immense painful heaviness from her belly. Phoebe let his familiar scent envelop her when he came to her and took her in a crushing embrace. She never wanted to let him go. His arms were a protective cocoon, making her safer than she'd ever been before. She would have happily stayed there forever but he slackened his hold, while he placed his forehead against hers, lightly brushing the tip of his nose against the tip of hers and gently tucking errant strands of her hair behind her ear.

"I love you, Phoebe. And the last thing I want you to do is give up your mission with the Movement. I know how important it is to you. It's been important to you since I met you all those years ago. The very first time I saw you, you were reciting the knight's oath. A remarkable thing for such a wee lass. It's ingrained in you, a part of you, your need to fight oppression and control. And as one who loves you, I have to let you do as you must. My only request is that you let me escort you for safety, and when I am unable to, you take three or more MacLean escorts with you," he said.

Phoebe blinked, stunned into lightheadedness. She was speechless, her muscles frozen for a second. He understood her, like no one else ever had. She recalled the escorts Falcon had sent for her that day at Hortons. The MacLean escorts would have to be cleared by the Movement, but it would work, not only to lessen Slade's worry but to increase her safety.

"How could I have been so lucky that you chose me for a wife. It's a miracle. You are my miracle," Phoebe said, her tone soft and disbelieving.

"And you are the most welcomed surprise of my entire life. My dearest little friend who grew up to be my dearest love. I will do anything to make you happy and keep you safe. I would kill every last redcoat, if you asked me to. But you are also my savior, Phoebe. A chance to make amends for my past sins. And I'll thank all the saints for you each and every day for the rest of my life," he said.

A strange sensation tightened Phoebe's chest. Hot and cold swirled in her belly. She pulled her forehead away from his and gently palmed his cheeks, focusing on the darkness in his eyes. What she saw there not only took her breath away, it broke her heart. It was the lovely ghost that had been haunting them for a decade.

"What sins? What is it, *mo ghaol?*" she whispered, her thumb running gentle strokes along his chiseled jawline.

He took both her hands, kissed each of them, then stepped away to remove his jacket, neckcloth, and waistcoat, as if they had turned heavy on his body, dropping them one after the other on a nearby chair while she waited with a thumping heart, holding her breath.

He raked a hand through his thick hair, leaving it in a delectably disheveled state, then he rubbed his temples before speaking. "Sylvia's ... my former betrothed's father was ... is a high-ranking English officer, and he demanded she not marry me ten years ago. I'd never even met the man back then, but he'd already decided against me for a son-in-law because I am a Scotsman."

Disbelief rattled her insides as she stared at her husband. "I … I didn't realize he objected," she said.

"Vehement objections from her absentee father. She was born out of wedlock, you see. Her father demanded she not marry me, and I demanded she forsake her father and marry me regardless; to prove she loved me more," he said. His voice was hard as stone.

Her stomach dropped, as coldness climbed up her spine. She knew what his next words would be when a flash of raw pain tightened his beautiful mouth.

"Sylvia didn't want to lose the measly scraps of love her father threw at her whenever he deigned to visit the Highlands. And she didn't want to lose me, the man she loved. Out of despair and desperation one night she drank a bottle of hemlock, because I had pressured her to decide—in my favor, of course, out of pure selfishness. I might as well have handed her the hemlock myself. I killed her," he said.

Phoebe's mouth opened, but nothing came out for a full ten seconds. The pieces of the puzzle that hadn't fit, when she had learned that Bolingbroke was Sylvia's father, now fitted perfectly into a terrible picture. She now understood the hatred she'd always sensed in Slade, whenever he spoke Bolingbroke's name.

She finally managed to find her voice. "I met Mistress Willoughby while you were away. She said Bolingbroke was Sylvia's father, but she said nothing about his objections to the marriage," Phoebe said, her tone light with incredulity.

But then Phoebe was at Slade's side, slipping her hands around his waist, pulling him into her arms and resting her cheek against his chest. She ran her hands up and down his tall lean back in soothing strokes. His body melted into her embrace.

"I would never speak ill of the dead, *mo ghaol*, but if I were Sylvia, you would always be my choice. The only sin you committed was to expect your love to choose you and she didn't, and that's no sin at all, it's just love. Love is as perfect, or as imperfect … as we are. It's beautiful, freeing, full of light, hope, and sacrifice. But it's also dark, selfish and can bring you grief, disappointment, sadness and even bitterness. But we still should hope for everything from and for those we love. Love is hopeful, after all," Phoebe whispered.

"I shouldn't have pressured her," he said, his voice low and defeated.

CHAPTER 71

"You shouldn't have had to," Phoebe said.

"I have replayed it in my head so many times over the years. What I might have said differently, what I might have done differently. I should have been more patient with her, she was innocent, and she felt everything deeply. I should have been more understanding of the difficult position her father was putting her in. I should have been more supportive, and less forceful with having my own way. I regret that the most," Slade said, pulling back a fraction, his brows creased, his expression haunted.

Phoebe's heart went out to Slade for taking on such a monumental burden that wasn't his. It was no one's fault Sylvia took her life. Unfortunately, tragedies existed without it having to be anyone's fault; they just, are. She recalled what Breena had said that Egan thought of Slade. Slade MacLean is an honorable and courageous man. He would never cause harm to the woman he loved. His sense of what is right and wrong is too nauseatingly overinflated.

Then Phoebe recalled a detail about the conversation she'd had with Mistress Willoughby.

Phoebe pulled Slade closer, looking up at him. "Mistress Willoughby said something else to me which I think you should know."

"Oh?" he asked.

"She said that her Sylvia would be pleased you were married and had someone. She said that Sylvia would have wanted you to have a good life, a happy life," Phoebe said.

Slade blinked at her, and she saw the moment his beautiful lips went slack as he considered her words, or rather, the words Mistress Willoughby had spoken.

"She said that?" Slade asked with raised brows, looking equal parts shocked and dazed.

Phoebe smiled. "She did, indeed."

"Well …" Slade cut off, seeming at a loss for words.

"Despite what happened back then, I think you are taking on a burden that is not yours. It's no one's. It was just a terrible tragedy, *mo ghaol*."

Phoebe pulled him closer still, desperately wanting more of him after being away from him for so long, resting her cheek on his chest, feeling his chin coming to rest lightly on her crown. They held each other for a few minutes as she let him consider her words. Slowly the tension seeped out of his body, and she felt the moment his body relaxed.

She had to make sure Sylvia wouldn't haunt them for the rest of their lives. "Do you miss her? Do you miss Sylvia?"

"I am grateful for having known her, grateful for what she has taught me about myself. It has allowed me to be a better person, to be a better husband for you. But I wouldn't say I miss her. Part of me will always remember her, and I hope with more fondness in the future and with less gut-wrenching guilt. But you, Phoebe, without you my life would be dark, desolate, and pitiable. It would kill me not to have you by my side. Saying I love you, seems so inadequate to convey the depth of my adoration, love, and my shear awe of you," he said.

Phoebe's heart swelled with so much warmth and love; she could barely speak. "Oh, my love …"

"You are my redemption. I believe it's time for me to move beyond my past," he whispered.

Then he was crushing her in his arms again, so tightly Phoebe could hardly breathe, but she welcomed the deprivation, for it was heaven to be held so closely against his hard body.

"I need you, and I'll die if I have to wait a second longer," he whispered, his voice gruff.

He proceeded to shower kisses on her crown, her forehead, her temple, her cheeks and then his lips found their way to her mouth. An involuntary low moan of pleasure erupted from Phoebe's chest and the kiss turned greedy and carnal.

It was neither smooth nor sweet. It was hard and hungry. A stark welcomed invasion of her senses ticking up her heartbeat and laboring her breath. They clawed at each other, her hands going for his neck then pulling him in closer, and closer. His arms were like a vise around her waist, then kneading her derriere and sliding up in strong strokes to her shoulders. A gratifying sound escaped his mouth as she savagely kissed him back. It was too much, but not enough. It sparked a fiery tumult in every cell of her body.

The kiss shifted her world with its voraciousness. And nothing but Slade existed, his steely embrace, his hot mouth plundering hers and her need for more, and more. His hand cupped the back of her head, bringing her yet closer and more flush against him. He increased the pressure of the kiss, tilting his head to press more into her lips, his teeth grazing her mouth. It was wildly intoxicating.

She was desperate for more. Her desperation was mirrored in the wild volcano burning in his eyes as he scooped her up.

He deposited her on the soft bed, sliding in above her, one knee on either side of her thighs. "I fell asleep to the memory of your naked body each night I was away from you. It was torture of the acutest kind," he said, kissing her jaws, clavicles, and the slope of her neck. It wasn't tender, soft, or sweet. He bit down on the pulse point at her neck, that must have been beating like a frantic fluttering bird. It wasn't enough to hurt her, but the shock from his teeth made her gasp. The rawness of pleasure rippled down her. Then he licked and gently sucked the spot he'd bitten, his hot, fast, uneven breath burning her skin. It unleashed Phoebe's recklessness. She wanted even more of his mouth. She tugged at his shirt, yearning for his skin against her skin, for the weight of him directly on top of her, for the friction of him inside her.

"*Mo ghaol* … your clothes," she said, her breathing dangerously ragged.

He raised his head. His beautiful eyes were desperate and wild, his lips damp and his hair mussed. It hit her that she'd been tangling and tugging at his thick dark locks with her fingers.

Slade urgently tugged at the opening of his breeches. And, out of desperation for him, she hiked up the hem of her gown, fabric bunching at her midriff, exposing herself to him. There was no decency in the gesture. Nothing but unbridled desire drove her to part her legs, like a feline in heat. Her core throbbed with need and emptiness.

He growled as he stared down at her core. "Sweet Saints, I have never seen anything more beautiful."

The raw heat in his voice would have knocked her off her feet had she not already been lying on the bed.

He tugged down his breeches. Fabric bunched at his knees. And he was on top of her, kissing her and moving between her legs.

His knees parted her thighs further, his body's weight supported by his limbs, then as his eyes bored into hers, his shaft sank deep into her core with a single steely thrust.

Phoebe gasped with unbridled pleasure at his thick rigidity filling her to the brim.

"You are heaven, and I've been in hell without you," he said, in a low growl.

Her body screamed in pleasure as he started to move. She arched upwards to meet him as her fingers dug into the flesh of his back, her inner muscles contracting around his girth.

They moved together, her arching desperate thrusts meeting his deep frantic plunges.

The raw hunger in his expression, the frantic, delicious friction of their accelerated movements, and the fact that she was starved for him pushed her over the edge. Her body erupted in cascading spasms. Wave after wave hit her as Slade drove into her deeper and harder. Their combined release was brutal and ragged, their labored breaths a disjointed symphony, culminating with her in weightless bliss.

Slade slumped on her, and she welcomed his delicious weight. But then he slid to lie next to her. He pulled her closer into the crook of his arms. And they lay there for some time, Phoebe more content than she'd ever been.

Slade shifted and Phoebe opened her eyes. He'd propped himself up on an elbow to gaze down at her, his eyes dark with renewed passion, and his smile lazy and seductive.

"I've never been that desperate. I promise the next time will be slower and sweeter," he murmured, gently fingering a lock of her hair.

"We have all the night, and the rest of our lives," she said, rising to kiss the tip of his nose.

He was utterly unconcerned by the way his breeches bunched at his knees, his middle exposed. His handsomely disheveled appearance tugged a warm smile from her as she detangled herself from him and slid off the bed, her own garments bunched ridiculously at her waist, her thigh-high hose clad legs visible and her middle similarly exposed. But the one thing that bothered her was her boots. Rather than being a necessity, they felt clunky on her feet. She bent down, unlaced each and left them by the side of the bed, with her hose. Her bare feet enjoyed the coolness of the stone floor. When she straightened again, it dawned on her that she didn't have the need to run. She didn't have the need to be ready anymore. She could finally stop running. She marveled at the fact that she was finally safe and at home with Slade. Slade was her home.

Phoebe went to get a drink of sherry from the sideboard, utterly parched. Slade declined whisky. Then she smiled coquettishly as she removed her rumpled garments and pulled on a plush red velvet dressing gown, tying its belt at her waist.

Slade leisurely rubbed his thumb against his bottom lip, eying her like an eagle sizing up his next meal, a deceptively lazy smile stretching his mouth, but then his eye took in her state of dress. "I don't recall seeing you in red before, but I certainly recalled your disinclination to take off your boots in the bedchamber," he murmured.

Phoebe laughed, twirling around. "Don't you like my new dressing gown?"

His eyes hungrily raked the length of her, then his brows hiked up. "The color suits you very well, but despite that fact, I'm going to take pleasure in disrobing you shortly, especially since it appears you've decided to take off your boots and stop running," his voice was slow, and silken, with a hint of intrigue.

A silly grin lifted the corners of her lips as her insides warmed. He understood her like no one else ever had, understood the significance of her bare feet. Phoebe looked down at the robe, briefly fingering its softness, then her eyes travelled to her feet. Her old fears had started to fade. "I've decided to stop running, and to embrace freedom and colors again. To take control of my wardrobe, so to speak."

Since Faye Ross's death, Phoebe had reconsidered her hate of red. It was just a color after all.

He considered for a breath. "I like this new look for you, it has an air of grand victory about it," Slade said, with an overdone flourish of his hand.

"It does, doesn't it." Phoebe chuckled, warmth cascading down her body.

Slade sat up in bed, detangling himself from his own garments. His expression sobered. "I had to see wily old Bullfinch on my way back and received news which he wanted me to share since it is relevant to your mission. Prince Charles Edward Stuart was arrested in France by the French authorities while attending the opera at the Théâtre du Palais-Royal. Under the new rules of the Aix-la-Chapelle Treaty, France and Britain are now allies. A rebel of Britain is now an outlaw in France."

Phoebe gasped, shocked. Her right palm made a move to cover her mouth, as she dropped down on the nearest divan. "Oh no. We must get him out."

"The Movement is doing so as we speak. Bulfinch said also that the elusive and dangerous Ossifrage is on his way to the Highlands. Bulfinch plans to stay out of his way. Ossifrage tends to be a harbinger of bad news," Slade said.

Blue Jay had described Ossifrage as elegant, exceptionally intelligent but also devious and deadly. As the spymaster of the west region, he is known for being ruthless and taking on missions no one else could accomplish, not above utilizing bribery and fraud amongst the highest echelons of society to get what he wanted, even extending to the King himself. Thankfully Phoebe had never had the displeasure of meeting him. He sounded like a veritable villain.

"With Prince Charles Edward Stuart being an outlaw, is the future of the Movement in jeopardy? Is that why Ossifrage is coming to the Highlands?" Phoebe said.

Was Scotland's rebellion over? Had King George II, the English government, and the Whig party won? *Blast it all to hell*

Slade came to kneel in front of the divan where she sat, taking both her hands in his and kissing her knuckles. His nearness completely rid her body of worry and her head of rational political thoughts.

"Uncertain times indeed, especially for those of us who wanted things the way they were before the signing of the Union," he said, his eyes hungrily resting on her lips for a moment before he leaned in and took her mouth with his. This kiss was slow and seductive. His tongue gently plundered her mouth, deliciously spinning her head and sending whirls of sensations down her body all the way to her toes.

He cupped her breasts over the soft fabric of the dressing gown and growled. Phoebe was panting when she broke the kiss, Slade's eyes were dark but questioning. It took tremendous strength of will to focus her mind back to the Movement. "Will funding from France for the Movement stop?" she asked breathlessly.

His brows wrinkled, as he stood up and went to the sideboard. It seemed he needed a drink after all. "I doubt it. Outwardly they will make a show of support for Britain, but inwardly still harbor hopes of weakening the British Empire," Slade said.

She would have guessed the same. Phoebe tried to focus her thoughts on the future of the Movement, but her eyes strayed to the delicious sight of Slade's exposed skin.

"I'll have to get new orders from Falcon, but I fully intend on continuing my fight against the redcoats," she murmured, distracted by his lips on the tumbler as he downed the liquid in one gulp. She licked her own lips as her body's temperature notched up and her core contracted, in emptiness.

She stood up and closed the distance between her and Slade. Heat enveloped her body as she slid her arms around her husband's narrow waist, raising her eyes to meet his dark ones. She'd worry about Falcon's orders later.

"Make love to me," she said.

"With pleasure, my Warrior Goddess," he said.

His smile was slow and wicked as his mouth came down on hers. Their next bout of lovemaking wasn't slow or sweet, it was rough and delicious. Slade did however manage to keep his promise of slow and sweet loving, the third time around.

ACKNOWLEDGMENTS

Cheers to Tanya, Kim, and the entire team at Oliver Heber Books for getting this story published.

ABOUT THE AUTHOR

Award winning author, Roma Cordon came to New York in the 1990's where she earned a graduate degree at NYU. She's been a voracious reader since her teenage years, but it was after taking a writing course with the late great Anne Rice in the early 2000's that she started to dabble in the craft.

Life got in the way, as it does, and it would take Roma until 2022 to publish her first historical romance novel.

Bewitching a Highlander was published by CamCat Books in 2022 and won the IPPY gold medal, and a silver medal from IBPA Benjamin Franklin in 2023. It hit #1 in Scottish Historical Romance with Amazon Kindle in December of 2023. It will soon be translated to French! Tragic struck and CamCat Books was bought out after losing its founder, Sue Arroyo. Roma returned to the market and found her new home with Oliver Heber Books in 2025. Her latest historical romance *A Highlander's Secret*, a continuation of the Scottish Highland Warriors series, will be released by OHB later in 2025.

Roma is a member of the Women's Fiction Writers Association, Romance Writers of America, and the Historical Novel Society. She attended a number of Writer's Digest Conferences and was at the 2024 Romance Writers of America Conference in Austin, Texas. She's done several on-line author interviews, podcast interviews and spoke on two author panels, the most notably being Library Journal Day of Dialogue.

Look for her on X, Instagram, Facebook, Book Bub and Goodreads, and learn more about her work on romacordon.com.

Roma lives in New York City with her husband and two kitties adopted from local shelters. She works in the finance industry to pay the bills while pursuing her passion of writing.

A small press bound by the belief that every voice matters.

Sign up for our newsletter to learn about new releases and more.
https://oliver-heberbooks.com/subscribe/

Follow us on social media:

facebook.com/oliverheberbooks
instagram.com/oliverheberbooks
amazon.com/oliverheberbooks
youtube.com/@OliverHeberBooksPublisher